SHARDS OF YOU AND ME

TANYA BIRD

For every ex-Jehovah's Witness grieving someone they left behind.

1

ANNIE

It's no easy feat to hold a tune when there's a demon behind you. Sister Maria is laid out on the floor in the back room, an elder praying on either side of her. I don't need to be in the room to know what's happening. The demonic attacks are a regular occurrence.

I keep my eyes forwards and try to bring some extra volume to my voice. So does Sister Ava beside me, although she sounds like she's singing an entirely different song. When I sneak a glance at her, I notice spit gathered in the corners of her mouth. She usually ducks out into the kitchen for a drink after the public talk, but since no one is going near the back room today, she's gone without.

The song comes to an end, and Sister Ava holds the final note—off-key—for a few seconds longer than everyone else. It makes the young sister in the next row giggle. A throat clears, and the room falls silent for prayer. I bow my head and close my eyes.

A moan cuts through the silence, and I can't help but look over my shoulder. Brother Oliver has Sister Maria pinned to the ground with his knee, his prayers growing more urgent. Mum jabs me with her elbow, and I whip my head forwards, pressing my eyes shut and wishing I could cover my ears as well. The brother on the platform does remarkably well under difficult circumstances and keeps the prayer nice and short. Finally, there's a collective murmur of amens followed by the relief of conversation filling the room.

'Poor Sister Maria,' Mum says, tutting. 'I might drop a hot meal over this afternoon. I can't imagine she'll be up to cooking.'

A four-wheel drive pulls up at the door, and the driver jumps out to open the boot. The back seat is laid flat, and a moment later, a disorientated Sister Maria is helped out to the car. Her daughter isn't allowed to go with her, so Sister Jane takes the crying girl to the far end of the Kingdom Hall to pray. The boot is closed, the car pulls away, and everyone resumes their conversations.

'Annie.'

I turn to find Brother Oliver, one of two elders in our congregation, standing at the end of the row of seats. He's wearing his favourite blue suit and trademark smile that never quite reaches his eyes. My hands immediately turn clammy. 'Hi.'

'Can we have a private word in the back room?' he asks. 'You can bring your mum along if you like.'

I glance at Mum, who's also managing to smile—even if it doesn't quite fit the moment.

'Happy to sit in,' she says, ushering me in his direction.

My feet obey. Only my feet.

All eyes land on me as we head to the back of the hall. The glass doors slide closed behind us, indicating that the conversation is of a more serious nature. No one can hear us, but everyone can see us.

He doesn't sit, so I don't either. Instead, he turns to face me, ready to impart his wisdom. 'It's been wonderful seeing you regularly at the meetings,' he begins. 'I know year twelve can be very demanding, and there's always pressure from teachers to put your worldly studies before your spiritual needs, so well done on keeping your priorities straight.'

The only person putting pressure on me right now is *me*. I *want* to do well. I want to feel like the previous thirteen years of school weren't a complete waste.

I'm waiting for the 'but'. He hasn't brought me in here to point out the things I'm doing right. He could have done that out there with everyone else.

'Annie's very smart,' Mum says, pride in her voice, 'and she enjoys school, but she's more focused on getting baptised at the next assembly.'

Brother Oliver nods slowly, then focuses back on me. 'I wanted to ask you what you think about the skirt you're wearing.'

This I wasn't expecting.

I glance down at the black pencil skirt that I picked up at a thrift shop in Turram a few weeks ago. What do I think? I mean, the fabric's a little itchy, even with stockings. It's fitted. Perhaps that's the issue. 'To be honest, I haven't really thought much about it.'

'It's a very popular style among the sisters right now,' Mum adds.

'I won't pretend to be up with the latest fashions,' he replies light-heartedly. 'What I will say though is that it's worth sitting down in the skirts when you're trying them on to see where the hem ends up.'

Length. This is about the length. The skirt sits well below the knee when I'm standing and slightly above when I'm sitting. But who's looking at my knees when I'm seated?

'We must consider everyone in the congregation when selecting clothing for the meetings,' Brother Oliver continues. 'There are many young brothers who need our help staying focused on the talks.' He says this last part with a knowing smile.

'Did someone complain?' my mother asks nervously.

He meets her gaze. 'No, no. Everyone was focused on the spiritual food on offer this morning. But since I gave the morning talk, I had a unique view from the platform.'

It's *his* complaint. *He* noticed.

I take a small step back, shame swallowing me.

'We appreciate you bringing it to our attention,' Mum says.

He opens the Bible that I hadn't noticed he was carrying and starts flicking through the pages until he finds what he's looking for. '1 Timothy 2:9–10. The women should adorn themselves in appropriate dress, with modesty and soundness of mind, not with styles of hair braiding and gold or pearls or very expensive clothing, but in a way that is proper for women professing devotion to God, namely, through good works.'

He doesn't have to worry about me wearing anything expensive. I turn the leather bracelets on my wrist. It gives my hand something to do.

'I know this can be a very uncomfortable topic for sisters,' he says, sounding sincere, 'but it's an important conversation to have.'

What's uncomfortable is that he brought me in the back to tell me that he noticed my knees during his talk this morning. My *knees*.

'Perhaps I can take the hem down,' Mum offers.

Brother Oliver walks over to the glass doors. 'We're very lucky to have so many sisters with sewing skills in the congregation.' He slides open the door and gestures for us to go ahead of him.

Such a gentleman. A true beacon of light to young brothers.

I walk across the floor where Sister Maria lay fitting minutes earlier.

'Will you be joining us for field service today?' he asks before I have the chance to flee.

I have an assessment due in three days, but that's not the right answer. 'Yes,' I say, pausing at the door.

He's visibly pleased by my response, and Mum is visibly pleased at him being pleased.

'First day of sunshine we've had in a long time,' she says, following me out. 'Perhaps we can eat outside if the lawn's dry?'

I loathe eating lunch as a congregation. Soggy rolls and eternal rotations of stale fruit cake. What I don't understand is the older sisters have spent *years* perfecting their sponge cakes. So why always fruit cake?

Mum and Brother Oliver exchange a few more pleasantries. The second he steps away, I head for the exit.

'Where are you going?' Mum calls to me.

Out. Out of the hall. Out of sight. Away from the stares. 'To get my cardigan from the car. I'm going to need something to cover my knees with.' I tug my skirt down as I walk. The exit's a few steps away.

'Annie.'

Ignoring Mum, I rush through the door and don't stop until I reach the car. When I try the handle, it doesn't open. Slapping the door, I drop my forehead to the glass window. Only once my breathing slows do I return inside for the keys.

2

HUNTER

I'm heating baked beans in the kitchen when I hear the gunshot. A chill starts behind my eyes and runs through every bone, organ, and vein before exiting my fingers and toes. Flicking the stove off, I jog to the front door, stepping into my boots on the way out. Dad's supposed to be pulling ragwort. That's what he said two hours ago as yet another beer hissed open in his hands.

'I'll cook dinner when I get back,' he'd said before leaving.

Liar. I can't remember the last time he was sober enough to cook.

The sheep disperse when I leap over the gate and start running. I'm prepared for anything at this point— I've been prepared for years. Though imagining his death is one thing, seeing it up close will be quite another.

But he's not dead. He's sitting up, head in his hands and the rifle lying in the grass next to him. I freeze when I see a bloodied and lifeless kelpie twenty feet away.

'What the fuck did you do?' I ask, heading straight for the dog.

He looks up, red-faced and clearly drunk. 'I thought it was a fox.'

It looks nothing like a fox. I bend down to ensure it's dead, then walk back to Dad, snatching up the rifle. 'Go home.'

He blinks up at me. 'Whose dog is it?'

I open the bolt and empty the remaining cartridges onto the grass. 'Likely the Wilsons'.' It tends to wander.

Dad stands up and sways on his feet. 'I'll take it to them.'

I fight the urge to push him back down. 'Really? You're going to show up at their house, still drunk, and hand them their dead pet that you just shot?' I sling the rifle over one shoulder and go to collect the animal. It's still warm, and that makes me even angrier for some reason. 'I'll go.'

'I can clean up my own messes.'

'You couldn't last night,' I say, referring to when he was sick beside the toilet. 'Go home and sober up.'

Without a backwards glance, I keep walking all the way down to the creek that separates our farm from the Wilsons' acreage. There's a railroad tie posing as a bridge across the water. Only their dog crosses it, so I've no idea why it's even there. Once a family of four, the Wilson family has dwindled to two—Annie and her mum. They're Jehovah's Witnesses, so the only time they step foot on our property is when they're either looking for their dog or when they're knocking on doors with bullshit messages about God, hope, and the meaning of life.

I head up the hill, swearing at a blackberry bush that snags my clothing. When I reach the top, I spot Annie in the horse paddock filling the water trough. She stills when she sees me, gaze dropping to the dog in my arms. She stares at it for a long moment before turning off the hose.

'Your dog was on our property again,' I say, stopping a few feet from her. 'You know we have new lambs. I thought he was a fox.'

I expect her to cry or pray or fall to her knees, but she tucks locks of copper hair behind her ears and continues to stare at the animal with that sad expression on her face.

'What's your dog's name again?' I ask. 'Moses? Noah?'

She lifts her gaze, her amber eyes reflecting the light. 'My dog's name is Banjo.'

I had it in my head that it was a Bible name. Now I look like I was being a smart-arse.

This is the part where I'm supposed to apologise and show some kind of remorse, but I don't really do apologies—or remorse, for that matter. 'Want me to bury him?' I'm always happy to dig a hole in place of words.

She draws a long breath. 'I don't want you to bury my dog, no. You'll need to ask the Davises about this one.'

Confused, I look down at the corpse in my arms. 'This isn't yours?'

She shakes her head, and her hair comes loose. 'Fairly sure it's the Davises' new working dog. *Her* name is Millie.'

I check the gender of the dog. 'Ah.' Probably should

have done that before presenting her with a bloodied corpse.

Annie whistles, and a moment later, a very much alive Banjo comes bounding up to us. His tail stops wagging when he smells the blood, and he walks over to sniff the dog I'm holding.

'Well, make sure yours stays this side of the creek,' I say, pushing her dog back with my foot. 'Consider this a preview of things to come.'

She crinkles her nose. 'You know, I saw your dad wandering around with a rifle earlier.'

'So?' It's messed up that I can be angry at him and protective of him in the same breath.

She shrugs. 'So maybe it wasn't you who shot the dog.'

And we're done. 'Next time I'll throw the carcass in the creek and save myself the headache.'

Annie tilts her head. 'You could've done that this time.'

'Aww.' I smirk. 'You trying to find the good in me, Wilson?'

'Simply pointing out the facts.'

It's time for me to leave, but I don't. 'I'd dispose of it now, but we both know your impeccable conscience will have you fishing it out of the water and taking it to the Davis farm yourself.'

'Most people just call that common decency.'

Turns out Annie Wilson's a bit of a smart-arse. 'You're free to call it whatever you want.' I look in the direction of the Davis farm. 'Just do me a favour and don't mention anything to anyone about seeing my dad with a rifle, okay?'

'You want me to lie?'

I return my gaze to her. I can't tell if she's being serious or simply trying to get a rise out of me. 'Don't stress. If news travels around town that I'm killing people's dogs, no one's going to come and ask you anything.'

She swallows and searches my eyes. 'Do you want me to come with you?'

'Where?'

'To the Davises'.'

Her words reek of kindness, which I'm absolutely not prepared for. 'For what reason?'

She shrugs. 'Moral support.'

I stare at her a moment. 'I thought your kind aren't allowed to be alone with the opposite sex?'

Her gaze falls to the dead dog in my arms. 'I think I'd be reasonably safe in this instance.'

Why she thinks she would be safe with the guy who just confessed to shooting a dog, I've no idea. 'I don't need your Christian charity.'

She appears unfazed by my words, but I doubt much would faze this girl. I've heard the things people say to her at school, and I can only imagine what people say when she comes knocking at nine o'clock on a Saturday morning.

'Annie!'

We both look in the direction of the house, and there's her mum, standing at the back door, squinting in our direction.

'Just be honest,' Annie says, increasing the distance between us. 'They'll understand if you tell them the truth.'

I roll my eyes as I turn away. 'Why don't you just pray for me instead?'

'And hide the gun,' she adds, ignoring my last comment. 'For your dad's sake.'

My feet stop, and when I look back at Annie, I see pity. We don't get much pity around these parts nowadays. It ran out long ago. You get maybe a year to grieve and fall apart after losing a loved one, and then you're supposed to get on with things. And I did, mostly, but Dad couldn't. He fell apart even more in the second year. And a little more every year since.

I nod once at Annie, then walk on.

3

ANNIE

'Annie, wait up!'

I stop short of my locker, dread pooling in my belly, then turn to watch Donna striding towards me.

'Have you had lunch?' she asks.

The bell went three minutes ago, and I haven't even reached my locker. 'Not yet.'

'Great. Let me get mine. We'll eat together.'

Donna Hughes is the only Jehovah's Witness at my school close to me in age. That's the basis of our friendship. But if you ask anyone in the congregation about us, they'll tell you we're best friends. Never mind the fact that Donna annoys me 95 percent of the time. I'm not entirely sure why. Perhaps it's the way she tells stories. They always lack a punchline. Sometimes she'll even laugh despite nothing about it being funny. Or maybe it's the way she eats a sandwich by tearing small pieces off instead of taking bites. Even her constant ponytail annoys me. She's worn her hair the same way every day since she was eight.

I could write an essay on all the things that annoy me about her, and I'd go well over the word limit.

'I'll meet you at the tables outside,' I tell her, forcing a smile.

She touches my arm as she passes me, in that best friend kind of way, and my smile fades the second her back's turned.

When I step up to my locker, I find Tamsin Stevenson watching me curiously. She's rearranging her books in the locker next to mine.

'Why do you hang out with her if you don't like her?' she asks me, her voice low.

It's a worry that other people are picking up on the fact. 'I like Donna.' I hesitate. 'Just not all the time.'

Tamsin gives me a look that suggests she doesn't believe that. 'Right.'

She's one of the few girls at this school who's always been nice to me. Most people don't even realise they're being nasty. It can be so subtle, like simply asking a personal question in front of a large group of people.

'So you've *never* eaten an Easter egg?' or 'Don't you get tired of people telling you to fuck off when you knock on their door?'

If Tamsin's around, she usually shuts question time down, sparing me having to answer. Hopefully she knows how grateful I am without me explicitly telling her each time.

Her gaze goes to the bracelets along my arm. 'Those are cute. Where did you get them?'

I close my locker door. 'I made them.'

Her eyes widen. 'Really?' She catches hold of my wrist, inspecting the bracelets up close. 'Leather?'

'Yeah. Mostly recycled leather from belts and bags I find in thrift shops. Though this one's made from an old horse bridle,' I say, pointing to it.

'Clever thing.' She lets go of my arm. 'You know, people pay a lot of money for that kind of jewellery.'

'I can make you one if you want.'

She tilts her head. 'Aww. I'd love that.' Glancing back at her friends who are waiting for her, she adds, 'You should come down to the courts and shoot with us.'

I pull my bag down and retrieve my sandwich. 'I'm not much of a netballer.'

She laughs. 'You don't need to be sporty to join in. We just mess around.'

I wouldn't know if I'm sporty. I've never been allowed to play team sports. 'I told Donna I'd meet her.'

Something behind me catches Tamsin's eye. When I look over my shoulder, I find Hunter with his friend Sammy walking down the middle of the corridor. Yes, the middle. You can do that when all the other students scamper out of your way. I can't remember ever seeing him break stride for anyone.

Hunter glances in my direction, eyes brushing over me. Nothing changes on his face. Then he's looking forwards again and gone from sight a moment later.

'Is it just me, or does Hunter look to be in a mood?' Tamsin asks.

I return my gaze to her. 'I thought he only had one mood.'

She laughs at that and leans on her locker. 'Everyone's going to Trent's place at Whistle Beach on Saturday night. You should come.'

I tug at the corners of my gladwrapped sandwich. 'You know I don't go to parties.'

'I know your religion has rules and stuff, but you're eighteen—an adult. You can legally decide for yourself if you want to come hang out with me, right?'

I swallow. 'Right.'

'If you don't want to, that's another matter entirely.'

Of course I want to, but I'm not supposed to associate with people outside the religion. 'No' is my automatic response to the few party invitations that come my way. It's the right answer every time. Most people in this town figured out years ago not to bother asking, but I'd be lying if I said I wasn't curious to go just once. It's not a birthday party, after all, or part of any pagan celebration. It's just a simple get-together.

This is the lie I tell myself.

'It'll be the last party until exams are done,' she adds. 'You could get ready at mine, and we could go together. I'll see you through the entire thing.'

It feels a lot like Satan extending his hand right now.

I've never been to a get-together outside of those organised by our congregation, where people gather around the piano and sing kingdom melodies and discuss their field service successes.

'Pray continually, so that you may not enter into temptation'—Matthew 26:41.

'I really can't,' I say. 'But thanks for the invite.'

She searches my eyes, then nods. 'I think I'll keep asking, in case you change your mind.'

———

Donna's telling me how she watched *Titanic* with Sister Kelly on Sunday. They ended up turning it off because of the love scene in the car.

The urge to roll my eyes is strong. 'I watched it. You don't even see anything,' I say, picking at the soggy lettuce in my sandwich.

'The fog on the windows was very suggestive. The hand sliding down the glass was the final straw for Sister Kelly.' She tears off a piece of sandwich and flattens it between her thumb and forefinger before popping it into her mouth.

I place mine down on the gladwrap and look across the oval to where kids are disappearing into the trees. 'You missed the best part of the movie if that's where you stopped it.'

Donna tears off another piece of her sandwich. 'Let me guess. They hit an iceberg.'

That might have been funny coming from anyone else. I nod in the direction of the trees. 'Do you think there's a fight happening?' The clearing between the school and the golf course is a common place for airing grievances.

She tosses her ponytail over her shoulder and squints in the direction of the trees. 'Probably. I saw Mason Clarke throw an apple core at Sammy Carter earlier. No idea why. Hunter stepped in, always the guard dog. Then

Mason said something about Hunter's dad being a drunk and his mum dying of embarrassment. A moment later it was on. Mr Petros separated them, but it was fairly obvious they weren't done.'

I'm stuck on the part where Mason told Hunter his mum died of embarrassment. Hunter's mum died of breast cancer six years back. She had fought hard for three years before it spread to her lymph nodes and lungs. 'You think it's a fight between Mason and Hunter?'

Donna shrugs. 'Hunter's always looking for an excuse to clock someone.'

I pick up my sandwich and toss it into the bin. 'I'm going to wander over.'

Her eyes widen. 'What? Why?'

It's a reasonable question. 'To see what's happening.'

'You can't leave the school grounds without a lunch pass.'

'The whole school is leaving the grounds right now.'

Donna stands up. 'They'll be *fighting*.'

I start walking because I know she'll continue all day if I don't. 'I'll see you later.'

'I'm going to find Mr Petros,' she says, smoothing down her oversized school dress.

Ignoring her, I head for the trees. I hear the fighting well before I see it, people shouting and cheering. When I step out into the clearing, I see everyone gathered in a giant circle. No one's trying to stop them, which means every person there is a spectator. I squeeze my way through so I can see who's fighting. It might sound crazy, but I swear I can feel Hunter's energy before I lay eyes on him.

I still when I see him in the middle, Mason circling him. At least it appears to be an even fight. I flinch when Hunter lunges forwards and punches Mason in the face —not once but twice. Blood smears his teeth. That should be the end of it.

You hit him in the face, Hunter.

You drew blood.

You win.

But Mason's stepping up for more, and Hunter looks like he's just warming up. I've never seen violence in real life like this before—or even on TV, for that matter. It's a lot. I should leave, but I don't. I stand there watching, still and mute.

Hunter finally takes a step back from Mason and asks, 'Are you done?'

Mason runs at him, preparing to tackle him to the ground. Hunter shoves him back, feet moving again and eyes trained on his opponent. Those eyes flick briefly in my direction, and his fists drop a few inches. Mason takes advantage of the distraction and throws a punch into Hunter's stomach. It's the only one he's landed since I arrived—and I suspect it's my fault.

Hunter has Mason on the ground a beat later, pressing a knee into his ribs. Mason covers his face with his arms while Hunter lays into him.

Just when I think I'm either going to faint or vomit, Mr Petros pushes through the crowd of students.

'Hey!' He pulls Hunter off Mason and shoves him back, jabbing a finger in the direction of the school. 'Mr Trest's office—now!'

I half expect Hunter to start punching him too, but he

backs up, eyeing Mason before turning away. His blazing eyes are a startling shade of blue as they meet mine. His face is glistening with sweat, but there's not one mark on it. I drop my gaze and move aside as he brushes past me and sets off for the principal's office.

Students are dispersing like uncovered mice around me now. Donna was right. I should never have left the school grounds. I'm not a rule breaker. I'm having trouble looking away from a very pale and bloodied Mason, who's now being helped to his feet.

'I expected better from you, Annie,' Mr Petros says, glancing in my direction.

That's when I realise I'm the only student still standing there.

'Sorry, sir.' And I mean it. I'm sorry I left school grounds, sorry I stood idle while someone was hurt, and sorry for the relief I feel that Hunter walked away mostly unscathed.

Mason spits blood onto the ground and wipes angry tears off his cheeks.

'Grab his shoe, would you?' Mr Petros says, nodding towards the black runner lying a few feet away. I didn't even see it come off.

I run to retrieve it, then follow a stern-faced Mr Petros and limping Mason all the way to the infirmary. Mason sinks down into the chair and hangs his head in his hands. Because I have no idea what he needs, I slide the sick bucket close to him, then place the discarded shoe beside it.

'You can go,' Mr Petros tells me.

I back out of the much too small room, almost

colliding with the school nurse in the process. As I pass the principal's office, I glimpse Hunter through the open door. My feet stop involuntarily when he looks in my direction, his expression completely unreadable.

'Close the door,' I hear Mr Trest say.

Hunter rises from his chair and walks slowly over, watching me the whole time. A moment later, the door clicks shut between us.

4

HUNTER

The school banned me from catching the bus at the beginning of year eleven because I got into a fight with someone over something I can't even remember. The ban was only a year, but now I'm so used to walking, I haven't bothered with the bus since. It's not that far. Forty minutes if I'm dragging my feet, which is most of the time. My home is not the kind you rush home to—especially today.

The principal called Dad to tell him that Mason's parents are within their rights to press charges, and I can't decide if that phone call will make him drink more or less this afternoon.

I move off the road and head down the slope towards the tall gums that shade the creek. My feet slow when I see Annie Wilson sitting atop her school bag at the creek's edge, watching the water. I don't know if she's thinking or praying or what. All I do know is that we've seen enough of each other today. I'm guessing she got more than she bargained for when she showed up at that fight. Her horror was written all over her face.

I'm about to head back to the road when I hear a male voice say, 'You drop your Bible in the water?'

I look to the creek and see Lee White and two of his dickhead mates on the other side.

Annie rises, picks up her bag, and walks away. That should be the end of it, but the trio start to follow her.

I've gotten into enough trouble today, so the best thing for me to do is leave—but I don't. I'm curious to see how she'll handle this, so I head back down the slope towards her.

J-dubs believe in turning the other cheek and all that shit, so Annie's well-rehearsed at polite silences. I've watched her navigate these types of situations with an annoying amount of grace my whole life.

'I heard you came to Trent's house on the weekend,' Lee calls to her. 'With one of your little pamphlets.'

His friends smile at the ground.

'His mum said you stepped in cow dung on your walk up the drive,' Lee continues. 'Their house smelled like shit for days.'

Annie glances in their direction but doesn't say anything.

'I heard his dad used the leaflet to wipe his arse,' Lee keeps going when he doesn't get a response.

I'm almost at the creek when I reply, 'If he's using junk mail to wipe his arse, that might explain the smell in the house.'

All eyes are on me now, all smiles gone.

Annie turns to face me, her expression guarded.

'Let's go,' I tell her.

Her eyebrows come together. 'Where?'

'Home.'

She glances again in the direction of the others, then runs to catch up with me.

I look over my shoulder to make sure the others aren't following and see their retreating backs. Turning back to Annie, I ask, 'Why don't you just tell them to piss off and be done with it?'

'Easier to just ignore them.' She watches the trail. 'You should try it some time.'

I roll my eyes in her direction. 'Must be so lonely up there all by yourself on that high horse.'

'It's not so bad.'

My lips twitch. 'Should've let Lee walk you home.'

'I'm honestly surprised you didn't.' She watches me a moment. 'Did you get hurt today?'

I shake my head. 'Was surprised to see you there.'

She dodges a puddle before falling into step with me once more. 'I regret going. Hearing about these things is one thing. Seeing it in person is something else.'

I'd never admit it, but I was distracted by her being there. I'm not really sure why. 'Well, I certainly didn't invite you.' I look down at her feet when I notice her limping slightly. 'What's wrong with your foot?'

'Nothing. I think there's a stone in my shoe.'

I stop and turn to her. 'Then get rid of it so we can get home before dark.' The agitation in my voice isn't because of the delay but because she didn't speak up sooner.

She balances on one foot and tugs off her shoe,

shaking it until a stone falls out. When she begins to tilt, I grab hold of her backpack to keep her steady because I don't think she'd appreciate my hands on her.

Her eyes travel up to mine as her foot lands back on the ground. 'Thanks.'

We resume walking.

'How much trouble did you get into?' she asks.

'I didn't get suspended, which's surprising. I got something far worse.'

She looks up. 'Worse than getting suspended?'

I nod. 'I'll be cleaning tables during lunch for the rest of the month.'

Her eyebrows come together. 'How is that worse?'

'Because someone's going to make a smart-arse comment about it, and then I'll probably end up in another fight.'

She holds on to the straps of her backpack. 'You could be the bigger person and ignore them.'

I glance sideways at her. 'And run away, like you?'

'Should I have stayed and fought them?'

I note the glint of amusement in her eyes. 'That depends. Could you win?'

'I do have God on my side.'

The corners of my mouth lift. 'You'd want to be damn sure before taking on three of them.'

She's watching her feet again. 'What do you get out of it? The fighting?'

That's a ballsy question. I'm not obligated to answer, but I do. 'I get people leaving me alone for a while.'

She looks up at me. 'That makes no sense. You're the most left-alone person at the school.'

'Because when I'm unhappy, I express it.'

She watches me. 'You really hurt Mason today.'

'I also taught him a valuable lesson.'

'Oh yeah? What lesson's that?'

'To think twice before he opens his fucking mouth.' I see her flinch. It's subtle, but I see it. 'I know being bullied comes with being a J-dub, but do you have to make it *so* easy for people?'

She shrugs. 'I'm kind like that.'

'Well, it comes across as weak.'

Her elbow bumps my arm, so she widens the distance between us. 'You think beating someone up makes you *strong*?'

It's rhetorical, so I don't answer.

'It takes more strength to remain silent,' she says, looking around. 'Return evil for evil to no one.'

'That a quote from one of your pamphlets?'

Her eyes return to me. 'Yes, actually.'

I hold her gaze. 'That's how you want this conversation to go? You want to preach at me?'

Her cheeks colour. 'No.'

'What would you be saying if your God couldn't hear you right now?'

'He's not *my* God.'

I look heavenwards. 'Fine. If *the* God couldn't hear you right now, what would you say to me? Since it's a hypothetical question, your reply doesn't count as saying it.'

'Haven't you ever heard the phrase "God is everywhere"?'

I shake my head and notice her looking over her shoulder. 'What's wrong now?'

She stops. 'We're far enough from them now. You should go on ahead.'

I turn, noting the discomfort on her face. 'Is that because you'll get in trouble for walking home with a *boy*?'

She looks away. 'I've already endured a lecture on clothing choice this week. Not in the mood for a second topic.'

I regard her much-too-big clothes. She could do with sizing down, but it's hardly worthy of a lecture. 'What's the problem?'

She hesitates, then swallows. 'Modesty.'

My mouth turns up. 'Someone lectured you about *modesty*? What, did you flash an ankle or something?'

She stares at my chest, not answering.

The rules this girl lives by are crazy. 'Could you walk home with me if I were a J-dub?'

'No. We have to be chaperoned with all men, all the time.'

I let out a long whistle. 'How are so many of you married if you can never be alone?'

'It's a long answer that you probably aren't interested in hearing anyway.' She gestures for me to start walking. 'And since you have the emotional maturity of a toddler, I think I'll save my breath.'

'Wow. That's not very Christian of you, Wilson. What happened to return evil for evil to no one?'

She steps past me, deciding to walk ahead of me instead. 'I suddenly remembered Matthew 5:38. "Eye for an eye."' She lifts her hand in a wave while walking away. 'Have fun cleaning tables at school.'

My mouth curls into a smile. 'And you have fun at Bible study. Chaperoned, of course.'

Annie glances over her shoulder, then breaks into a jog.

5

ANNIE

'What are you doing up so early?' Mum asks, flicking the kettle on and dragging the container of teabags to her.

I rub my eyes and glance at the clock. 'I have exams coming up, remember?'

She gets two mugs from the cupboard above her and drops teabags into them, despite the fact that I prefer to drink coffee in the mornings. Nowhere in the Bible does it say we aren't allowed to drink coffee. The organisation tells us to make our own decision about it and not judge others for theirs. But at some point, Mum made the decision for both of us, and turning eighteen doesn't seem to count for much. So when she places the tea in front of me, I say thank you and drink it.

'Do you know Tamsin from school?' I ask as I'm packing up my books.

Mum rests a hip on the bench, watching me. 'Her dad's a solicitor, yes?'

I nod, barely believing what I'm about to say. 'She invited me over tomorrow night.'

'To her house?'

Another nod.

Mum blows on her tea. 'Do you have a school assignment together or something?'

'No. She invited me to just… sleep over and hang out.'

I'm met with a worried sigh.

'That's just asking for trouble. We all know how worldly girls that age spend their Saturday nights.'

I scrape my teeth over my lip. 'I don't, actually. I've never been with any of them on a Saturday night.'

Mum's face pinches with worry. 'Annie. Please be smart. I'm sure Tamsin's a lovely girl, but she doesn't live by Jehovah's moral standards.'

Irritation pulses through me. 'That doesn't mean she's without morals.'

Another sigh. 'I know it's tempting, but why make life harder for yourself?'

My foot bounces furiously under the table. 'Can I ask you something?'

'Of course.'

'The other day, when Brother Oliver spoke to me about my skirt, did you agree with him?'

She frowns at the question, clearly not following. 'When he commented on the length?'

'Yes, when he commented on the length.'

She turns the cup in her hands. 'I mean, I could see his point once it was brought to our attention. Why are you asking about that now?'

'Because *I* thought it was ridiculous.' I should stop there, but I don't. 'And inappropriate.'

'Inappropriate how?'

My hands are clamming up. 'They're knees, Mum. And he's the only person who noticed them.'

'Because he was on the platform looking down, a bird's-eye view.'

'They're *knees*.' I'm not sure why I think emphasis will help her understand my point. 'Never mind.'

She sets her cup down. 'They must draw a line somewhere, or we'll have sisters walking around in miniskirts.'

I stand up, stuffing my books into the open bag on the next chair.

'"The women should adorn themselves in appropriate dress," Mum says, "with modesty and soundness of mind." 1 Timothy 2:9. These are Jehovah's wishes, not Brother Oliver's.'

I zip up my bag. 'Okay. Well, I'm going to stay at Tamsin's house tomorrow.'

She looks stunned for a moment. 'What's actually going on here?'

'Nothing's going on. I'm simply letting you know my plans for the weekend.'

Her lips flatten into a thin line. 'Do you need to talk to someone?'

'Like who?'

'Like one of your spiritual sisters.'

'Why? So they can set me back on God's path?' Guilt floods me as I leave the room, but I don't back down. I swim in it. Thankfully, swimming lessons were on the approved list of extracurricular activities growing up.

Mum follows me to my bedroom. 'Sister Jane said you can call her anytime if you need someone to chat to.'

Sister Jane smells permanently of tinned soup and hasn't lived in the real world for more than fifty years. She has both elders on speed dial in order to report any suspicious behaviour within the congregation.

'I'll ask her to come visit after school today,' Mum says when I don't reply. 'It'll be good for you, and she'll love feeling needed. It must get very lonely living up in those hills by herself.'

'That's on her. She *chose* to cut off her entire family.'

Mum stiffens in the doorway, confirming I've gone too far.

'Sorry,' I say quietly.

She straightens. 'Sister Jane's spiritual family extends all over the world.'

'Then I guess she's very lucky.' I wonder if Mum actually believes half the things that come out of her mouth. Does she really think her spiritual brothers and sisters will ever replace the husband and daughter missing from this house?

Mum watches me change my clothes and step into my sneakers. I don't bother with the laces.

'Why are you leaving so early?'

'Because I need to use the computers at school.' *And I can't breathe in this house.*

'You haven't had breakfast.'

'I'm not hungry.' I swing my bag over my shoulder. 'And I'm working after school today, so please don't call Sister Jane.'

She follows me to the front door. 'What time will you finish work?'

'Normal time.'

'You'll be here for dinner?'

The panic in her voice makes me look back at her. I'm all she has left, and spending a night with a worldly acquaintance threatens that. 'I'm always here for dinner, Mum.'

She nods, her grip on the door frame easing. 'We can prepare for the *Watchtower* study since you won't be here tomorrow night.'

I take the olive branch. 'Okay.'

———

I get caught up in the computer room trying to get the printer to work, which means I'm late to 2D art. Rushing in, I look around at the full tables. Tamsin's not here, but Hunter Reed is. This is the only class I have with him, and so far, we've managed to ignore each other entirely during that time. Hunter usually has a table meant for eight people all to himself. He prefers it that way. How do I know? Because of the death stares he casts at those who dare to approach.

Given the convenient location of the table, my late-ness, the lack of alternatives, and the fact that he was willing to be seen in public with me yesterday, I wonder if he might make an exception this time.

He glances in my direction, acknowledging my exis-tence briefly. Encouraged, I approach, sliding into the chair opposite him.

He looks up abruptly. 'What are you doing?'

I open my pencil case and rifle around for a grey lead. 'Art.'

He stares at me. 'I hope you don't think because I saved your arse down at the creek last night that we're friends now.'

I meet his stare. 'And I hope you don't think that me sitting in the chair farthest from you at this enormous table when there are no other options is an extension of friendship.'

Nothing changes on his face. 'I need a lot of space to draw.'

'And I need quiet.'

His eyes remain on me for a few more seconds. Then he returns his attention to his sketch pad.

Miss Talbert looks up from where she's fiddling with the VCR. 'You can get on with your projects, guys. I'm just setting this up for later.'

Tamsin rushes into the room, giving Miss Talbert an apologetic look and mouthing, 'Sorry.'

'Find a seat, please,' Miss Talbert says, crouching in front of the power point.

Tamsin spots me, then looks at Hunter. Her eyebrows lift slightly. 'Generous of you to share your table,' she says to Hunter as she slides into the seat next to me.

He looks up briefly. 'Oh, I didn't share. Wilson just can't take a hint.'

Tamsin gives me a look.

Ignoring Hunter's comment, I say, 'Is that invitation still open for tomorrow? If not, that's fine.'

A grin splits Tamsin's face. 'You're really going to come?'

Her smile is contagious. 'Only if you haven't made other plans.'

She waves off the suggestion. 'Even if I had, I'd change them. This is huge. Annie Wilson's stepping out.'

Hunter leans back in his chair, looking across the table at me. '*You're* going to a party.'

I nod.

He looks almost annoyed. 'Why?'

'I need a reason?'

He makes a face. 'There'll be drinking, smoking. People hooking up.'

'There'll also be dancing and fun,' Tamsin says. 'Stop scaring her.'

Hunter's eyes never leave mine. 'Am I scaring you, Wilson?'

I shake my head. 'No.'

He returns his attention to his work.

Tamsin leans in and whispers, 'We'll just go for a few hours, and we can leave whenever you want. What do you like to drink? I'll pick something up for us.'

'Wilson doesn't drink,' Hunter says without looking up.

I cut my eyes to him. 'Just because I don't get drunk doesn't mean I don't drink.'

He looks up. 'Oh yeah? What's your poison?'

'Are you asking as a friend?'

We stare at each other a moment, breaking eye contact only when Miss Talbert claps her hands. Everyone falls silent and looks in her direction.

'Right. Well, I can't seem to get the VCR working, so we'll just keep going with our final pieces. I know some of you are struggling, so I might pair you guys up for the lesson so you can share ideas with your partner. Work through any problems you have. Get inspired.'

Hunter crosses his arms and tips his head back. No surprise that he's not a fan of study partners.

'Tamsin, you can go with Amy,' the teacher says, walking between the tables. She stops when she reaches me, then looks at Hunter.

I know what she's going to say before she says it.

'Annie, I'm going to put you with Hunter. You have very different styles and ideas. I think that will help you both.'

Hunter sits up straight. 'I don't need a partner. I've got plenty of ideas.'

Saw that coming a mile away.

'Well, Mr Reed, I'd know that if you had submitted your plan to me on time.' She walks on, calling out more names.

Tamsin picks up her books and says to Hunter, 'Be nice,' before walking over to sit with Amy.

'Okay. Let's go,' Miss Talbert calls, clapping her hands again. 'I want lots of feedback and sharing of ideas.'

Hunter doesn't move, so it falls on me to do so. I rise, picking up my stuff and walking around to the other side of the table. The closer I get to him, the brighter his eyes burn in my direction. It feels a lot like approaching an aggressive dog and trying to read their body language to know if you're about to be bitten.

He reaches for the chair next to his, dragging it back

from the table. The legs screech against the floor for endless seconds, drawing the attention of everyone in the room. I lower myself into it.

The second my book hits the table, he picks it up and flicks through it. 'I don't think we're going to be much help to each other judging by these pretty little drawings.'

I take it from his hands.

'Why are you going to this party tomorrow?' he asks.

The question catches me off guard. 'Because I haven't been to one before.'

'So you're rebelling?'

I give him a tired look.

'Most kids rebel *before* they're legally allowed to do whatever the hell they want,' he says.

I reach for his sketchbook. When he doesn't stop me, I flick through it. Ink drawings of slaughtered pigs hanging on butcher hooks fill the pages. 'These are... disturbing.'

'You feel disturbed?'

'Yes,' I say, closing it and handing it back to him.

He nods. 'Good.'

'That's *good*?'

'Yeah. You felt something. That's the point of art, isn't it?'

I swallow. 'I see. This is your way of saying you didn't feel anything when you looked at mine.'

'Besides bored?'

I look down at my drawing of a young woman with her horse, then mutter, 'Let's just work independently.'

'And disobey the teacher? You really are rebelling.'

'Technically *you're* disobeying the teacher by being rude instead of helpful.'

He leans his elbows on the table. 'I was being honest. Your technique's good. The subject matter's just a bit dry.'

I look down again, studying the drawing. 'What would you change?'

'The girl.' He pauses. 'And the horse.'

I tilt my head at him.

He exhales. 'Fine. What do you want people to feel when they look at it?'

'It's a reunion. I want people to feel happy.' When he doesn't say anything, I look at him. He's staring at the page, the skin between his eyebrows pinched. 'What?'

He brushes a finger down his nose. 'Is that Bridget?'

It's a logical conclusion, but I'm not ready to hear my sister's name—especially from Hunter Reed's mouth. Bridget's a true horse girl. She only cried once the day she left, and it was when she was saying goodbye to her beloved Charlie. I'd watched through the window as her face collapsed before she buried it in the gelding's mane. Her shoulders shook for a full minute.

'Looks like your horse,' Hunter says, gesturing to the page.

I touch the drawing. Charlie's the reason I hold out hope of seeing her again. Mum was so confident her eldest would come crawling back. That's the reason we still have him.

It's been three years.

'The girl looks a bit like Bridget,' Hunter adds, 'if she were a puppet.'

My mouth falls open as I meet his eyes once more. 'That's… so rude.' But as I say it, I can't keep from smiling.

'It's the muppet mouth,' he says, pointing.

I swat at his hand, glimpsing a smirk as he retreats. It's gone as quickly as it came.

We work independently for the rest of the class, the silence between us not as uncomfortable as one would expect. When the bell rings at the end of the period, he's gone before I've even finished packing up.

'Was it awful?' Tamsin asks, appearing beside me.

I glance at the door Hunter exited through moments earlier. 'No. No, it was fine.'

6

ANNIE

Sunday morning meeting, Sunday afternoon field service, Monday night Bible study with Sister Jane, Tuesday night Bible study with half the congregation, Wednesday night preparation for Thursday's meeting, Friday night preparation for Sunday's meeting, and Saturday field service. This is the time I give to Jehovah each week. And I've done so my whole life without resentment, fitting the rest of my life in around these priorities. However, the resentment is creeping in. I'm not entirely sure who or what I'm resenting, but I'm feeling a little robbed of life lately.

We meet at Brother Sam's house for field service at 8:45 a.m., passing the oval on the way there, where families are settling in for a day of netball, footy, meat pies, and socialising. This is how people my age spend their Saturdays. Soon, we'll visit their empty houses and make a note to come back. Or perhaps someone will be home to tell us they're not interested. Or they won't bother answering the door at all, and we'll pretend we didn't just see the curtain move.

Everyone takes a seat, and as I look around the circle, I see they're genuinely happy to be here. Seeing others embrace this life with enthusiasm evokes a loneliness so deep that my bones ache with it.

'Any preferences for groups?' Brother Oliver asks, looking around.

Sister Jane's hand shoots up. 'I'd like to work with Annie.'

I look accusingly at Mum, but she's conveniently busy flicking through the *Watchtower* magazine in her lap. When Donna raises her hand and asks if she can go in our car, I have to stop myself from rolling my eyes. There's no escaping her—unless I leave the school grounds to watch a fight.

Mum joins the party, and the four of us climb into Sister Jane's Holden Camry. The door's hinges are rusted, and it requires two hands to pull it shut.

'Door's not closed properly, love,' Sister Jane says into the rear-view mirror.

I wince as it screeches open, then pull it hard.

'Still not shut,' Donna says beside me.

I open it again, slamming it harder. The light above the door remains on.

Sister Jane laughs. 'Put some muscle into it, dear.'

This time, I slam it so hard my mum jumps a foot in the air and the car rocks through the aftershock. Finally, the light is off.

'I think that got it,' Sister Jane says, turning the key in the ignition.

I glance sideways at Donna because she's staring at me. 'What?'

'Are you okay?'

I nod and look out the window.

Mum and Jane begin talking about the swooping magpies outside the Kingdom Hall. Donna leans in and says quietly, 'I hear there's going to be an announcement at the meeting tomorrow.'

I look back at her, taking the bait. 'About what?'

She flicks her gaze to the front to ensure the others aren't listening. 'Sister Carly has been seen a number of times with a worldly guy from Turram. Always unchaperoned. Brother Bill apparently saw them at that fishing spot past the rocks at Whistle Beach.'

I wait to feel some semblance of outrage at this news, but I feel nothing. 'Maybe they were fishing.'

Donna waits for the conversation in the front seat to resume before responding. 'I mean, they had fishing rods, but who knows? They were well away from the main beach.'

I nod slowly. 'Dad used to catch flathead there at high tide. They'd just swim right up to him.'

Her face contorts with pity. 'Have you spoken to him lately?'

'He phones every week.' We just have little to say to each other. He's moved on from this life, the religion, his friends. His family. I know he's seeing someone because there's always telling noises in the background when we speak on the phone. The clink of dishes or the distant hum of a vacuum cleaner. Not the noises of a guest but a resident. He's never mentioned it, and I've never asked.

We don't talk about anything outside of school, work, and the pets. Not Mum. Not Bridget. Even post-graduation plans are off limits. Contentious.

'I thought we might call upon Kevin Reed,' Sister Jane announces.

I snap my gaze to the rear-view mirror.

'He wasn't in a good way last time I called with Sister Marie,' she continues. 'We agreed a morning visit might be a better idea.' She exchanges a knowing look with Mum when she says this part.

'Was he intoxicated last time?' Donna asks, leaning forwards.

'It did appear and smell that way, but let's not contribute to gossip. Goodness knows there's enough of it in this town.' She meets my eyes once more. 'Would you like to come with me, Annie? Hunter's in your year at school, isn't he?'

'He is.' My voice barely carries.

He *was* a year above me through primary school, but he missed so much of year seven after his mum passed that he ended up having to repeat it.

'Such a troubled boy,' Mum says, tutting. 'But he might be more willing to listen if Annie's with you.'

The fact that Mum thinks Hunter would listen to me shows how little she knows him.

Sister Jane turns the car onto the dirt road that leads to the farm. 'There's nothing quite like bringing people hope of seeing their dead loved ones again.'

I can barely hear her over the thrumming of my heart.

'I know it can be a little awkward witnessing to other

students,' Sister Jane says, 'but Jehovah never tests us beyond what we can bear.'

That's not true. I couldn't bear it when Dad left, and I certainly couldn't bear it when Bridget left. I can't bear the hollow feeling I wake up with every morning or the sense that I'm living a life meant for someone else. And right now I can't bear Donna staring at me.

I can't bear any of it.

'Here we are,' Sister Jane says when the house comes into view. 'Ute's here, so someone's home.'

My entire body tenses up when I spot Hunter chopping wood at the side of the house. He's wearing a torn Red Hot Chili Peppers T-shirt, which is clinging to his lean frame, and faded jeans with Blundstones. His hair's a sweaty mess.

And I can't look away.

He lowers the axe when he notices the car. I try to shrink down into the seat, but he sees me, eyes narrowing with suspicion. He drops the axe on the ground and walks to the front of the house, arms crossed as he waits for us to exit the car.

'Good luck,' Donna whispers.

There's a slight tremble in my hands as I struggle with the door yet again. It takes me three tries to push it open, and I only succeed with Sister Jane's help. We walk towards Hunter, Sister Jane smiling warmly and me trying very hard not to appear as outwardly mortified as I feel on the inside.

'What are you doing here?' Hunter asks me in place of a greeting. His gaze sweeps the full length of me as he awaits my answer.

I wrap my cardigan tighter around me, covering as much of my hand-me-down blouse as I can. 'Is your dad home?' I've forgotten to say good morning, to tell him that we're calling on him and his neighbours, and the many other things I'm supposed to say. Maybe because I know he wants me to get straight to the point.

Sister Jane looks awkwardly between us, then says, 'I had a lovely conversation with your father on Wednesday. I left him with some reading and wanted to see if he had any questions.'

Hunter looks at her, and his expression makes me want to retreat to the car. 'He's still asleep, and he didn't read your leaflet, because I binned it.'

Sister Jane's face falls.

'*Do You Have an Immortal Spirit?*' he says. 'That was the title, wasn't it?'

Jane clears her throat. 'That's right. It talks about—'

'I know what it talks about.' He shifts his weight. 'It said the spirit dies with the body. That when we lose people, they don't go to heaven. They're 100 percent gone. Noted. Thanks for coming all this way to share the good news.'

Sister Jane had good intentions when she left that tract with Kevin, but people grieving don't want to hear that their loved ones are simply rotting in the ground and the only way to see them again is to upheave their life, abandon their friends, and come worship a God they don't know.

Sister Jane takes a step back from him. 'I think we'll come back another time.'

Hunter shakes his head. 'I wouldn't bother. Everything Dad worships comes in a can or a bottle.'

I drop my gaze, unable to look at him any longer.

'Perhaps you could let him know that we came by.' Sister Jane gestures to the pile of wood he's dragged up from the creek. 'I hope you get through that before the rain arrives.'

Hunter nods in place of a reply, then turns and heads for the chopping block.

I return to the car, feeling hot now despite the cold air, and tug once, twice, three times on the door. I stop and draw a long breath as Sister Jane slides breezily into her seat without any problems and reaches for her seat belt. I yank at the door again with no success. Donna makes a move to help me, then freezes.

What is she doing?

An arm appears around me, two fingers sliding under the handle next to mine. Hunter opens it on the first go, then keeps hold of it, waiting for me to get inside. When I look up at him, I'm met with an annoyed expression. This isn't an act of chivalry. He simply wants us off his property—now.

'Thanks,' I say before dropping into the car.

The door slams shut, and I watch him stride away through the window. He snatches up a piece of wood and places it on the chopping block.

I hear the axe come down as we pull away.

7

ANNIE

Tamsin's bed is scattered with all the types of clothes I'm not allowed to wear and the kinds of CDs I'm not allowed to listen to.

'You like Silverchair?' she asks as she slips her midriff top over her head and turns to check her reflection in the mirror.

I've heard Silverchair songs enough times on the radio to recognise them. 'Sure.'

She points to the bed. 'Put *Freak Show* on.'

It takes me a moment to find it. I flip it over and read the song titles on the back as I make my way over to the player.

'What do you think?' Tamsin asks, turning in a circle.

My gaze falls to her belly piercing and continues down her 26 Red jeans to the white Reeboks peeking out at the bottom. 'You look really good.'

'So do you,' she lies. 'You should take your hair out, though. It looks gorgeous down.'

I reach up and tug at the elastic, brushing my hair out with my fingers.

Tamsin assesses me. 'Do you want to borrow something to wear?'

'You just said I look good,' I reply, teasing her.

Her nose crinkles. 'You do, but we're going to a party, not hanging out at the courts.'

I wouldn't know what girls wear to either. My wardrobe is divided into two parts: meeting clothes and nonmeeting clothes. Meeting clothes are long skirts, blouses, cardigans, conservative dresses, and sensible dress shoes. Nonmeeting clothes are oversized T-shirts, flannel, jeans, leggings, riding pants, and cheap sneakers. They're mostly thrift shop finds and hand-me-downs from my sister.

I bet Bridget has an amazing wardrobe now.

Tonight I'm wearing a Billabong T-shirt I found at a sale, Levis, and R. M. Williams boots. 'I'm okay in this.'

Tamsin walks over and lifts the hem of my T-shirt, inspecting the jeans. 'Such a great arse. These are actually a good cut for you, but you can't see that with your T-shirt hanging to your thighs.' She twists the bottom of the T-shirt and ties a small knot, then steps back to admire her work. 'That's so much better.'

I turn to the mirror and tug the T-shirt down so it meets the top of my jeans. It does look better. I imagine what people in my congregation would think if they saw me like this. The things they would say.

'You want some make-up?' Tamsin asks, holding out her mascara.

I take it and move closer to the mirror to apply some.

1 Peter 3:3 pops into my mind: 'Do not let your adornment be external.' The consensus in our congregation seems to be it's fine to wear make-up to meetings, so long as it doesn't *look* like you're wearing make-up.

I pick the red lipstick, a colour I most certainly wouldn't wear to a meeting.

'Oh my God, yes. Perfect colour for you.'

She's right. It's bright and fun, and it suits me.

'Ready?' Tamsin asks. 'Mum will drop us off.'

'I can drive.'

She tilts her head. 'No, you're drinking with me, remember?'

As tempting as it is to drive, I want this experience. And I trust Tamsin. That does nothing to stop the guilt that hits me from both sides, though.

'Let's go,' she says, grabbing my arm and tugging me along.

Tamsin's mum's name is Sue. She's kind, funny, and so... normal. She chats away the entire drive, asking me about my jewellery, school, and my plans post-school. Any lingering guilt is eaten up by this entirely comfortable moment.

It hits me then. What if temptation for me isn't a boy or a fancy career? What if it's a stable family to spend time with?

Well played, Satan.

We pull up in front of a small beach house decaying beneath a mountain of debris. The location more than makes up for the venue, as it's directly across the road from a quiet stretch of beach.

'See you at eleven,' Sue says as we climb out.

Tamsin makes a pouty face. 'Twelve?'

'Eleven or get a taxi.'

'There are no taxis in Whistle Beach.'

Sue gives a triumphant smile. 'Oh, I know. That's why I'll see you at eleven. Don't make me come inside and get you.'

We watch her pull away, then head for the house. Alanis Morissette's 'You Oughta Know' pours from the open door. Some kids from school are sitting on stained couches out front, cigarettes hidden from the view of the cars pulling up.

My stomach tightens as we enter. Nerves meshing with... excitement? It's been so long since I've experienced excitement that I barely recognise it anymore. People look curiously in my direction before returning to their conversations.

'If you're looking for the Kingdom Hall, it's the next town over,' Trent says as we enter the kitchen.

My eyes meet his, and I can tell he's just looking for a laugh.

'Don't be a dick,' Tamsin says, swatting him.

He slides a bottle of Jim Beam in her direction. 'We've run out of Coke.'

'That's okay.' She pulls room-temperature ginger ale out of her straw bag. 'I've come prepared.' She tugs two white cups from a plastic sleeve and gets to work.

And there's the guilt again, threatening to ruin the evening before it's even begun. It's not only the drinking triggering me but the whole worldly environment.

'What do you normally drink?' Tamsin asks as she pushes a cup towards me.

Trent leans on the chipped table. 'J-dubs don't drink, do they?'

I take the cup Tamsin hands me and smell it. 'Jesus drank.'

'Bourbon?' Trent asks.

Tamsin jabs him with her elbow.

He raises his hand. 'It was a joke. So you're a wine drinker?'

I drank red wine *once* and didn't much like it, but he doesn't need all the details. 'Sure.' I sip at the bourbon. It actually tastes better than it smells.

People continue to arrive in a steady stream, wandering into the kitchen to say hello—to Tamsin and Trent. It's fine. I don't belong here. They know it, and I know it.

Tamsin keeps looking to the door, like she's waiting for someone.

'Who are you looking for?' I ask.

'That would be Sammy,' Trent answers on her behalf.

'Really?' Sammy's the only guy I know who's brave enough to call Hunter a friend. He's nice enough. And by nice, I mean he ignores me entirely instead of making my life a living hell. He keeps to himself. We have that in common.

'You can stop pining now,' Trent says, stepping around Tamsin. 'He just walked in.'

Tamsin grabs hold of my arm, baring her teeth at me. 'Lipstick check.'

I bite back a smile. 'You're good.'

When I look to the door, I see Hunter's here also. The pair are talking to some girls from school. Well, Sammy's talking. Hunter's looking around the room. His eyes land on me, and he looks immediately annoyed, despite knowing I was coming. His gaze falls to the drink in my hand, then away.

'Ah, what was that?' Tamsin whispers.

I look at her. 'What was what?'

'*That.*' She gestures towards Hunter. 'That little exchange.'

'There was no exchange.'

She gives me a sceptical look. 'Okay. Well, just know there are far safer choices here tonight if that's where your mind is going.'

My cheeks heat. 'That's not where my...' I drink until my cup is empty.

'Oh, okay,' Tamsin says. 'We're proper drinking now, are we?' She empties her cup, then takes the empty from my hand. 'Better refill while we can.'

Trent returns to the kitchen, glancing at me as he swings the fridge open. 'Looks like someone'll be hitting the confessional tomorrow.'

'We don't have a confessional,' I reply dryly. 'That's a Catholic thing.'

Amused, Trent steps up to the table and into my personal space. 'Then how does a good girl like you repent for her sins?'

I go to step back and collide with a wall of chest behind me. I turn and my eyes travel all the way up to Hunter's disapproving face.

'You actually came,' he says.

I swallow. 'I did.'

He glances at Trent, who retreats to the other side of

the kitchen. I immediately increase the space between myself and Hunter. I'm starting to recognise his scent, and that scares me for some reason. It's a combination of whatever deodorant he wears, fresh hay, and... him.

Tamsin raises her drink in greeting. 'Hunter.'

'Tamsin.'

Hunter intercepts the drink she hands me and smells it. 'You plan on throwing up on the driveway later? Maybe finish with a skinny-dip?'

Tamsin laughs behind me. 'No one's throwing up anywhere.' She takes the drink from his hand and gives it to me. 'The skinny-dip is absolutely an option, though.' She raises her chin and meets Hunter's gaze. 'What are you doing here? I thought you were too cool for these kinds of events.'

'I drove Sammy.'

'Hunter prefers to play the role of chauffeur and security at parties,' Tamsin says to me. 'You'll never catch him drinking on the job.'

That's not surprising given what he's facing at home. 'Security, huh? And yet I feel *less* safe since he arrived,' I say.

Hunter angles his head at me. 'Then I'd suggest limiting your drinks. The first rule of drinking is to make sure you're safe before getting legless.'

'She's very safe with me,' Tamsin says. 'Why are you guys behaving like such arseholes tonight? Let her enjoy herself.'

Hunter shifts his weight. 'Guys? Who else was being an arsehole?'

Trent raises his hands, feigning innocence.

Tamsin shakes her head and drags me from the kitchen. When I look over my shoulder, I meet Hunter's turbulent blue eyes before he disappears from sight.

———

Hunter

Annie Wilson should be home studying her Bible, not here drinking bourbon. Talk about a fish out of water. She's behaving like a thirteen-year-old. And even though it's none of my business, I'm wondering what prompted all this. It might have something to do with her sister. She fled town around the same age. No one knows where she went. I'm not even sure Annie knows.

I'm not one for parties, and I didn't want to come to this one. But when Sammy asked me, I found myself saying yes. And now I'm watching Annie, wondering if she might be the reason I'm here. I guess I was curious to see her in this environment. So I came. Now I've seen her. Done.

So why do I continue to watch her? Why am I distracted when she's in the room and distracted when she's not? When she steps out front, my eyes go to the window. When she's refilling her drink for the fifth time, my gaze drifts to the kitchen. And when she's in the room, I'm noticing the sliver of skin between her jeans and tee that flashes every now and then. I keep looking. And I'm not the only one. Annie's forbidden fruit, and every guy here knows it. Maybe they've always looked, and I've just never noticed it before.

Tamsin's well on her way to drunk now, but Annie seems to be holding up better than I expected. She's a fairly relaxed drunk, it turns out. I watch her soak up the conversation, jokes, and endless flirtation going on around her.

If only I could read that mind of hers.

When the music's turned up, I take that as my cue. People are going to start dancing soon, and I have no interest in joining them, so I slip from the house and cross the road, heading down to the beach. I'll wait here until I hear the music's turned down, a signal that it's safe to return.

Sinking down onto the sand, I draw my knees up and listen to the waves crash in front of me. They're extra violent tonight.

I've barely had a chance to settle in when I sense someone behind me. I glance over my shoulder and make out Annie's familiar frame standing a few metres away.

'This your idea of being safe, Wilson?' I say. 'Wandering around in the dark, drunk, at an abandoned beach?'

She walks over, dropping down onto the sand beside me. 'It's not abandoned. You're here. Why'd you leave?'

Normally I'd be annoyed at the unwelcome company, but I'm not annoyed at Annie. 'Not much of a dancer.'

'Oh. Is that what they're doing?'

My lips twitch. 'You're not going to join in?'

'I wouldn't know how.'

'You just raise your arms and shout the lyrics as loud as you can while spilling your drink everywhere.'

Her teeth flash in the dark. 'Well, I don't know any of the lyrics.'

'Neither do half the people singing right now.'

She laughs. I've heard laughs described as pretty before, but I've never really understood what it meant. Annie Wilson has a laugh that sounds like the wind chime that once hung on our veranda when Mum was alive.

She peers into her cup. 'This was full a moment ago. I must have spilled it on the way here.'

I keep my eyes ahead. 'I think you've had enough.'

She rests her cheek on her knee and watches me. 'I'm sorry about this morning. I didn't want to get out of the car.'

'You didn't want to get back in it either judging by your terrible attempt.'

She laughs again, and it makes me look in her direction.

'That car has the worst doors,' she says. 'I finished the morning feeling like I'd lifted weights for three hours.'

I study her face. 'Does your mum know where you are?'

She shakes her head and looks at the water. 'I don't need her permission.'

I doubt that's true. 'Why'd you really come tonight?'

'Just to see.'

'See what?'

She doesn't reply straight away. 'To see if I feel better here with these people than with my people.'

'And do you?'

She looks at me. 'I don't think these people like me very much.'

'I wouldn't take it personally. They don't like me very much either.'

She sighs. 'It feels better here, on this beach. Even if the company is a little rough.'

My gaze meets hers in the dark. Neither of us speaks for the longest time.

Annie's first to break the silence. 'I'm safe on this abandoned beach with you. Right?'

I nod. 'For now.'

She smiles and looks back at the water. 'Will they really go skinny-dipping later?'

'Can't tell you how many drunk twats I've pulled from that water.'

'Really? Bully by day, hero by night.'

'I've also been tempted to leave a few as shark food.'

She rests her head on her hand, observing me. 'Would you pull *me* out of the water?'

I wouldn't let her get in to begin with. 'Don't you have a God for that sort of thing?'

She laughs silently, her arm brushing mine. It's not like me to notice stuff like that, but I notice it tonight.

'Do you think I could have the skinny-dipping experience without the skinny-dipping part?' she asks.

'I'm going to assume you're drunk and don't know what you're saying.'

She sighs. 'I know what I'm saying. I want to go in but keep some clothes on.'

I watch her, trying to assess her level of drunkenness. 'Yeah, we just call that a swim 'round these parts.'

She stands up and begins unbuttoning her jeans. 'Come in with me.'

I reach up and still her hands. 'You're not going in the water.'

She lets go of her jeans and sits down again. 'You might be right. I think I've had enough to drink.'

My shoulders relax.

'They warn us about these worldly parties,' she says. 'They're supposedly wildly immoral, bursting with temptations.'

'Worldly parties? That's what they call a bunch of teens hanging out?'

She nods.

I lean back on my hands. 'I mean, they're not entirely wrong. Someone will likely be lighting a joint or sneaking off into one of the bedrooms by now.'

'But not *every* person. I mean, you're sober, and you have zero temptations because you're stuck here with me.' She flashes me a cheeky smile.

That last part isn't entirely true. Annie Wilson's proving to be a small temptation in her own right. But only a fool would go there. Only an idiot would try to compete with a God.

She leans back on her hands also. We're eye to eye when she whispers, 'I think I'm having doubts.'

It takes me a moment to realise she's talking about her religion. 'I'm guessing that's also a sin?'

'Yes,' she replies. 'I can't help but wonder if Bridget did the right thing in leaving. I mean, she hasn't come back, and everyone assured me she would. Maybe she's happier outside of it.'

I have no idea how to respond to that. If I were capable of pity, I might be inclined to throw some her way.

'Annie!' Tamsin calls behind us. 'You down here?'

Annie rises to her feet. 'Yeah.'

'It's quarter to eleven. We need to sober up.'

'Coming!' Her gaze falls on me once more. 'Thanks for keeping me on dry land.'

I'm eye level with the exposed skin above her jeans, so I keep my focus on the water ahead. 'Enjoy your first hangover, Wilson.'

8

ANNIE

My head's throbbing, and I'm painfully thirsty. I crawl from the mattress beside Tamsin's bed and creep to the kitchen for a glass of water. The clock reads 7:55 a.m. If I don't leave now, I'm going to be late for the meeting.

'I have to go,' I whisper to a sleeping Tamsin when I return to the bedroom.

'I'll walk you out,' she says without opening her eyes or making any effort to move.

I suppress a smile. 'That's okay. You go back to sleep.'

She's drifted off again before I've even left the room.

Sue's pottering around the kitchen in her dressing gown when I emerge from the bedroom this time. The house smells of freshly ground coffee.

'You're up early,' she says.

'I have to get going.'

'Church this morning?'

I don't correct her. Church is what most would call it. 'Yeah.'

'You're good.' She sips from her mug. 'Don't mind us heathens over here.' She gives me a playful wink.

I thank her for having me, and she tells me I'm welcome anytime.

As I'm driving home, I brace for the guilt, regret, and remorse. But it doesn't come. I'm not sorry I went, only that I didn't fit in. But I don't think Hunter fit in either. Despite his initial hostile greeting, he ended up being perfect company for the latter part of the night. He clearly wasn't happy about my being there. I could feel his eyes following me from room to room. Sadly, a part of me enjoyed holding his attention. Under the gentle buzz of a few drinks, I liked being the one he watched. It felt good to be seen. It felt good to be seen by *him*.

What does that say about me?

Mum is largely silent when I enter the house, so I head straight to the shower. I put on a long-sleeve dress with stockings and black flats. The clothes I wore to the party go straight into the washing machine. I'm paranoid they smell of cigarettes and bourbon, but when I sniff them, they smell of salt and sand—and Hunter Reed.

I'm in the car at 8:40 a.m. because I don't want to give Mum any more fuel to throw on the fire.

'You didn't have breakfast,' she says as she slips into the passenger seat.

I start the car. 'Had something at Tamsin's.' That's a lie, and I told it directly to her face.

We're halfway to the Kingdom Hall when she asks, 'So, what did you girls get up to last night?'

'We went to the beach.' It's the truth. I simply choose not to mention the party. Or the drinking. Or the fact that my T-shirt was tied up and no one judged me for it. I definitely don't tell her that I liked that version of me better than this one.

The morning talk is titled 'Kindness—Essential in the Sight of God'. The whole time Brother Peter's speaking, I can't help but think about the brother seated at the back of the Kingdom Hall who we're all shunning right now due to a rumoured gambling addiction. *That* doesn't feel very kind. It never has. It doesn't align with anything being taught to us right now.

'Let's turn to Matthew 5:38,' Brother Peter says.

There's a rustle of pages across the hall.

'It says, "You must accordingly be perfect, as your heavenly Father is perfect."'

I think about the terrible way he speaks to his wife and let out a long breath, prompting Mum to look sideways at me. Leaning in, I whisper, 'He's a bit of a hypocrite.'

Her eyes widen slightly. Then she shakes her head at me before returning her attention to him.

After the talk, we sing another song, marking the halfway point of the meeting. Then comes the *Watchtower* study. The children around me are starting to squirm in their chairs, their parents dipping their heads constantly to remind them to sit still and listen.

Two hours is too long for kids.

Two hours is too long for me.

When the final amen is uttered, the children burst from their seats and go in search of their friends. I pick up my bag and say to Mum, 'Do you mind if we go? I've got to finish my final assessment piece for 2D this afternoon.'

She gives a reluctant nod. 'I'm still not sure why you chose that subject. Seems like a waste.'

'It's all a waste, Mum. Every subject is a waste if I do nothing with the knowledge.' The words come out snarkier than I intend. I hook my handbag on my shoulder. My pounding head isn't helping my mood. 'Sorry.'

Sister Jane appears at the end of the row of chairs. 'Not joining us for field service this afternoon?'

The self-control required on my part to not groan aloud is enormous.

'Annie has some things to finish for school,' Mum says.

Sister Jane smiles. 'Well, at least you came for your spiritual food first.' She's not one to pass judgement. 'More fruit cake for the rest of us.'

I really need to get out of here.

Unfortunately, our exit coincides with the four-wheel drive pulling up to collect Sister Maria. She's ushered past us and loaded into the car after another demonic attack during the *Watchtower* study. Her tired eyes meet mine briefly as she passes, then again when she's laid carefully in the boot of the car by two ministerial servants. She looks so defeated.

'Poor love,' Mum says as the car pulls away. 'It's not only at the meetings, you know. They attack at home in front of her daughter. Can you imagine how scary that must be for her?'

We're almost to the car now. I check over my shoulder before saying, 'What if it's *not* demons?'

Mum gives me a confused look.

'People have seizures for all kinds of reasons. I assume she's been to see a doctor.'

'The elders know what they're doing.' Mum stops walking and turns to me. 'Sister Maria used to visit mediums prior to finding Jehovah. When the seizures began, the elders went through all her belongings and found tarot cards. That's an invitation for trouble if I've ever heard one. The cards were burned, but Satan doesn't give up easily.'

She resumes walking, and I follow her to the car.

When we arrive home, I tell Mum I'm going for a ride.

'I thought you needed to finish your piece.'

'I do, but Charlie needs some exercise.'

She drops her handbag onto the bench and looks out the kitchen windows to where the horse is visible through the trees. 'It's probably time he was sold.'

She's been saying this for years, but she never goes through with it. That gelding is all we have left of Bridget.

Mum turns back to the bench. 'I'll make you a sandwich while you change.'

The pain's still there, always present despite her efforts to hide it. Acknowledging it would be her undoing. Uttering the words 'I miss her' might finish us both.

I put on riding pants and a flannelette shirt and snatch the sandwich from the plate on my way out. 'Thanks.' I haven't eaten since the night before, and my appetite has returned in full force.

Banjo leaps up from his bed when I step outside, and we walk between the weeping willows towards a waiting Charlie. I sometimes wonder if he's still waiting for

Bridget to return, expecting her to appear through the trees with a lead in hand and a giant smile.

'Only me,' I say as I halter him.

I lead him over to the tiny shed, the one Bridget used to jokingly refer to as the tack room, and saddle him. As I finish, I hear a motorbike across the creek. I lead Charlie to the top of the slope and spot Hunter.

He stops the bike when he sees me, so I walk Charlie down the slope towards the water. Hunter kills the motor, climbs off, and heads to the edge of the creek. He's wearing black tracksuit pants with worn knees and a blue hoodie that he fills out perfectly.

We're standing on opposite sides of the creek looking at each other, and I don't think either of us knows why.

'Can I ask you something?' I say.

He nods. 'As long as it's not "Would you like a free Bible study?"'

I suppress a smile and check over my shoulder before speaking. 'We went to Melbourne in August. Mum had appointments, so we spent the weekend there. When she was out, I went to the state library. Told Mum I needed to do some research for an assignment.'

He nods. 'That's not a question.'

'I asked one of the ladies there for info on Noah's ark.' Pausing, I draw a breath. 'Turns out there's no scientific evidence that an ark that size existed. No evidence of a global flood. In fact, many scientists say it would be impossible.'

He frowns at me across the water. 'Still no question.'

I nod, gathering my thoughts. 'If we're wrong about that, what else might we be wrong about?'

Hunter continues to watch me. 'What explanation did your mum give?'

'I didn't ask her. I couldn't.'

'Why not?'

I'm embarrassed by the answer. 'Because we're not allowed to look outside the organisation for answers.'

He rests his hands on his hips. 'Well, that's messed up.'

'It's for our protection. To avoid misinformation.'

'Misinformation.' He nods slowly. 'Right. So they don't want you focused on school, don't want you heading off to uni, and don't want you to learn anything outside of what they tell you is true.' He pauses. 'One might suspect them of trying to keep you uneducated.'

I press my eyes shut. While the organisation encourages the basic education necessary for supporting oneself, my doubts are the direct result of me venturing too far when they explicitly tell us not to. Higher education is considered a moral and spiritual threat.

'You all right?' Hunter asks.

I open my eyes, nose burning from the build-up of tears that I absolutely refuse to let out. They may never stop coming if I do. 'Yeah. Fine.'

He looks far from convinced. 'You shouldn't keep that shit bottled up, you know.'

'Well, not all of us have the luxury of violence as an outlet.'

'I have other outlets.' He glances upstream. 'Do you know the bend in the creek past the Davises' property? At the base of the hill where our land ends?'

I nod.

'Let's go,' he says, turning away and heading back to his bike.

'Why?'

'You'll see when we get there.'

I look down at Banjo before mounting Charlie.

Hunter starts his bike and follows the trail that runs adjacent with the water. I push Charlie into a trot to keep up. When Hunter revs his bike, it scares the gelding into a canter. I glance across the water, wondering if he did it on purpose. Judging by his amused expression, I'd say yes.

When the track ends on the other side, Hunter's forced to navigate the high grass. He's standing up because the paddock is uneven, but he still manages to stay ahead of me. I lean forwards and loosen the reins, and his stride lengthens. The moment I pass Hunter, he revs his bike again.

And now we're racing.

Hunter navigates the potholes and flies over bumps while Charlie leaps over shrubs and debris. Banjo's living his best life, tongue flying like a wet flag. I'm starting to have fun without meaning to. When I look over at Hunter, I swear I see him grinning. It's difficult to tell with him flashing in and out of view, though.

We slow down when we reach the bend in the creek. Charlie's snorting and heaving, and Banjo's panting and happy. The heaviness in my chest has eased, making it a little easier to breathe.

Hunter sits back on his seat, chest rising and falling fast. 'That horse can move.'

'He can.' I clap Charlie's neck. 'So what are we doing here?'

'You have to cross the creek.'

I cast a suspicious glance in his direction before navigating my way down to the shallow part of the creek. We both dismount on the other side.

'Now what?' I ask.

'Now we climb the hill.'

I walk at Hunter's side, Charlie and Banjo trailing behind me. When we reach the top, we descend into the basin below. The sheep scatter when they see us coming, and twice I have to recall an excited and poorly trained Banjo.

The ground is squelchy beneath our feet when we reach the bottom. Hunter turns to me and says, 'You can yell, scream, do whatever you like down here. No one'll hear you. The hills are like walls.'

Frowning, I look around. 'I don't understand. You want me to… yell?'

He taps a fist to his sternum. 'Just let it out. Whatever's stuck in here.'

I furrow my brow. 'That's not a good idea.'

'Why not?'

'Because it'll be ugly.'

He searches my eyes. 'So you'd prefer to let the ugly rot inside you? Make you miserable? *Bitter?*'

I shake my head. 'My feelings are private.'

'It's not a narrative. You can just scream and swear if you want.'

'I don't swear, remember?'

He shrugs. 'Maybe you should.'

I scrape my teeth over my lip, wondering if I'm brave enough to partake in this insanity.

'I'm not waiting here all day,' he says on a sigh.

'Fine.' I can't believe I'm actually agreeing to do this. 'Turn around.'

His eyebrows lift slightly. 'Why?'

'I don't want you to see me. Hearing it's one thing, but a visual is something else.'

With a roll of his eyes, he turns his back to me. 'Remember, from the chest.'

I stare at his back a moment. Having *him* in sight doesn't work for me either, so I turn around also. 'What do you normally say?'

'I normally say "fuck" a lot. I guess you'll have to be creative.'

I shift my weight from foot to foot, wondering if I have it in me to cuss aloud. 'What's the least offensive swear word, do you think?'

He looks over his shoulder at the same time I look over mine. 'You could go with something classic, like "shit".'

Facing forwards again, I ball my hands and close my eyes. 'Shit.' The word comes out as an embarrassing squeak.

Hunter bursts into laughter behind me. 'What the hell was that? Either do it properly or don't do it at all.'

I squeeze my eyes shut and shout, 'Shit!'

He doesn't laugh this time. 'Better, but I think you've got more in you. You've gotta drag it out until there's no air left to expel.'

Drawing a deep breath, I look heavenwards and shout, '*Shiiiiiiiiiiiiit!*'

'Keep going,' Hunter instructs me.

This time it's a primal roar from deep in my belly that makes Charlie scurry away from me.

'Are you angry?' he asks.

'Yes.' A tear falls down my cheek, and I brush it away as quickly as it appears.

'Because I can't quite hear it.'

'I'm angry!'

Banjo begins to whine.

'What are you angry about?'

'The constant rules!'

'What else?'

I turn to face him. 'The elders. The elders with their patronising voices and stupid words!'

He turns also, crossing his arms. 'And what else?'

'The whole organisation! It's taken everything from me. My childhood—all of it. And my whole future.' I inhale sharply. 'It even took my family.'

Hunter's eyes never leave mine. 'What do you want to say to the organisation, Wilson?'

I shake my head, hating the sensation building in my throat.

'Don't you dare filter yourself now.'

'Fuck you,' I whisper.

He leans in. 'You talking to me or the organisation?'

I swallow. 'Both.'

'Because I definitely can't hear you,' he shouts.

'*Fuck you!*' I stagger backwards with the force of the words, holding on to my waist for balance.

Hunter stares calmly at me as I stand panting before him. 'You done?'

I lick my lips and drop my gaze. 'I think so.'

He emits a long whistle. 'You have a very foul mouth, Wilson.'

I snap my eyes to his.

'You better go home and say your prayers,' he says with a wink. Then he steps past me and climbs back up the hill.

9

ANNIE

Tamsin's leaning against her locker, books hugged to her chest, throwing questions at me. 'So you followed him to the beach, and he didn't tell you to get lost?'

It's clear she wants every detail about the time I spent with Hunter on Saturday night. I think back to how comfortable that moment felt with him. 'Not directly, but it's possible I missed non-verbal cues in that state.'

Her eyes are shining with mischief. 'It's also possible Hunter Reed tolerates your company.'

I roll my eyes in her direction. 'Forgive me, because I'm new to this, but am I supposed to be flattered when a boy tolerates my company?'

'Not *a* boy. Hunter Reed.'

I close my locker and turn to her, wondering if I should mention that I saw him again yesterday. *That* was a very different exchange.

'You're so far from his usual type it's laughable,' Tamsin says, 'but I'm definitely picking up on some weird chemistry between you two, and I'm not usually wrong about these things.'

We start walking to our classes. 'What's his usual type?' I've never seen Hunter with a girlfriend before, so I'm curious.

She thinks for a moment. 'Well, firstly, he doesn't date girls at this school. I'm not certain about the reason why, but some say it's so when he breaks up with them, he can cut ties completely.'

That seems cold and a contrast to the guy I raced along the creek yesterday. The Hunter from yesterday is complicated, not cruel.

As we round the corner, I almost run straight into the man of the moment. My eyes travel up to meet Hunter's glare, but the moment he recognises me, the edges of his face soften. We stare at one another.

This is the part where I'm supposed to look away, stutter out some sort of apology, move aside and flee to safety. That's the correct response for someone in this situation.

Look away.

Move aside.

But I don't do either of those things. I do hold my breath, though. His eyes bore into mine for one long, intense moment before he steps around me and keeps walking.

He steps around *me*.

'Wow,' Tamsin breathes. 'I bloody knew it.'

I realise that the other students have all fallen silent and are staring at me like a person who's just revealed their superpower.

Lee's first to break the silence. 'So the rumours are true, then?'

I pinch my eyebrows together. 'What rumours?'

'Ignore him,' Tamsin says.

Lee turns to Sammy, whose locker is next to his. 'Must have been some good head on that beach.'

Tamsin produces a pencil, from goodness knows where, and throws it, hitting him squarely in the head. 'Don't be gross.'

Lee laughs. 'Relax. I know for a fact that J-dubs have a sense of humour.' He meets my eyes. 'That's why you come knocking again after being told to piss off, right?'

Sammy shakes his head and exits the scene. His next class is biology with Hunter. Hopefully he doesn't say anything. I'm embarrassed enough without Hunter finding out.

'Not cool,' Tamsin says to Lee. She grabs me by the arm and pulls me away from all the stares. When we're out of sight and earshot, she asks, 'You all right?'

I nod, even though my heart's racing. I'm used to jokes about my religion. They're easy to ignore and shrug off. Jokes about me and boys is new territory.

Mr Petros steps out of a nearby classroom. 'The bell rang five minutes ago, ladies.' His eyes narrow on me briefly.

Heads down, we flee the corridor.

———

Hunter

'So nothing happened between you two on Saturday?' Sammy whispers. 'You just sat there in the dark?'

I'm trying to focus on Mr Brown's refresher on macromolecules ahead of our exam, but for whatever reason, Sammy's come to class full of questions for me. 'We spoke. That's it.'

'Right.' He taps the end of his pen on his notebook. 'So are you guys friends now? What have I missed here?'

I draw a slow breath and ignore him.

'There are four types,' Mr Brown is saying. 'Carbohydrates, lipids, nucleic acids, and proteins.'

When he turns back to the board, Sammy pokes me with his pen. 'You should probably know that the rumour mill's churning.'

I smack the offending pen from his hand. It lands a few feet from our desk, prompting Mr Brown to turn and look straight at us.

'Exams are in two weeks,' he says. 'I suggest you both pay attention.'

I wait for him to turn back to the board. 'You know I don't give a shit what people say about me.'

'I know, I know. It's just that Lee was mouthing off at Annie at the lockers.'

That gets my full attention. I lean back in my chair. 'And what did the little fucker say?'

A slow smile forms on his face. 'Ah. So you do like her. I mean, I wouldn't have picked that in a million years, to be honest.' He frowns. 'Wait. Is that even allowed?'

'What did he say?' I repeat, slower this time.

Sammy makes a crude gesture with his hand and mouth.

When I say my temper flares, I mean it goes from zero to a hundred in one blow job motion. I know how damaging that rumour will be for her. It could get her into serious trouble with the old fools at her church who run her life in place of capable parents.

'Maybe I shouldn't have said anything,' Sammy says. 'Now your jaw's doing that twitchy thing.'

'I appreciate the heads-up.'

I concentrate as best I can for the rest of the class, but the second that bell rings, I snatch up my books and head out into the corridor.

'Hunter,' Sammy calls to my back, knowing me too well.

I head for the lockers, scanning every face I pass on the walk there. Eventually I spot Lee coming in the other direction, chatting up some year eleven girl whose name I can't remember. My shoulder clips his—hard—and his books go flying. His face goes rigid and flushes red. He turns to me, preparing to run his mouth, then stops when he registers my expression.

'You should watch where you're going,' I say, getting in his face. 'And while you're at it, maybe be a little more careful about the things that come out of your mouth.'

He looks around at the students who've paused to watch the exchange. 'Funny, I was just telling Annie that she should be more careful about the things that come *into* her mou—'

I have him up against the lockers with my arm pressed to his throat before he's finished speaking.

Leaning my full weight on him, I say calmly, 'Who the fuck are you trying to impress?' I nod towards the wide-eyed girl he's been chatting up. 'Her?' Then to the gaping students on the other side of the corridor. 'Them?'

'Mr Reed!' comes the principal's familiar voice.

I look in his direction, easing the pressure on Lee's throat.

'My office—*now*.'

I step back from Lee, and he starts to cough. His face is now fully flushed—a nice bonus.

Swinging my books to my side, I head off towards the principal's office. I spot Annie standing to one side, hugging her textbooks tightly. She meets my gaze briefly before looking away. I sense her disapproval and don't have it in me to give a shit.

She's walking away before I even reach her, and she doesn't look back.

10

ANNIE

The phone rings after school, and I can tell it's Dad by Mum's stilted responses. I can also tell the second he asks after Bridget, because she turns slightly away so I can't see her face.

'No, Tom. No one has heard from her.'

Mum believes Bridget's lost and miserable without Jehovah—or perhaps she hopes. After all, my sister won't come back if she finds happiness out there. But I don't want her to be lost and miserable. I want her to prove everyone wrong.

'Hi,' I say into the phone when Mum hands it to me.

'Hey. How was school?'

And so begins our safe exchange. He has a way of asking about my life but never about me. He never asks how *I* am. I think he's afraid that I'll answer truthfully. In turn, I don't ask about the Super Mario music I can hear in the background, sounds that make my stomach sink all the way to my feet.

Replacing a wife is one thing. Replacing your children is...

'I'll give you a buzz before exams,' he says, wrapping up the conversation.

'What for?' I realise I sound like a snooty thirteen-year-old.

There's a long, uncomfortable silence before I hear, 'Because I'm your dad, and I want to wish you luck.'

I press my eyes shut. 'I only need to pass.'

'Just because you've decided not to go to uni, that doesn't mean you don't try.'

He makes it sound like it was my choice. 'That's exactly what it means.'

He sighs into the phone.

'I've spoken to Maggie about next year,' I tell him. 'I'll be working there four days a week starting from January.' The fifth day will be spent doing field service.

'Well, if that's what you want, what'll make you happy, then I support you.'

He knows the decision has nothing to do with happiness. Very few people grow up dreaming of being a sales assistant in a field they have no interest in. My happiness will supposedly come from serving Jehovah. That's what I've been told all my life.

After I hang up the phone, I tell Mum I'm going to feed Charlie.

'Everything all right with your dad?' she asks.

I nod. 'Yeah.'

She doesn't want the truth anyway.

I head outside, drawing greedy lungfuls of air. As I'm nearing the paddock, I hear a motorbike idling in the distance. I bypass Charlie and go down to the creek. Kevin's sitting in the tall grass, holding his head, the motorbike on its side a few feet from him. Something feels off about the scene.

'You all right?' I call across the water.

He looks up, and I see his face is streaked with blood. My breath catches. A moment later, I'm crossing the railroad tie bridge and jogging up the hill towards him. He blinks in my direction.

'Did you come off?' I ask, crouching beside him. The smell of drink almost has me standing again. My throat closes in protest.

'Bloody bike,' Kevin mutters. 'Wheels need aligning.'

I inspect the cut above his ear. There's so much blood it's difficult to tell how bad it is. 'You might need stitches.'

'No stitches.'

It's clear I'm not going to get him to a doctor. 'Is Hunter home?'

He shakes his head.

Rising, I walk over and switch the bike off, then stand it upright so it's easier for Hunter to find later.

'Go home,' I tell Banjo.

The dog doesn't move.

I return to Kevin. 'Let's get you cleaned up.'

He doesn't protest as I attempt to get him to his feet. He's also no help. When I finally get him upright, he leans his full weight on me.

'I'm going to need you to lock those knees for me,' I tell him. 'I'm not as strong as I look.'

He chuckles softly, and it throws his balance slightly. 'That bloody kid's always in trouble.'

I'm struggling to get him to walk straight. 'Hunter?'

He nods.

It appears that Hunter's earlier run-in with Lee has landed him in trouble once again. I'm fairly certain it had something to do with the rumours. People have said far worse about him though, so I'm surprised he responded the way he did. A part of me wonders if perhaps he was being protective of me, a notion that makes my chest feel light and my stomach tighten at the same time. It's both mortifying and pleasing. I could barely look at him earlier, yet I haven't stopped thinking about him since.

Eventually I get Kevin into the house and sit him down on one of the green vinyl dining chairs in the kitchen that looks like something out of a seventies movie. Then I go to fetch a bowl of warm water, adding some table salt to it.

Now to find a clean cloth.

The linen cupboard is filled with everything except linen, but I do find a threadbare hand towel in the bathroom that appears somewhat clean. Returning to the kitchen, I find Kevin half asleep, chin resting on his chest.

'Pretty sure you're not supposed to nap straight after a head injury,' I say, rousing him.

He gives me a confused look, taking a moment to register my face. 'Annie Wilson.'

'That's me.'

He blinks and continues to study my face. 'You look just like your sister but with red hair.'

I wring out the cloth and bring it to his head. 'She was probably my age the last time you saw her.'

He nods sleepily. 'Where'd she go? Melbourne?'

'Brisbane.' Talking about her makes my chest feel heavy. I dunk the towel into the bowl and watch the water turn red. 'I assume she's still there. She'd be finished with her degree by now. Hopefully working in some fancy art gallery.'

'She sure could paint. I remember they displayed the year twelve pieces at the local gallery. Bridget's really stood out.'

I meet his eyes. 'You went to that exhibition?'

'God, no. Saw photos in the paper.'

I smile to myself.

'Always seemed a bit down,' he adds. 'I remember that about her.'

My smile disappears. It's tough hearing that, especially from someone who only ran into her every now and then at the chemist where she worked after school.

He sighs. 'Not everyone wants to live forever. It's easy to assume they do, but it's too long for some.'

I still mid-rinse of the cloth. He's of course referring to our belief that Jehovah's people will live forever on a paradise earth. 'You really wouldn't want to live forever?'

He shakes his head. 'Some of us are just trying to survive the short time we're here.' Scratching his nose, he adds, 'And where are all these people going to fit, anyway? The planet needs us to die.'

We've all asked that same question at some point, but we're supposed to trust Jehovah's plan. 'The wound's still bleeding. Do you have something to cover it with? A bandage?'

He waves the suggestion away. 'It'll heal quicker without one.'

I go to the sink and wash the bowl out. 'I can stay with you until Hunter gets home.'

He stands slowly. 'I'll be fine,' he says, sauntering from the kitchen, clipping the door frame on his way out. I hear the creak of a bed a moment later.

I stand awkwardly in the kitchen for a few minutes, then go to check on him. He's asleep on the bed, legs hanging over the edge. I get a towel from the bathroom to place under his head, then go to remove his boots. He doesn't even stir.

Returning to the kitchen, I grab the pen by the phone and write a note on the back of the cornflakes box.

Wake your dad when you get home and check the wound on his head. Your motorbike is in the paddock near the creek.

Annie

Glancing around the kitchen a final time, I exit the house.

———

Hunter

I'm leaning against the door frame of Dad's room, watching him sleep and feeling too much at once. The fact that I can't even get through detention without him nearly killing himself is making me crazy. Dark thoughts rush in, like the image of me holding a pillow over his head to end this misery for both of us. He'd welcome it. I know he would.

My chest and eyes are burning, and I'm petrified that my emotions might present as something other than anger. I take hold of the door frame to steady myself while looking down at the cereal box and rereading Annie's note. And now I'm angry at her. How dare she come into my home and stick her nose into my business? Annie with her superior morals. Annie, who's the reason I was in detention in the first place, because she's too piss-weak to stand up for herself.

Can I be angry at her and grateful to her at the same time? Would I be angrier if she'd left him bleeding in the paddock? Maybe I'm angry at myself for being at school or for caring enough to act the way I did. For caring at all about anything.

I look back at Dad and feel that anger multiply. I'm definitely mad at him. He didn't even get through work before writing himself off. Now it falls to me to finish everything on my own—yet again.

He's a shit farmer and a shit dad. He used to be a great farmer, and he used to be good at the parenting stuff too. When I was young, he'd read with me in the mornings while Mum made eggs and coffee.

'Tastes better than the expensive stuff they sell in town,' he'd say when she handed him instant coffee in a chipped mug.

And she'd always reply with 'It's all in the milk.'

Mum used to walk to the Davis farm each morning, jug in hand, and take milk straight from the vat in the shed. Then on weekends, she'd drop over a cut of lamb.

That all died with her. The only thing we exchange with the Davises now, especially since Dad shot one of their working dogs, is awkward glances.

I head to the kitchen and open the fridge to see if he at least made it to the supermarket to get a few groceries for dinner. It's empty aside from a few cartons of long-life milk.

How the mighty have fallen.

The cupboard isn't much better. My eyes go to the cornflakes box I just placed on the bench. *Ladies and gentlemen, I present dinner.* But there's work to be done before I indulge in such luxuries.

Slamming the fridge closed, I go to retrieve the bike.

The sun is low in the sky. I squint against it as I head for the creek. The sound of a chainsaw draws my eye to the other side of the water. And there's Annie, hacking through blackberry bushes that have gotten well out of control. She straightens when she sees me and turns off the chainsaw. I doubt it's a coincidence that she's down here.

'How's your dad?' she says when I'm within hearing range.

I run my eyes over the bike, surveying it for damage. 'He'll live.' When she moves to restart the chainsaw, I add, 'You didn't need to do that.'

Her eyes return to me. 'Should I have left him bleeding on the ground?'

'How else is he going to learn?'

She shifts her weight and switches the chainsaw to her other hand. 'You know, there's places that can help if he can't stop.'

'He doesn't have the time or money for that shit.' I crouch to inspect the back wheel. 'I'm surprised you didn't leave one of your little pamphlets, use it as a teaching moment.'

I'm such an arsehole.

She shakes her head and turns away, starting up the chainsaw.

There's a tightening sensation in my throat. It feels a lot like guilt, and I don't like it.

'Hey,' I call.

She looks tiredly in my direction.

'Thank you.' Two words. Two words that are so hard for me to say.

She stares at me a long moment, then turns the chainsaw off. 'Do you want some soup?'

That's not the response I was expecting.

'What?'

'Mum made a batch of soup to last the week. The sooner we get through it, the sooner I get to eat something else.'

She got the cornflakes box out of the cupboard, so she likely knows there's no food in the house. 'I don't need your Christian charity.'

'It's not charity, you idiot. I'm being neighbourly.'

My eyebrows lift. 'Are you allowed to say idiot?'

She shrugs. 'It's in the Bible.'

I look away so she doesn't see my almost smile. She might be weird, but she's also occasionally funny.

I want to say no, but Dad probably needs some proper food in him. 'Fine. I'll take the soup.'

She sets the chainsaw down. 'Wait there.'

I watch her climb the slope, watch her until she's out of sight. I've been doing that a lot lately. I don't quite understand the draw. Yes, she's attractive, but so are other girls at our school, and I rarely look twice at any of them.

When she reappears, I make my way down to the water so she doesn't have to walk up the hill on this side. Tupperware container in hand, she navigates the railroad tie bridge with ease, then raises those pretty amber eyes to me as she steps off it. I ignore the lift in my chest.

She hands me the container before turning slightly and pointing above us. 'See that large branch that stretches out across the water?'

I look up. 'Yeah.'

'It's perfect for a rope swing.' Her eyes return to me. 'Every winter my dad used to announce that he was going to put one there in summer. Then summer would come and go. The year he finally bought the rope for the project, Bridget told him we were too old for swings.' She gives me a weak smile. 'And I didn't want to contradict her.'

The Tupperware container is almost too hot to hold. I pass it back and forth between my hands. 'How old were you when she said that?'

'Eleven.'

Of course Annie still liked swings at age eleven.

I hold up the container, trying to see its contents. 'What kind of soup is this?'

'Pea and ham.' Her expression is apologetic.

'The worst flavour ever invented.'

'Why do you think I'm giving it away?'

My eyes move between hers, and there's that damn feeling in my chest again.

'You can just return the container to me at school tomorrow,' she says. When I freeze, she smiles. 'That was a joke.'

'Ah.'

Her smile fades. 'Why did you get in a fight with Lee today?'

'I think you know why.'

She exhales. 'Since when do you care what people say about you?'

'But it wasn't just about me, was it?'

She searches my eyes, turning the leather band on her wrist. 'I don't need you getting into trouble for me.'

This conversation's too much. 'Okay, well, next time I'll let the whole school think you blew me on a beach.' I start to turn away.

'What do you mean by "blew me on a beach"?'

I still. For the first time ever, I'm completely speechless. Surely she's heard that phrase before.

I open my mouth to respond, but no words come. How do I explain a blow job to a J-dub who's never even kissed a boy?

A mischievous smile spreads across Annie's face. 'Gotcha.'

I release a breath. 'Jesus, Wilson.'

She skips backwards, looking very pleased with herself. 'Hunter Reed. Lost for words.'

'I'm still not convinced you know what it means.'

She laughs all the way to the creek.

11

ANNIE

I'm seated in Miss Talbert's class staring down at my final assessment piece, the one I stayed up until 3:00 a.m. finishing.

The subject's forehead rests on the horse's, her eyes closed and fresh tears on her cheek. This version of joy is different to the one Hunter saw last time. This one is subtle. It's the kind of joy that hurts a little when it rises to the surface.

This version is a fantasy.

Someone drops into the seat beside me. I assume it's Tamsin, but when I look up, I see Hunter. He's not looking at me, though. He's staring at the drawing.

'Are you lost?' I ask, angling my head at him.

He meets my gaze. 'Is this it? Your final piece?'

I nod.

His mouth turns up. 'It's good.'

The compliment catches me off guard. That's high praise from him.

I look back at the piece. 'I did it in one sitting last night.'

'Well, you fucking nailed it.'

I wait for the backhanded remark, but it doesn't come.

'I finished mine last night too.' He pulls a large piece of card from his art folio and drops it on the desk.

My eyes move over the pig carcass hanging from a hook drawn in black and red. It's graphic and bloody and disturbing, but there's one difference from the last time I saw it. Below the carcass is a single piglet, happy, oblivious to what's hanging above him.

I look at Hunter. 'You added hope.'

I see him swallow as he picks up the drawing and places it back in the folder.

Tamsin walks in, looks between us, smiles, then goes to sit at another table.

'You gonna study art like your sister?' Hunter asks me.

I put my pieces away also. 'Art was Bridget's thing, not mine.'

'Then what's your thing?'

I hesitate, then hold my wrist up so he can see the eight braided bands I'm wearing today. 'I make jewellery.'

He reaches up to touch one of them. Tiny bumps appear on my arm when the tip of his finger brushes my skin. He must notice, because he immediately withdraws his hand. 'You made those?'

I untie one and hand it to him. 'I started when I was ten and haven't really stopped since.'

'You only make bracelets?'

'Bracelets, necklaces, anklets.'

He inspects it closely, then surprises me by trying it on. 'Leather?'

I nod. 'Recycled.' He goes to take it off. 'You can keep it if you want. I have a drawer full of them and no one to give them to.'

He knots the leather, then shakes his sleeve down over it. Of course he doesn't want anyone to see it. I'm not even sure why I told him to keep it.

'It's just a hobby,' I say.

'Doesn't have to be.'

I straighten my pencils on the table. 'I've already agreed to work four days a week at Maggie's next year.'

He looks disappointed. 'Selling shoes?'

'Yeah.'

'What a waste.'

I frown. 'Of what?'

'A life. At least work in a jewellery shop if you're going to limit yourself to retail. I mean, are shoes the dream?'

I tilt my head. 'Actually, everlasting life's the dream.'

He doesn't even try to hide his amusement. 'I almost forgot about your "paradise earth, never growing old" thing.'

I shift in my chair. 'We're taught to prioritise *spiritual* education. We don't have to go off and become doctors. We save lives by going door to door.'

Hunter blinks. 'Do you actually believe that?'

I open my mouth to answer, then close it again. *Why am I hesitating?* 'Yes.'

He does not look convinced by the weak response.

'We don't chase worldly goals,' I say.

His brow pinches. 'You've explained worldly parties. What are worldly goals?'

Sometimes I forget he doesn't speak our language. 'Like wealth and material possessions.'

'You think J-dubs invented the "money doesn't buy you happiness" philosophy?'

'No, but I think we live by it more than most.'

He lets out a long breath. 'So superior.'

I note the beginnings of a smirk. 'Okay. Well, what are your plans after graduation?'

'I'm a fifth-generation farmer. What do you think?'

I chew my lip. 'You don't want to try something else? Maybe go to uni?'

'Luckily, no.'

'Luckily?'

His brow creases. 'Obviously I couldn't go off and study right now even if I wanted to.'

'Because of your dad?'

His scowl deepens, and he turns to face the front. 'I think share time's over, Wilson.'

'So only you can ask personal questions?'

Miss Talbert comes rushing into the room. 'Sorry I'm late, guys. Got stuck at the photocopier.'

Hunter doesn't speak another word to me for the rest of the class.

———

When I get home from school, I find Mum leaning on the kitchen bench, flicking through the local paper. She slides the container of biscuits towards me when I walk in.

'Your favourites,' she says without looking up.

I stare down at the jam biscuits. 'Actually, these are Bridget's favourites.'

That makes her look up. 'What do you mean? You love these.'

I pull the container closer and take two. 'I like them. They're just not my favourite.'

She watches me eat them. 'Which ones are your favourite, then?'

'The lemon biscuits with the icing.'

A pained expression passes over her face. 'Oh. Well, Sister Joy dropped some lemons over yesterday. I'll make those next.' She returns her attention to the newspaper.

My gaze falls to the embroidered logo on her uniform. Cleaning's the only paid job she's ever had. She never complains about it, never talks about wanting to do something else, wanting something *more*. She's too humble.

'What would you do for work if you weren't a cleaner?'

She looks up again and tilts her head. 'You mean if the work dried up?'

'Or maybe your back goes? Or your knee? Or you lose your driver's licence?'

She appears utterly confused by the direction of the conversation. 'Why would I lose my driver's licence?'

'Or perhaps you simply get sick of it and want to do something else.'

'We all get sick of working sometimes, but we all need to make a living.'

I roll my eyes. 'If you had to pick something else.'

She thinks a moment. 'Maybe ironing. Or mending. People with too much on their plate are outsourcing those things nowadays.'

I hate her answer. I hate that she limits herself to Cinderella duties. I guess that makes me an enormous hypocrite.

'Where's all this coming from?' she asks.

I can see the topic has made her nervous, which wasn't my intention. 'Just making conversation.' I grab one more of Bridget's favourite biscuits before stepping back from the bench. 'I'm going to get some studying done before the meeting.'

She nods, then straightens suddenly. 'Oh. I noticed there's a swing hanging over the creek. Did you put that up?'

I blink. 'A swing?'

'You didn't put it up?'

I shake my head, thinking back to my conversation with Hunter yesterday. Surely he wouldn't do something so... human.

'Kevin probably did it while intoxicated,' Mum says. 'He's lucky he didn't drown in the process.'

I head for the back door. 'I'm going to take a look.'

'It's just a piece of rope hanging from a tree. Don't you have to study?'

I glance over my shoulder as I open the door. 'I'll only be a minute.'

With Banjo at my heel, I head down to the creek,

stopping when I see a thick piece of rope with a foot loop at the bottom swinging gently over the water. It's hanging from the exact branch I pointed out to Hunter yesterday, confirming my suspicions.

I make my way down to the creek and can do nothing to stop the smile that's taken over my face. Hunter Reed made me a rope swing. But when? He must have come back after dinner.

My eye catches on a Tupperware container sitting at the base of the tree. I walk over, pick it up, and open it. Inside is a torn-off piece of paper with a note.

Better late than never.

I shove it into my pocket and drop the container onto the ground. It's time to test the swing. Hopefully it's properly secured and he's not hiding somewhere, waiting for me to fall into the icy water below.

Using a long stick, I catch hold of the rope and walk backwards, pulling hard in all directions to ensure it's sturdy before even thinking about putting weight on it.

It's secure. Turns out he doesn't want me to die today.

I move to the edge of the creek and step into the foothold. Then, gripping the rope with both hands, I draw a breath and swing out over the water. A childish thrill blooms inside me, a smile splitting my face. I tip my head back, watching the branches above. My surroundings whoosh by. I stretch one arm out and start to spin in a slow circle. A laugh escapes me as I close my eyes, enjoying the falling sensation.

The rope begins to slow. I open my eyes and see I'm now falling short of the creek's edge. I attempt to use my body weight to get moving again, but my timing is off, and I end up going side to side before eventually coming to a stop in the middle of the creek.

Releasing a frustrated breath, I rest my forehead on the rope for a moment. There's only one way to get off this thing, and that involves me getting wet, then having to explain to Mum the reason why.

'How are you so bad at this?'

I snap my head up and see Hunter standing on his side of the creek, arms folded, watching me. 'It didn't exactly come with instructions.'

His gaze drops to the water below. 'Bit cold for a swim, isn't it?'

'It is, actually. Maybe you can help a girl out?'

'I did find a spare length of rope last night.' He brings a hand to his chin, pretending to think. 'Now, what did I do with it?'

'Ah. Handy with a rope *and* funny. Who knew?' I sigh. 'Can you just grab a stick or something?'

His eyes are shining with amusement. 'Afraid not. You see, my side of the creek's a lot neater than yours.'

'Then cross the bridge. There's all kinds of debris over here.'

He doesn't move.

Is he waiting for me to beg? 'Can you please help me?'

His arms fall to his sides. 'All right. I'll help.'

'Thank you.'

Hunter proceeds to leap off the edge of the creek, arms outstretched. I squeak as he grabs hold of the rope, and we're launched sideways. His feet are dangling above the water, his arms doing all the work.

'We're going to fall,' I manage to get out. 'Can the rope even hold the weight of both of us?'

He starts to spin us. 'Let's find out.'

I can't stop the squeals coming from me. He uses his foot to push off the bank, and we're swinging off in the other direction before I have a chance to dismount.

'So far so good,' he says.

My eyes are pressed shut, and I'm too breathless to answer.

He keeps swinging us back and forth and round and round until we're both dizzy and windswept, our hands raw.

'Had enough?' he asks.

I open my eyes, struggling to focus on him. 'Definitely.'

He dismounts on my side of the creek and catches me before I can swing away. I'm laughing as I climb off, my hands trembling and my legs like jelly. He takes hold of my arms to steady me.

My laughter dies.

I'm suddenly aware of how close he is, how *wrong* this moment is. He's still holding me, and the heat from his hands through my shirt is a foreign warmth I've never felt before. It reaches all the way to my bones. I'm afraid to look up, afraid of what I'll see, but more afraid of what *he'll* see.

When he doesn't let go, I lift my gaze, paranoid that he can feel me trembling. He's not smiling now. He's watching. The intensity of his stare only makes the trembling worse.

His gaze drops to my mouth, and I feel the full weight

of it. I know I'm inexperienced with these things, but it feels like that moment in a movie just before the couple kisses. I've watched plenty of movies about people falling in love. I've just never seen movies about people *making* love.

The draw is a lot—too much. This is what comes of being alone with a boy. This is the temptation they're always warning us about. Over and over and over and—

Hunter reaches up to free a piece of hair stuck to my cheek. His movements are slow and cautious. The sensation of his fingers barely touching me crawls across my skin and travels down my spine. My breath hitches, barely, but he notices. He releases his hold on me and takes not one but two steps back.

We both look away.

He clears his throat and picks up the stick I used earlier, retrieving the rope in the same manner. 'I'll tie it to your side so you can practice.'

As the heat and adrenaline start to dissipate, I feel a bit sick. Sick because I'm in this high-risk situation to begin with, but more so because he was the first one to step back. That should have been me. I should have stepped back weeks ago. I've let it build to this. And while I have no idea what *this* is, I do know it's wrong.

'Just so we're clear,' he says, 'I'm not going to be that guy.'

It takes a moment for his words to land. 'What guy?'

His eyes return to me. 'The guy you rebel with.'

'I'm not...' Heat floods my cheeks. 'I told you already. I'm not rebelling.'

He nods, then heads for the bridge.

'Why did you build me a swing?' I call to him, regaining some of my confidence.

He stops at the edge of the bridge. 'I certainly didn't do it to get in your pants.' He gives me a half smirk before crossing.

12

HUNTER

What kind of idiot gets himself in that kind of situation with a J-dub?

This idiot, it turns out.

Yesterday was too close. *She* was too close. Her breath was hitting my face with each burst of laughter, and she smelled of strawberry jam and sugary biscuits. She smelled of my childhood before Mum passed. I think I just got caught up in that feeling of freedom that kids experience before life gets real. And I suppose I liked that she was caught up in it too.

It was refreshing to watch her squeal like a banshee, to see those permanent lines on her forehead smooth out for a few seconds. To hear her laugh.

That laughter has a way of pacifying me.

But I refuse to be the topic of her prayers or the person who pulls her off course. She'd hate me for it later. I'd prefer to keep her *out* of trouble. She can hate me for that instead.

'Where are you going?'

I'm halfway out the front door when I hear Dad behind me. It's a little after 7:30 a.m., and I was hoping to sneak out before he rose. I had to pick him up off the floor last night and carry his drunk arse to bed. Then he pissed himself as I was leaving his room. I could smell it. I left him to sleep in it, to wake in it—and I'm not sorry. The least he can feel is shame. But even though I want him to feel it, I don't want to witness it. It's embarrassing for both of us when it really should only be embarrassing for him.

'Library opens at eight, and it's our last week of class-es.' I say all this without looking at him.

He might've changed his clothes, but he hasn't had a shower yet. The smell of piss lingers in the air between us.

He's silent a moment, like he's wrestling with his words. 'Okay. Well, have a good day.'

'Yep.' Relieved by his dismissal, I flee.

It's been a long time since I've spent time in the library—especially for studying purposes. I feel Mrs Pritchard, the school's librarian, watching me the whole time, like she's waiting for me to steal something or carve my initials into the table. But when the bell rings and I'm heading for the door, she says, 'Good luck with your exams, Mr Reed.'

I pause and look back, noting her sincerity. 'Thanks.'

When I show up at the science room to clean tables at lunchtime, I find Mr Trest waiting for me.

Now what?

'Mr Reed,' he says.

I nod in place of words, bracing for whatever's coming next.

'I think the tables in here look pretty good,' he says. 'You're free to go and enjoy your lunch break.'

I'm fairly certain this is some kind of test. 'Wouldn't I just go to the next room, then?'

'The goal isn't clean tables, Mr Reed, it's clean students.' He offers me an extraordinarily rare smile. 'Mrs Pritchard came to see me today. She mentioned you were in the library before school.'

I'm not following. 'I didn't break in or anything. It was open.'

He laughs quietly. 'I'm aware of that. And this is me acknowledging your effort. While it might be late, and long overdue, it doesn't go unnoticed. Off you go.'

My hands go into my jean pockets as I take in his expression, which closely resembles pride. 'Right.' I nod. 'Okay.' I step outside and head for my locker.

When I pass the computer room, Annie flashes into view. I stop, backtrack, and watch her through the small glass window. She's typing away at one of the computers. I should keep walking, but instead, I push the door open and step inside. Why I would deliberately throw myself in her path after avoiding her all morning, I can't really fathom.

She looks up when I enter, fingers stilling on the keys.

'Hey,' I say.

She's understandably wary after yesterday's encounter at the creek. 'Hey.'

I lean my back on the door. 'You don't have a computer at home?'

She shakes her head. 'Nope.'

I watch.

She waits.

When I don't say anything, she says, 'What do you want, Hunter?'

Fair enough. 'About yesterday—'

'What about yesterday?'

It's clear she's embarrassed or angry about what happened. 'I was just trying to keep ahead of the bullshit. We'll have to share this town after graduation. No point making things awkward.'

'Why would they be awkward?'

She's not going to make this easy for me. 'You'd be reminded of your regrets every time we run into each other at the post office.'

She tilts her head. 'Why at the post office?'

'Or the supermarket. Petrol station. The bank.'

She leans back in her chair, crossing her arms. 'We get our groceries in Turram, and Mum fills her car up at the feed supply place on the highway because it's a few cents cheaper than town. The bank's a possibility, though. Imagine having to pass each other a few times a year.'

Definitely more anger than embarrassment. 'You know what I mean. You're a J-dub. I won't be responsible for you going to hell.'

'We don't believe in hell.'

I forgot about that small, important detail. 'Missing out on everlasting life, then.'

'What an awful lot of power you think you have.' She sits forwards and returns her attention to the screen. 'You were right about one thing, though. I am testing some boundaries.'

I watch her type. 'Because you're having doubts?'

She stops, thinks. 'I guess. Or maybe I just want to try to figure some things out before I'm baptised. The consequences will be more severe after that.'

This is news. 'You're not *baptised*?'

She shakes her head.

'You weren't baptised as a baby?'

'It doesn't work like that. It has to be our decision.'

I'm learning a lot today. 'What age do people get baptised?'

She shrugs. 'It varies, but there's a lot of pressure when you reach adulthood. The next assembly's in April. I think everyone's expecting it to happen then. Mum certainly is.'

'Huh.' I cross my feet. 'It's a literal baptism? In water?'

'Fully submerged in a pool in front of thousands of people.'

I sit with that image for a moment. 'So people just line up in their bathers and get dunked in a pool?'

The faintest smile comes and goes. 'Actually, they wear clothes over their bathers. The human form can be very tempting, after all.'

I rub my forehead. 'Of course. You can't have thousands of people running off to the bathrooms to scratch an itch.'

She shakes her head. 'That would never happen, because masturbation's a sin.'

'A *sin*?'

'Yeah.'

I laugh once. 'You can't make fornication *and* masturbation a sin. It's one or the other.'

She suppresses a smile as she swivels side-to-side on her chair. 'I'd like to drink some beer.'

I never know what's going to come out of this girl's mouth next. 'So drink some.'

'My mum doesn't drink, and I'd get a lot of questions if I just randomly came home with a six-pack of Victoria Bitter.'

She's painfully adorable. 'Don't drink VB. Drink something decent.'

'Like what?'

It's like we're thirteen. 'I don't know, anything. Crownies are always a safe bet.'

'Okay. I'll keep that in mind if I ever get the chance.' She continues to watch me.

I let out a resigned breath. 'Fine. I'll get the beer, and I'll drink *one* with you.'

'But you don't want to be that guy, remember? The one I rebel with?' Her tone is teasing.

I stand up and grip the doorknob. 'I won't be the guy who *ruins* you. There's a big difference.' And yet the more time I spend with her, the more I want to be that person. 'Can you meet me at the creek after dinner?'

Her eyes light up. 'I think so.'

'Then I guess I'll see you later.'

13

ANNIE

I'm trying to exit the school, but Donna has bailed me up at the gate. Now I'm forced to stand here enduring one of her well-meaning speeches that feels a lot like a lecture.

'Hunter's the epitome of worldly, and 1 Corinthians 15:33 tells us that bad associations spoil useful habits.'

She's quoting the Bible at me as if I'm not familiar with every scripture in it. 'Is this because I didn't eat lunch with you today? I was typing up study notes, not smoking in the bushes.'

'I went past the computer room, and it didn't look like much studying was happening.'

So that's what this is about. Anger curls inside me. 'You were checking up on me?'

'It's not like that.' She touches my arm. 'I'm looking out for my spiritual sister. These people will be gone from your life once exams are over. You have me for life.'

If that's meant to make me feel better, it doesn't. And I

don't have her for life. I have her until I don't. Her sisterly love is conditional. She'll be there for me 100 percent, unless I turn my back on God. Then she'll shun me alongside the rest of the congregation.

'I have to get to work,' I say, stepping past her.

'Will I see you at lunch tomorrow?'

I wave in place of an answer, keep walking, and don't look back.

The walk from school to the main street is only ten minutes. Maggie's Shoes is opposite the milk bar and next to the bank in what some might describe as a great location. Maggie's on the phone when I walk in. I wave, and she pauses mid-fluff of her perm and waves back.

It takes me two hours to sort the delivery that arrived that afternoon and restock the shelves above the displays. When the sign is turned to 'Closed', I help her with the books.

'I can't wait to have you here four days,' she says, sitting on the stool to rest her tired feet. 'I might finally be able to eat dinner with my husband again.'

I want to say that I can't wait either, but the lie sticks in my throat. She's been so good to me over the years, hiring someone else to help on Saturday mornings because she knows I can't ever work them.

'All done,' I tell her. 'Everything balances.'

She squeezes my arm, then notices my bracelet. 'Oh. This one's new. I like the blue thread through it.'

I look down at the band I finished last night when I couldn't sleep. 'Thanks. I've been experimenting with colour.'

'It's gorgeous. I'd sell those right here in this shop.'

I smile as I dip below the counter to collect my school bag. 'I'll see you Friday after school.'

She stands and winces. Her knees aren't what they used to be. 'Yes, go. I've kept you late again. Exams start next week. You've got studying to do.'

And beer to drink with Hunter.

She locks the door behind me, and I start the long walk home.

Mum's unusually chatty at dinner. She's telling me about a new client, an older gentleman who failed to notice he had maggots in his house.

'He was suitably embarrassed,' she says. 'Turns out there was a dead rat in the wall. They were just crawling out from beneath the skirting boards.'

My chest grows heavy as I listen. She deserves more than dead rats and maggots.

After we finish eating, I wash the dishes, and Mum settles herself in the lounge room with a Cary Grant movie. She'll fall asleep in ten minutes, and she won't wake up until I tap her on the shoulder later and tell her to go to bed. So I loiter in the kitchen, rearranging tins in the cupboards and wiping the sticky circles left by the sauce bottles. It's nearing eight when I pop my head into the lounge room and find her asleep. I quietly tug on gumboots, then slip out the back door. It's still light thanks to daylight saving.

'Stay,' I tell Banjo.

The dog pauses, waits until I'm a few metres ahead, then resumes following me.

When I arrive at the swing, I find Hunter seated on the grass on his side of the creek, beer in hand. He's wearing a long-sleeve Rip Curl T-shirt, khaki pants, and muddied boots.

'Should I use the bridge or swing across?' I ask him.

He swigs from the bottle in his hand. 'Swing.'

I untie the rope and slip my foot in the loop, landing gracefully on the other side.

'Improvement,' he says, fetching a beer from the cardboard box beside him. He pulls his keys from his pocket and opens the bottle with one before handing it to me. When I sit, he taps the neck of his beer to mine. 'Cheers, Wilson.'

'Cheers.' I smell it before tasting it. It's slightly repulsive, but in a good way—like Vegemite. I take my first sip. It's more bitter than I was expecting, but it's also cold, fizzy, and refreshing.

'What do you think?' Hunter asks.

'I suspect it's an acquired taste, so I'll drink more of it before passing judgement.' I watch him take a sip. 'I wasn't sure if you drank.'

He's looking ahead at the creek. 'I just don't drink at parties.'

'Why not?'

'Because I don't trust drunk people—especially a crowd of them.'

I'm certain his dad is the reason for that. 'Well, I'm well behaved, so you can relax with me.'

'Good to know.' He drinks again. 'So what's next on your list of things to try?'

'Skinny-dipping.'

He coughs mid-drink.

'It's all right. You don't have to hold my hand for that one.'

He regards me. 'Then you better do it somewhere sensible where you won't drown.'

I drink, then look over my shoulder at the motorbike parked behind us. 'You know, I've never ridden a bike before.'

He follows my line of sight. 'That can't be a religious thing. Fairly sure I've seen J-dubs on bikes before.'

'So long as it's for practical reasons and not thrills.'

He shakes his head. 'They just suck the fun out of everything, don't they? The Davises have a nice, safe four-wheeler they'd probably be happy to put you on.'

I laugh. 'A four-wheeler? Why not a dirt bike like yours?'

'It's not safe.'

'It would be with you.'

He regards me for a moment, then stands up with a sigh. 'All right. Fine. Put your beer down and get up.'

'Really?'

'Hurry up. Before I change my mind.'

I prop my bottle against the beer box and leap to my feet. He empties his, then drops it on the ground before walking off in the direction of the bike. I hurry after him.

He climbs on and looks at me, waiting until he has my full attention. 'First some basics. Anything related to braking is on the right side. Basically anything related to the control of the bike is on the left.' He points to something. 'This is your front brake up top.' He points down.

'This is your rear brake. If you're going down a hill, or just going too fast, and you grab the front brake, you're going over the handlebars. If you use only your rear brake, you may slide a little. Use both.' He points again. 'This is your kick-starter. It's how we turn the bike on.' He pauses to check if I'm keeping up. 'This is your clutch. You'll need that to change gears.' Pointing down, he adds, 'Shift lever.'

Climbing off, he gestures for me to get on. I'm excited, but that excitement turns to something else when he climbs on behind me. He reaches down and guides my feet to the footrests. 'First thing you're going to do is turn the fuel on.' He points to a switch, and I bend down to turn it on. 'Good. Now we're going to make sure the bike's in neutral.'

He takes hold of my foot again, and I'm acutely aware of the hand wrapping my ankle as he explains how to tell what gear it's in.

'If you're unsure, push the bike forwards a little. If it moves freely, it's in neutral.' He rolls forwards a foot. 'Okay, we're good.'

His hands go over mine, his chest pressing against my back. I'm nestled between his thighs. It's a lot all at once.

'You want to kick-start it?' he asks.

It takes me a moment to register the question. I look down as he positions my foot again.

'Straight down,' he says. 'Nice and hard.'

The bike starts on the first go, and the vibration travels up my body. It's noisy and thrilling.

'Clutch,' he says into my ear. 'That's it. Now you're going to push the gear shifter down into first.'

I continue to follow his instructions.

'Good. This next bit's important,' he says. 'You're going to very slowly let out the clutch while you give it a little bit of fuel.'

The bike immediately stalls, and Hunter's chest rumbles with laughter.

My cheeks heat. 'Sorry.'

'It's normal when you're learning. Let's go again.'

It doesn't stall this time. We move forwards, Hunter's feet hovering above the ground, ready to steady us.

'When do I go into second?' I shout over the noise.

He shakes his head. 'You don't. Just focus on not killing us at this speed.'

Slow is fine. Hunter behind me is fine. His voice in my ear is fine. His breath in my hair, prompting tiny goosebumps to break out everywhere, is more than fine. I have the strangest urge to tilt my head so I can feel his breath on my neck.

These are thoughts I've never had and things I've never felt before. It's making concentration nearly impossible, and I'm scared of crashing the bike but so desperate for this moment to stretch on.

'You all right?' he asks.

I swallow and nod. This is wrong, and me not doing anything about it is even more wrong.

His fingers reach for the brake, and the bike stops. 'You sure you're all right?'

I'm definitely not all right, and apparently that's obvious to him. 'I need to get off.'

He immediately dismounts, keeping a hold of the

bike while I climb off. I walk in circles, trying to expel all these feelings from my body.

'What's going on?' he asks.

Lust, I think. 'Just a little short of breath.'

He looks concerned. 'Were we going too fast?'

Much, much too fast. Not the bike. My mind and body. 'No. It was... No.'

He turns the bike off, kicks the stand down, then walks around so he's in front of me. 'Wilson.'

I stare at the ground. 'Yeah?'

'Look at me.'

I'm not sure I can, but I do it anyway.

He searches my eyes. 'Did I do something?'

'No.'

'What, then?'

He's waiting for an explanation, and when he doesn't get one, he steps closer. I'm barely breathing. My gaze falls to his lips, and I'm hot, and his scent is suffocating me. And then he whispers my name. Not Wilson—my *name*.

'Annie.'

It's the first time I've heard it from his lips, and it's perfect and breathy.

'Annie,' he says again.

Then two of his fingers wrap two of mine.

It's a loose grip, so easy for me to pull away—but I don't. Instead, I close my eyes and thread all five of my fingers through all five of his. His tighten blissfully around mine.

So this is what holding hands feels like. It's wrong because he's worldly, wrong because we're not courting, and wrong because there's no mutual goal of marriage. We're just two people with absolutely no plan at all. And now it feels like the only way to end this torturous moment is to complete it.

'Do you want to kiss me?' I ask.

His fingers slide between mine. 'So you can hate me afterwards?'

I shake my head. 'I could never hate you.' I tip my face up, like they do in the movies. I'm fairly sure he can see my heart thudding in my chest through my jumper.

He dips his head, lips hovering a centimetre from mine. He's so close I can smell the beer on his breath.

'It's okay,' I whisper, sensing his hesitation.

The second his lips touch mine, the heat that's been building inside me ignites into flames. My stomach clenches, and my knees soften. I've got no idea what I'm doing, but it doesn't seem to matter. He knows. He knows *exactly* what he's doing. I simply follow his lead.

He opens his mouth, tongue sweeping across mine. My breath catches. He breaks the kiss, dropping his forehead to mine. And that's when I notice his change in breath also. That's when I realise I'm not alone in these feelings. This heat, this desire—it's shared.

'Annie.'

My heels lift off the ground, lips finding his once more. I want as much of him as I can get before my mind clears and the guilt hits, before the shame drowns me where I stand.

His free hand goes into my hair as he deepens the kiss, and my palm lands on his chest. I'm ready to push him away. Any moment now, my good sense will surface, a line will be crossed, and I'll know it's time to stop.

Any moment now.

He draws me closer still. It's like we're siphoning oxygen from one another, and if we stop, we'll die. It's a push-and-pull of breath and heat. I slide my arms around his neck, extinguishing the safety barrier between us. When our bodies come together, desire and guilt war inside me.

Desire wins.

It's Hunter who breaks the kiss. Apparently he's the only one with enough self-control to do it.

'Why are you stopping?' I pant, frustrated by the interruption. I lean into him to retain what heat I can.

His hands are still on me, holding me in place. 'You gotta tell me where the line is before this goes any further.'

I shake my head to clear it of the lust fogging my brain. 'The line. Right.' I wet my lips. 'We can't... I can't have sex.'

He kisses my jaw and says, 'There's so much between here and there, Wilson.'

Of course there is, but I can barely think past my physical needs right now. 'I'll know when I get there.'

His mouth goes to my neck, and he runs his tongue down it. 'You sure about that?'

My head falls back, welcoming the sensation. My legs are no longer of any use, and I start to sink to the ground. Hunter catches me, sits down, and drags me onto his lap. My knees land on either side of him as he pushes my hair back from my neck, his mouth returning to my scorched skin. I grab hold of his hair with both hands, eyes closing.

'I trust you,' I say.

He stops kissing me. 'Don't say that.'

I look him in the eye. 'I trust you.'

His expression is tortured, his eyes heavy with desire. 'Okay.' He nods. 'Okay.'

14

ANNIE

Tamsin sits opposite me in the library, perched on the edge of her seat, head strained in my direction. 'I thought it was all just rumour?' Her voice is as low as she can make it while still being audible.

I look around before replying, paranoid that Donna's hiding behind one of the bookshelves, listening. 'The other stuff is rumour. Nothing happened on the beach.'

A smile plays on her lips. 'And then last night everything changed.'

I keep swinging between exhilaration and nausea. I'm praying for forgiveness one minute, then touching my lips, trying to recapture the sensation the next. 'Not everything. We just kissed and stuff.'

She's wide-eyed and needing more. 'What *stuff*?'

While I don't want to share every intimate detail, Tamsin's also the only person I have to talk to about this. 'Just some touching.'

'Oh really?' She's drinking this up.

'I mean, he touched, and I...' *Had no idea what I was doing.* Hunter, on the other hand, knew exactly what he was doing, bringing me to a life-altering finish within minutes using only his hand. 'I would've liked it to have been mutual,' I admit.

'None of us know what we're doing in the beginning.' Tamsin laughs. 'You just have to tell Hunter that you want to learn. I suspect he'll be an eager teacher when it comes to you.' She rests her chin on her hands. 'You know, this whole thing feels very Romeo and Juliet.'

I laugh. 'Hardly.'

'It's the star-crossed-lovers story of our time.'

I stand, gathering my things. 'I need to check these books out before the bell rings.'

'The Jehovah's Witness girl who falls in love with the troubled boy from the wrong side of the creek.'

I shake my head and look at her. 'Romeo and Juliet might be a love story, but it's also a tragedy.' I pause. 'You can't say anything to anyone about this.'

She stands. 'Don't worry. I know what's at stake, and I won't tell a soul.'

As we walk to the front desk, I look around the library. 'I can't believe tomorrow's our last day of classes. A few weeks of exams, and then you'll be moving to the city with pretty much everyone else from our year level.'

'Except Hunter.' She gives me a coy look.

I don't respond.

'You could come, you know. You don't have to stay here. You could still apply to a TAFE or get an entry-level job somewhere else.'

I could move to the city, but it would be a very

different life to the one she's describing. 'It's not that easy, unfortunately.'

Tamsin gives me a sympathetic look. 'I wish I could say I understand, but I don't.'

'That's okay. You don't need to understand. You just need to not forget about me when you leave.'

'Never.'

As I join the queue of students at the desk, I say, 'You go. I'll see you later.'

She presses a hand to her heart. 'Parting is such sweet sorrow.'

'Stop.'

She starts backing away to the door. 'That I shall say goodnight till it be morrow.'

———

Hunter

I try to focus on other things, anything but Annie Wilson. But she pushes her way into every thought and every minute of my morning. I don't know if seeing her will make it better or worse.

Worse, surely.

I've never been with a girl so responsive to my touch, someone who stops breathing with the slightest change of pressure or adjustment of my hand. I've also never been in a situation where it was 100 percent about her, and I didn't mind one bit. Did I have to take care of business when I got home? Sure. But seeing her come for the first time was the reward. And now it's all I can think about. I'm fifteen again.

But now it's done. She had her rebellious moment, then likely went home and prayed herself to sleep before coming to her senses. And I'm supposed to pretend I don't want to back her up against the lockers, slide my hands inside her jeans, and watch the replay. I'd settle for a kiss, a moan, a hand tugging my hair.

As I'm having these thoughts, Annie appears next to my locker. 'Hey.'

I turn to her, searching for signs of remorse or embarrassment and finding none. Her eyes are pure gold in this light. 'Hey.'

She makes herself taller, like she's working up the courage to say something. 'I was wondering if you're free after school?'

What is she doing? Why is she pretending that yesterday was the beginning of something when it can only be the end? 'Why's that?'

'I thought you could come over.' When I don't reply, she adds, 'My mum's working until six.'

'Why would I come over?' It might seem harsh, but her pretending we can be anything more than Bible study partners is an arsehole move on her part.

Her cheeks redden. 'Never mind.' She starts to turn away.

I catch her arm, a reflex. Everything's a reflex with her. She looks down at my hand, then up at me. And there's that look in her eyes—the one from last night. I immediately let go of her before I embarrass myself.

'Why do you want me to come to your house?' I ask.

She waits for the girl on the other side of me to close her locker and leave before replying. 'I have some more things I want to tick off my pre-baptism list. I thought you could help.'

My pulse quickens, which is maddening. Maybe she wants me to introduce her to heavy metal or host a seance. 'Okay.'

Her lips turn up. 'Yeah?'

I couldn't say no to her even if I wanted to. 'Yeah.'

And so begins the longest afternoon of my life, waiting to be alone with Annie so I can find out what's next in her crazy rebellion plan.

After school, I go in search of Dad and find him in the hay shed. He's still working, which is rare nowadays. But I don't miss the open beer can sitting on the bale by the door.

Clearing my throat, I say, 'I'm going to Annie's.'

He drops the bale he's holding and looks at me. 'Annie's? As in Annie Wilson?'

I nod.

'To her house?'

'Yeah.'

He rests his hands on his hips. 'Mate, she's a nice girl...'

Here it comes.

'But she's also a J-dub,' he finishes.

I draw a long breath. 'We're just hanging out, not getting married.'

He looks awkwardly around the shed. 'Is Dawn home?'

'Jesus, Dad. I'm letting you know as a courtesy, not asking your permission.'

He nods slowly and reaches for the bale. 'Just be careful, would you?'

I shake off his words and leave, knowing he's right. Meeting up with Annie is a bad idea. It was a bad idea yesterday too. That doesn't stop me from going, though.

When I arrive at Annie's, I find her sitting on the dog bed by the back door, presumably waiting for me. Banjo runs to greet me, and I give him a quick pat. Annie stands as I approach, arms crossed and shoulders lifted. She looks nervous. Her hair's slightly damp, like she's just had a shower. I try not to read too much into that.

'Come in,' she says, leading the way.

I follow her into the kitchen, looking around at the aged cupboards and stained benchtop. Everything's clean, though. A fruit bowl sits on the counter, full of mandarins. It's strange that I've lived across the creek from her my whole life, but I've never seen inside her house.

I rest my hip on the bench and look down at her. 'What's next on the list, Wilson?'

She uncrosses her arms. 'I'd like to watch a horror movie.'

'Today?'

She shakes her head. 'I'd want to go to a cinema, probably in the city. I know Turram is closest, but I can't risk being spotted there.'

I nod slowly. 'And you want me to come with you?'

'If you want to. We could go after exams.'

I watch her carefully. 'Okay.'

She shifts her weight. 'And I thought I might skip to the next thing on the list in the meantime.'

'Which is?'

She drops her gaze to the ground between us. 'I'd like to know how to... reciprocate.'

My entire body is paying attention now. 'Reciprocate?'

Colour rises to her cheeks. 'I feel bad about yesterday.'

'Because of what we did?'

She still won't look at me. 'Yes. But also for what we didn't do.' She swallows audibly, then clears her throat. 'What *I* didn't do. I just didn't know...'

She's the sweetest thing—and she's killing me. 'Did it seem like I wasn't enjoying myself?'

Finally she lifts her eyes to me. 'No, but—'

'It's not a debt to be settled.'

'I know.' She clasps her hands together to stop from fidgeting. 'Did *I* seem like I was enjoying myself?'

The memory of her back lifting off the grass and her fingernails pressing into my scalp flashes in my mind. 'I think so.'

She tilts her head. 'And did you like that?'

I fucking loved it. 'Sure.'

'Because I think I'd like it too. Seeing you, I mean.'

The affection and lust I feel for this girl right now are unsettling. 'I suppose I could teach you, since you don't appear to hate me after yesterday.'

'I don't have time to hate you. Self-loathing is a full-time job.' She offers me a weak smile.

It's funny and tragic at the same time.

'Mum will be home at six,' she says. 'Will that be enough time?'

I laugh. 'It's four o'clock. I think we're safe.'

She steps up to me, threading her fingers through mine. This is how it started yesterday. This is what she knows. The fact that the gesture already feels familiar blows my mind.

Pushing up on her toes, she whispers against my mouth, 'Tell me what to do.'

I reach between her legs, touching her through her jeans. 'There's something I need to take care of first.'

15

ANNIE

There's gladwrap over the seats in the toilets and two cows loose in the tennis courts. I'm always surprised at what students get away with on their last day of school.

It's muck-up day, and all the year twelves have dressed up. Most of the guys have come as footy players and musicians. There's a lot of eighties-style wigs around the place. Tamsin and I dress as two of the teachers. It was her idea, and a funny one. The teachers are good-humoured about it. I wasn't planning on dressing up at all, but it's nice to be part of the fun for once instead of an awkward bystander.

One girl is dressed up as a Jehovah's Witness. She wears an ugly brown skirt that sits mid-calf and a cream blouse with shoulder pads. I'm not sure what the shoulder pads are about, but the skirt's on point. Her hair is parted in the middle and pulled tightly back in a bun. She might be getting Jehovah's Witnesses confused with the Amish. But what ruins the costume for me is that the

Bible she's carrying around is the Old Testament instead of the New Testament.

Rookie mistake.

Of course, Donna learns of this costume and reports her to the principal. It doesn't bother me. I'm not offended, so I'm not sure why Donna took it upon herself to get involved. She even lectures me about my costume choice and setting a good example for the younger Witnesses who attend the school.

She's right, but I just don't have it in me to care. This day isn't about her or the organisation. It's a celebration. This is a piece of my life finished, and there's some sadness around that. Soon Tamsin will move, and I'm sad that we were at school together for thirteen years and have only just become friends. I'm also sad about weird things, like having never been to a blue light disco. If I had my time over, I would sneak out to one. I wouldn't regret it. I know because I've been waiting to regret the time I've spent with Hunter, and I don't. How can I when these past few days have been the most exhilarating of my life?

After school, I head to Maggie's and work until six before making my way home. Mum is curled up on the couch watching a Jeanette MacDonald and Nelson Eddy movie.

'How was your last day?' she asks when I pop my head in to say hi.

'Fun.'

She studies me, like she's looking for evidence of un-Christian behaviour. 'Good. I'm glad. Now you just have a few exams and you're all done.' She almost sounds relieved.

'Yeah.' There's that empty feeling in my gut again.

'Dinner's in the microwave.' She looks back at the television. 'Savoury chops.'

I push off the door frame. 'Thanks.'

While my dinner is heating, I go to my bedroom and get my psychology textbooks out, preparing for a night of revision.

I'm about to head back to the kitchen when I hear a tap at my window. I turn my head and see Hunter standing outside, looking every bit the bad influence with his hair falling over one eye and his black hoodie tugged up. A smile spreads across my face as I walk over to the window.

He knows Mum's home, so the window remains closed. We don't speak, just look. I notice he has this new light in his eyes that wasn't there a few weeks ago, and I'm hoping like crazy that I'm the reason for it. We both know this is temporary, that we're stealing moments that don't belong to us, but neither of us wants to let go before we have to. Maybe he *wants* to drown alongside me.

I've tried to cleanse myself of these feelings, to rationalise them away. I've prayed more in the past two weeks than I have in my entire life. I know what a cliché I am. The Jehovah's Witness girl led astray by desire. It's wrong. I'm wrong. I can't even point the finger at Hunter, because he didn't lure me away from God. I stepped away willingly, dragging the worldly boy down with me.

Not only do I not have a plan, but I don't even have enough remorse to make one. Easier to wait for him to betray me, tire of me. Break me. Then I'll come to my senses, retreating with my tail between my legs, having learned my lesson the hardest way possible. I'd be truly remorseful then, returning to Jehovah, to my *real* life. Then I'll spend the rest of my days warning young sisters like myself against the dangers of temptation. Until then, I'd quite like to race this boy along the creek, swing with him across the water until I'm dizzy from laughter, and lie in the grass kissing him for hours on end.

'Tomorrow?' he mouths.

'After witnessing,' I mouth back.

He nods, winks, then jogs off, leaving me with a smile on my face and my heart soaring.

16

HUNTER

I spend Saturday morning helping Dad repair fences around the property, then throw down a sandwich before heading to the creek to wait for Annie. Technically, I should be studying for my biology exam all weekend. It's crazy how much my priorities have shifted in the past few weeks.

The creak of the rope swing has me looking up, and my eyes meet Annie's as her feet land on my side of the creek. She has this huge smile that turns my insides to pulp. I stand up, surprised when she runs to me instead of walking. No one's ever run to me before. No one's ever been this excited to see me. Except maybe Mum.

Annie greets me like we're a couple instead of two misfits fooling around, kissing me and taking my hand. I'm not scared of much, but the ease of our interactions scares the shit out of me. I think she's forgotten that this isn't a relationship. It's easy enough to do.

'What are we doing?' she asks.

We're hiding from the world, touching in secret,

pretending we're not limited to the farm and this moment isn't fleeting. 'How long do you have?'

'An hour. Two at most.' She startles suddenly. 'Oh, I know. You could show me the dam, the one you used to swim in when you were a kid.'

'How do you know about that?'

She tilts her head. 'Because we were in a combined grades three and four class together, remember? You told everyone during show and tell.'

I don't remember that, and I can't believe she does.

'Come on,' she says, pulling me up the hill. 'Sun's out. We can take our shoes and socks off and sit on the jetty.'

We follow the sheep tracks to the next paddock, then head down to the dam. It's sitting at around 80 percent capacity after a wet winter, which is great as we head into summer.

'I didn't know you had a boat,' Annie says, pointing to the beat-up tinny tied to the jetty. 'Can we go on it?'

I used to row Mum around in it when I was a kid, and I haven't been in it since. 'It'll probably be full of water.'

'Then we'll empty it,' she replies, undeterred.

We take off our shoes and socks and spend a few minutes scooping dirty water out of the bottom. The tinny's rusted and filthy, but Annie doesn't seem to mind. She might not come from a farming family, but she's a country girl at her core.

When we've gotten most of the water out, I help her into the boat, then climb in after her. 'Ready?' I ask as I place the oars in the water.

She nods. 'Ready.'

I row us out into the middle of the dam, then pull the

oars in. Annie turns her face up to the sun and closes her eyes. It reminds me of Mum. When she was going through chemo, she told me it helped with the nausea. I don't think it made much of a difference towards the end, though.

'Will you be happy here working on the farm?' Annie asks, looking at me.

I squint out at the water. 'Yeah, I think so. It's not the place, but the life you build, right?'

She draws her knees up. 'And what kind of life will you build?'

'Something simple, peaceful.'

She watches me a moment. 'Just think, one day your kids might be playing in this boat.'

Discussing anything in the future feels like dangerous territory. 'Hopefully I can afford something a bit better by then.' I lean forwards. 'Just need to dig us out of this financial dumpster fire first.'

'Are you guys managing okay? You won't lose the farm or anything?'

I shake my head. 'Nah. Once I'm done with school, I'll get on top of things. There's money coming in. Dad just...' I don't finish. I don't have to because she knows.

It's warm in the sun, so I tug my jumper off. Annie's gaze falls to the leather band she gave me in class last week. I haven't taken it off since. She does me the favour of not mentioning it.

'How long have you had the boat?' she asks.

I have to really think about that. 'Santa delivered it Christmas Eve in 1988.'

'So you were nine?'

I nod.

She looks around the tinny. 'And what age did you learn that Santa wasn't real?'

My eyebrows come together. 'Wait. What do you mean, not real?'

There's a brief moment of panic on her face before she realises I'm joking. She dips her hand in the water and flicks it at me.

'I had doubts when I was around eight,' I tell her. 'But I chose to remain blissfully ignorant for a few more years. I guess the first Christmas without Mum truly burst that bubble. Dad tried, but he just couldn't pull it off like she could. Drinking and present wrapping don't mix.'

Annie gives me a sympathetic smile.

'What was it like growing up without Christmas?' I ask.

She thinks for a moment. 'It was tough when we were younger. You know Santa's not real, but it still feels like you're missing out on some kind of magic. Once the magic is gone for everyone else, it's easier. Then you're only missing out on new clothes and CDs.' Her eyes move between mine. 'You're Catholic, right?'

I nod. 'No one in my family has stepped inside a church since I was baptised, but yes, we're Catholic.'

'That means you'll still get a fancy church wedding. Kingdom Halls don't have the same charm, I'm afraid.'

It should be strange to sit here talking about marriage, but it's not. I guess she hasn't forgotten this is fleeting after all.

'For the record,' she says, 'I can't come to your wedding. I'm not allowed to go into churches.'

'Why's that?'

'There's usually a sermon of some kind discussing "unscriptural ideas". Or maybe they make the sign of the cross or pray to a false God. Anything that might cause us to stumble spiritually is a no-go.'

My mouth turns up. 'That's okay. I probably won't go to your wedding either, because I won't be invited.'

She laughs, then goes quiet. 'It's obviously inconvenient that I'm not allowed to date you, but it's crap that we can't even be friends.' She shrugs. 'I like you.'

It's more than crap. I want to say I like you too, but I simply nod.

She looks down at her feet, and her face falls. 'Was that water already inside the boat?'

I feel it then, water at my feet. It's seeping in through the rust. 'Shit.'

'Are we sinking?' She shoots up, and the boat rocks violently.

I pull her back down and drop one of the oars in the process. We both reach for it at the same time, and the boat leans right, taking in water. The oar is pushed away on a wave as the tinny levels itself.

'Sorry,' Annie says.

I start paddling with the one oar I still have, trying to get us back to the jetty. We're ten feet from it when the boat starts to go under.

'Jump,' I tell Annie. 'Go.'

She leaps into the water, and I jump in after her, then return to the boat, trying to pull it to shore. I can't bear to see it sink.

Annie grabs hold of one of the wooden piles and

looks back at me. 'Let it go. It'll drag you down.'

She's right. It slips beneath the surface and starts to pull me down with it. Swearing, I let go and watch it sink. When the bubbles stop rising, I swim over to Annie.

'You okay?' I ask.

She nods. 'Can you help me up?'

I get a better grip on the foundation pile and take hold of her leg with my other hand. When I hoist her up, she grabs hold of the jetty, then pulls herself up onto it. She stands no chance of lifting me, so I swim to the water's edge, where I'm forced to navigate the mud. My legs and feet are covered in it by the time I step onto dry land. I look back at Annie and see she's untied the rope we use to secure the tinny.

'What are you doing?' I call to her.

She glances in my direction. 'I'm going to tie it to the oarlock. Then we can pull it up.'

I watch as she prepares to dive in. 'Absolutely not. Stay where you are.'

'It's not that deep.'

I head for the jetty, eyes locked on her. 'Wilson.' Her name is a warning from my lips—one she doesn't heed.

She dives, disappearing into the murky water.

I take off at a run, feet slippery with mud, looking for her the whole time. When I don't see her, I dive in. I'm not exactly sure what my plan is given I can't see my own hand in front of my face, but I search for her anyway. I search until I can no longer hold my breath, then surface with a sharp inhale. And there's Annie, treading water a few feet from me.

'What are you doing?' she asks. 'I was going to throw

it up to you.' She holds up the end of the rope. 'I'm not the best at knots, but it should hold.'

I swim to her, snatching the rope from her hand. 'What the fuck? I told you not to get in.'

She backs up from me. 'And I ignored you.'

'Why?'

'Because I knew I could do it.'

I run a hand down my face and draw a calming breath. 'I want you out of the water.'

She watches me with this wounded expression.

'*Now*,' I tell her.

She swallows. 'Can you help me up again?'

I'm tempted to make her go through the mud but nod instead. Once she's safely on the jetty, I'm able to relax a little.

'Throw the rope up,' she calls.

I toss it to her. 'Don't do anything until I get there.'

She listens this time.

When I reach her, she hands me the rope. It takes us a few attempts, but eventually the rusted tinny surfaces. We drag it alongside the jetty until it's safely lodged in the mud.

'What if you hadn't surfaced?' I say, turning to her. 'I couldn't see a thing down there.'

'I know I'm not known for my athletic abilities around school, but I can swim.'

'Why didn't you just leave it?'

She searches my eyes. 'I didn't want Santa to get mad at you.' She looks down at the boat. 'Your recent behaviour hasn't been great. Anything we can do to get you off his naughty list is helpful at this poi—'

My lips crash down on hers. She tastes of muddy water and bad jokes, and I can't get enough of it. My hands go into her wet hair, my body seeking hers. It's not cautious this time—it's urgent. I'm pissed off and falling for this girl harder by the minute.

Annie doesn't pull away. She doesn't ask what I'm doing. Instead, she fists my wet shirt, drawing me closer, teeth scraping my lips with a hunger that matches my own. We go to our knees, and she brings my hand to her breast.

'I can't...' she pants, momentarily breaking our kiss.

'I know.' No sex. The line hasn't moved. And that's fine. I'll take whatever she'll give me and satisfy her in any way she'll let me.

We're a tangle of wet limbs and hungry mouths and urgent hands and soft moans. It's all over far too quickly, but neither of us had the restraint to finish any other way. It's enough, yet I want more of her. I don't tell her that, though, because she doesn't need to feel any more torn than she does. The conversation is futile. Instead, we lie in the sun, shoulder to shoulder, watching the clouds pass overhead, until she inevitably rolls to face me and says, 'I have to go.'

She kisses me for a full minute before getting to her feet. 'At least our shoes are dry.'

I walk her back to the bridge and realise I don't want her to leave. This is new territory for me. She mustn't want to leave either, because she doesn't cross.

'Did you like today?' she asks, looking up at me.

I'm drowning in those eyes. 'Sure. Except for the bit where you jumped in without me.'

She smiles. 'You don't have to worry about me. I can take care of myself in the water.'

'What about out of the water?'

She opens her mouth to answer but doesn't get the chance to.

'Annie?' comes a voice.

Her head whips in the direction of the water. On the other side of the creek, her mum stands holding a bypass lopper, looking thoroughly confused.

Annie takes a hurried step back from me, almost tripping over her own feet in the process. I don't reach for her, don't dare touch her.

'Mum.'

Dawn looks between us, her confusion melting into suspicion. 'What are you doing over there?'

It takes Annie a beat too long to come up with an answer. 'I was just chatting to Hunter about exams.'

She's a terrible liar. Her voice is too high, and she can't keep her hands still.

Dawn looks her daughter up and down. 'Why are you wet?'

'She fell off the swing,' I say. I can tell a lie just fine. 'My attempt to help wasn't overly successful, as you can see.' I gesture to my own wet clothes.

Dawn stares at me—hard.

'I should go,' I say, looking back at Annie. 'Good luck next week.'

She nods. 'You too.'

I turn away, and under no circumstances do I look back.

17

ANNIE

The exams are held at the footy club rooms in town, because it's the only venue equipped for it. My first exam is psychology, and I walk out feeling relieved instead of worried, so I guess that means it went okay.

I did end up doing a lot of studying for it—mostly to avoid Mum's scrutiny. Ever since she saw me with Hunter, she's been oddly quiet but extra watchful. Safer to hide away in my bedroom than risk questioning.

As I'm descending the steps, I spot Hunter leaning against the rail at the bottom. He straightens when he sees me. I can't tell if his serious expression is due to the fact that we're in public or if something's actually wrong.

'How'd you go?' he asks when I reach him.

'Okay—I think.'

He gestures towards the empty part of the car park under the clubhouse, and we head there. The second we're out of sight of everyone, he turns to me.

'Did you get in trouble?'

It's clear he's no longer talking about the exam. 'On Saturday? No.'

'I came to the creek yesterday looking for you.'

He was likely concerned, but it's always hard to tell with him, because every emotion comes out as anger. 'I had to lie low. Mum was watching me like a hawk.'

The creases on his face deepen. 'She tell the elders?'

Definitely sounds like concern. Angry, Hunter-style concern. 'Tell them what? She found us talking.'

'I thought you couldn't be with a guy unchaperoned?'

I touch his arm. 'It's all fine. I'm not in any trouble.'

He steps out of reach. 'And what if she'd found us kissing? Would she have told them then?'

I let out an exasperated breath. 'Probably. Or one of the sisters. I don't know.'

A car drives by, and we fall silent until it passes.

'What happens when you're brought before the elders?' he asks.

I draw a breath before replying. 'We're not lashed or starved, if that's what you're asking. It's just a lot of talking, reading of the scriptures, and prayer.' Guilt. Shame.

'What about shunning?'

I feel hot suddenly. 'You're only shunned if you're baptised.'

'Like your sister?'

I drop my gaze. I don't know what this is, what he's doing. And I don't know how to fix it. 'I need you to explain what's going on here.'

He links his hands atop his head. 'It's just messed up. I can't contact you to find out what happened, and you have all these bullshit consequences, half of which I don't understand.' He shakes his head. 'I don't like the lies.'

'You think I do?'

'And I don't like sneaking around.'

Panic rises in me. This feels a lot like an exit. 'When exams are over, we'll go to the city and watch that horror movie. We'll do whatever we want, and we'll do it out in public. We won't have to worry about anyone seeing us.'

He doesn't react or say anything, and now my stomach feels like I'm about to walk into another exam. His silence is more unsettling than Mum's. 'Hunter.'

He blinks slowly. 'And then what?' His tone has a hard edge to it.

'You mean after the movie?'

'After our perfect day in the city. What happens when we're back in this town living our normal lives?'

Suddenly we're here, in that place we didn't want to be, and I'm gutted. 'What are you doing?'

'I'm asking you a question.'

I nod slowly, taking a small step back from him. 'Well, I don't know what you want me to say, because I don't have any answers.'

His bottom lip disappears between his teeth, and he looks up at the overcast sky. 'And when *will* you have answers?'

'I don't know. I just walked out of an exam, and you're hitting me with this. I don't have the headspace for this conversation.' Because I'm a coward.

He continues chewing that lip of his. 'Your mum's not an idiot.'

'I know that.'

'Then how long do you think until she figures out that her only daughter still in the organisation is being fingerfucked by the guy across the creek while she's at work?'

I flinch. I flinch so hard the action feels like a convulsion. Hunter's sworn in front of me plenty of times, but this phrase from his mouth is too much. It makes me feel dirtier than anything we've ever done.

I stand there waiting for him to realise what he just said, to realise he's overstepped. I'm waiting for the remorse to show on his face or an apology of some kind, but it doesn't come. Instead, he's standing there waiting for *me* to respond.

'I can't believe you just said that to me.' I'm upset at his choice of words, but I'm more upset that we've reached our expiration date so soon.

He stares at me. 'What do you want, Wilson?'

What I want is to go back in time, for this conversation to never have happened. 'I have to go.' I start backing away. 'I have my second exam tomorrow.'

He pinches the bridge of his nose. 'You don't have five minutes to finish the conversation?'

'No. No, I don't.' I turn and walk away. His boots crunch on the stones behind me.

'This isn't just you ticking shit off your rebellious acts list anymore,' he says.

I keep walking. 'I know that.'

'And I just told you I don't want to sneak around.'

I throw my hands up. 'So don't.'

He catches my wrist, spinning me to face him. 'Stop. Running.'

'Why? Do you have some more vulgarities you want to throw at me before I leave?'

He searches my eyes, his grip on me loosening. 'You *want* me to be the one who ends it, don't you? That way all your fears will be justified. Is that it?'

I shake my head, even though everything he's saying is true.

'Then you can go running back to the safety and comfort of your cult.' He releases my arm. 'If I don't end it, if it turns out I'm not so bad, that makes things tricky for you, doesn't it?'

My eyes begin to burn. 'Did you just say *cult*?'

'Yes, cult. Any organisation that isolates its members from the real world looks suspiciously like a cult from where I'm standing.'

I lean in. 'It *protects* its members.'

He laughs in my face. 'From what? Real life?'

I jab a finger in his direction. 'From people like you.'

Not one muscle moves on his face. 'You think I'm the threat here? You hold all the power, Wilson. You always did. And I was stupid enough to hand it to you.'

I swallow, straighten. 'How can you say that as you back me into a corner, forcing me to choose between you and my whole life?'

He looks away, and I'm finally able to draw breath.

'You're right.' He nods slowly. 'It isn't fair to make you choose. So *I'll* choose.' His eyes meet mine once more. 'And I choose to be done with this bullshit.'

Never have words landed so hard.

'I'm not driving two hours just so I can hold your hand in public,' he continues, 'only to be tossed aside when this phase of yours is over.' He gestures between us. 'Me calling it should make things real easy for you.'

I blink, paralysed by his words.

He shakes his head, appearing defeated. 'You're a long way from figuring your shit out, and I don't want to be a factor.'

My hands hang heavy at my sides. I wonder if he's breaking his own heart as well as mine with this speech.

'Wait,' I manage to get out.

He starts walking backwards. 'Good luck.'

I take a step after him. 'Stop talking like I'm not going to see you in a few hours.' When he turns away, I panic. 'Can't you just... can't you just give me some time to think?'

'Take all the time you need. This decision isn't about me,' he says over his shoulder. 'It's about whether you want to stay in the religion or not. You don't need me around for that.'

He tugs up the hood of his jumper and heads for the ute.

18

HUNTER

The exam period turns into the longest two weeks of my life. I haven't seen Annie since the fight in the car park, since I ended things. But ended what? We were never really a thing. We were just teetering close to the edge of something real and all-consuming and fucking terrifying. I did what I had to do, what she didn't have the strength to. And I remind myself of this over and over, but it does little to move whatever's lodged in my chest.

My last exam is 2D art, and I can't tell if I'm on edge because I'm so close to the finish line or because I'm going to see Annie. I don't know if she's angry, upset, or completely over the whole thing. And I don't know which one would be worse.

She's last to arrive and first to leave. She doesn't so much as glance in my direction, while my eyes seem to drift constantly in hers. It's crazy to miss something you never had.

I'm intentionally slow getting down the stairs after the

exam, and I'm rewarded by the sight of Annie driving away in her mother's car. I guess she's not one for awkward encounters either.

The rest of the students are standing in a group with relieved smiles on their faces and bags under their eyes. They're laughing at things that aren't funny. It's the adrenaline of the past few weeks working its way out of their bodies. More year twelve students pull up in cars, wanting to share this moment. Sammy's among them. He jumps out of Trent's car and walks over to me, pulling me into a hug.

'We're done,' he says, clapping me on the back.

My mouth turns up, his cheerfulness contagious. 'We are.'

Releasing me, he crosses his arms, looking around at the others. 'Feels weird, doesn't it?'

'Yeah. Yeah it does.'

I can see Tamsin standing beside Trent's car with her friends, their gestures animated as they make plans for the evening. She glances in my direction, then steps away from the group to come speak with me—or, more likely, Sammy.

'Hey,' she says. 'You guys coming to celebrate tonight?'

Sammy perks up. 'Where?'

'Whistle Beach.'

'I'm keen,' he says.

Me, not so much. 'Who else's going?'

Tamsin gives me a look. 'I would've invited Annie, but she fled so fast I didn't get a chance.' There's a hint of accusation in her tone.

'I'll come for a bit,' I tell her.

'Great.' She looks at Sammy. 'I'll see you later.' She heads back over to Trent's car.

When we're alone, he turns to me and says, 'Let me guess. You're the reason Annie fled.'

'No comment.' I start walking to the ute. Sure, it's possible I regret some of the words that spilled from my mouth a few weeks back, but I don't regret the end result. Annie needs me out of the way while she figures out how she wants to live her adult life.

'Can you drop me home?' he asks.

'Sure.'

'Then pick me up later?'

I roll my eyes. 'Fine, but I'm not hanging around all night.'

It's nearing five in the afternoon when I finally walk in the door, and Dad's nowhere to be seen. I don't know why, but I expect him to be waiting for me. This feels like one of those moments he should be present for.

I go check if the bike's in the shed. Thankfully it is. I then set off in search of him, calling to him like he's a lost toddler instead of a forty-five-year-old man.

'Dad!'

I eventually find him slumped against a rail of one of the sheep pens. He doesn't appear to be injured, so that's something. I nudge his leg with my boot, and he groans. And he's alive.

Grabbing hold of his arm, I drape it around my shoulders and pull him to his feet. 'Gonna need you to walk,' I say.

He attempts to cooperate.

I think back to the time Annie managed to get him from the creek paddock all the way to the house by herself. It would have been pure stubbornness more than strength.

We make it back to the house, and I lay him on his bed to sleep it off. I remove his muddy boots before going to shower, then check on him before I leave. He hasn't moved at all.

'I'm going out for a bit,' I say, knowing I won't get a response. 'Sleep it off, old man.'

It's after six when I pull into Sammy's driveway. He jogs out of the house and jumps into the passenger seat. 'What's wrong with you?' he asks.

I wave to his mum, who's just pulled up beside me, then turn the car around. 'Usual.'

'Ah. Kev not in a good way?'

'Nope.'

He fiddles with the radio until he finds Triple J. 'You know, there's a rehab place in Turram. Might be a bit of a wait to get him in, but the sooner you put his name on the list, the sooner he'll get help.'

I focus on the road ahead. 'He has to *want* the help.'

'You have to do an intervention so he knows there's a problem.'

I glance sideways at him. 'Oh, he knows there's a problem.'

Sammy leans his head back on the seat. 'Tell him you want him to go. Maybe he needs to hear that. Then he'll get sober, have a proper look at himself, and come looking for forgiveness.'

'I think I'm busy that day.'

He chuckles. 'Don't really blame you. You've put up with a lot more than most people would.'

It's not like I have a choice.

The party's on a quiet section of the foreshore far from the main beach. The nearby car park's already full, so we park on the side of the road. From the moment we step down onto the beach, it's clear that most of the party-goers started their celebrations well before we arrived. There's a fire going with a hotplate laid over the top. A cooler sits nearby containing everything one needs for a barbeque: cheap sausages with ingredients you should never question, fresh white bread, and a few bottles of cheap sauce. Nirvana blares from a portable CD player.

I spot Tamsin seated on a towel, an open Strongbow in hand. She turned eighteen in the middle of the exams, so this is her first social bash since ticking over to legal age. She waves us over when she sees us.

'Coming?' Sammy asks when I hesitate.

I reluctantly follow him over to the group. The girls greet us with a high-pitched drunken 'Hiiiiii', which confirms that I absolutely do not want to remain here past a few basic pleasantries.

Tamsin stands and drunkenly hugs us both. She smells of bourbon and menthol cigarettes. 'You caaaaame.'

I roll my eyes in Sammy's direction. 'I was just dropping Sammy off.'

'You can't go yet,' Tamsin says. 'This is technically my birthday party.'

Sammy gives me a look that clearly says stay.

I ignore it.

'Are you at least going to say hi to Annie before you head off?' Tamsin asks.

That was well played. I take the bait. 'Annie's here?'

'She was a moment ago.' She's swaying a little as she looks around. 'Wait, I remember. She went off with Andy somewhere.'

I try very hard not to react to that statement. 'Andy Collins?' She doesn't even know the guy.

'Yeah.' Tamsin turns to the other girls. 'Did they go in?'

My eyes go to the water. 'What do you mean, *in*?'

One of her friends gestures to the rocks at the far end of the beach. 'I saw them walk that way.'

Tamsin turns back to us, momentarily taking Sammy's arm for balance. 'I'll go find her.'

'That's not a good idea,' Sammy says.

I draw a slow breath. '*I'll* go find her.'

Tamsin gives me an adoring look. 'Aww. You're such a sweetheart.'

I glance once at Sammy, then head off in the direction of the rocks.

There's no one at that end of the beach, and no one in the water that I can see, so I climb up for a better view. When I still don't find her, I scale the rocks to the beach on the other side, dropping down onto the sand and looking around.

The sound of voices has me turning. I follow the rock line around, stilling when I spot Annie and Andy standing at the water's edge. I watch them a moment, like a stalker, tensing up when she begins unbuttoning her jeans.

What the... If she thinks she's skinny-dipping with Andy fucking Collins, then she's about to be sorely disappointed. I wouldn't have picked Andy as a pervert, but what do I know?

I head off across the wet sand, intending to tell Annie to do her pants up before calmly removing her. But that's not what happens. Andy tugs his T-shirt off and stands there watching Annie undress. My eyes never leave him. He knows he's in trouble the second he looks up, the moment his eyes meet mine. He opens his mouth to speak right before my fist connects with his face, then drops to the sand beside his surfboard, hands going over his face as he emits a long groan.

'Hunter!' Annie says on an inhale, stepping between us. 'What are you doing?'

'Start walking,' I say, eyes still on Andy. 'I'm taking you home.'

She shakes her head. 'What? No.'

I look at her. 'Start. Walking.'

Her eyes narrow into a glare. 'I'm not going anywhere with you.'

I gesture to her unbuttoned jeans. 'And do your pants up.'

Ignoring me, she turns to Andy. 'Are you okay?'

'He's fine,' I say, pulling her to the other side of me. 'Let's go.'

Andy sits up and spits blood onto the sand. 'What the hell was that for?'

'You made him bleed,' Annie says behind me.

I roll my eyes. 'I didn't break anything.'

She releases this helpless, exasperated laugh. 'I'm so sorry,' she tells Andy. Then she turns and walks away.

'Salt water will do wonders for that,' I add before following her.

Annie doesn't wait for me. She starts to climb, flying over the rocks, her bare feet slipping and shins crashing against stone.

'Slow down,' I call to her.

She ignores me entirely.

I'm sure she'll appreciate what I did once she's had a chance to calm down. 'The ute's on the road.'

Again I'm ignored, but she does head in the right direction. I guess it falls on me to let the others know that I now have her and I'm taking her home.

'She all right?' Tamsin asks when I tell her. 'She didn't hurt herself surfing, did she?'

I blink. 'She wasn't surfing.'

She makes a face. 'Oh. I thought Andy offered to teach her.'

Now that she mentions it, there was a surfboard at the scene. My anger dissolves.

Sammy claps me on the arm. 'I'll catch a ride home with someone else later.'

I nod. 'Yep.'

Annie didn't bother waiting for me. I find her leaning against the ute, arms crossed. She steps aside when I unlock her door, careful not to make eye contact with me. She climbs in and pulls the door from my hands before I have a chance to close it. Drawing a long breath, I head for the driver side. Perhaps I should have gone with my original plan, but it's too late now.

When I climb in, she has her head in her hands, and I'm fairly sure she's crying. I grip the steering wheel, knowing I'm 100 percent responsible for these tears.

'I thought you were going skinny-dipping,' I say, as if that excuses my behaviour.

Her hands drop to her lap, and she leans her head back on the headrest, looking up at the roof. 'I mentioned to Andy that I'd never surfed before. He was being kind.'

I swallow my guilt. 'You were taking off your clothes...'

She meets my gaze. 'So? I'm wearing bathers under my clothes. And even if I wasn't, it's nothing to do with you. I can surf or skinny-dip with whoever I like.'

I turn the key. 'That's fair.'

'That's fair?' She shakes her head. 'How about "I'm sorry"?'

'You want me to apologise for looking out for you? I didn't know if you'd been drinking—or if he had.'

She reaches back for her seat belt, but it keeps locking every time she pulls it. After releasing a frustrated groan, she pauses, breathes, and tries again. The second the seat belt clicks into place, she says, 'Can we go please?'

I put the ute into gear and pull out onto the road. She doesn't say a word as we head back to Chirnside, she simply stares out the window.

'You going to ignore me the whole drive?' I ask.

'I'm not ignoring you. I just don't have anything to say to you.'

We drive in silence for a few more minutes.

I glance sideways at her. 'You pissed at me about today or the things I said last time?'

'I'm not angry at you.' Her voice is quiet. 'I'm angry at me.'

I hate everything about that answer. 'What does that mean?'

She shakes her head, clearly not wanting to elaborate. 'I'm just so tired.'

I don't know if she's tired from exams, of life, or of me. And I'm not sure I want to know the answer.

'I miss you,' she says at the window. 'Even after everything.'

I stare hard at the road ahead, palms heating the steering wheel. It takes me a moment to respond. 'Like I said, you need to figure shit out, and I'm in the way.'

She turns her head and looks at me. 'Do you miss me?'

More than anything. But it's one thing to feel it and another to admit it aloud.

When I don't respond, she reaches for the door latch. 'Just let me out here. I'll walk the rest of the way.'

I don't want to let her out, because once she leaves this car, there won't be any more moments like this. 'It's dark.'

'I don't care. Please pull over.'

There's a frantic edge to those last words that has me indicating and pulling off onto the side of the road.

'I can't be seen alone in a car with you.' She meets my eyes briefly before pushing the door open.

'Wilson,' I say as she's climbing out.

She turns back to me, waiting.

All the things I want to say to her, I can't. 'I'll drive back to the beach, make sure Andy is okay.'

She nods, then closes the door. It doesn't close properly, so she has to backtrack and try again. She looks visibly relieved when it closes this time.

I watch her walk off in her rolled-up jeans and scuffed Aerosports. She hugs herself against the cold and picks up speed. I watch her climb the embankment on the other side of the road and disappear into the trees.

I drop my head to the steering wheel for a moment, then head back to the beach.

The first thing I do when I finally arrive home is go check on Dad. I can smell the vomit before I see it. At least he did it on the floor and not all over the bed and himself. As much as I'd love to leave it for him to clean up in the morning, I don't. The smell is all through the house, and it lingers long after I finish cleaning. I have to open all the windows and doors, dousing the place with bleach in an attempt to disguise it.

And now the house reeks of bleach.

I can't sleep in this stench, so I snatch my duvet off the bed and head for the hay shed. Our working dog, Tess, whines at me as I pass her, so I cave and let her off her chain. She can keep the mice off me. I close the shed door, then, wrapping myself in my covers, flop down onto the hay and sleep.

19

ANNIE

I made sure I scheduled in some downtime between exams and starting work. Not for Bible study or field service, but to ride, read, watch old movies, or to simply lie under our budding peach tree and wait for the mosquitos to find me.

It feels a bit like freedom.

'Why don't you come help me for the day?' Mum says on Tuesday. 'You could earn a bit of extra cash.'

I don't want money. I want time. 'I thought I might go riding, then see if Tamsin wants to go to the beach in the afternoon.'

'Tamsin?' Mum's porridge-loaded spoon pauses mid-air. 'What about Donna? She loves the beach.'

I sigh inwardly. 'Actually, she doesn't love the beach. She complains endlessly about the sand sticking to everything.'

She sets her spoon down. 'You know, I understand the need to have someone at school, in your own year level, going through the same things you're going through. But school's over now. It's pointless to put effort into worldly friendships.'

I watch my Weet-Bix soak up milk in my bowl.

'Tamsin's a nice girl, but she's about to go off and pursue her worldly goals,' she continues. 'That might make you question your own path.'

I don't need Tamsin for that. I've been questioning my path since I was fifteen. 'I understand where you're coming from, but it doesn't feel right to cut her from my life without cause.'

Mum picks up her bowl and carries it over to the sink. 'I can only offer you advice, not force you to take it.' She starts rinsing dishes.

'Leave those. I'll do them.'

She smiles at me as she collects her handbag from the counter.

'I thought tomorrow I might call the real estate agent and organise a viewing of one of those vacant flats near the school,' I say as she's preparing to leave.

'They're vacant for a reason. Rat-infested mould hubs.'

'I guess a rat-infested mould hub will be all I can afford next year.'

Mum walks by me on her way to the door. 'You're always welcome to stay here, you know. Pay a bit of board. Buy some groceries occasionally. Much cheaper.'

Nothing will change if I stay here. My life will be exactly the same. *I'll* be exactly the same. 'I'll keep that in mind, thanks.'

'You can do dinner since you have all the time in the

world,' Mum says on her way out. 'There are chops in the freezer.'

When the front door finally closes, I release a long breath. Finally, some peace. I scrape my soggy Weet-Bix into the bin, then do the dishes.

With the chops now thawing, I change into riding clothes and head to the creek paddock to saddle Charlie. He's pawing at the gate.

'Only me.' I still feel the need to say that, and I'm certain I can sense his disappointment.

In the distance, I can hear the sound of panicked sheep being rounded up. I sneak a look and see Hunter on his bike and Tess doing her best to maintain order, but there are sheep dispersing in all directions. I have no idea what Hunter's doing or why he's doing it alone, but I can hear his frustration in his instructions to Tess.

'Round the back. Round the back!' is carried on the breeze.

Sighing, I mount Charlie and head down to the water, raising my feet so they don't get wet when we cross. Thankfully Banjo's on the chain, because I'd intended to go out on the road and didn't want him getting hit by a car.

Hunter's at the top of the paddock, watching the sheep pass through. I spot four huddled together in the shade away from the flock, so I head for them, waving my arm to get them moving. 'I think you're wanted in the top paddock, ladies.'

They take off up the hill, and I follow them to ensure they don't get distracted on the way.

Hunter looks in my direction as he wipes the sweat off

his face. It's not overly hot, so it's safe to assume it's stress related.

'Where's your dad?' I shout.

'Sleeping.'

He means sleeping it off. I look around at the flock. 'Where are they going?'

'It's shearing day.'

I frown. 'Please tell me you're not planning on shearing two thousand sheep by yourself.'

'I've got two shearers arriving in half an hour.'

I look to the hill paddock past the pine trees. 'Want me to help you get the rest?' I can see him wrestling with his pride. 'I don't mind, really.'

He nods, then whistles to Tess. 'Push up!'

I turn Charlie around and head to the other side of the flock. Between the horse, the dog, and the bike, we manage to get the first four hundred sheep into the pen closest to the shed. I push the gate closed when the final one runs through, and Hunter pulls up to latch it.

Then we head off again.

We're still rounding up sheep when the shearers arrive, and Kevin's nowhere to be seen. Thankfully the two men don't ask questions. They simply get on with the job. By the time we've brought the last of the sheep in, there's already a pen filled with freshly shorn sheep.

I could leave. I've done what I said I would do, but Hunter's still a man down for the day, so I put Charlie in one of the pens and follow him inside. I bag the wool while Hunter tends to the other tasks.

By midday, I'm pouring with sweat and covered with some kind of oil. It's a hundred degrees inside the shed despite the large fan in the corner. The men are all shirt-less, so I strip down to my singlet. Hunter wanders over with a cup of water. He watches me drink, and I watch him right back. There's something about him in that state, sweat-soaked and peppered with fleece, that makes my pulse quicken. I notice his gaze drop to the neck of my singlet as I hand him the cup back.

'You good?' he asks.

I nod. 'Yeah.'

Kevin enters the wool shed, looking like death. He's sweating for very different reasons. 'Fellas,' he says, greeting the shearers. There's a brief exchange before he comes our way. He nods at Hunter. 'Thanks for getting things started.'

Hunter turns away from him. 'Didn't have much choice.' His eyes meet mine. 'You go. We've got it from here.'

'You sure?'

'Yeah.'

I still hate leaving him. How can that be after every-thing? 'Good luck.'

'Thanks for helping out,' Kevin says quietly when I pass him.

I force a smile. 'No worries.'

Charlie's thoroughly exhausted from his morning of pretending to be a workhorse, so I skip the ride and return him to his paddock.

In the afternoon, Tamsin picks me up in the Rav 4 she got as a graduation present, and we spend a few blissful hours swimming, sunbaking, and talking about what she's wearing to the graduation I'm not attending. She tells me how Sammy's new place is only a short tram ride from where she'll be living. I lie with my eyes closed, enjoying the warmth of the sun on my skin and the sound of her voice. She sounds so happy.

I wish I could sound like that.

She drops me home a little after four o'clock, and I start on dinner. I stare out the back window, in the direction of the creek, while the chops in the frypan spit fat at me. It's been like this every day since the fight. I'm not looking for him—I'm *feeling* for him.

I still have an hour before Mum gets home, so I turn the hotplate off and put a cover over the meat before heading down to the creek. And there he is, sitting in the grass on the other side, bare chested and wet skin glistening. His hair is a dripping mess going in all directions. He must have gone for a swim.

I've stopped walking to stare at him. He doesn't look the slightest bit surprised when he spots me. It's almost as if he was waiting for me. Or perhaps he was feeling for me too.

Loneliness hits then. I want to sit at his side, hold his hand, kiss his rough cheek. But I want to do all those things without an internal war constantly raging inside me. Surely we've both earned some peace.

I ask myself every day why I stay in the religion when I'm so deeply unhappy and always doubting my beliefs. But that's not the right question. The question isn't why do I *stay*? It's why can't I *leave*? And the answer carries more shame than my lack of faith. I'm a coward. I don't want to end up like my sister. I don't want to be an outcast, alone. Unlovable.

Hunter frowns, like he can hear the whisper of my thoughts but can't quite make them out. He stands up and takes a few steps in my direction. My brain goes quiet. The relief is bliss. I head for the water, for him. If Hunter's willing to have me in this moment, then I'm willing to hate myself a little more after it.

I walk straight into the water, boots and all. 'Are you coming in?'

He hesitates, and I understand why, but then his need to feel good for a few minutes must win, because now he's coming towards me too. His eyes are heavy with exhaustion and resignation. His eyes are heavy *on me*. Any so-called progress we've made over the past two weeks is about to be undone.

Hunter knows it. I know it.

He wades into the creek, his cargos taking on water until he's submerged to the waist. The closer he gets to me the shallower my breathing becomes. Then he's reaching for me, dragging me to him, lifting me. I've missed these hands so much. He guides my legs around him so we're as close as we can physically be. But it's still not close enough.

I peel my T-shirt off and throw it onto the creek bank. Then I do something I've not done before—I take off my bra. Yes, he's touched my breasts, many times, but I've never been this exposed to him before.

He drops his gaze, unashamedly taking in the sight.

'You're so beautiful,' he says.

I've never really heard tender words from his mouth, and the emotion it conjures catches me off guard. He lowers us into the icy water so only the tops of our shoulders are visible. I shudder as he draws me closer, and now we're skin to skin, and it feels so good and so right.

He kisses me, and I kiss him back.

Then we're *really* kissing—more than kissing. We're inhaling each other's pain and loneliness, cleansing ourselves. The heat we're generating is blurring the line before me. Suddenly there are no rules, only him.

He's touching me through my pants, and I'm impatient to be rid of them. As we're tugging wet clothes off one another, I know I'll want to keep going, because I want more of him. I want him without restrictions.

We're falling all over the place. Then we're laughing, and it feels *so* good to laugh with him again.

Finally, he tosses my jeans triumphantly aside.

'Your turn,' I say.

He gathers me in his arms, smile gone. 'Where's the line, Wilson?'

'Gone,' I whisper.

He pushes hair back from my face, eyes searching mine, then buries his face in my neck. 'Annie.' He slides his hand up my thigh and tugs down my underwear. The cold temperature of the water is a delicious contrast to the heat building inside me. He kisses along my collarbone, and it feels like his mouth is everywhere at once. My eyes sink shut as he—

'Annie!'

I gasp violently when my mother's voice rings out around me and drop low in the water. Hunter releases his grip on me, and I stagger off him in the least graceful way possible.

Mum's mouth hangs open, her eyes filled with horror. *Horror.* Like she just discovered me feasting on a child.

'Oh my goodness,' she breathes out before clapping a hand over her mouth.

Hunter stands, thankfully still wearing pants. 'I told her to come in. She didn't want to.'

I can't think while naked in front of her. 'My T-shirt,' I manage to say, sounding small and pathetic.

He rushes to retrieve it, turning it the right way out before handing it to me. He passes my bra to me under-water, but it's pointless because my mum already knows I'm not wearing it.

'Get out of there,' Mum says, her voice shaking. 'Right now.'

I'm struggling to get my T-shirt on. Hunter moves to help me, but I shake my head.

He looks back at Mum. 'This is on me.'

'Stop,' I tell him. 'It won't make any difference.' I finally have my T-shirt on, but I still have to get out and collect the rest of my things. *Where are my socks?* I don't care.

This is like the walk of shame I've heard mentioned in movies, but I'm fairly sure this particular walk tops anything Hollywood can dream up. Firstly, the audience is my Jehovah's Witness mother. Secondly, my undies are see-through, and my T-shirt is clinging to my naked form like translucent skin. Everything's on display right now. My body, my sins, my shame.

I pick up my pants and empty the water from my boots. My feet squelch in the mud as I walk towards her.

She doesn't look at me but waits for me to pass by. Perhaps she doesn't trust me to follow her.

'You stay away from her!' she hisses at Hunter.

I turn. 'Mum, stop. This is my mistake, not his.'

'Get inside the house!' Her voice cracks with emotion as she yells at me.

My face collapses as I turn away, and I start to cry.

20

ANNIE

There are two elders in our congregation, and I can't for the life of me figure out why Mum has phoned Brother Oliver. She knows he's my least favourite, if such a thing were allowed. I don't like his voice, his stare, his words, his smile. His mannerisms make me uncomfortable. And now he's sitting before me discussing intimate details of my life, and there's not a thing I can do about it.

'So there was some mutual masturbation?' he asks, leaning slightly forwards as he awaits my reply.

I nod—barely.

Mum's next to me, staring down at the open Bible in her lap. On the coffee table sits a pot of tea and a plate of jam biscuits. Brother Oliver has poured himself some tea but has the decency not to stuff his face with biscuits while asking me for details about my sex life.

'Is this the first time you've given in to temptation?' he asks me.

Mum looks up, bracing for my reply.

I don't lie for myself—I lie for her. 'Yes.' I wet my lips, but it doesn't help much. My mouth is so dry. 'Not the first time we've hung out, just the first time we went that far.' That part is true.

He nods as though he understands. 'It appears the temptation has been there for quite some time. I imagine you now see the importance of associating with people who have the same set of morals you do, along with the value of a chaperone when spending time with the opposite sex.'

'Yes.' I'll agree with anything he says at this point. I just want this conversation to be over.

'I'm glad your mother called me so we were able to get on top of this before any more damage was done.'

That's what I am now. Damaged.

'I think the best thing to do at this point is ask for Jehovah's forgiveness and strength, then make a plan to keep you focused on your baptism goal.'

I close my eyes and bow my head, trying to focus on the words he's saying. He spares little detail as he spells out my sins for Jehovah, as if he hasn't witnessed every misstep first-hand.

I am sorry for a lot of things—just not this.

Brother Oliver suggests upping my contribution to the congregation. I'll spend my free time visiting sisters, run errands for the elderly, help the busy mums with childcare and Bible study, increase my hours of field service. Eat some fruit cake. Pray more. I'll be so busy giving of myself to others that I won't have time to fornicate. I think that's the gist of the plan.

Mum sees Brother Oliver to the door, turning the

outside light on and waiting for him to pull away. Then she returns to the room where I'm still seated and starts clearing away the tea and untouched biscuits.

'They can just go back in the container,' she says.

I watch her carry them away, hear the opening and closing of the Tupperware. And then silence. Or perhaps that's the sound of heartbreak.

I stand slowly, adjusting the blouse Mum made me put on before he arrived, and walk out to the kitchen. She's leaning against the bench, eyes closed and a hand pressed to her forehead.

'I have to go talk to Hunter.'

Her head snaps in my direction, confusion in her eyes. 'What?'

'I can't leave things like this. We need to talk.'

She can barely hide her disgust. 'Oh, I think naked in a creek is a very sensible place to leave things. Did you listen to a word Brother Oliver said?'

The nausea's overwhelming. It's the shame trying to work its way out of my body. 'None of this is Hunter's fault. He doesn't understand this life.'

'This is his fault!'

I shake my head, eyes welling up. 'I did this—me.'

'Because of *him*.'

'No, Mum. Not because of him.' I blink, and a few tears escape the corners of my eyes. 'This isn't even really about him. What you saw is just a symptom of other things.'

'What other things?'

'Doubts I've been having.'

She grips the edge of the bench. 'What *doubts*?'

'Probably the same doubts Bridget had, but I wouldn't know because we don't talk about her.' I swallow. 'I don't know that I believe all the things they teach us.'

She purses her lips so tightly they lose all colour, then says, 'You are being tested. Satan's testing you. Now is the time to turn to Jehovah for strength, not away from him.'

I'm shaking my head the whole time she's speaking. 'I don't even know if I believe in Satan.'

She reacts as though I reached out and slapped her. 'Annie...'

'I wish I didn't have all these doubts,' I whisper. 'I really do. It would be so much easier not to question a thing.'

'Then don't. Have faith.' She looks down at her hands. 'Or perhaps you think I haven't lost enough family members.'

I start to cry, but it's mostly from relief at having finally said some of these things aloud. A tiny piece of *my* truth is now out there in the world.

'Don't go to that boy when you're at your weakest,' she says, looking back at me.

I give her a feeble smile. 'I'm not at my weakest.' In fact, she might be witnessing my first glimpses of strength.

This moment is breaking her. I can see it all over her face and in the way her knees are now pressing into the cupboard for balance.

'I'm sorry,' I say as I head for the back door.

———

Hunter

We messed up. I mean, we *really* messed up. This is what Annie's been afraid of all along, and now it's happened. She's across that creek, her life in ruins, and there's not a damn thing I can do about it. If I go over there now, it'll 100 percent make things worse for her.

'Dad?' I call as I step into the house. I have no idea what I'm going to say to him, but I need to talk to someone.

He doesn't answer.

'Dad!'

I check the kitchen and find him slumped in a chair with a beer can still in hand. He can actually do the advice thing well when he's sober, or even part-way to drunk, but he can't even hear me right now. I'm completely alone in this.

As I'm pacing in the doorway, willing him to wake up and help *me* for once, the house starts to feel too small. I begin to overheat, so I tug my jumper off and draw a few long breaths, trying to slow my heart down.

Is this really my life now?

I stop and lean against the door frame, staring at my dad while my future plays out like a movie in my mind. Him drunk every day. Or worse, drinking himself to death. Annie living across the creek, always in sight but never within reach. She'll have no choice but to shut me out now. Or she might choose to leave the religion. It's a possibility. She might choose to walk away from that life and live another one. She might leave her mum, her community, her friends, her safety net. She might even choose to include me in that new life. But I can't be the reason for her leaving. I'm not enough of a reason, and I shouldn't factor at all.

I head to my bedroom, looking around at the unmade bed and peeling walls in need of paint. It's not a homely room. It serves the purpose of sleep. It hasn't felt homely since Mum was alive, when she used to hang pictures and buy duvet covers in prints of things I loved. Aeroplanes, motorbikes, drums, surfboards. Then after she passed, my interests changed, but my duvet cover didn't.

Dad was too sad to notice. Then he was too drunk.

I took the pictures down when I outgrew them, and there was nothing to replace them with. Blu-Tack marks on the walls are the only evidence of a childhood. The current duvet cover is a striped print, purchased by my aunt who came to visit a few years after Mum died.

I'm doubting my ability to live this miserable existence, putting Dad to bed each day and single-handedly running the farm. I don't want to do it, but what I want doesn't matter. No one else is going to pick his drunk arse up off the floor. Though maybe waking up on the floor in his own spew in an empty house, with no one else to do the work, would be the 'rock bottom' everyone keeps banging on about. Perhaps I really am enabling him.

That thought plays repeatedly in my mind.

I'm pacing again. Where would I go if I left? What would I do? How heavy would the guilt be? And how long would I have to carry it?

Maybe I don't need to have all the answers now. Maybe I just need to get out of everyone's way and figure the rest out later.

One thing I know for sure is that Annie needs time and space to get her life in order. She can't do that with me distracting her. If one day she works up the courage to leave, then we can see what's between us—not now. Right now I need to bow out.

I open my cupboard and set my eyes on the duffel bag up top. The idea is taking shape before I've even figured out if I have the courage to see it through. Pulling the bag down, I sit it on my bed and unzip it. Then I step back, arms folded, staring at it for the longest time.

'Fuck it.'

I start opening drawers and grabbing clothes, shoving them into the bag. Then I pick up the pile of CDs beside my bed and a handful of books that'll never make it back to the library and stuff those in too. On top of that, I drop a towel, my wallet, my Walkman, and a freezer bag filled with toiletries. My heart is racing as I zip it up. I carry it into the kitchen and see Dad hasn't moved. I want him to wake up so I can tell him I'm leaving to his face.

'Dad.'

He doesn't stir.

I take hold of his shoulder and shake him. His head tips back, and the can falls from his hand. Beer fizzes out all over the floor. As tempting as it is to clean it up before leaving, I don't. I do get him into bed, though. One final time. The next time he opens a drink, he'll do it knowing I'm no longer around to help, so that decision will be all on him. For now, I do what I've always done.

After settling him in bed, I go into the kitchen and pull out the shopping list pad I bought Mum at a Mother's Day stall when I was ten and write Dad a note. Dropping the pen onto the bench, I reread it, then snatch up my duffel bag and walk out.

———

Annie

I'm halfway to the creek when I remember I'm wearing a blouse. At least Mum didn't make me put a skirt on. Gumboots are my shoe of choice, because they were the only dry footwear available at the back door. There was no way I was going back through the house in search of sneakers.

The light's fading outside as I navigate the railroad tie bridge and begin the long walk up the hill to the farmhouse. The ute and bike are both there, so I know he's home. The house is quiet as I step up onto the veranda. I glance over at a whining Tess, whose food bowl is filled to the top. That's far too much kibble for a dog her size.

'Don't you eat all that in one go,' I tell the kelpie.

I knock and wait, but no one comes to the door. I knock again, louder this time, and listen for movement inside. All is still.

Stepping off the veranda, I go check the hay shed, the workshop, and shearing shed, but can't find him anywhere. If he was venturing any farther, he'd take the bike, and if he were moving sheep, he'd take Tess. My eyes return to the bowl of dog food, and an unsettling feeling climbs my spine.

Walking back to the house, I knock once before stepping inside. 'Hello? Hunter?'

It's possible he doesn't want to talk to me, but that's too bad, because there are things I need to say. Floorboards creak underfoot as I make my way to the kitchen. I stop when I notice a pool of beer on the floor.

'Kevin?'

Again, no reply.

I spot a notepad on the bench with writing scrawled over it. While I know I shouldn't, I make my way over to it, stepping around the spilled beer in the process. The words 'Shopping List' are printed at the top, and below that is Hunter's barely legible handwriting. I run my eyes over the words.

Dad,

You wanted me to finish school, so I finished. We've never really had a proper conversation about after school. I think we both made a lot of assumptions instead of a real plan. You were right to assume I would follow in your footsteps. Farming's in my blood. I'd stay for that job, but not the other one I find myself doing.

I'm leaving for a while. There are a few reasons why, but you know the main one. It's time for you to get sober, and right now you don't have a reason to.

You're going to need to employ someone to help out. There are plenty of willing apprentices around here. Just remember that their job's to take care of the farm, not you.

See you when you're sober.

H

I snatch up the pad and reread the note, heart racing. Dropping it onto the counter, I steady myself on the benchtop as I try to process what I've just read. Hunter's going. No, he's *gone*. Though he can't have gone very far without a car. Maybe Sammy picked him up or he took the bus somewhere.

My gaze snaps to the clock on the wall. It's 7:47 p.m. I'm trying to remember what time the V/Line passes through town each night. Eight? Eight thirty? Perhaps he's waiting at the bus stop.

I race out of the house and sprint down the hill, flying across the bridge. By the time I climb up the other side, my chest is burning. But I don't slow down. There isn't time.

When I burst into the house, Mum straightens with a look of alarm. 'What happened?'

'Did he come here?'

She shakes her head, confused. 'Who?'

'Hunter.'

Of course he didn't come here. He knew I would talk him out of leaving or suggest something crazy like going with him. And in my current state, that's a very real possibility. Running away would be so much easier than facing my mother's shame each morning. I think he knew that. I think he wants me to do it the hard way, because in his eyes, that's the proper way.

Snatching the car keys off the bench, I glance at the clock on the stove—7:54 p.m. I run for the front door.

'Where are you going now?' Mum calls behind me.

'Town.' My hands are shaking as I slide into the car and try to get the key into the ignition. It takes me multiple attempts, and then I forget which way to turn it. My eyes are welling with tears as I slip the car into reverse and speed off down the driveway.

As I pull out onto the road, I panic, because I'm fairly sure the car clock is a few minutes slow. Or is it fast? I accelerate harder.

The bus stop is outside Robinson's Furniture Shop, so I take the shortest route possible to the small car park behind it. I come to a jolting stop and yank the keys from the ignition before shouldering the door open. I'm really regretting my gumboot decision now because they're so difficult to run in.

As I'm rounding the side of the shop, I hear the bus idling out front. I have no idea if it just arrived or if it's preparing to leave, but at least I haven't missed it. I pass the corner just as the door hisses closed.

No, no, no.

I slow, searching for Hunter as I pass the windows. Maybe he's not even on there. Maybe Sammy gave him a ride to the Turram train station. Perhaps he hitchhiked.

My feet falter when I catch sight of a figure seated next to the window with the hood of their jumper pulled up. His form is so familiar to me now that I'm certain it's him. My suspicions are confirmed when he drags his hood back and slips on a pair of headphones.

The bus starts to pull away.

'Hunter!' I wave my arms just as he tugs the hood of his jumper up again. I run towards the door. 'Wait! Stop the bus!'

But the driver is looking the other way. He's focused on what's coming in his other mirror.

'Stop the bus!' It speeds up before I reach the door, and I slap the side of it in frustration. 'Stop!'

The bus keeps going.

Hunter flashes into view once more, head resting on the seat and eyes closed. He doesn't see me.

How do you leave your home without a single glance back?

I'm running alongside the bus. 'Hunter!'

I'm here. Look at me. Look *at me.*

Don't leave.

Don't leave me.

21

ANNIE

'When you're done serving Gary, come to the window,' Maggie calls to me from the other side of the shop.

I slide Gary's new dress shoes into a bag and hand them to him with a smile. 'Enjoy the wedding.'

'I'd want to enjoy it. Cost me enough,' he adds with a wink before heading for the door. 'See ya, Maggie.'

'Bye-bye,' she calls back.

I make my way over to the shop window, where Maggie's bent over sweeping a pile of dust and fluff into a dustpan.

'Amazing how dirty it gets in just a month,' she says.

I nod. 'Want me to run it to the bin?'

She straightens, pressing a hand to her chest as she catches her breath. 'No need. I can do it.' She looks around at the freshly cleaned space. 'Now, these past six months, you've really proven yourself, and the customers clearly adore you.' She makes a face. 'I mean, Jenny White is a nice lady and all, but she's always brought her kids in here to be fitted and sized for school shoes, then driven to Turram where they're a bit cheaper. She doesn't know I know, but I do.' She tuts before continuing. 'I really believe the only reason she bought those two pairs of shoes the other day is because you impressed her with how good you were with her kids.' She reaches out and pats my arm. 'My point being I think you've earned the opportunity.'

I have zero idea what she's talking about right now. 'Which opportunity is that?'

Maggie makes a large sweeping gesture with her arm. 'You are in charge of the display window this month.' She's beaming at me now.

Unfortunately my excitement doesn't come anywhere close to matching hers. 'Wow. Thank you.' I find a smile. 'That's... I appreciate everything you just said.' And I do. Everyone wants to feel valued.

'I'll leave you to it.' She pats me again, then waddles off towards the counter.

I look down at the display risers stacked to one side and try to muster up some enthusiasm for the task. There are still two more hours until we close, and then it's home to prepare for field service tomorrow. I'm starting the morning with four return visits, which Mum casually mentioned to the sisters in the congregation after the meeting on Sunday. I think it's safe to say she's proud of where I'm at spiritually right now.

After arranging the risers, I head out back and select some netball and footy boots to display. It's that time of year, and Adidas released new styles that arrived earlier in the week. I also grab a box of Blundstones before returning to the shop window.

'Do we still have that box of toys and balls out back that your grandkids play with when they come in on school holidays?' I ask Maggie as I pass the counter.

She looks up, thinking. 'I think they're in the cupboard under the fax machine.'

I dump the boxes by the window and return to the back, sifting through the random assortment of items. As I'm heading back to the window, the doorbell sounds, deafening all in a twenty-metre radius. I did once politely suggest to Maggie that we could turn it down and still hear it from the back, but her hearing isn't what it used to be, so it remains at the highest possible volume. I peer around the pile of balls I'm carrying and almost drop them when I see Kevin Reed standing awkwardly inside the door.

All the heartache I've spent the past few months burying bubbles to the surface in one glance. That's all it takes. One reminder of him to bring it all up again.

'Annie,' Kevin says by way of greeting.

'Hi.' I've only seen him twice since Hunter left. He tends to stay away from town, and town tends to stay away from him. 'Let me put these down, and then I'll be right with you.'

'No, no,' Maggie says, walking around from behind the counter. 'You keep going with your display.' She gives Kevin the same welcoming smile she gives all her customers, ignoring the odour of drink taking over the air. 'You need some dress shoes for the wedding too?'

Kevin gives her a blank stare. 'Wedding?'

Maggie's face falls, and her cheeks turn red. Every farmer in the district is going to Gary's daughter's wedding. Every farmer except Kevin Reed. She waves a dismissive hand. 'Never mind. My old brain getting confused. Time for some new work boots?'

'Size eleven. Wide fit. Thanks.'

Maggie nods. 'I'll have to check. I've got a feeling we sold our last pair of elevens yesterday.' She disappears out back, and Kevin's eyes drift in my direction.

The silence is far from comfortable, but I'm struggling with what to say. 'How's the new farmhand working out?'

He shoves his hands into his pockets and takes a few steps in my direction. 'Well, he shows up, so that's a big improvement on the last one.'

His last farmhand was Greg Dawson, who was a year above me at school. I heard his mother tell Maggie that he wasn't learning much and that Kevin was usually still in bed when he arrived in the mornings. 'That's positive.'

Maggie reappears. 'I was right. Sold them yesterday. We do have an order arriving this afternoon. Courier said he'd get here before closing. You want to pop back then?'

We all know he'll be in no condition to drive later.

'I could drop them over to you after work,' I offer.

Maggie's face fills with pride. 'Isn't she great? If she keeps this up, she's going to make employee of the month fifth month running.' She laughs at her own joke as she heads back to the counter. 'Happy to fix it up now?'

Kevin glances at me as he follows after her. 'Sure you don't mind?'

'It's fine, really.' Better that than him driving around drunk.

'You heard from that boy of yours?' Maggie asks as she presses buttons on the till.

I still, listening for his response.

There's a bit of a pause before Kevin replies. 'He's busy seeing a bit more of the world.'

'I'm sure he'll be back when he runs out of money. That's how these things usually play out.'

Kevin knows as well as I do that Hunter would sleep on the street before ever returning for financial reasons.

'How long's it been?' Maggie asks.

I look in their direction and watch Kevin count out cash.

'Six months.'

I guess neither of us has heard from him. It's tragic that I'm still starving for any crumb of information about him. At some point I'm going to need to stop caring.

Kevin thanks Maggie and gives me a small wave.

'Dear me,' Maggie says after he's left. 'He's not in a good way.' She smells the air. 'Might need to get the spray.'

An hour later, I call her over to the window to have a look at the display. She insists on viewing it from the street, even going so far as to shield her eyes so she doesn't see it prior. I watch through the glass as her expression melts into motherly pride once more. She's grinning ear to ear, rocking on her heels as she takes it all in.

'You like it?' I ask when she comes back in.

She moves over to look from another angle. 'I love it.

It's so clever. The balls, the little netball skirt made out of tissue paper.'

Clapping a hand over her mouth, she turns to me, wide-eyed. 'I almost forgot.' She rushes off in the direction of the counter.

I follow her. 'Forgot what?'

Maggie opens the till and pulls out a five-dollar note, placing it gracefully in the middle of the counter. 'This is yours.'

I pick it up and look at her in question.

She leans her elbows on the counter. 'Keely Thompson bought one of your bracelets while you were out at lunch.'

My eyes go to the display of leather jewellery on the counter—Maggie's idea. She wanted to prove to me that people would buy them.

'I didn't say a word about them,' Maggie says, raising her hands. 'She saw them there when she was paying and added it herself.'

I place the note back down on the counter. 'This is your shop. I'm supposed to get a cut, not the whole amount.'

'Pfft.' She waves the notion away. 'The shoes are my bread and butter. The jewellery is your side hustle. Anyway, they're grossly underpriced given the work that goes into them.'

I put my hand over hers. 'Thank you.'

'What for?'

My throat thickens. 'For everything.'

She tilts her head. 'Go clean up those boxes before you make me cry.'

I smile as I slip the money into my pocket.

Maggie leaves around five, and I stay behind to clean, do the books, and wait for the delivery. The driver helps me carry everything inside, and I put it all away so Maggie won't have to do it in the morning. After locking up, I head to the Reeds' farm.

It's strange going up the driveway and seeing the house. I hate that Hunter's not a part of this scene anymore. I hate that I miss him.

'Door's open,' Kevin calls from inside when I knock.

I enter, trying not to feel things, and make my way through the kitchen. 'Here they are,' I say, handing him the shoes. 'Size eleven. Wide fit.'

He sets his beer down and opens the box. 'That's them.'

My gaze drifts to the dirty dishes covering the bench. The floor's sticky beneath my feet, but I don't look down. I don't want to embarrass him. He has a lot to manage with Hunter gone.

'Had a cleaner for a while there,' he says, reading my mind, 'but she stopped coming.'

I don't need to ask why. Looking around, I say, 'Why don't I give you a hand with the dishes before I go? At least then you'll have something to cook with.' Though I suspect most of his meals are liquid nowadays judging by the weight loss.

'You don't have to do that,' he says, turning red.

'I know.' I walk over to the drawers and find a clean tea towel, holding it out to him. 'You can dry.'

He looks thoroughly uncomfortable as he takes it. I turn to the sink and start removing all the dirty dishes from it so I can fill it with water. He rises slowly and joins me. I wash, and he dries and puts away. Neither of us speaks.

Once all the dishes are clean, I walk over to the food cupboard and have a look at his dinner options. It's slim pickings, but I find a tin of baked beans. I heat them on the stovetop.

'I can do that,' he tells me, still standing by the sink.

I glance in his direction. 'But will you?'

His mouth turns up, and he drops his gaze. 'Probably not.'

I put the hot beans into a clean bowl and place it on the table with a fork. 'If you clean your plate, you get your beer back,' I say with a smirk, then take the can with me to the sink. I fill the basin with fresh water and wash the saucepan.

'My wife used to hate these beans,' Kevin says quietly.

I turn and lean against the sink. 'All tinned beans or just this brand?'

'All. She used to make her own.' He scrapes the sauce at the bottom of the bowl. 'Good quality butter beans and molasses were her secret ingredients.'

The grief is still present, despite all the time that's passed. 'I'll have to remember that.'

He stands up and takes his empty bowl to the sink, washing it himself. 'Have you heard from him? Since he left?' He doesn't look at me.

'No, I haven't.' I don't know if that'll make him feel better or worse.

He's silent a moment. 'Didn't see it coming. I know that's probably surprising for you to hear, but I thought we'd at least have a conversation before we got to that point. "Shape up or I'm outta here" kinda thing.'

Guilt twists in my stomach. It's clear he doesn't know everything that happened that day. 'I saw him before he left.'

Kevin stills and looks at me, waiting for more.

'We were in the creek.' I swallow. 'Mum found us, and there was a bit of a scene.' I pause, finding Kevin as unreadable as his son. 'I think he felt responsible for me getting into trouble.' This is the first time I've said this aloud to anyone other than Tamsin. 'I worry *I'm* the reason he left.'

He places the bowl in the dish rack. 'I don't remember anything about that afternoon. I woke up in my bed the next morning, where he put me.' He wipes his hands on the tea towel. 'There's no doubt in my mind that if I'd been sober that day, he wouldn't have left.'

We stand there with our mutual pain for a moment.

'I'm going to come back tomorrow afternoon and clean the floors,' I say. 'But there's a catch.'

He raises an eyebrow.

'The bathroom needs to be clean, and you need to be sober.'

His eyes move between mine. 'I can see why Hunter fell for you the way he did. You're a good egg, with a good heart.'

The hollowness in my chest grows a little bigger. 'Clean bathroom and sober.'

He nods slowly. 'Clean bathroom and sober.'

22

HUNTER

I point the gun at his head and try hard not to look him in the eye. It's the worst part of this job. He knows what's about to happen.

'Sorry, mate.'

I pull the trigger, and the rifle kicks back into my shoulder. The young steer emits a short, sharp bellow and falls still.

'Bloody ticks,' Pete says behind me.

I look over my shoulder, not realising I had an audience. Despite treatment, some of the younger steers developed tick fever. Thankfully, only one needed to be euthanised.

Pete's large frame appears next to me. He brushes a finger down his sunburned nose as he looks down at the corpse. 'Let's get him buried.'

I place the rifle in the ute and grab some shovels from the back. We dig in silence for thirty minutes, then drag the steer into the grave. I lift my hat and wipe my brow before starting the tedious task of filling it. Despite the arrival of cooler temperatures, I still sweat a lot of the time. It's going to take me longer than six months to adjust to the climate.

Six months.

Aside from a couple phone calls to Sammy, I haven't seen or spoken to anyone from home since I left.

Pete had been understandably suspicious of a loner with nothing but a duffel bag showing up at his door asking for work. 'What brings you north?' he'd asked.

'The weather,' I lied.

My aunt in Perth has always told me I'm welcome there, but I knew if Annie ever worked up the courage to leave the organisation, she'd come looking for her sister in Brisbane. So that's where I went. I made enquiries at farms closest to the city, then worked my way west, eventually coming across an asparagus farmer in Ripley who told me about a cattle farm five minutes down the road.

'Their youngest has just left home for the big smoke.'

It amused me hearing Brisbane described as 'the big smoke'.

The Leroys' farm had immediate appeal. I remember walking down the long driveway, past lush paddocks with mountain backdrops, and thinking, *This'll do.*

'Can't pay you much,' Pete told me, 'but we have a separate bungalow you can use, and my wife's the best cook this side of Ipswich.'

I didn't even ask what the salary was. A roof over my head and guaranteed food after two weeks of sleeping in bus shelters and eating food from packets was all I needed. And 'not much' ended up being not too bad.

'Hungry?' Pete asks as we toss the shovels into the back of the ute.

'I could eat.'

'Good. Sue made pies.'

Sue's one of the hardest-working women I know. She raised four kids while being a full-time farmhand to her husband, as well as being the beating heart of the local community. If someone's sick, she's the one dropping soup at their door.

All their children have left home now, but they return home regularly to be doted on and fed. They were wary of me at first, but once they realised I'm safe company and here to work, they accepted me as part of the furniture.

'Forgot to tell you. Bridget Wilson called for you earlier,' Pete says on the drive to the house.

I look at him. 'She did?' I've been trying to track her down since arriving here, calling various galleries and institutions with no success. Then last week someone suggested I call the Queensland Arts Society. The woman I spoke to on the phone confirmed that not only does she know her, but Bridget works there. So I left my details with her and waited.

'This the girl you've been trying to find?'

Sue and Pete always leave the room to give me privacy on the phone, but it doesn't stop them listening. 'Yeah.'

'She a friend of yours?'

'Old neighbour. She lives in Brisbane now.'

Pete does me the favour of not asking any more questions.

When I enter the house, Sue meets me at the door, handing me a piece of paper with Bridget's contact details.

'Friend of yours?' she asks.

Pete smiles to himself. 'Old neighbour.'

'Oh.' Sue looks me over. 'Well, lunch isn't quite ready, so kitchen's all yours. We'll make ourselves busy in the living room.'

I doubt that. 'Thanks.'

I head to the phone hanging on the kitchen wall, dialling the number on the page. It's a mobile number, and Bridget answers on the fourth ring.

'Bridget speaking.'

She sounds so much like Annie that it throws me for a second. 'Hey. It's Hunter.'

There's a long pause. 'Hi.'

'Hi.'

She clears her throat. 'You left a message for me to call you?'

I tell her that I've moved to Brisbane, that I'd heard she was living up here now, and that it would be great to see a familiar face.

She's quiet on the other end. 'Who told you I was in Brisbane?'

'Annie. I mean, she didn't know for sure.'

More silence.

'You had a conversation with my sister about me?' She's understandably sceptical.

'We were hanging out a little before I left.'

'*You* were hanging out with Annie?'

It's not my place to tell that story. 'A little.' My hand goes briefly to the leather band around my wrist.

'I forgot you were in the same year at school.' She pauses. 'Did she graduate?'

It's safe to say she hasn't heard from her sister. I push down the disappointment. 'Yeah.'

'Is she still living at home?'

'Think so.' I only know what Sammy's told me, and he only knows what Tamsin's told him. 'Last I heard, she's working at Maggie's.'

Bridget exhales into the phone. 'Right.' Another pause. 'What about you? Where are you living?'

'Ripley. Working as a farmhand.'

'I assumed you'd stay in Chirnside and work at your own farm.'

I close my eyes briefly. 'That was the plan, but plans change.' I lean on the wall. 'Listen, if you ever want to meet up, it'd be great to see a familiar face.'

We're not friends, so this is awkward for both of us. But the guarded woman on the other end of the line is my only remaining tie to Annie since I've severed all the others.

'I'm sorry to be blunt,' she says, 'and I might be missing the mark here, but I have zero interest in dating right now.'

I smile into the phone. 'That's not what this is.'

'And if it's a friend you're looking for, I'm not very good at that either.'

'We have that in common. I didn't mean to come across like that. I don't know anyone up here and thought I'd reach out.'

She sighs. 'I know what it's like to be alone in a new city. What are you doing this weekend?'

'Actually, I thought I might head into the city tomorrow. Thinking about buying a mobile phone. I'd appreciate some tech-savvy company if you have the time.'

'Fine. City hall. Two o'clock. Wear comfortable walking shoes. I'll give you a walking tour while we shop.'

'So no high heels?'

'No high heels or strappy sandals.'

It sounds like something Annie would say.

When I hang up the phone, Pete walks in. 'Take the ute tomorrow. The bus'll take forever.'

So much for privacy. 'Thanks.'

'I think getting a mobile phone is a very sensible idea,' Sue says, appearing behind him. 'Every man and his dog has one nowadays.'

They may as well have stayed in the room since they heard every detail of that conversation.

'I'm sure your dad would love to be able to call you,' Sue adds, taking the pies out of the oven.

She has a sixth sense when it comes to family relationships. Plus she's a fixer by nature. She's managed to squeeze some information out of me over time, though they know only that my mum passed, I'm an only child, and that I'm giving Dad some space to work on himself.

Pete gestures for me to sit. 'Hunter can decide who he wants to speak to on the telephone.'

Sue puts a plate in front of me. 'All right, all right. I won't say another word about it.' She collects the other plates from the counter and hands one to her husband before taking a seat. 'Family's important is all I'm saying.'

'That was six more words,' I tell her. 'Eight if you count the contractions.'

'And I've made my point now.'

Pete and I smile down at our plates, then dig into our lunch.

23

ANNIE

'They're lemon biscuits,' Mum says, making a pattern with them on the plate. 'Your favourite.'

Yes, they're my favourite, but they're not really for me. Brother Oliver's on his way here. The biscuits are for him.

There's an assembly in November, just six weeks away, and this is the meeting that he'll confirm if I'm to be baptised or not. There's no reason for any further delays. I've done the work, everything they asked of me. I've proven myself in Jehovah's eyes over and over again and not set one foot wrong.

Everything's moving in the right direction.

Happiness is within reach.

'That sounds like his car,' Mum says when headlights flash through the lounge room window.

My stomach tightens. Nerves. Totally normal. This is a big moment, and I've worked hard to get here. I press a hand to my stomach and take a few slow breaths.

'Come on in,' she tells Brother Oliver when she opens

the front door. 'No need to take your shoes off. Leave them on.'

She hates people wearing shoes in the house.

'Annie, Brother Oliver's here,' she calls casually as she brings him through. Her voice is all sing-songy. She's so relieved, excited, and proud that we got here. And I'm happy for her. She's earned this moment.

Finding a smile, I walk into the lounge room carrying the tray of tea and biscuits. 'Hi.'

Brother Oliver seats himself in the largest chair, like a king settling on his throne, and looks in my direction. 'Evening, Annie. Ah, these smell good. Which one of you has been baking?'

I place the tray directly in front of him. 'Mum. I prefer to do the eating.'

He chuckles. 'Well, it's a tough job, but someone has to do it.' He picks up a biscuit while Mum pours his tea, his eyes on me. 'Great to work with you out in the field on Sunday. Do you ever rest these days?'

If Mum puffs up any bigger, she's going to topple off her chair.

Brother Oliver takes a bite of the biscuit and pauses midchew. His expression is far from complimentary.

Mum's face falls. 'They're made with olive oil instead of butter. The flavour's not for everyone.'

He sets it down on the plate. 'A little salty for my palate.' He washes it down with scalding-hot tea.

Mum picks up a biscuit and takes the world's most polite bite. She stops chewing and looks accusingly at the biscuit. 'Annie, when I told you to get the sugar out of the cupboard, did you check the label?'

'I think so.'

'No, you must've gotten the salt.'

For some reason, this sets me off laughing. 'Really?' When I see Mum's horrified expression, I fall silent. 'Sorry about that.'

Brother Oliver gives us a reassuring smile. 'It makes the tea taste extra good. Don't be offended if I don't finish it, though.'

Mum's out of her seat and whisking the plate away a moment later. We sit in silence while she flitters about the kitchen, returning with a few Scotch Finger biscuits on a fresh plate.

'Apologies, Brother Oliver,' she says, taking a seat.

We spend the next forty minutes discussing my spiritual growth and my goals for the year ahead. When he brings up the upcoming assembly, Mum's clasped hands turn white.

'I think baptism is a wonderful idea for you, Annie. The congregation is very much looking forward to seeing you commit to this wonderful way of life and serving Jehovah.'

There they are. The words my mother has waited nineteen years to hear. And I'm so focused on her reaction, her joy, that I barely register my own feelings. My face is frozen in one expression, and my lips are a little numb, but I don't think either of them notice. It's probably relief surfacing.

A few more minutes pass, and then Brother Oliver stands, says a few kind words, makes a final joke about the biscuits, and heads for the front door.

'See you at the meeting,' he says as he steps

through it.

Mum closes the door and leans her forehead on it briefly before turning to face me. 'Biscuits aside, I'd call that a raging success.' She waits for me to agree.

'Yeah.'

She studies me, her smile wavering slightly. 'I thought you'd be more pleased.'

'I am pleased.' I'm just not experienced in the art of happiness. I smile—for her.

'We're going to have single brothers lining up at the door to court you when word gets out.'

There's that familiar feeling in my stomach, like I'm missing home even though I'm standing in it.

'That was a joke,' Mum says, reading my face.

'I know.'

My reaction must make her nervous, because she adds, 'You don't even have to get married if you don't want to. Plenty of sisters remain happily single.'

It's true. There are two sisters in our congregation who appear happy with that choice. I don't think I would be, though. Imagine never experiencing falling asleep beside someone you love and waking up with them every day. Imagine depending on females for companionship for the rest of your life and *never* experiencing sexual pleasure in any form.

Mum heads for the kitchen, squeezing my arm as she passes me. 'I think this calls for a fresh batch of biscuits—made with sugar.'

Yes, that's what this calls for. Biscuits.

I catch my reflection in the arched window of the front door. The woman staring back at me is the same sad-looking girl from a year earlier. The image crushes me. I'm supposed to look different. I did everything they asked, handed my life over to them and trusted them to fix it.

Turning away from my reflection, I follow Mum into the kitchen.

24

HUNTER

My phone's ringing somewhere near my head, but I'm struggling to locate it. It feels a lot like my eyelids were glued together overnight. As I'm feeling around for it, my hand touches a warm body, and my eyes spring open.

Shit.

I forgot that I didn't come home alone last night. The brunette who beat me at pool is naked beside me, clothes discarded all over the bungalow. I snatch my mobile off the floor, trying to answer it before it wakes her. I'm not ready for that yet. I'd like to remember how we ended up here first.

'Yeah?'

'Really? That's how you answer your phone?' Bridget's voice sounds in my ear.

I look back at the sleeping woman, covered to the waist with a sheet. 'Sorry. Hi.'

'Why are you whispering? And why does your voice sound weird?'

I press my eyes shut. 'I was asleep.'

'But I thought farmers rose with the sun.'

I glance at the clock. It's nearing ten. *Ten*. I haven't slept past 6:00 a.m. since arriving in Queensland. Kookaburras make the best alarm clocks—when not intoxicated. I don't usually drink more than a beer or two at most. And I definitely don't drink scotch. This is what happens when the Leroy boys come home for the weekend and insist I come to the pub for one drink.

'You still there?' Bridget asks.

I stare at the naked brunette beside me. 'Yeah, I'm here.'

'Next weekend is my birthday, and some people at work have talked me into celebrating it.'

'You mean your friends?' She has a bad habit of referring to people in her life as colleagues or artists or something equally as vague.

'Real friends don't make friends celebrate their birthdays.'

'Fairly sure that's not true, but go on.'

She draws a breath. 'Would you like to come to a barbeque at my apartment?'

My mouth turns up. 'That was hard for you, wasn't it?'

'Yes.'

My lips twitch. 'You left the religion four years ago and haven't celebrated a birthday yet?'

'Firstly, not your business. And secondly, haven't you ever heard the expression "old habits die hard"?'

I still when the woman next to me stirs and turns her head to look at me.

'Morning,' she says sleepily.

What's her name? Kylie? Kylie seems right. 'Morning.'

'Do you have company?' Bridget inhales sharply. 'Oh my goodness. That's why you're still in bed. Well, this is awkward. Sorry.'

'It's fine.' I clear my throat and look away from my bed companion. 'I'll be there. At your birthday.'

'Will you be bringing someone?'

My mouth flattens into a line. 'No. Just me.'

'Okay. Well, Sunday the fourteenth. Midday onwards. You remember how to get here?'

'Yeah, I remember.'

'And I've told everyone no gifts.'

I rub my forehead. 'It's a birthday. They'll bring one anyway.'

'But I told them not to.'

'Well, no one wants to be the arsehole who shows up empty-handed.' I look back at Kylie and find her watching me. 'I gotta go.'

'Of course. Enjoy your... lie-in.' She hangs up before I can respond.

I put the phone down and look around for my boxers. Thankfully they're within reach. I really don't want to have this conversation naked.

'Sorry about that,' I say as I pull my boxers up beneath the sheet. 'If you get dressed, I'll give you a lift wherever you need to go.'

The cute smile on her face vanishes, replaced with embarrassment. 'Wow.' She takes the sheet with her as she climbs off the bed. 'I see.'

This isn't going to go well. 'Listen, Kylie—'

'It's Carly.'

So close. I go to fetch a clean T-shirt and jeans from the cupboard. As I'm dressing, I notice my knuckles are red and swollen. I turn to Carly. 'What the hell happened last night?'

'You don't remember getting into a fight?' She tugs her singlet down. 'Troy Baroud knocked Heath's drink out of his hand, so you knocked out one of his teeth.'

Heath is Pete and Sue's youngest son, and Troy Baroud is a local twat. And now that she mentions it, I do recall Troy falling backwards over a barstool. 'Ah.'

'The bartender threw you out. I babysat you while Heath was convincing the manager not to call the cops.'

It seems she babysat me a little too well. 'Do you live locally?'

She pulls her jeans up with angry jerks. 'Are you seriously asking me that? I'm at that pub every Friday night, and we've had multiple conversations about where I'm from.'

'Well, I'm not great with faces.'

'Or names,' she mutters.

I grab my keys off the table by the door and wait for her to put on her shoes. She casts a death stare in my direction when I start jiggling the keys.

'Heath told me you were a nice guy,' she says as she heads for the door. 'Guess he lied.'

Heath would have thought he was doing me a favour saying that. I sigh. 'I'm not trying to be a dick here. I just have work today.'

She yanks the door open. 'Go work, then. Heath can give me a ride home.' Looking over her shoulder, she adds, 'He knows where I live because he pays attention when I talk.'

The door slams shut.

I have no idea what I'm supposed to do next. Maybe follow her out, apologise, and insist on driving her home. But I don't have it in me. It's easier to let her hate me. Then if I'm ever allowed back into the pub, she won't waste her time.

My gaze falls to the leather band on my wrist, and guilt hits. It shouldn't, but it does. I suspect last night's drunken antics were less to do with Troy being a dick and more to do with the news I got about Annie yesterday. Sammy ran into Tamsin on the weekend. She told him Annie got baptised. That snippet of information landed like a punch to the stomach.

Moving to Brisbane was a fool's mission, and now it's time to let go.

I guess Carly was my first attempt at doing that, and Troy... Who am I kidding? I probably would have punched him in the face anyway.

When I step out of the bungalow, I come face to face with Pete. He's got that disappointed father look going on. I'm about to cop a speech of some kind. I'm really regretting the booze right now. The blinding sun has my head spinning and stomach turning.

'Carly left in a hurry,' he says, glancing in the direction of the car now pulling away from the house. 'Why's Heath driving her home?'

I nod. 'I offered to drive her.'

'Offered a little too quickly, perhaps.' He studies me a

moment. 'First girl you've shown any interest in, and you chase her out the door instead of offering her breakfast?'

I rub my dry eyes. 'I'm no gentleman.'

'Bullshit. I've seen the way you behave around my wife and daughter. You might not be a romantic kind of fella, but you *are* a gentleman. I suggest you remember that next time you bring a lady friend home.' He goes to leave, then stops. 'I'm starting to wonder if maybe you left that heart of yours back in Chirnside.'

I swallow and say nothing.

'That's what I thought.' He rests his hands on his hips. 'She end it?'

Last night's booze swirls in my stomach. 'You can't end something that never really began.'

He stares at me. 'You could always give her a call on that fancy phone of yours.'

I really don't want to talk about Annie with him—or anyone, for that matter. 'We starting with fences this morning?' I ask, changing the subject.

Pete shakes his head. 'You're starting with a trip into town.'

'What for?'

'To apologise to Troy and thank him for not going to the cops this morning and pressing charges.' He looks around. 'Listen, I don't know what kind of bad behaviour you got away with back home, but if I hear any more reports of you starting fights and breaking teeth, I'll let you go.' His stern eyes meet mine. 'Understand?'

I nod and step past him, heading for the ute.

25

ANNIE

'So, it's $120 a week, plus bills,' Cheryl says. 'The previous tenant left the bed and the couch behind. You're welcome to those, or I can have them removed.' She runs a hand over the top of the threadbare couch and waits for my response.

Cheryl Patel is the rental property manager for Chirnside's only real estate agency and has been since I was born.

'I think we could get a second-hand one that's a bit cleaner than that,' Mum says, stepping up next to me.

I'd wanted to come by myself, wanted the experience of getting my first rental to be mine alone. But Mum seemed so excited to be involved that I hadn't had the heart to tell her no.

I walk through to the kitchen. It's dark, smells of grease, and the stovetop is covered in rust patches. 'The oven works?'

Cheryl walks over to it and turns a few knobs. 'Just needs a fresh gas bottle.'

This place needs a fresh everything.

Mum taps the wall, and a few paint flakes flutter down onto the countertop. She looks in my direction and makes a face.

'I can ask the owner about giving it a coat of paint before you move in,' Cheryl says. 'He's wanting a two-year lease.'

I look at her. 'Two years? That's a big commitment.'

Mum gives me a puzzled look. 'What's the difference between one year and two?'

'One year,' I reply.

Mum tuts.

I'm hesitant to commit to one year of living this way, let alone two. I remember having a conversation with Bridget when I was fourteen and she was seventeen. We planned to move out together once I finished school. I'm gutted that she's not here hating this place with me. Though we might have made a home of it with two of us.

'You don't have a lot of options in Chirnside,' Mum whispers. 'You can't afford anything fancy while you're saving for a car.'

I could if I worked five days instead of four, but I don't say that. I look up at the ceiling, which is blistered from water damage. 'Then maybe I look outside of Chirnside.'

'Don't be silly,' Mum says. 'You can just about walk to work from here.'

Cheryl looks between us. 'I could speak to the owner about a shorter lease.'

I shake my head. 'I'm so sorry to waste your time.' I can't believe my options are this or living with my mother forever.

Mum's mouth drops open. 'At least let Cheryl ask the question.'

I'm already heading for the door.

'We'll be in touch,' I hear Mum say behind me.

I practically fly down the chipped concrete steps and go to wait by the car.

'Annie,' Mum says, walking over to me. 'That was a bit rude.'

It was. I nod in agreement, then turn in a circle, breathing in as much fresh air as I can manage.

Mum's eyes move over me. 'You know, it's normal to feel a bit apprehensive about leaving home for the first time.'

'I know.'

'I thought this is what you wanted?'

I slow my breathing. 'It is.' Partly.

She looks back at the unit, where Cheryl's standing on the steps pretending she's not listening to us. There's no such thing as privacy in this town. Lowering her voice, Mum says, 'They always seem worse when they're empty and smell like the previous owners. You'd be surprised what some fresh curtains will do for the place.'

If only curtains were the fix.

'I actually didn't think it was *that* bad,' she continues.

I shake my head. 'It's not the unit. I know I could clean it up.'

'Then what is it?'

I don't know how to answer because I'm not actually sure. 'What if something goes wrong? What if I need to leave, but because of a lease I'm stuck in this town with people who hate me?'

She's visibly confused. 'Leave? What are you talking about? What people?'

I lick my lips, embarrassed to taste tears. 'I'm baptised now. That changes things. If I step away from the religion, and I'm stuck here in this town, they'll pass the shop window every day, intentionally never looking inside. They'll cross the street to avoid me, make me feel small, because that's what will ultimately drive me back to Jehovah. Not my remorse or change of heart, but the shame and loneliness I wake up with every morning and carry around with me all day. The guilt I drown in going to sleep at night.'

One look at Mum's face tells me she understands perfectly now. Her hand goes to her forehead. 'Oh, Annie.' She takes a moment to collect herself, then lowers her hand. 'You've barely been baptised a week.'

I don't blame her for being devastated by the words spilling out of me. I'm all she has left. The day I climbed down into that pool was one of the happiest of her life. 'What if I made a mistake?' The question comes out as a shame-filled whisper.

Mum releases a shaky breath. 'It's a little late for doubts.'

'Haven't you been listening? I've been having doubts for years.'

The colour drains from her face. Her only movements are the rapid rise and fall of her chest. 'This is because of your sister.' She nods emphatically. 'You watched her get baptised, then watched her life unravel.' There's a pause. 'I should've listened to the elders, told her not to go to university. She had a wonderful job opportunity at the chemist, but it was never enough for her. She always wanted more.'

I shake my head. 'Don't do that. Don't talk about her like she became an addict and ran off with her pimp, like she threw her future away.' I wipe my face. 'Bridget's only sin was her love of art and her curiosity to learn everything she could about it. She didn't want to work at the chemist. She wanted a job that fed her soul. She wanted to be happy in *this* life instead of waiting for the next one.'

Mum throws her hands up. 'She could've worked in a gallery. That wasn't the issue. You think *that* was the issue? You think Jehovah's Witnesses aren't allowed to appreciate art?'

'Well, you need a degree for those kinds of jobs nowadays, so what would you have her do?'

'I can tell you what she was *not* supposed to do. She was not supposed to abandon Jehovah for some job, to throw away her chance at everlasting life for a few pretty paintings and some interesting historical facts.'

I drop my gaze, and we both fall silent.

'You're being tested,' she says, lowering her voice. 'You've been tested before, and you came through it. You can do it again.'

She might be right. This might be a test. But I'm so tired of being tested. 'I want to go home.'

Mum fishes around her handbag for the car keys as she heads for the driver side. She fumbles with the lock, then gets in and starts the car. I stand there a moment, collecting myself, then climb in.

'We're going to pray before we go anywhere,' she says, reaching for me. Her hand is clammy and suffocating.

I hesitate, then close my eyes and bow my head.

'Dear Jehovah,' Mum says over the hum of the engine. 'We come to you in prayer now to ask for your strength.'

Great. I could do with some strength.

26

ANNIE

I kneel in front of the toilet, waiting to vomit, but nothing comes up. Leaning my back against the wall, I glance up at the small window above me. It's light outside, morning. And suddenly I'm doubting my ability to see this through.

A knock on the door makes me jump.

'Annie, are you okay? You've been in there for ages.'

No. No, I'm definitely not okay. I'm sad and scared and barely holding it together.

Standing, I take a few deep breaths and open the door. 'Morning.'

She takes in my clammy face. 'Are you sick?'

I shake my head and step past her. 'Just a bit tired.'

She follows me to my room. 'Maybe you should call in sick.'

'Because I'm tired?' I force a smile. 'All good. No need to worry.' I pull some clean clothes from the drawer and head to the bathroom for a shower.

When I enter the kitchen twenty minutes later, I feel

Mum watching me, smell her fear. It's almost like she knows.

'I'll see you later,' I say—like I always do.

'No breakfast?'

I'd only throw it up. 'I'm running late.' I back up and grab a banana from the fruit bowl to appease her. 'I'll eat this on the way.'

Her eyes follow me all the way to the door. 'Have a good day.'

Maggie's out back when I arrive at work, talking to herself while she sorts old stock.

'Morning,' I call to her.

She peers around a pile of shoeboxes. 'Morning, love.' Then, registering my expression, she asks, 'You all right?'

I shake my head, close to tears before I've even started speaking.

'Oooh, sweetheart.' She navigates the mess and makes her way over to me, taking my hand. 'What's the matter?'

There's no point beating around the bush. 'I'm so sorry to do this to you, but I'm leaving town—today.'

Her eyes widen as she processes this sudden announcement, but she keeps hold of my hand. 'For how long?'

'I don't know.'

Maggie lets out an emotional breath. 'Are you leaving town or leaving that church of yours?'

I scrape my teeth over my lip. 'Both.'

She nods slowly, eyes sympathetic.

'I'm really sorry I didn't tell you sooner. I've known I was leaving for a few days but couldn't risk certain people finding out. I know we're a few weeks from Christmas, your busiest time—'

'Don't you worry about that. I've managed things solo before. I can do it again.' She rubs the back of my hand. 'This has been brewing for some time, hasn't it?'

Years.

I nod.

'Does your mum know?'

'I'll tell her when she gets home from work, once I'm packed and ready to leave.'

Maggie's face creases with worry. 'Where will you go?'

'Brisbane.'

'To your sister?'

I nod.

'She know you're coming?'

'I don't even know if she's still there.'

Maggie thinks a moment. 'What about your dad? You could go to Melbourne.'

I could. I'm sure Dad would open his door to me if I needed him to.

'I need to find my sister.'

She pulls me into a hug. 'Course you do. I bet she'll welcome you with open arms. And I'll be cheering you both on. You girls deserve a life of your choosing.'

A life of my choosing.

I'm crying now, body shaking with the effort of trying to cry quietly. She holds me until I stop, holds me in the way she knows my own mother won't.

Stepping back, I wipe my face with the sleeve of my jumper. 'Again, I'm sorry I couldn't give you more notice.'

She waves the apology away. 'I know you don't have

that kind of luxury. I won't pretend to understand your beliefs, but I've been around your kind enough times to know it's more complicated than most realise.' She wipes her eyes. 'Oh, dear. I'm going to look a mess for the day now. Come on out front. We'll get your pay sorted.'

I don't feel comfortable taking money from her after dropping this on her, but I also need every cent owed to me for this next part. I'll be relying on my car savings because any leftover money after expenses has always gone into the contribution box at the Kingdom Hall, and I've no idea how long it'll be between jobs. She pats my back a few times, then waves me towards the door.

Maggie takes cash directly from the till and counts out four hundred dollars. 'So far as the tax department's concerned, you finished up last week.' She hands it to me with a wink.

The kindness of this woman is overwhelming, but I hand some of the money back. 'I've only worked three days this week, and it's too much for four anyway.'

She pushes my hand away. 'It's for the remaining jewellery sitting on the counter right there. I'll have no way to pay you otherwise.'

I bite down on my lip and nod. 'Thank you—for everything.'

When the doorbell chimes on my way out, I can't help but smile. It'll be a long time before I'm deafened by that sound again.

On my way home, I deliver some farewell letters. I don't have the time or emotional bandwidth for good-byes. It's close to midday when I get to packing, and my hands are shaking as I fill a large suitcase with all my clothes and important belongings. I make sure every-thing I pack belongs to me, because I can't predict Mum's reaction, and I don't want to be stopped by the police before I even make it to the 'Thank you for visiting Chirnside!' sign.

It's tempting to just leave. It would be so much easier. But I refuse to run scared. I have to be able to live with myself later, to look back on my departure with some degree of pride.

I have two hours until Mum gets home from work, and I spend that time cleaning the house, washing linen, feeding Charlie carrots, and committing Banjo's scent to memory.

'I'm so sorry,' I tell him. 'Maybe if I get a place with a big yard one day, you can come live with me.'

He's turning his head back and forth, desperately trying to comprehend what I'm saying. I think he senses I'm leaving, but he just doesn't know why or for how long.

I take a final look around the house, then wheel my suitcase out front. I'm seated under the veranda rubbing Banjo's head and listening for Mum's car, telling myself she'll be all right. She has an entire congregation to take care of her.

My palms go clammy when I hear her car pull into the driveway. She spots me, turns the engine off, but doesn't get out. Her eyes go to the suitcase beside me, and then we're watching each other through the glass. I'm patient with her, because I understand the enormity of this moment and how hard she's working to keep it together right now.

Finally, the door swings open and she climbs out. But

she doesn't come towards me. Instead, she closes the car door and leans against it.

'I'm surprised you waited,' she says, her voice heavy with disappointment.

I wet my lips. 'I couldn't leave without saying a proper goodbye.'

Nothing changes on her face. 'You didn't even make it to two weeks.'

She's referring to how long I've been baptised. 'I'm sorry.'

She pushes off the car and takes a few steps in my direction. 'You're sorry.'

'Yes.'

She nods, holding back tears. 'You were doing *so* well.'

'I'm sorry.'

'You said that already.'

I knew this was coming, but it doesn't make it any easier. 'Just know that I'm leaving the organisation, not you.'

'Right.' She blinks a few times. 'Where are you going? To your dad's?'

'Brisbane.'

I think that hurts her more than my leaving. Going to Bridget is a cruel form of betrayal in her eyes. 'I doubt she'll even want to see you.'

I don't reply to that—I can't. Instead, I reach down and stroke Banjo's head.

'Don't go getting any ideas. Banjo stays here. He belongs to the family, not you.'

Doesn't she realise she's the only one left? 'Okay.' I'm not getting into a fight over the dog. I'll never win.

'I can't believe this. Both daughters.' She shakes her head at the ground. Her collective disappointment weighs heavy.

I swallow down tears. 'I tried. I really did, but the feeling never goes away. It's always there, and it's... exhausting.'

Mum presses her lips together and walks straight past me to the front door. 'You'll have to make your own way to the bus stop. Dinner won't cook itself.'

I knew to expect all this, but it still stings. They say every child's worst fear is being rejected by a parent. Turns out that fear doesn't go away as an adult.

'So that's it?' I call to her. 'You're done with me?'

She pauses at the door and calls Banjo's name. He trots over to her, and my heart splits in two.

'You're turning your back on Jehovah,' she says. 'It's just unimaginable after everything we've been through.' She pushes the door open, and I see her face collapse as she steps through it. I know she's crying on that side of the door while I'm crying on this side of it.

I wipe my shaking hands on my jeans, then tug up the handle of my suitcase, wheeling it along the edge of the veranda towards the drive. The wheels jam the moment it hits the gravel, and I have to half drag, half carry it all the way to the road.

The walk takes me twelve minutes.

Twelve minutes of physical, mental, and emotional struggle until I'm finally standing on the asphalt. I did it. I left. Now I'm sweating all over and trying very hard not to throw up. It's difficult choosing this when I know I could turn around and beg Mum to help me stay on the right path—and she'd do it. Without hesitation, she would help me. But I've chosen the coward's path too many times. It's time to be brave.

Adjusting my backpack, I start dragging my suitcase along the road in the direction of town. I slow when I see a Rav 4 parked on the shoulder up ahead. The driver door opens, and out steps Tamsin in low-rise jeans and heeled sandals, her hair in a slick ponytail.

'Need a ride?' she calls from twenty metres away.

'What are you doing here?' My voice is drowned out by the rumble of my suitcase wheels.

'Mum saw you drop a letter for me in the letterbox.' She slides her hands into her back pockets. 'I asked her to read it to me over the phone.'

This is the friend the organisation warned me against, the bad association. The only person to show up for me.

When I reach the car, she helps me wrestle the suitcase into the boot.

'Please tell me you didn't drive all the way from Melbourne because of that letter,' I say.

She shrugs. 'I was coming down for Trent's birthday tomorrow anyway. I just came a day earlier.' She slams the boot shut. 'So, where to?'

'Brisbane.'

She scrunches up her nose. 'That might be a stretch.'

'How about the milk bar to buy a V/Line ticket, then?'

She gestures for me to get in. 'So you can wait three hours for the bus? Have enough time to change your mind? I don't think so. I'll drive you to Turram. They have a bus that will take you all the way to Cann River. From there you can catch a bus to Canberra, then take the train to Brisbane.'

'The bus is cheaper.'

She climbs into the driver seat and closes the door. 'Sure, but the train is so much faster. You know, if you need money—'

'I don't need money.' I click in my seat belt. 'I just need to be sensible with what I have.'

Her eyes sweep over me. 'Fine, no money.' She starts the car. 'You look good, by the way. I like your hair shorter.'

I reach up and touch the ends of it. I've had long hair my whole life and decided to cut it just below my shoulders a few months back. It's noticeably wavier at this length.

'And new clothes—that fit,' she says with a smile.

I've slowly been replacing items in my wardrobe. Of course, now I wish I had saved the money instead.

The drive to Turram is around forty minutes. Tamsin spends that time filling me in on all her news—months' worth. Entire months that I'd intentionally cut her from my life, and she still showed up. Though some in my congregation might have shown up if they believed I could be talked off the ledge, but the only place they would drive me would be to an elder's house for counselling.

'I'm sorry I missed all those things,' I tell her.

She glances sideways at me. 'Stop. I know why. I'm utterly irreplaceable, and I knew you'd be back eventually.'

'Utterly irreplaceable, huh?'

She flashes a smile at me, then asks, 'Are you going to come back here if you don't find your sister?'

I look out the window. 'I can't. Not unless I'm coming back to all of it.'

'You mean the religion?'

I nod.

'That pisses me off.'

My lips turn up. 'Me too.'

'You know you're always welcome at my house, right? My mum adores you.'

'Thank you, but if I can't find Bridget, the plan is to keep looking.'

'I think that's a great plan.'

When we arrive at the depot, I tell Tamsin to drop me out front, but she insists on parking and coming in. I buy my ticket, and then we head to the small cafe next to the booth. Though cafe is probably too generous a word for what is essentially a display of fried food and a coffee machine.

'My shout,' Tamsin says, handing a twenty to the lady.

We sit on the bench in bay twelve, eating greasy potato cakes and hot chips, sipping coffee from disposable cups. More passengers start to trickle in, and eventually the driver shows up to open the luggage doors. Ticket in hand, I wheel my suitcase over and join the queue.

'Before I forget,' Tamsin says, pulling a pen out of her handbag and taking the ticket from me. She writes her mobile number on the back of it. 'Call me any time you want or need to. And make sure you let me know your new address once you're settled so I can come visit next time I'm up north.'

I hug her, holding on for a long moment. 'Make sure you visit.'

'You make sure you call.'

I hand my suitcase to the driver. He slides it into place, then checks my ticket. I'm holding up the line, so I have no choice but to board.

'You've 100 percent got this,' Tamsin says with an encouraging smile.

I nod and step up onto the bus, finding a seat halfway down. Tamsin continues to wait, and I watch her through the window. I'm grateful that someone is here waving goodbye while at the same time hurting over my mother's final words to me.

Not surprised, but hurt.

It's not her fault. There's no one to blame. It would be so much easier if there was. I can't resent her for her way of thinking. These aren't political views that can be swayed with education. These are deeply rooted values and beliefs that bring meaning and purpose to her life. To support me would be a betrayal to herself and the God she loves wholeheartedly. The personal cost would be too great.

And yet I want it anyway.

I wave to Tamsin as the bus backs out of the bay. She walks alongside it for a bit. I continue waving until she disappears from sight, then bury my face in my backpack and cry all the way to Cann River.

27

ANNIE

Bush, coast, farmland, suburbia. I watch the landscape change all the way to Canberra.

It's surprisingly cold when I finally step off the bus in the sleeping city, especially given how far north I've travelled. There are no skyscrapers, but there are plenty of trees.

'What time does the bus depart?' I ask the woman in the booth when I buy my ticket.

'Six sharp,' she replies without looking up.

I thank her and glance down at my watch—1:37 a.m. Suitcase in hand, I make my way over to the coffee vending machine and dig around in my pockets for coins. I carry the hot cup to some empty chairs and get my coat out of my suitcase. Then I sit with both hands wrapping the cup and people-watch for the next four hours. I need to stay awake, so whenever I run out of coffee, I go and grab another cup.

So much for drinking it in moderation.

Whenever Mum thought I was drinking too much of

it, she would simply forget to buy it or say she was waiting for it to go on special. I ended up buying my own jar and keeping it next to the kettle at work. When Maggie realised I was bringing my own coffee in, she bought the largest tin of instant she could find to ensure I never ran out.

I'm on my sixth cup when I hear the announcement for those travelling to Sydney to make their way to bay fifteen. My blood buzzes as I stand, and I pray to a God who's no longer listening to me that I don't have a stroke on the bus.

Four hours later, I arrive in Sydney. I barely have time to register the chaos and noise before I'm climbing aboard another bus and pulling back out onto the road. I stare out the window, eyes blinking with fatigue, watching people and cars moving in all directions. When the Opera House appears across the water, I sit up straight and stare. Then a minute later we're crossing the Harbour Bridge. I can't help but smile. I've just crossed two items off my bucket list, and it was all included in one sensible ticket fare.

As we exit Sydney, I start to come down from my caffeine high. I thread my arms through the straps of my backpack so it can't be stolen and place my jacket between my head and the window.

Finally, I sleep.

———

Sixteen hours and thirty-four minutes later, I step off the bus in Brisbane. The air's different, thick and wet. I take my suitcase from the driver and wheel it away from the small crowd, then strip off as much clothing as I can. I'm going to need a map, because wandering aimlessly will most certainly result in dehydration. I find one at the information booth, and when I step outside again, it's raining. Not just a shower but a full torrential downpour.

'Welcome to Brissie,' a man says as he passes me.

I sit undercover to wait it out, but it doesn't stop. It just falls and falls and falls. With a resigned sigh, I put the map in my backpack and step out into it. I'm thoroughly drenched within seconds, so there's no point trying to rush. Every few blocks, I stop to check the map. Eventually, I find my way to the heart of the city. I have no idea where Bridget is. I only know that if she is here in this city, she'll be close to the cultural hub. But that search will take planning and time, and right now I need a place to sleep.

I'm standing outside what appears to be a pub. The sign says Imperial Tavern. I enter and look around. This is my first time in a venue like this. The man behind the bar looks up, eyes travelling down me, all the way to the water pooling at my feet.

'Can I help you?' he asks.

The man has one of those friendly, approachable faces. Judging by the grey peppered through his hair, I guess him to be around forty.

'Sorry.' I look down at the mess I've made. 'It's really coming down out there.'

He throws me a clean tea towel. 'Here.'

'Thanks.' I clean myself up, then bend to wipe the

floor. 'Do you know where I might find some cheap accommodation?'

He regards me as he's drying glasses. 'Motel cheap or hostel cheap?'

I'm distracted by another staff member appearing to pour a beer. It's fast, messy, and completely fascinating. 'Ah, whichever one's cheaper.'

'Hostel's cheaper if you don't mind sharing a room.'

Do I mind? I assume it's safe if other people do it. 'I don't mind sharing.' If it's awful, I can always leave.

He points. 'River Backpackers is a few doors down. They usually have plenty of beds. Plus there's a rooftop pool.' He observes me a moment. 'Can I get you a drink? Food?'

I've survived on coffee and processed food for the past two days. I desperately need some proper food, but I also need to be really careful with my spending.

As though reading my mind, he says, 'We have a $10 steak special on Sundays if you order before five thirty. Comes with salad and a pot.'

I salivate at the mention of meat. 'A pot?'

He holds up a glass. 'Of beer. Or soft drink if you'd prefer.'

I stare at the glass in his hand. 'Is that what I ask for if I want a beer in a pub? A pot?'

The corners of his mouth lift. '285ml is a pot.' He holds up a larger glass. '425ml is a schooner.' Then he gestures to a stack of glasses nearby. '570ml is a pint.'

I'm guessing by his amused expression that this is common knowledge. 'Any chance I can get a large coffee instead?'

The bartender nods once and walks to the other end of the bar where a coffee pot sits. I pull a soggy ten-dollar note from my pocket and place it on the counter. He takes it when he returns with the coffee. 'Cutlery's over there.' He gestures to a table in the corner.

Fifteen minutes later, a plate lands in front of me. The fatty T-bone steak is a decent size, and the salad fills the rest of the plate. As I eat, I'm hit with a wave of homesickness that steals my appetite. I'm sitting in a bar in the middle of the day—on a meeting day—and there's not a fruit cake in sight. I barely recognise myself.

I force the rest of my food down because I have no idea when I'll be eating next. He keeps asking me if I want anything else, and I feel bad telling him no. Ten dollars is my limit.

When I stand to leave, he says, 'If for some reason they don't have a bed, come back here. There are a few other places I can direct you to.'

I thank him before heading off, relieved to find that it's stopped raining outside. It makes the walk slightly more comfortable.

The hostel has clear signage, so I have no issue locating it. Inside, people lounge on couches and armchairs around the foyer. Some have luggage by their feet. I walk over to what looks to be the counter and wait a long time for someone to come before noticing the bell in front of me.

Once I ring it, a lady with purple hair appears, her smile warm. 'Hey there.'

I ask her what the cheapest accommodation is, and

she informs me that a bed in an eight-share room is sixteen dollars per night.

I pull out a twenty. 'One night, please.'

She gives me change, then disappears out back for a moment, returning with a pile of linen and a key. 'Follow me. I'll show you around.'

We head up some squeaky stairs, and she points out the communal laundry and kitchen. When we reach the top floor, she shows me the bathroom next to the room I'll be staying in. The room itself is large and contains four bunk beds. There's a young woman reading on one of them. She looks up and smiles briefly before returning to her book.

My host hands me the pile of linen. 'First time?'

'That obvious?'

She smiles again. 'Think of it as school camp for grown-ups.'

I've never been on a school camp, so that's no help at all.

She gestures to the poster on the wall. 'House rules are right there. Come find me if you have any questions. You can take any bed that isn't made up.'

I head to the bed farthest from the door, stomach swirling, and sink down onto the leather mattress. I'm so far out of my comfort zone, so exhausted, and so completely alone.

One step at a time. Just do the next thing, then the next thing, then the next thing.

Rising, I make my bed. The linen's clean. The room's clean. The people are fine. No one's going to rob me. It'll be okay. I'll take a shower, sleep, and then tomorrow I'll start looking for Bridget.

It's a sensible plan—the only one I have. Or I return to the bus depot and buy a ticket home.

This is better.

This will eventually be better.

28

ANNIE

The bartender's name is James. He's forty-four, part owner of the pub, divorced, and has two children aged fourteen and sixteen. He lives in the apartment above the pub and drives to Kingscliff a few times a week to see his kids. During the five afternoons I've been eating here, always before five thirty, he's also become my only friend in this city. Though I'm not sure he sees me the same way. I'm that annoying patron who comes for the special and drinks the free tap water available on the counter.

I have my map of the city open next to my empty plate, crossing off two galleries I visited today whose staff had never heard of Bridget Wilson. I'm quickly running out of art-related establishments. I've even phoned every university and TAFE within one hundred kilometres of Brisbane.

James wanders over and leans on the bar, running his eyes over the map. He points to a spot a few blocks back from the river. 'Have you tried the Queensland Art Society?'

'It's not on the map.'

'It's hardly a landmark but worth checking out.'

I mark the spot and make a note to go there tomorrow. 'Thanks.'

I've also been calling shops asking about casual work, but no one wants to employ someone living in a hostel, and I don't blame them.

James places a fresh cup of coffee in front of me. 'This one's on the house.'

I push it away. 'No, you don't have to do that. I already had one.'

'Well, I can't put it back in the pot, so unless you want to see it go down the sink, drink.'

I exhale, a little embarrassed. 'I could wipe the tables down for you if you like. Work off my debt,' I joke.

He looks over at me. 'If you're looking for work, I could find you something to do around here.'

I sit a little straighter on my stool. 'But I don't have any experience in hospitality.'

'You just said you can wipe tables.'

'Not well, according to my mum.'

He laughs. It's a friendly sound that makes me warm to him even more. 'Well, you'd have to learn on the job, then.'

'If you're serious, I'm up for anything you have the patience to teach me.'

He leans his weight on the bar and frowns in my direction. 'It'll be a lot of not very fun work initially. Dishes, toilets.'

'I've been known to excel at things that aren't very fun.'

He chuckles. 'That right? Can you be here midday Monday for a trial?'

'Yes, of course.'

He nods. 'Good. It's a nice quiet day to learn.'

I slide off the stool and fold up the map. 'I'll be here at twelve.'

'Black pants and shoes you won't tire in. I'll have a T-shirt for you.'

This is the first thing to fall into place since I left, the smallest seed of hope. 'Thank you.'

He goes to serve a customer at the other end of the bar, and I leave, heading straight to Kmart. I buy some black pants and manage to find a pair of shoes my size in the clearance section. I'm work-ready for less than twelve dollars.

The following morning, I throw down some cereal before heading off. It's a fifteen-minute walk to the Queensland Arts Society, and the building is still closed when I arrive. McDonald's is across the road, so I head there because it's the cheapest place to buy coffee. I sit by the window and drink two cups while watching the other side of the road.

A few minutes before nine, a middle-aged woman arrives with keys to unlock the door. I'm off my chair and jogging across the road before she makes it inside.

'Excuse me!' I call to her.

She frowns in my direction. 'We don't open for another ten minutes.'

'I know. Quick question.' I stop in front of her, slightly

out of breath. 'I'm trying to track down my sister, Bridget Wilson. I wondered if you might know her.'

The woman lets go of the door and turns to me. That's recognition on her face.

'Sister?'

'You know her?'

Her expression has turned to suspicion. 'The Bridget I know doesn't have a sister.'

I don't let that deter me. 'She has light brown hair and the same colour eyes as me. Quiet type, dry sense of humour. Irrational fear of cats.'

She looks at me tiredly. 'I'm afraid I can't give out employee information.'

When she turns away, I block the door with my arm. 'Wait. She works here?'

'I'm going to need you to remove your hand from the door.'

I withdraw it. 'Sorry.'

She pushes the door open.

'Does she work on weekends?' I say to her back. 'I can just wait here.'

The woman is halfway through the door. 'She doesn't work weekends.'

'Oh.' I'm so close. 'It's just that having to wait another two days might break me.'

The woman looks back, lips pressed into a thin line. 'Kurilpa Point Park,' she says, nodding in the direction of the river. 'Cross the footbridge and look for a group of people with sketch pads. It's one of those drawing groups. Anyone can go along. Bridget goes every Saturday.'

This tiny piece of information means everything to

me. She used to get in trouble for doodling on her *Watch-towers* and *Awakes* during meetings, and now she spends Saturday mornings drawing in the park.

'Thank you so much,' I breathe as she disappears inside.

I don't run towards the river—I *fly*. My feet barely touch the footpath. People step out of my way, and I shout apologies at them over my shoulder. When the river comes into sight, I don't wait at the pedestrian crossing with everyone else. I dash between cars, ignoring the blaring horns in my trail. As I jog across the bridge, I look for any signs that say Kurilpa Point Park but find none.

As I step down off the bridge, I stop a man walking his dog and ask him for directions. He points west, and I'm running again, searching for her. My feet carry me across the grass until I spot a group of people seated beneath the shade of a giant fig tree, sketchbooks in hand. I stop and turn in a circle. This will be the first time I've laid eyes on my sister in nearly five years, and there are emotions bubbling up inside me that I wasn't prepared for.

Breathe.

Breathe, and don't throw up.

I press my eyes shut, then open them as I turn to face the group. Everyone's so absorbed in what they're doing that they don't even notice me. I look from face to face as I move slowly towards them, stopping when I see Bridget. She's leaning against the trunk with one leg pulled up, using it like an easel. Her skin is lightly tanned, her hair out and so long now. She has it tucked behind her ears, her pensive expression on full display. She pauses drawing to stretch out her neck and hands, her mannerisms so familiar that it's hard to believe I've not witnessed them in years.

She glances briefly in my direction before returning to her drawing. But a beat later, she lifts her eyes to me again. I see them narrow and then watch the shock register on her face. She doesn't light up, doesn't smile. She simply stares. I lift a hand in a small wave, in case she doesn't know for sure that it's me. But she knows.

Placing her pad and pencil on the ground, she says something to the person next to her before standing. Then she's walking in my direction, wary eyes looking me up and down. She stops a full metre from me, a safe distance, and crosses her arms.

That's fair.

Neither of us speaks—probably because we don't know what to say.

A full minute passes before Bridget says, 'What are you doing here, Annie?'

It's clear that seeing me has triggered a negative reaction for her. I hate that. I hate it, but there's nothing I can do about it. 'Looking for you.'

'Why?' She's naturally suspicious.

I'm not really sure what to say. There are a hundred reasons I'm here, and some of them she won't be ready to hear. 'I got baptised.'

Her eyebrows lift slightly. 'Congratulations.'

'Then I left.'

More staring. 'You left what?'

I swallow. 'Everything.'

She takes a moment to process this. 'So why are you looking for me?'

The sting in my nose is instant. She should understand better than anyone, but I'm feeling more and more alone with each passing second.

Because I really don't want to cry in front of her, I turn and walk away.

'Annie,' she calls instantly.

The edge in her voice makes me turn back.

I see her swallow, and then she looks over her shoulder. 'Let me get my things. Wait here.'

I watch her walk away, feeling slightly better.

She returns a moment later, her sketchbook in hand. 'My car's parked down the road. I'll take you to my place.'

She has a place. And a car. 'Where do you live?'

'Fortitude Valley.'

That doesn't mean much to me. 'I don't know my way around yet. Is it close?'

'Ten-minute drive from here.'

We arrive at a red Ford Laser. Bridget climbs in and reaches over to unlock my door. We drive along the streets that I've been walking every day this past week searching for her. Ten minutes later, we pull into the car park below her apartment building, and I follow her to the door. She puts in a code, then hip and shoulders the door.

'It sticks in this weather,' she explains.

There's no lift, so we walk up six flights of stairs to apartment 36. Inside smells familiar—like her, and a little of home. I want to lie down on the floor and breathe in the comforting scent. Obviously, I don't do that. I stay very much on my feet and follow her through to the kitchen. She doesn't give me a tour, simply puts the kettle on and drags a jar of teabags to her.

'Tea?'

I spot the plunger nearby. 'Coffee if you have it, please.'

She pushes the jar back in place and grabs the coffee plunger. 'Bet Mum doesn't like that.'

'No, she doesn't.'

She puts the kettle on and spoons some ground coffee into the plunger. I watch her, bracing for the inevitable questions.

'Does Mum know where you are?' she asks.

And so it begins.

'She knows I'm in Brisbane, but she doesn't know where.'

Bridget leans against the bench on the far side of the kitchen. 'When did you get here?'

'Sunday.'

'Sunday? Where are you staying?'

'River Backpackers.'

Her eyebrows rise slightly. 'You're staying at a hostel?'

I shrug. 'It's cheap.'

She pours boiling water into the plunger, then turns back to me. 'You weren't tempted to look up the local congregation and stay with one of your spiritual sisters?'

I lift my chin. 'Is that what you did?'

Her eyes never leave mine. 'I shared a place with some other students.' She regards me a moment. 'I'm not going back.'

'I know.'

'I didn't "fall out" of the truth, like they said. I educated myself. I intentionally chose this life instead of that one.'

I nod. 'Bridget, I know.' She's never experienced me outside of the religion before, and she clearly doesn't trust this version of me. 'I'm not here to bring you back in. I'm here because I left it too.'

She leans on the bench. 'Why did you leave?'

What answer to give? A persistent gut feeling that never subsides? Conflicting beliefs? Lust? Questioning if there's even a God? 'I guess I just want to live a life shaped by something other than guilt and shame.'

She turns to pour the coffee. 'How do you take it?'

'Milk with one.' Just like her.

She finishes making the drinks, then hands me one of the mugs. 'It doesn't go away when you leave, you know.'

My eyebrows come together in question. 'What doesn't?'

'The guilt. The shame.'

I take a sip of my coffee, savouring the taste. 'It must ease at some point.'

'I think you just learn to live with it.' She watches me over her cup. 'I still can't watch TV in the evenings. When I was studying, it was fine. I replaced one form of study for another. When I graduated, suddenly I had all this time. Nothing triggers guilt more than time spent doing something for yourself.'

I look around the perfectly organised kitchen. 'Do you still pray?'

She shakes her head. 'I took up journaling instead. Clears your mind the same way.' She taps a finger on her mug. 'It'll take you a while to break the habit. Or maybe you won't break it. Maybe you'll keep that part.'

To stop is an admittance that you no longer believe, that there's no one listening. 'What do you believe now?'

She stares at the microwave. 'I believe it's okay to not have all the answers.' There's a pause. 'I believe you don't need to belong to an organisation to be spiritual, and that a person's beliefs, and their relationship with God, or complete dismissal of him, is no one else's business.'

I lift my eyebrows. 'Fair enough.'

She's tapping on her mug again. 'Why didn't you go to Dad's?'

'Why didn't you?' I catch the hurt in her eyes before she looks in the direction of the terrace, but I don't dare ask about it. 'He's seeing someone.'

She doesn't react at first. 'Surprised Mum didn't put him off women forever.'

Those words hang between us for a moment.

'I can't hold your hand through this,' she says, changing the subject again. 'It has to be a hundred percent you.'

Feels like she's wiping her hands of me before I've even asked for help. 'I don't need you to hold my hand.' *Though it might have been nice.* 'We've not talked all these years because you were out, and I was in. Now we're both out. That's why I'm here.'

She sets her cup down. 'I guess now we pretend I wasn't cut out of your life and just go back to being sisters.'

I blink. '*I* didn't cut you out of my life. I was fifteen when you left. What was I supposed to do?'

She swallows and looks away. 'I guess I could clear out my studio if you need a place to stay short-term.'

I love the addition of 'short-term'. With a subtle roll of my eyes, I take my empty cup to the sink. 'I wouldn't want to get in the way of your art.'

'Well, you can't stay at the hostel.'

'Why not? They're a lot more welcoming there.'

We realise at the same time that we're standing too close to each other, and we both take a step back.

She looks up at the roof and draws a long breath. 'You can stay here.'

I note the softening of her tone. 'Okay.'

Her eyes return to me. 'I really hope you've thought this through. What will you do for work?'

'Actually, I got a job at a pub in the city. I start tomorrow.'

Bridget suppresses a smile. 'At a *pub*? How on earth did you get a job at a pub?' She waves a hand. 'You know what? Never mind. It's really none of my business.' She picks up her car keys, then turns to me, clearing her throat. 'Also... it's my birthday tomorrow.'

Naturally, I'd forgotten this. Remembering has always been futile. 'Okay.'

She appears uncomfortable. 'I'm having people over.'

'Oh.' This is new. 'Like a birthday party?'

'No.' She shakes her head. 'More of a barbeque.'

'So a birthday barbeque?'

She scrunches her nose up. 'I guess if you have to give it a name.'

Now we're both uncomfortable. 'Do you want me out of the apartment for it?'

'No,' she says quickly. 'Unless you'd prefer to not be here. I don't want it to be awkward. It's a big leap from recently baptised to birthday parties.'

'I thought you said it wasn't a party.'

She presses her lips together and lifts her chin. 'You should also know that I eat the Easter eggs people give me now.'

It feels a lot like she's testing me. 'Even the creme ones that look like real egg yolk?'

She scowls. 'Of course not. I'm not a complete Satan worshipper.'

We watch each other for a moment, like we're daring the other to smile.

'Do you put a Christmas tree up?' I ask.

She shakes her head. 'No tree. No turkey. No lights. No carols—except Mariah Carey.'

I'm relieved to hear that with Christmas being a few weeks away. It would be a lot and too soon. 'Then what do you do on Christmas Day?'

'Last year I painted on the terrace and ate tuna from a tin because I forgot all the shops are closed.'

The corners of my mouth lift.

Bridget jingles her keys. 'Let's go get your things before one of us changes our mind.'

29

HUNTER

The moment Pete mentioned he was getting a new ute, I asked what he was doing with the old one. It had low kilometres, and I knew he'd taken care of it. Pete named his price, which I later realised was too cheap after seeing similar utes for sale in the classifieds. Half of the amount I already had in savings, and the other half has been coming out of my pay each week. Yesterday I made the final payment, which means today I drive myself to Bridget's birthday not owing a cent to anyone. I prefer the freedom that comes with having no financial ties.

I stop at a bakery in Ipswich to buy a birthday cake because I know Bridget won't buy one for herself. She's still figuring out how to do this stuff. The act of having guests at her house to celebrate her birth is already well out of her comfort zone.

'Need some candles?' the woman asks me.

'Yes, please.'

Cake in hand, I jog back to the ute and head to

Brisbane.

I'm already late thanks to a broken pump this morning, and there's nothing I can do about it. Thankfully, traffic is kind. I'm parked outside Bridget's apartment thirty-five minutes later and almost to the door when I remember the cake and have to run back and get it. This makes me officially an hour and twenty minutes late by the time I knock on her door.

Music drifts out from beneath the door—if you can call it that. It's exactly the type of music I'd expect artsy people to listen to. I've prepared myself for the fact that this won't be my usual crowd. There's going to be people talking about brushstrokes and light.

The door swings open, and my lungs still. Standing before me is Annie. I blink, certain I'm hallucinating, but she doesn't disappear. Her hair's shorter, clothes better, but those flame-licked eyes are exactly the same. She's wearing make-up too. I know, because her freckles aren't visible.

The glass of champagne she's holding slips from her hand, splashing up the door as it hits the carpet. She doesn't react, just continues to stare at me. And I'm staring back, wondering why she's here and what the hell we're supposed to do now. I should probably clean up the mess if she's not going to—assuming she lets me inside.

'Wilson,' I say.

She keeps a hold of the door. 'What are you...' She can't even get the question out.

'I'm here for the barbeque.'

She shakes her head, visibly confused. 'What?'

Bridget appears beside her. 'Hey, you came.' Her toe

hits the glass on the carpet, and she notices the mess at Annie's feet. 'Oh.'

That seems to bring Annie out of her trance. 'Sorry.' She bends and picks up the glass. 'I'll get something to clean it up.' Then she retreats to the kitchen.

Bridget pulls the door wide open. 'You coming in?'

I step inside, eyes still on Annie. She's frantically opening and closing drawers and cupboards. 'I think I surprised her.'

Bridget looks in the direction of the kitchen. 'That's my fault. I completely forgot to tell her you were coming.' She leans in. 'It's been quite the weekend.'

'I see that.' My heart is pounding.

'Come in.'

I follow her into the kitchen. 'I got you a cake,' I say, placing the box on the bench.

'I told you no presents.'

'Which is why I brought a cake.' I'm trying not to look at Annie, because I can see she's struggling to keep it together, and so am I.

Bridget opens the box and peers in. 'I don't want people singing.'

'If there's a cake, they'll sing.'

Picking up on the tension in the room, Bridget looks between me and Annie. 'What did I miss?'

Annie exits the kitchen to avoid answering, so Bridget looks to me instead.

'I thought you said you guys were friends,' she says.

'No, I said we hung out.'

She gives me a confused look. 'What does that mean?'

Annie returns to the kitchen before I can reply to

rinse out the cloth.

'What's wrong?' Bridget asks her.

Annie glances over her shoulder. Not at me, of course. 'Nothing. I'm just surprised to see Hunter this far north—at your barbeque.'

Bridget continues to look between us, like she's trying to put pieces together. 'He moved up here last year and reached out. We've been hanging out, like you guys used to.'

Annie glares in my direction. 'Is that right?'

'*Not* like we used to,' I clarify.

Annie grabs the spray from under the sink. 'I need to finish cleaning up before it stains.'

When I look back at Bridget, she's staring hard at me. 'What?'

'Don't "what" me.' She lowers her voice. 'Did you hook up with my sister?'

I shake my head. 'It's not like that.'

'So that's a no?'

I draw a breath. 'Not in the way you think.' I'm sweating from running up six flights of stairs—and other reasons. 'Look, I don't want to ruin your birthday. I'll just leave.'

'But you just got here.' When Annie re-enters the kitchen, Bridget says to her, 'Hunter says he's going to leave. Do you want him to go?'

Annie folds the cloth, hangs it over the tap, then turns to face me. 'Stay. Go. Makes no difference to me.'

Bridget touches a hand to her forehead. 'You know what? I think I'll leave you guys to figure this out. Not my business.' With that, she retreats to the terrace.

Annie and I stand awkwardly at opposite ends of the kitchen, looking at each other without looking at each other.

'What are you doing here?' I ask.

She holds on to the sink behind her. 'I live here.'

'Since when?'

'Since yesterday.' She doesn't appear to be joking.

'I don't understand.'

'Nothing new there.'

I press my teeth together. 'Why are you here?' My frustration is creeping into my voice.

There's a long silence before she says, 'I left.'

My mind is buzzing. 'What do you mean, you *left*?'

'My job, my home.' She swallows. 'And the religion. I left it all.'

I raise a hand, trying to process this. 'Sammy told me you got baptised.'

'You still speak to Sammy?' She looks so wounded by that.

I wait for her to answer my original question.

She sighs. 'I did get baptised. Then I guess I changed my mind.'

Then she changed her mind. She changed her fucking mind.

Bridget returns to the kitchen and fetches a bottle of wine from the fridge. 'Are we good?'

I wait for Annie to answer. If she wants me gone, I'll go without a word.

'Of course,' Annie says. 'We've both moved on from high school.' She looks at me. 'Right?'

'Absolutely,' I say with confidence.

Bridget nods. 'Great. Then you can come meet my work colleagues.'

'I think the correct term is *friends*,' Annie says, stealing the words directly from my mouth. 'You guys go ahead.'

'You're just going to stay in here by yourself?' I ask.

'If I want to.'

Bridget ushers us both towards the terrace. 'Just go. Both of you. They're debating whether graffiti is art.'

I blink slowly and follow the girls out of the kitchen.

I use the opportunity to check Annie out from behind. She's wearing a long skirt, but not like the ugly ones she used to wear. This one's yellow and flowy. On top she has a simple white singlet with an elaborate leather necklace threaded with colourful beads, which I assume she made. Bracelets in various designs cover both arms. She's gotten better.

The names of the people I meet go in one ear and out the other. The older guy keeps asking if I've seen this exhibition and that exhibition. I tell him repeatedly that I'm a farmer and don't get into the city much.

Annie positions herself as far away as is politely possible, and my eyes keep going to her like they always do when she's in the same room. I want to speak to her, ask her a million questions, but it's not the right time.

At one point she disappears into the kitchen and returns with a plate of lamingtons. She moves from person to person, leaving me until last. She somehow manages to avoid all eye contact in the process.

When she goes to leave, the older gentleman says, 'You know, we didn't even know our Bridget had a sister.'

Annie has no choice but to have this conversation in front of me. 'I think I succeeded in surprising her.'

The man laughs warmly. 'It's nice to see her like this.'

'Like this?'

'Happy.'

Annie drops her eyes to the plate. 'Well, it is her birthday.'

He takes a second lamington. 'Where'd you stay when you got here?'

I love this man for asking the questions I can't.

'At a hostel,' Annie replies.

I brush a finger down my nose to hide my irritation. 'You were staying at a hostel?'

She meets my eyes. 'Yes.'

'And I heard you found a job already,' the man says. 'Good for you.'

'What job?' I ask, unable to help myself.

'At a pub, in the city.'

I shift my weight. 'You're going to work at a *pub*? Serving beer to drunks all day?'

She rolls her eyes in my direction this time. 'They're patrons, not drunks.' She looks back at the man. 'I actually met the owner the day I arrived. Walked into his pub, dripping wet, and he was kind enough to not throw me out.'

My jaw works. 'You didn't happen to be wearing a white T-shirt at the time, did you?'

She ignores me entirely and keeps talking to the man. 'I've eaten there pretty much every day, and he was nice enough to give me a job.'

If she's trying to make me jealous, it's working. 'Did you impress him with your beer-pouring skills?'

'He offered to train me,' she replies.

The man smiles encouragingly at her. 'Sounds like he saw potential in you.'

I nod in agreement. 'I bet he did.'

'He's a nice guy,' she says, defending him. 'I could do with some nice men in my life.'

I'm about to ask for the address of this establishment, so I can set it alight, when a woman wanders over to get a lamington from the plate. She notices Annie's necklace.

'This is lovely. Very unique.'

Annie reaches up to touch it. 'Thank you.'

'Oooh, you've got the whole set,' the woman says, lifting one of Annie's arms to inspect the bracelets. 'Brisbane has some great markets if you like this kind of thing.'

'She makes them herself,' I say.

'Really?'

Annie looks at me. 'Yeah. It's a hobby of mine.'

Bridget wanders over to see what we're talking about.

'You didn't mention what a clever sister you have,' the woman says. 'Two creative girls in the family.'

Bridget stares at the necklace. 'You've gotten really good.'

'And I see you have one too,' the woman says, coming over to me.

I attempt to put my hand in my pocket, but the woman catches it with surprising speed, lifting it to display the worn band to everyone.

Annie stares at it while the conversation continues around her, then steps back from the group. 'Excuse me.'

I know I should leave her be, give her a chance to process everything, but I don't. I go looking for her, finding her in the kitchen. She's studying the cake I brought.

'I didn't think to get a cake,' she says, not looking up.

I grab a glass from the cabinet and fill it with water, leaning against the sink as I drink. At least she's speaking to me. 'Why would you?'

She carefully lifts it out of the box and sets it on a plate. 'How does the song go again?'

It takes me a moment to realise which song she's referring to. I speak the lyrics for her. 'Happy birthday to you. Happy birthday to you. Happy birthday, dear Bridget. And don't forget to hold the note for her name.' I pause. 'Happy birthday to you.'

She watches me a moment longer, then looks down. 'They're all expecting cake, right? That's why they're still here?'

I move closer, stopping when I see her tense up. Slowly, I reach for the candles and hand them to her. 'Yes, they'll be waiting for cake. It's rude to leave before.'

Annie presses a single candle in between the strawberries, and I fetch the matches from atop the fridge.

'What now?' she asks, lighting the candle.

'Now you carry it out. Be sure to shield the flame with one hand on the walk. Start singing when you enter, and everyone will join in.'

She picks up the cake. 'Can you start the song?'

I normally hide at the back, not singing, but I nod.

'Sure.'

It's an awkward cake moment. Bridget's like a deer in headlights as we step out onto the terrace. Annie forgets both the tune and lyrics of the world's most unforgettable song and ends up standing there silent for the entire thing. Plus I forgot to tell her about the 'hip hip hooray', and that has her looking around in a state of confusion and panic. Then Bridget forgets that she's supposed to blow the candle out. Everyone's shouting at her to make a wish, and you can tell she just wants this to be over.

Finally, everyone's eating cake—except Annie and Bridget, who are pushing it around their paper plates.

My phone rings, and I sneak off into the kitchen to answer it. It's Pete asking a question about the water pump. When I hang up, I turn to see Annie standing in the doorway, eyes on the phone in my hand.

'You have a mobile phone?' she asks.

I nod. 'Yeah.'

Her eyes meet mine, and I see the anger in them. 'You didn't think to call your dad and let him know you're okay?'

I'm a little taken aback by her reaction. 'I know he's still drinking and that nothing's changed. Sammy keeps me up to date.'

She turns the tap on and starts angry-washing the dishes.

I watch her a moment. 'Something you want to say?'

She turns the water to full hot. 'Nope.'

'Wilson.'

She doesn't look at me.

'*Annie.*'

'What?' She's still not looking at me.

Her hands are turning red under the water. Walking over, I turn the tap to cold. 'Are you pissed at me for not calling Dad or pissed at me for not calling you?'

She's focused on the plate in her hand. 'You left without even saying goodbye. I'd be an idiot to expect a courtesy phone call from you.' She turns the tap back to hot. 'You should go socialise.'

I draw a breath for patience. 'I don't want to talk to them. I want to talk to you.'

'Well, you're a year too late.'

I turn the tap off completely. 'And I don't play these fucking games. You should know that about me by now.'

She turns to me, eyes like two flames. 'I don't know you at all. You're just a boy I liked for a minute in high school who ran away.' She leans in. 'I don't play games either. I don't have the headspace for it. You want to be friends with my sister? That's fine. I'll tolerate your company for her sake. But to be clear, she's the only thing we have in common now.'

My phone vibrates in my pocket, and Annie turns back to the sink.

'You should answer that,' she says. 'It might be important.'

And that's my patience used up. 'Tell your sister goodbye.'

Annie continues washing. 'Maybe you should send her a text message. It's so easy to keep in touch with those things.'

I press my teeth together. 'All right, Wilson. You win.'

My fist hits the kitchen cupboard on my way out.

30

ANNIE

My head is filled with Hunter Reed once more. I can't think past him, and I can't figure out how we ended up here, with him a part of my sister's life but not mine. It's been a year since I last saw him, so why do the anger and hurt still feel so fresh? Maybe because he didn't say any of the things I'd imagined him saying when I saw him again, such as, 'It's so good to see you again. I'm sorry for leaving. How can I fix this?'

'Earth to Annie,' James says, waving a hand in front of my face.

'Sorry.' I try to focus.

'Have a go,' he says, stepping back from the beer tap.

After a week of cleaning tables and collecting glasses, James has decided I'm ready to learn the bar. Now to do this without embarrassing myself.

'Remember, if there's too much head'—he laughs—'like there is right now, just keep the tap going a little longer.'

I watch the froth spill over, then hold the glass up to inspect it. 'You really don't need to wipe it?'

A smile flickers on his face. 'No, you most definitely don't need to wipe it. That's why we have runners all along the bar.' He takes the glass from me and carries it down to one of his regular patrons. 'On the house, Tony.'

Tony salutes him.

'Okay. Time for a lesson on wine,' James says when he returns.

Another week passes in a blur of sticky tables and drunk patrons hitting on me as I collect their glasses. James must notice, because at the end of my second week, he moves me permanently to the bar.

At the end of each shift, I arrive home exhausted.

'How was work?' Bridget asks me every night.

And I give her the same answer each time. 'Good. You?'

Her responses are a little more varied. 'Fine' or 'Slow' or 'Busy'. Then she proceeds to paint until bedtime.

'You haven't made any jewellery since you arrived,' she says to me randomly one night.

'I don't have any materials.'

'So get some.'

I watch her mix purple on the paint palette. 'I'll need to raid some thrift shops.'

She looks up at me. 'I could take you on Saturday.'

'Okay. Thanks.'

And just like that I have a date with my sister.

The following Saturday, Bridget drives me around Paddington and Newstead, where I stock up on old leather belts and handbags.

On the drive home, we're stopped at a set of traffic lights when she asks, 'Have you spoken to Mum since you got here?'

'No.'

I think she's waiting for me to change my mind, to run home, to leave her. Perhaps she's waiting for me to break her heart like she did mine.

She drops me at work on the way back. James asked me to work a Saturday shift, and I didn't hesitate in saying yes. I prefer to be busy. Being idle leaves room for thinking, and I definitely don't want to do that.

The Saturday night shift turns out to be fun. The weekend staff are all around my age. Students, mostly. Plus it's busy, which makes the time fly by. When we close, everyone helps clean the place up, then settles at the bar for a drink. This is what normal people do, and I don't have to be the girl who leaves anymore.

'What'll it be?' James asks.

I think back to some of the drinks I've made tonight. 'Vodka, lime and soda. Ta.'

'Oooh, yes please,' one of the other girls says, taking the seat next to me. Mandy is twenty-one, in her final year of studying architecture, and absolutely rocks her prescription glasses.

James gets out two clean glasses and makes the drinks, dropping a short straw into each. It tastes pretty good and goes down easy. I sip away while Mandy tells me all about her Christmas plans with the boyfriend. Thankfully, she doesn't ask about my plans.

'Another?' she says when our glasses are empty.

I shake my head. 'I have to go. My sister will be wondering where I am.'

'I'll drive you,' James says, fetching his keys from the hook above the till on the other side.

I stand. 'You don't have to do that.'

'It's Saturday and close to midnight. I'll be driving you.'

I don't argue.

Saying goodbye to everyone, I pick up the handbag I scored at a thrift shop today and follow him. He holds the door open for me, and I step past him out onto the street.

As we're heading for the car park next door, I spot Hunter up ahead leaning against a ute. I know it's tragic, but I still get the same lightness in my stomach and chest that I used to get in high school. I hate that all this time has passed and that still happens. When will it stop?

Hunter moves to the middle of the footpath when he spots me, eyes on James.

'What are you doing here?' I say as we approach.

His gaze slides to meet mine. 'Bridget said you were doing a late shift, so I came to pick you up.'

James stops beside me and sizes Hunter up. 'Friend of yours?'

How to answer that? 'We went to school together.'

'Oh. Small world.'

Hunter nods slowly. 'You the owner of the pub?'

'One of them.' He extends a hand. 'James.'

Hunter stares at the hand for a long moment, then takes hold of it briefly. 'Hunter.'

'Hunter,' James repeats. 'Annie's never mentioned you.'

'Really? Because I've heard all about you.'

My cheeks are burning now. 'You can go back inside,' I say, turning to James. 'He'll give me a ride home.'

James looks uncertain. 'You sure?'

'She's sure,' Hunter replies for me.

James glances briefly in his direction before saying to me, 'Thanks for helping out tonight.'

'Any time. See you Monday.'

James smiles. It fades when he turns back to Hunter. 'Nice to meet you.'

Hunter nods once.

Only when I hear the pub door close behind me do I say, 'What was that?'

He walks over to the ute and opens the passenger door, waiting for me to get in. I hesitate, but there's no point arguing when he's in a mood. The door closes the moment I'm inside, and Hunter's scent swallows me whole. Memories pour in like floodwater. I'm eighteen again, desperate for a glimpse of him at the lockers.

The driver door opens, and Hunter climbs in. 'Couldn't find a job at a shoe shop?'

I put my seat belt on. 'I happen to like it there. Everyone's really nice.'

'Yeah. You've mentioned that.' He checks the rearview mirror before pulling out. 'Why do you want to hang around a place like that?'

'I just explained why.' I sneak a glance at him. 'Bridget says you're working as a farmhand at a cattle farm. What's your boss like?'

'Nice—for a very different reason to yours.'

'What's that supposed to mean?'

He meets my eyes briefly. 'Guys like that will 100 percent take advantage of girls like you.'

'Girls like me?'

He changes lanes. 'Naive girls.'

I lean my head back and look at the roof. 'You sound ridiculous. Jealous.'

'Of the guy who's the same age as your father?'

I shake my head and look out the window. 'I'm not fighting with you again.'

He taps the steering wheel with his thumb. 'We need to talk eventually.'

'About what?'

He breathes out. 'I'm trying here, Wilson.'

Now he's trying. 'Your efforts might be a little late. Maybe you should've tried saying goodbye before skipping town.'

He's quiet a moment. 'I'd hoped you'd understand by now why I left the way I did. It had to be that way.'

I ignore the thickening in my throat. 'I saw you on the bus. The day you left.'

He gives me a confused look.

'I shouted your name, over and over. I chased that bus down the street.' I take a moment to rein in the emotion bubbling up. 'And you didn't even look back.'

He swallows. 'I didn't see you.'

'Would it have made a difference if you had?'

There's a small pause before he says, 'No.'

We fall silent for the rest of the trip.

When he pulls up in front of the apartment building, I reach for the door handle, and he reaches for me. It's the first time he's touched me in fourteen months, and I'm anchored by it.

'If you don't want to see or talk to me anymore, that's your choice,' he says. 'You can absolutely choose that. And you can think I'm a shit son, that I was an arsehole to your boss back there. That's valid. But what you don't get to do is be pissed off at me for leaving. It was the right thing to do. Leaving you at that time was the right thing to do. Staying away, not calling, letting you get to this point on your own, was the right thing to do.'

I'm limp in my seat. 'You completely abandoned me.'

He shakes his head. 'No, I *waited* for you.'

His hand is warm on my arm, his touch painfully familiar. It would be so easy to fall into old ways. 'Please don't lie to my face. I'm not strong enough.'

He releases me. 'I came to this hot box for you. I could've gone anywhere, but I came to the one place I knew you'd come if you ever worked up the courage to leave. I've been sweating my arse off in this city for over a year, waiting for *you*.'

My chest rises and falls rapidly. These words are better than the ones I've imagined. I sit with them for a moment, unsure if I can trust them.

A knock on the window has me jumping a foot in the air. I turn to see a visibly agitated Bridget.

'I drove to your work looking for you,' she says. 'You couldn't call?' She shakes her head and walks off.

I give Hunter an apologetic look, then reach for the door. 'I have to go.'

He rubs his forehead. 'I'll call you from the road in ten minutes so we can finish this.'

'Okay.' I climb out of the ute and go after Bridget.

I find her in the bathroom brushing her teeth. Our eyes meet in the mirror.

'You need to get a phone,' she says with a mouth full of toothpaste. 'For all I knew you were lying dead on the side of the road.'

It's her way of saying she was worried. It feels sisterly. 'I'm sorry.'

She rinses, then turns to me. 'What happened between you and Hunter back home?'

I barely know where to begin. 'We had a... thing. Mum found out. Things got messy.' I lean my shoulder on the door frame. 'Between everything going on with his dad and the drama with me... I guess he reached his limit. He wrote a note to his dad and left town.'

Her expression borders on sympathetic. 'But you didn't get a note?'

I shake my head.

'But he did come to Brisbane,' she says. 'Then he tracked me down, and now I understand why. He was hoping you'd come looking for me.'

I swallow. 'He says he was waiting for me.'

Bridget laughs once. 'I suppose that depends on your definition.'

'What does that mean?'

She walks over to me. 'Hunter's a *very* straightforward individual. I'm sure he'll clarify that for you.'

As if on cue, the house phone rings. I head to the kitchen to answer it.

'Can you talk?' Hunter asks.

I lean against the wall. 'Yeah.'

My sister flashes into view before disappearing into her bedroom and closing the door. 'Can I ask you something?'

'Sure.'

I play with the phone cord. 'What did you mean before when you said you were waiting for me?'

'Exactly that. I moved north in hope that one day you'd follow. Why do you ask?'

I shake my head. 'Just something my sister said. She told me to ask you about your definition of waiting.'

A long silence follows. 'She's likely referring to waiting in the sense of not seeing other people.'

The handset slips an inch in my hand. 'Oh.'

'A few weeks back—'

'It's fine,' I say quickly. I can't hear this story. 'You don't have to explain. We weren't together. We were never together.'

He's silent.

'So, to clarify, your definition of waiting is doing whatever you want with whoever you want, like you always have—just in another city.'

He makes an exasperated noise. 'You went and got baptised, but I'm expected to live like a fucking priest?'

He's right, but it still stings. 'I have to go. I'll speak to you later.'

He exhales loudly. 'When later?'

I hang up the phone and stand there processing. Only when I'm certain I have a handle on my emotions do I go to my bedroom and close the door.

31

HUNTER

I've been in a bad mood for the past two weeks. Pete likes to point out the fact in case I'm not aware.

'Something happen with Bridget?' he asks me one afternoon.

Fairly sure he thinks we're dating even though I've told him multiple times that we're just friends. 'Nope. We're good.' And that's true. I don't blame her for looking out for her sister.

'This about your dad?' Pete asks.

I shake my head.

'What, then?'

'I don't want to talk about it.'

He chuckles. 'I don't particularly want to hear about it, but I'm sick of you slamming gates and kicking dirt.'

I release a long breath and give in to his badgering. 'Bridget has a sister, Annie.'

'There's a plot twist I didn't see coming. She up this way too?'

I nod. 'She moved up here last month.'

'Ah. She the one from back home? The reason you kicked Carly from your bed a few weeks back?'

I look away, giving him his answer.

'You two have a fight?'

'One of many.' And I haven't heard from her since.

'So call her.'

I give him a tired look. 'You think I haven't tried?' Every time I phone, she's either working or out somewhere.

'Then go see her,' Pete says. 'Clear the air in person. Kicking fence posts around this joint isn't going to fix anything.' He waves me off. 'I can finish up here.'

It's not the worst idea in the world. I'm fairly sure she doesn't work Sundays, so I take him up on the offer. 'Thanks.'

After a quick shower, I drive into the city to have another go at this.

'James took her out for lunch and sightseeing,' Bridget says to me when she opens the door. 'He wanted to thank her for working sixty hours last week.'

That guy is begging for a smack in the face. 'What's he got her working sixty hours for? Eighty percent of his patrons are in bed by eight thirty.'

She gestures for me to come in, and we take a seat on the sofa.

'And he can't leave her alone after hours?' I say.

Bridget draws her legs up and tucks them beneath her. 'Careful. You sound jealous.'

'I just don't like seeing people get taken advantage of, and she's buying into his bullshit.'

She regards me. 'So you're the only one allowed to take advantage of her. Is that it?'

It seems Annie has told her something of our history. 'I've never taken advantage of her.'

She looks somewhat amused. 'I'm sorry for throwing you under the bus the other day.'

'It was never supposed to be a secret.'

Bridget nods. 'This is all new to her. She's never had to deal with jealous feelings before.' Her mouth twitches. 'And yet she's *still* doing a better job than you.'

I don't deny it.

'How serious was it between you two?' she asks.

I've got no idea how to answer that. 'More serious than it should've been.'

Keys rattle on the other side of the door, and a moment later, Annie walks in. She freezes when she sees me.

Bridget gets to her feet. 'How was the sightseeing?'

Annie enters the room. 'It was great. We drove around, had lunch at some Japanese place. First time eating sushi. And probably the last.'

At least lunch was a bust. He was likely trying to impress her with his superior, mature palate.

I can't sit here and listen to her go on about her amazing date with her boss, whose motives are becoming very clear. Standing, I say, 'I'm going to head off.'

'You don't have to leave on my account,' Annie says.

I meet her eyes, then look away.

'Did you happen to grab the mail on your way up?' Bridget asks.

Annie shakes her head. 'I'll get it now.'

I give Bridget a look that makes it clear I know the game she's playing. 'See ya.'

She gives me a victorious smile. 'Bye.'

I hold the door open for Annie, and she walks on ahead of me. I watch her as we descend the stairs, trying to read her body language. She's easy viewing.

When we reach the bottom, she holds the door for me this time, but I grab it and gesture for her to go ahead.

'Thanks,' she mutters.

Then we're side by side, walking along the path to the mailboxes.

I have a few minutes at most to say the things I need to say. I'm just not sure what those things are.

'You should be careful with your boss.'

That certainly wasn't on the list.

Annie gives me a tired look. 'Careful of what, exactly?'

'Spending your days off with him will give him the wrong idea.'

She checks the mailbox, then straightens with a sigh. 'It's Sunday. There's no mail on Sundays.' She frowns in the direction of her apartment, then turns to me. 'And what wrong idea am I giving him?'

'That you're available to him twenty-four seven, for one.'

'Well, right now I am. Work is all I have.' She crosses her arms. 'You know, since I don't make comments on the people you see in your private life, maybe you should show me the same courtesy.'

I give her a sarcastic smile. 'The thing is, I know guys a little better than you do.'

'Oh, he's very different to the guys you're familiar with —trust me on that.'

'Because he's fifty?'

'Actually, he's forty-four.'

My eyebrows rise. 'So, more than twice your age.'

'And one of the kindest people I know.'

I snort. 'Listen, a guy that age can sniff out a virgin with daddy issues a mile away. And he'll be *so* patient.' I'm sure there was a more tactful way of saying that, but it needed to be said. I watch the shock register on her face.

'I don't think that's how he sees me at all. But good to know that's how *you* see me.'

'I think I know you pretty well.'

'No you don't.' Her glare holds heat. 'You don't know me. The girl across the creek from you was not me. She was a suppressed version of the person I'm becoming.'

We stare at each other.

'And you're making a lot of assumptions about my sex life,' she adds. 'The lines are no longer there. I *left*. Yet you assume I'm a virgin.'

It's the kick in the gut I deserve, and I know I should bow out gracefully and go home. Naturally, I don't. 'Guess we know how you got that job.'

Her entire face collapses, then hardens. 'I think it's time for you to leave.'

I turn away. 'I don't know why I bothered.' I head for the ute.

'And *you're* the cliché,' she says to my back. 'You're just an angry little boy. Well, go find another punching bag.'

Because I absolutely deserve everything she's saying, I bite my tongue and keep walking.

32

ANNIE

'Hello, stranger.'

I look up from where I'm crouched on the floor restocking one of the fridges to see an immaculately dressed and grinning Tamsin. My mouth falls open. 'Oh my goodness.' I laugh as I stand and make my way around the counter to hug her.

She squeezes me tightly, then draws back to look at me. 'Oh, you are rocking the all-black ensemble.'

'How are you this much taller than me?' I drop my gaze to her *very* high heels. 'Ah.'

She turns one foot so I can fully appreciate the shoe. 'A gift to myself for surviving first-year exams.' She lets out an enormous breath. 'It's so good to see you. I actually went to your apartment and met your very lovely yet rather suspicious of strangers sister. She gave me the address and told me you finished at eight.' She taps her watch. 'Well, look at that. It's nearly eight.'

I'm smiling as I return behind the bar to serve a

customer. 'What are you doing in Brisbane?' I ask as I pour a pint.

'Quick Gold Coast trip with the fam. Mum and Dad are having dinner with friends nearby tonight, so I thought I'd come have dinner with you.'

A regular sitting at the far end of the bar gestures to his empty glass, and I pour another. 'You might need to wait a few minutes, if that's okay?'

'Sure.' She takes a seat on one of the stools and winks at the man seated at the other end—who's approximately two hundred years old. 'You have a fine breed of clientele here.'

I suppress a smile. 'Tuesdays tend to be a little quiet.'

James appears from out back as she says that. His eyes go to Tamsin, and he raises an eyebrow at me in question.

'This is Tamsin,' I say.

He nods a greeting. 'From down south?'

'I am,' she replies coyly. The moment he looks away she pretends to fan her face.

I shake my head.

'Welcome to the sunshine state,' James says. 'What are you drinking?'

'A good white, please. And I'm not sure about this sunshine state business. It's rained every day since we arrived.'

'It's all backwards up here,' I tell her. 'You want sunshine? Come in winter.'

James places a wine glass on the bar and pours a generous amount. 'She almost sounds like a local now.'

'I *am* a local now.'

James touches a hand to my back as he steps around me. 'What are you ladies up to tonight?'

Tamsin rests her elbows on the bar. 'Dinner and hopefully more drinks.'

'There's a Mexican place a few doors up,' I say. 'Cheap food. Open late. Unlimited sangria on Tuesdays.'

Tamsin raises her glass. 'Sold.'

Twenty minutes later, I drop the 'No Service Area' sign on my end of the bar and catch James's eye to let him know I'm going.

He waves. 'Nice meeting you, Tamsin.'

'You too.' She moves close to me as we head for the door. 'Total silver fox.'

'And my boss,' I whisper.

She waits until we're outside before saying, 'I sense a pay rise coming.'

'Stop.'

'What? He's obviously into you.'

I laugh. 'And you know that how?'

'The way he put his hand on your back when he passed you earlier.'

Hunter's comments from Sunday come back to taunt me. 'It's a tight space.'

'And a classic move.'

Five minutes later, we're seated at one of the outside tables with a jug of sangria between us. Tamsin tells me all about her exams and the guy she's very casually seeing, then catches me up on Chirnside gossip, which is a short conversation, because not much happens in Chirnside.

'Have you seen Mum?' I ask, turning the straw in my drink.

She exhales. 'No, sorry. Have you tried calling her?'

I shake my head.

'You don't think she'd want to speak to you?'

This is the difficult part to explain to people. 'I'm sure she *wants* to speak with me, but she knows she shouldn't, and she'll be strongly encouraged by others not to.' I'm not sure which would be worse, no contact at all or having her coldly end the call if I tried.

Tamsin makes a frustrated noise and refills my glass. 'At least you found your sister. And she's such a sweetheart.'

'You sure you knocked on the right door?'

Tamsin laughs. 'I'm dying for all the reunion details.'

So I tell her that story, then proceed to tell her the *Hunter* story.

'I'd heard vague reports from Sammy that he was up this way,' Tamsin says, eyes wide, 'but I never connected the dots.' She presses a hand to her chest. 'It's so romantic. The Romeo and Juliet saga continues.'

I take a long drink. 'No, that saga officially ended when he told me the other day that guys like James can sniff out a virgin with daddy issues a mile away.'

She scrunches up her nose. 'Poor word choice, I admit, but it sounds like he picked up on the same vibe I did.'

'There's no *vibe*. I think you just want there to be one.'

'What I want is for you to be happy. If that means crossing a few ethical lines'—she clears her throat—'and age barriers, then so be it. I'm honestly surprised you haven't just gotten all that out of the way.' She tops up our glasses, then leans in closer. 'Your first time will likely be a bust. I mean, I had no idea what I was doing. I thought Cullum would because he was a year above us at school and had a girlfriend for two years before we were together. I was wrong.'

I drink. 'I didn't even know you were together.'

'It didn't last long—and I'm not just talking about the relationship.' She clinks her glass to mine in recognition of her joke. 'He was a nice boy. Paid for a cabin at a caravan park, lit a few candles, and asked me what I *liked*. Not enough guys do that.' She pauses to drink. 'But I didn't have an answer. I didn't know what I liked because I hadn't done it before.'

The waitress arrives with our food, and we stop talking while she arranges plates on the table. The second she leaves, Tamsin continues.

'If you want my advice, find someone who's nice, who you trust—that part's important—and with *experience*, like silver-fox boss, and get it out of the way.' She gestures to the waitress for another jug of sangria. 'Then the next time someone asks you what you like, you'll have an answer.'

We're both a little drunk at this point, so I can't tell whether that's good or terrible advice.

I think back to that afternoon in the creek with Hunter. It might have been reckless, but I absolutely trusted him.

We eat a lot of tacos and talk until our throats ache. When we're finished, we stand up to go pay and realise at the same time how incredibly drunk we are. This is a first for me. I've never felt like this before. It's funny and unsettling at the same time.

'Okay,' Tamsin says, looking both ways down the street. 'Where can we get a taxi?'

I link my arm through hers because I'm fearful of her falling in those shoes. 'There's a taxi rank just past the tavern.'

I put my head down as we pass the pub, because I'm worried someone from work will see me and I'll be forced to have a conversation in this state. Unfortunately, Tamsin chooses that location to fall over and almost pulls me to the ground with her. She's laughing, which is entirely contagious. And now I'm laughing as I try to pull her up with little success.

'Christ,' says a familiar voice.

I look in the direction of the pub and see James standing sideways locking the door. Wait. He's not sideways, I am.

'Exactly how hard did you hit the sangria?' he asks, walking over and pulling Tamsin to her feet.

I try to appear sober. 'It's possible they were stronger than we realised. Do you mind helping us get a taxi?'

He shakes his head. 'No sane taxi driver's going to take you two anywhere. Come on.' He gestures towards the car park. 'I'll drive you.'

Tamsin wraps an arm around my shoulders. 'Aww. He's such a *nice* guy.'

All I can think is *Please don't call him a silver fox to his face.* Thankfully, she stops at that, and we make it to the car without incident. Tamsin calls her mum for the address of the hotel they're having dinner at, and her dad meets us out front.

The moment Tamsin steps out of the car, she says, 'It's all Annie's fault. You know what a terrible influence she is on me.'

Her dad shakes his head. 'Likely story.'

Tamsin winks at me over her shoulder. 'See you next time.'

'I think we'll be leaving you home next time,' her dad says as he leads her inside. 'Thanks, Annie.'

'Sorry,' I call to him.

'It's not our fault,' I hear Tamsin say. 'The waitress just kept bringing them out.'

I close the car door and apologise profusely to James.

'It's fine,' he says. 'You're a well-behaved drunk. Just don't throw up in my car, and we'll finish the night friends.'

I rest my head on the window. 'Tamsin's right. You are a nice guy.' I close my eyes. 'And I trust you.'

'Don't fall asleep yet. I need an address.'

My eyes remain closed as I tell him. 'And don't worry. I'm not going to have sex with you.'

He laughs softly. 'That's good to know.'

When I open my eyes, I see that we're pulled up in front of the apartment building. I feel dizzier than I did earlier, and the feeling makes me panic a little.

'You all right?' James asks.

I nod and reach for the door.

He comes around to help me, then walks me up all six flights of stairs. He's completely out of breath by the time we reach the top, and my inability to judge the steps may be the reason for that.

'Want to come in?' I ask.

He helps me with the key. 'Not tonight.'

'Not for sex,' I clarify. 'For coffee.'

He suppresses a smile. 'I think you should save the coffee for morning and opt for a large glass of water tonight.'

I lean my head against the door. 'Am I going to be really embarrassed tomorrow?'

'Nah. You kept the sangria down and made a point of *not* propositioning me, so you're good.' He backs away to the stairs. 'See you tomorrow.'

I watch him disappear, and Hunter's words come to mind.

'He'll be so patient.'

It's quiet inside the house. The only light is the lamp in my bedroom that Bridget has left on for me. I creep into the kitchen and pull the biggest glass from the cupboard, filling it to the brim with water. After a few tentative sips, I dump the rest down the sink. As I turn to leave, I notice my sister's mobile phone charging on the bench. I tell myself to keep walking, to go to bed. But I don't listen. Instead, I reach for the phone and scroll through her list of contacts until I find Hunter. I run my thumb across his name.

'Don't you dare,' I say aloud. Then I dial his number and press the phone to my ear.

He answers after a few rings, voice groggy with sleep. 'Bridget?'

I close my eyes at the sound of his voice. It's the most soothing sound in the world in my drunken state.

'What's going on?' he asks.

I don't speak, just listen.

'Annie?'

He knows. Of course he knows. He knows me better than anyone, even though I told him that he doesn't know me at all. 'Hey.'

'Hey.'

I swallow. 'I'm sorry.'

'For what?'

'Lots of things, but mostly for getting drunk tonight.'

'Ah.'

My back slides down the wall until I'm seated on the floor. 'You were right. I'm a cliché.'

He exhales into the phone. 'You're not a cliché. I'm an arsehole.'

We're silent a moment.

'Do you need me to come over?' he asks.

I shake my head.

'Annie?'

I forgot he can't see me. 'No, don't do that. I'm fine.' I listen for noise in the background. 'Is she there with you?'

'Who?'

I'm thirsty again. 'Her. The woman you tried to tell me about.'

'No. No, she's not here.'

I lick my lips and realise they're numb.

'You still there?' he asks.

'Yeah.' I'm not ready to hang up yet. 'Can I ask you something?'

'Sure.'

My thoughts are messy. 'Do you think I should go see my dad? Will that fix some of the broken bits?'

He's silent a moment. 'I don't know. What would you say to him?'

This time when I lick my lips I taste salt. 'Why didn't you ask me to go with you when you left?'

'Wait. Are you asking your dad this question or me?'

I blink. 'Dad... I think.'

He sighs. 'Did you want to go with him?'

The fog of alcohol is making it difficult to remember. 'I don't think so. I just wanted him to ask, wanted to see his struggle.'

'Well, maybe he struggles inwardly, like his daughters.'

I close my eyes and feel the lure of sleep.

'Annie.'

'Mm?'

'I need you to go have a drink of water, then go put yourself to bed,' he says. 'Can you do that?'

I nod.

'Annie.'

'Yeah, I can do that.'

I hear him exhale again. 'Get some sleep, and I'll call you tomorrow.'

I miss you. 'Okay.'

33

HUNTER

I'm on my way to meet Pete at the shed when my phone rings. I think it's going to be Annie, phoning to apologise for drunk-dialling me last night, but instead Sammy's name flashes on the screen.

'Hey,' I say into the phone. 'This is early for you.'

'Hunter...'

When he says my name, my feet stop. My first thought is Dad's dead. It's finally happened. I knew it might happen one day. But it still hits me like a fucking tractor. 'What happened?'

Pete hears me and wanders out of the shed. He leans against the sliding door, watching me.

'There's been an accident,' Sammy says. 'Your dad was driving back from town...'

And he's dead.

'He hit a car head-on.'

And he's dead.

'Ambos took him to the hospital with head injuries and a suspected broken arm and collarbone.'

He's not dead.

The relief has me doubling over, holding on to my knee for balance.

'The driver of the other car didn't make it.'

I close my eyes, hand tightening around the phone.

He's killed someone. My dad has killed someone.

'Was he drunk?' It's such a stupid question.

There's a long pause. 'I don't have all the details.'

'Who was the other driver?'

'Don't know yet.'

I straighten, eyes meeting Pete's. 'I'll be there as soon as I can.'

Sammy exhales. 'I'm sorry, mate.'

'Appreciate the call.' I hang up and shove the phone into my pocket.

Pete wanders closer. 'News of your dad?'

I nod. 'Car accident. He's in hospital.' I bring a hand to my pounding head. 'The other driver didn't make it.'

Pete closes the distance between us and takes hold of my shoulders. 'Go pack a bag, and I'll drive you to the airport.'

'I'll be leaving you in the lurch.'

He pats my arm and lets go of me. 'My kids can make themselves useful for a while.'

My mind is pure sludge. 'I can't fly. I have to drive. I'll need transport while I'm down there.'

'You're in no state to drive eighteen hundred kilometres.'

'I'll take breaks.'

Pete doesn't look convinced. 'You'll have to stop every two hours.'

I nod. 'Okay.'

Sue comes to help me pack, ensuring I have every-thing I need for an unknown amount of time. 'Don't you come rushing back here,' she tells me. 'Stay as long as you need to. Sounds like your father's going to be out of action for a while.'

She hugs me, and I stand there, arms at my sides. I've forgotten what maternal affection feels like. She's unde-terred by my lack of response, doesn't need anything back.

When she releases me, she brings a hand to my face. 'You keep us updated with what's happening and tell us if you need something.'

I feel the rise of tears, which I immediately blink back. 'Will do.' I don't know what I've done to deserve this family, but I'm grateful.

Pete's waiting by the ute to say goodbye. There's a cooler on the floor of the passenger's seat. 'Food and drinks for all those breaks you'll be taking.'

'Thanks.'

He hugs me too, which brings me dangerously close to losing my shit in front of them. Eyes down, I climb into the ute and drive away.

The drive takes me a little over twenty-three hours. I stop every two hours because I told Pete I would. I eat the sandwiches, the muffins, the honey-roasted almonds, all made by Sue. I drink the juices and bottled water. The only time I have to open my wallet is for petrol.

In Chirnside, I drive straight to the local hospital only to be told that Dad's been transferred to Turram Hospital because he needs surgery on his collarbone. When I get to Turram, the nurse behind the desk asks me if I'm family, then proceeds to tell me that the surgery went well, and someone will collect me from the waiting room when he's awake.

An hour later, a different nurse arrives and takes me to see Dad. His eyes are closed when I step inside, head shaved on one side, revealing a line of stitches. His face is a swollen mess. My chest hurts the longer I look at him. I can't help but think about how Mum would react if she were alive. She'd be devastated seeing him like this, but she would also be at his side holding his hand.

The nurse fiddles with some of the equipment, and Dad opens his eyes. He sees me, blinks, then closes his eyes again. Tears fall down both of his cheeks.

'Don't you go feeling sorry for me,' he croaks.

I move closer to the bed. 'Were you drunk?'

He opens his eyes and stares straight ahead, giving me my answer. I can't look at him now. Not because of the injuries but because he's a selfish prick.

The nurse gives me a sympathetic look before leaving the room.

'Who told you?' Dad asks.

'Sammy.'

He looks at me. 'Where'd you come here from?'

'Brisbane.'

He tentatively raises one hand and scratches his neck. 'You didn't have to come all that way. And you're certainly not expected to stick around.'

'I disagree. You're going to need help.' I take a seat in the chair by the wall. 'Who else is going to do it?'

'I'll be remanded. Sentenced.'

'I know.' I lean forwards. 'I'm gonna help you, but I need some things from you in return.'

He looks at me, waiting.

'I'll need you to make me power of attorney so I can run the farm the way I need to.'

He nods.

'And I need to know that this is your first day of sobriety. No more. No fucking more. Not one drink. There are no second chances. I don't have it in me.'

His face collapses momentarily, and then he nods. 'I swear to you. No more.'

Sammy appears in the doorway and waits for me to wave him in. I stand, extending a hand. He takes it, then pulls me into a hug, clapping me on the back before letting go. 'You drive down?'

'Yeah.'

Sammy looks over at my father. 'Listen, I don't know if this is the right time, or if there is such a thing, but I just found out who was driving the other car and thought you'd want to know.'

My stomach braces.

'It was Maggie Phillips.'

Dad's face contorts, and he starts to cry. It's a lot seeing your broken father break a little more. I back away to the chair and fall into it.

Maggie. The woman who fitted me for school shoes every year, then every second term when they wouldn't stop growing. Kind Maggie. Annie's Maggie.

I drop my head into my hands and wonder how I'll ever be able to look at my dad the same way again.

34

ANNIE

'You bought a phone,' Bridget says when she walks into the kitchen. She flicks the kettle on, then turns to watch me slipping the back of it in place after having wrestled the SIM card in. 'That's very modern of you.'

She doesn't know the reason why I got it, because that reason is Hunter. It's been three days since I phoned him drunk, and I'm trying not to read too much into the fact that he hasn't called me back despite the multiple voice-mails I left on his phone. 'Have you heard from Hunter by any chance?'

'No. Why?'

'I've tried calling a few times. He's probably busy—or hates me.'

'He doesn't hate you.' She crosses her arms and tilts her head, regarding me. 'Is that why you bought the phone?'

'No.' The pitch of my voice is too high. I clear my

throat and hold the phone out to her. 'Do you want to put your number in and be my first official contact?'

She takes it from me, thumbs moving over the buttons. Then she pulls her mobile phone from her pocket. 'I'll put Hunter and Dad in too.'

'Didn't think you spoke to Dad.'

'I don't, but that doesn't mean you shouldn't.' I have questions about that, but I don't want her to shut down the conversation.

I pull my purse from my bag and wander over to the sofa, adding Tamsin's number, work, and James's mobile. Opening a fresh text message, I think hard about what I want to say to Hunter since speaking on the phone is apparently not an option.

Annie: Hey, it's Annie. Sorry about the other night. Oh, and I got a mobile phone. In case you want to save my number.

I delete the message and type something else. Then I delete that and stare at the blinking cursor.

'Just call him,' Bridget says from the kitchen. 'He won't know it's you, and if he answers, then you'll know he's been avoiding you.'

'And what do I say if it turns out that he *was* avoiding me?'

She pours boiling water into the plunger. 'That guy moved to Brisbane on the slight chance you would one day. He's not going to be that easily deterred.'

I dial his number. It goes to voicemail, and I panic.

'Hi.' I look at my sister, and she gestures for me to keep going. 'I got a new phone, and I'm calling from it.' I press my palm to my forehead. 'And now you have my number.' I drop my hand to my lap and look at the ceiling. 'In case you didn't get my other voicemails, I need to talk to you.' I give my sister an exasperated look, and she signals for me to wrap it up. 'Give me a call back on this number. Only if you want to.' I press my eyes shut. 'It's Annie, by the way.' I end the call and drop the device onto the sofa.

Bridget's laughing in the kitchen. *Laughing*. It's the first time I've heard her laugh since I got here. The embarrassment was worth it for that reason alone.

'Smooth,' she says.

I drop my face to the cushion and groan into it.

———

Our work Christmas party is on a Friday. James has closed the tavern and organised an afternoon of lawn bowling at a nearby club. It's stormy and so humid that even the locals are complaining, but everyone's in good spirits because the beer's cold and our shoes are off.

I'm seated with Mandy at one of the outdoor tables in the shade, a pot of beer warming in my hand. I drink slowly because I haven't really recovered from Tuesday's festival of sangria.

James looks in my direction, declines the next game, then comes to sit beside me. Mandy goes to take his place.

'That the same beer I brought you earlier?' he asks.

I look down at it. 'Is three days the normal amount of time for a hangover?'

'It is when you get to my age. You should be bouncing back after a hot shower and a greasy breakfast.'

'I didn't know about the greasy breakfast. That's clearly where I went wrong.'

He grins. 'There's always next time.' His gaze falls to my phone on the table beside me. 'Expecting a call? You've been checking that thing every five minutes since we arrived.'

That's embarrassingly true. I haven't heard a word from Hunter since Tuesday night, and I've been over and over the things I think I said and can't pinpoint anything that would provoke such a drastic reaction. If he's angry at me or over me, I'm sure he'd tell me as much.

I turn to James, giving him my full attention. 'Are you heading to Kingscliff tomorrow to see your kids?'

'Sure am. I'm going easy too. I need to be able to drive in the morning.'

I rest an arm on the table. 'Plus you wouldn't want to embarrass yourself in front of your employees.'

He laughs. 'We couldn't have that.'

'Thank you for being so kind and patient the other day.'

His eyes move over my face. 'You're very welcome. Honestly, you've been such a breath of fresh air around the place.'

I can see he means that.

My phone rings, and I look down at Hunter's flashing name. I shoot up and step away from the table.

'Hey.'

'Hey,' he replies.

He sounds different. Tired, maybe.

'I've been trying to reach you. Is everything okay?'

There's a long pause—much too long.

'Not really.'

I wander farther away from the noise, blocking my other ear to hear him better. 'Where are you?'

'Chirnside.'

I think I misheard him. 'Did you say Chirnside?'

'Yes.'

'Is your dad okay?'

There's a long silence. 'He was in an accident, but he'll live.' He pauses. 'The person driving the other car didn't survive.'

I press my eyes shut. 'Had your dad been drinking?'

'Yes. Annie... the driver of the other car was Maggie Phillips.'

I suck in a breath and slap a hand over my mouth. *Maggie.* Big-hearted Maggie. Dead. And Kevin Reed killed her.

How do I process that?

'I'm sorry,' Hunter says, like it's his fault.

I peel my hand from my mouth. 'Are you okay?'

'Well, I'm neck deep in sheep and debt, waiting for my dad to leave hospital so he can be remanded. So...'

My heart squeezes. 'I'll fly down.'

'Don't you dare.' His response is immediate and firm. 'You just got out of this place. You're free.' He pauses. 'Honestly, the best thing you can do right now is lose my number.'

I wasn't expecting that. 'What? Why would I lose your number?'

'Because I'm gonna be stuck here for some time. I'm stuck here, in your past, and I want you to focus on your future. Go make a life, Wilson. And make it a good one.' He doesn't say goodbye. He simply hangs up.

I call him back, but it goes straight to voicemail. My hand falls to my side, and the phone slips from my fingers.

James rushes over, picking my phone up and moving to stand in front of me. 'What's going on? You okay?'

I open my mouth to speak, but no words are coming out. I've just lost Maggie and Hunter in one phone call. Hunter for the second time.

'Wait here,' James says. 'I'll grab our shoes and let the others know I'm taking you home.'

When he returns, he takes me by the arm and guides me through the clubhouse, saying to the guy behind the bar, 'Can you phone a taxi for James please?'

We wait near the entrance for the taxi to arrive and then climb into the back seat. I stare out the window, and James watches me with a concerned expression. He pays the driver, then takes my hand, helping me out of the taxi. He keeps hold of it the entire walk up. There's comfort in that, and I'll take any comfort I can get right now.

James fishes keys out of my pocket and opens the door. After placing me on the sofa, he goes to open the terrace doors because it's a billion degrees in here. Then he sits beside me. 'You don't have to tell me anything. I'm just going to stay here with you until I know you're all right.'

That sentiment is everything. It's exactly what my dad should have said the day he announced he was moving out. It's what my sister should have said before she left and Hunter before he boarded that bus. It's what my mum should have said the day we stood beneath the veranda, hearts breaking, instead of telling me to make my own way to the bus stop because dinner wasn't going to cook itself.

I bet she didn't even eat dinner that night.

Self-pity is swallowing me whole. I shuffle closer to James, who opens his arms to me. I sink into the comfort so generously offered, my full weight against him. He rubs slow, soothing circles on my back. My eyes sink shut at the sensation. Whatever comfort he's willing to hand out, I'll take it.

This continues for a few minutes. I look up when his hand stops, and for the first time, I see it.

Desire.

He brushes his thumb across my cheek, then looks unashamedly at my mouth.

I hear Hunter's voice in my head.

'Where's the line, Wilson?'

I don't know. I don't know where it is now, or if we've crossed it already, or whether I led him to this point. It's likely I did. And he's given me so much since I arrived here that giving him this small thing feels like the least I can do. He doesn't push me away or shut me out. He's consistent and steady and trustworthy.

'And patient,' I hear Hunter say.

So what? I've been told my whole life that patience is a virtue.

He dips his head slightly, like he's asking me a question, and I respond by kissing him.

There. That was easy.

Except I feel nothing. There's no excitement or heat, only a screaming mind and recoiling heart. But I push through it, deepening the kiss to see if that helps. It doesn't. And he reads it as excitement, as any man would. He lays me back on the sofa, his unfamiliar hands moving over my body. The safe feeling has dissipated, and now every part of me is retreating from every part of him.

My body's not fooled.

This isn't Hunter.

'I've waited so long to taste you,' James whispers into my mouth.

His words make it worse. Dirty, even. And when his hand ventures beneath my skirt, I know I need to stop. I prepare myself for the fallout. The comfort will be withdrawn. James will leave, and I'll be alone again.

Breaking the kiss, I shuffle back until his hands fall away. 'I'm so sorry. I can't do this—not today.'

Not ever.

He sits up, taking a few deep breaths.

'I'm sorry,' I say again.

'Don't apologise. It's all good. Just bad timing. I shouldn't have gone there knowing the headspace you were in when we arrived.' He's embarrassed.

I want to tell him that yes, it's simply a timing thing, that another day would be better. But I don't want to kiss him another day. I don't want him to taste me. It's not even his age or the fact that he's my boss. It's because he's not Hunter.

'Are you going to be okay if I leave?' he says, standing.

This is what I was afraid of. I've ruined things between us. 'I really am sorry.'

He forces a smile. 'It's not a big deal. Just rest up.' He hesitates. 'You know not to mention this to anyone, right? You're an employee—'

'Of course. I won't say anything.'

He nods, then leaves the apartment. The second the door clicks shut, I curl up into a ball on the sofa and do something I haven't done in a long time.

I pray.

35

ANNIE

I front up to work the following day thinking it's going to be fine because James is spending the weekend with his kids. Except he's not with his kids. He's waiting for me.

He gestures for me to follow him out back. We pass through the kitchen and step outside into the heat.

'How are you doing today?' he asks. 'I know yesterday was a mess... for a few reasons.'

I owe him an explanation. 'The lady I used to work for, Maggie, died in a car accident. That was the phone call I got at the Christmas party yesterday.' The news broke me, and then Hunter finished me.

James looks genuinely sympathetic. Of course he does. He's a good person who deserves better than me. 'I'm so sorry for your loss.' He rubs my arm. 'Let me take you out for dinner after work. We'll get some food, and you can tell me funny stories from your time working with her. Not everyone realises this, but humour and grief pair perfectly.'

It's tempting. I'd love to talk about Maggie, laugh and cry about her. And James would be an attentive audience. But I'd be misleading him—using him. I don't want a relationship with him, and he needs to know that.

The back door opens, prompting James's hand to fall away. A woman I don't recognise steps outside.

'Claire,' James says, taking a large step back.

She smiles at him, and then her eyes go to me. I mean, she *really* looks at me.

'What are you doing here?' James asks.

Claire tucks her dark hair behind one ear. 'We thought we'd surprise you, since you weren't able to make it home this weekend.' She smiles at me. 'Christmas is such a busy time.'

This must be James's ex-wife.

'I told you I'd drive down tomorrow,' he says, walking over to her.

Claire's still looking at me. 'You must be the new girl he's been so busy training.'

An uneasy feeling settles in my stomach. 'Annie.'

'Annie,' she echoes. 'Pretty name for a pretty girl.'

'Where are the kids?' James asks, taking a step towards the door.

She catches his hand and pulls him to her. 'In the kitchen with Craig.' She wraps her arms around his middle. 'Don't you have a kiss for your wife?'

He dips his head and kisses her awkwardly on the cheek. Then she kisses him on the *lips*.

Oh no. No, no, no, no.

She looks over at me. 'Would you mind organising

some drinks for us? The kids will be thirsty after the car ride.'

My eyes flick to James, who's a picture of guilt. 'Of course.' I head for the door, embarrassment and anger warring inside me.

He's not divorced. He's married. And a liar.

'I like my sav blanc with a few ice cubes in it, Annie,' Claire calls to me as I open the door.

She knows. She *knows*. Maybe not everything, but she came here looking for answers as to why her husband's been absent lately—and I think she found them.

There are two teenagers in the kitchen when I enter, chatting away with Craig. One of them is just three years younger than me. Knowing that in your head is different to seeing it in real life.

Mandy's pouring beers when I enter the bar area. I grab a wine glass and a fresh bottle of sav blanc from the fridge.

'You okay?' Mandy asks when I step up beside her for ice.

I nod absently as I pour the wine. 'Yes.'

Now what? Does Claire expect me to take it to her outside? Does James expect that? I stare down at the glass in my hand, unsure what to do.

I jump when James appears next to me, white wine splashing over my hand. He takes the glass from me and hands me a tea towel. I look into his shame-filled eyes, then to the door behind him, where Claire stands watching us.

'Everything okay?' she asks.

I can't do this. I really can't do this. Yesterday he told me he had waited so long to taste me. Now I'm serving his wife drinks.

I walk over to my bag, snatch it up, and leave.

'Annie,' James says.

I don't stop or even look back. Yanking the door open, I step out onto the street. The heat swallows me.

I hear the door open and close behind me, then footsteps coming at a jog.

'Annie.'

I pick up my pace.

'Will you just stop and listen?'

'Why? So you can lie some more?'

He steps in front of me, forcing me to pull up. 'We've been on and off for years, living apart for most of that time.'

'You told me you were *divorced*.'

'Because in my mind the marriage is over. We just haven't had the courage to break our kids' hearts yet.'

I search his eyes. 'So she would be okay with what happened between us yesterday?'

He closes his eyes and pinches the bridge of his nose. 'You can't possibly understand how complicated these things are. Not at your age.'

'I think I understand just fine.' I step past him. 'I'm going home.'

'It'll look very suspicious if you don't come back.'

I shake my head. 'That's not my problem.'

———

Bridget gets home from her Christmas fundraiser at a gallery a little after ten o'clock. I'm seated on the couch staring at the TV, which is turned off.

My sister looks between me and the black screen. 'Good show?'

When I don't reply, she sits on the sofa, studying me. 'Have you been crying?'

It's obvious I have. 'Yeah.'

Most sisters would shuffle over and offer some comfort in this situation, but Bridget prefers to do comfort from a safe distance.

'What's going on?'

'Besides Maggie dying, Hunter telling me to lose his number, and making out with my boss last night, today I found out he's still married.'

Bridget's eyes widen. 'You're kidding.'

'His wife came to visit him at work today.'

She sighs. 'What a jerk.'

I blink and tears fall down my face.

'Do you think she knows?'

'Without a doubt.'

Bridget crosses her arms. 'At least you found out before things went any further.'

I look over at her. 'Why do you always sit so far away from me? What do you think will happen if we acciden-tally touch?'

She shifts in her seat. 'I don't always sit far away from you.'

'Yes you do. You do it in the kitchen too. If I'm at the sink, you'll wait by the fridge. Will you combust into flames if our arms brush as you're getting a glass of water?'

She blinks. 'Don't lash out at me because you're angry at them.'

'It's a genuine question.' I turn to face her properly. 'Your sister's sitting before you in tears, and you're ensuring there's three feet between us at all times.'

She stares at me, not speaking.

I start to cry again. 'What did I do?'

Nothing.

I turn to her. 'What did *I* do? I didn't move out. I didn't leave. *You* did that.'

Her eyes turn shiny. 'I had to.'

'I know why you left the religion, the town, our home, your horse, Mum. I just can't for the life of me figure out what *I* did wrong.'

Bridget stands up. 'Well, you're not exactly the world's most affectionate sister either.'

'Travelling to Brisbane and sifting the city to find you wasn't enough of a gesture?'

She looks so wounded. 'Stop.'

I swallow and drop my head into my hands. 'I'm sorry.'

Bridget watches me a moment, then slowly returns to her end of the sofa, picking up the TV remote. 'Do you want to watch a Christmas movie? They're supposed to cheer people up.'

I look up, nodding. 'Okay.'

She flicks through the channels until she finds one, then reaches for her handbag, pulling out a large bottle wrapped with cellophane and ribbon. 'Someone gave me a bottle of Baileys at the party tonight. Want some?'

I nod. 'I'll get the ice.'

We sit with five feet and a bottle of Baileys between us, watching *Jingle All the Way*. As it's coming to an end, my phone rings. Tamsin's name glows on the screen. I pick it up and wander out to the terrace in hope of a breeze, but everything's still.

'Hey,' I say.

'Hey.' She sounds flat. 'I'm going to assume you know about Maggie.'

'Yeah.' I glance back at my sister, who's now tidying up. 'Hunter told me... right before he cut me from his life for a second time.'

Tamsin sighs. 'He's not in a good way. Probably doesn't help that his dad's the most hated man in Chirnside right now. His injuries haven't won him much sympathy.'

The tinkle of dishes drifts out through the open door.

'I just spoke to Sammy,' she continues. 'He was on his way to collect Hunter from the police station. Apparently he punched Keith from the service station in the face and broke his nose.'

I close my eyes. 'Why?'

'Keith is best mates with Maggie's husband, so he refused to serve him. Thankfully no charges were filed.'

'Wow,' I deadpan. 'Things are really looking up for the Reed family.'

Tamsin laughs, but it dies quickly. 'Yeah.'

I hate that Hunter's getting into fights again. It says a

lot about his mental state right now. 'It's ridiculous that Keith would refuse him service when he was in Brisbane at the time of the accident.'

She sighs. 'Apparently Keith told Hunter that if he'd stayed on the farm like he was supposed to, then Kevin wouldn't have driven drunk.'

'That'll do it.'

'We're flying back early for Maggie's funeral. If you can get some time off, you could travel with us.'

I'm supposed to be working every day until New Year's, but I know that today marks the end of James and the Imperial Tavern. I can't go back there now. 'It just so happens that I have some time off.'

'Really?' Tamsin asks, surprised. 'You don't even have to see your mum if you don't want. You can just hide away with us.'

We finalise our plans, and when I hang up, I turn and find Bridget standing at the terrace doors. I can tell by her expression that she overheard.

'You're going back there?' she asks.

I nod.

'Oh.' She hugs herself as though it's cold. 'When will you be back?'

I think of everything Hunter is going through and has ahead of him. 'I don't know.'

She nods and looks away. 'I guess you won't be returning to work, so you've all the freedom in the world.'

'I'll be coming back. I just can't tell you when.'

She steps back from the doors. 'Make sure you say bye before you leave.' Then she walks off to her bedroom.

A moment later, I hear the door click closed. She thinks if I go home, I'll never come back, like you only get one chance to escape. She thinks I'm abandoning her, but I'm not. I'll come back. And maybe when I do, she'll pull me into her arms and finally hug me.

36

HUNTER

I'm sitting on the veranda flicking through the classifieds in the local paper when I hear a car coming up the driveway. I assume it's Sammy, because he's the only one brave enough to be seen on our property, but then Tamsin's Rav 4 appears. Rising, I wander over the steps and lean against the post. I'm really not in the mood for visitors.

The car rolls to a stop in front of the shed, and I glimpse Tamsin through the tinted glass. She waves but doesn't turn the engine off or make any move to get out. Instead, the passenger door opens, and Annie steps out of the car.

Annie.

Her eyes meet mine as she walks to the boot and proceeds to pull out a suitcase.

'Call me,' Tamsin tells her through the window before putting the car into reverse.

Annie nods, then turns to me. She's wearing knee-length denim shorts and a white Sportsgirl T-shirt. Her hair's in a messy bun, and she's makeup free, which means all those delicious freckles are on display. She walks slowly towards me, eyes narrowing on the bruise beneath my eye. I let Keith get one in, because he really needed it.

She stops at the bottom of the steps and says, 'Good afternoon. My name is Annie, and we're just calling around to people in your neighbourhood asking them the question, is violence really the answer?'

My lips twitch. 'Where's your leaflet?'

She pretends to hold one out. 'Jehovah tells us in Proverbs 22:24, "Do not keep company with a hot-tempered man or get involved with one disposed to rage."'

'Is that a real scripture?'

'Of course.'

I shake my head. 'How the hell do you still remember that?'

'I'm sure if you spent nineteen years dissecting the Bible, you would pick up a few verses too.'

I drink in the sight of her. 'What are you doing here, Wilson?'

She lets go of her suitcase and climbs the steps until she's standing on the one below me. Reaching up, she touches the colourful mark on my face. 'Can't believe someone finally got you.'

I catch her wrist. 'I said, what are you doing here?'

She doesn't try to pull her hand free. 'I came for Maggie's funeral, and I'm staying to help you.'

'With what?' My tone is sharper than it should be.

'With whatever you need.'

My fingers relax around her. 'What I need is for you to fly home after Maggie's funeral.'

Very slowly, she steps up onto the veranda beside me and threads her fingers through mine. 'I know your fight-or-flight response is in full swing right now, but I refuse to fight with you. And if you run, I'll chase you.'

I don't want her in this town or anywhere near my mess, but I also don't have the strength right now to push her away. Annie Wilson is the epitome of comfort, from her homely scent to her PG-rated humour. So instead of pushing her away, I pull her to me and bury my face in her neck. Her arms go around me, and I breathe her in. Minutes go by, and I feel my mind growing quieter with each one that passes. Finally, I draw back to look at her, and I see tears on her cheeks.

'What's wrong?' I ask her.

She wipes her face. 'I think people with pain recognise people with pain. That's always been our draw.' Her fingers go to my bruise again. 'Let me stay. Let me help.'

I have to look away. I'm so undeserving of the kindness and devotion she's extending to me. 'Your mum know you're here?'

She shakes her head. 'Not yet.'

'This town's swarming with J-dubs armed with crosses and garlic. Are you really up for that?'

'I think you're confusing Witnesses with vampire slayers. They don't own crosses because they believe Jesus died on a stake.' She pauses to think. 'Garlic might be effective, though.'

I drop my mouth to hers. She tastes like lemonade

and bad jokes. I've forgotten how well our mouths fit together, and our hands. And our hearts.

She doesn't hesitate in kissing me back. She's not shy or cautious. Her mouth seeks mine the same as it did a year earlier when we were submerged in that creek making bodily promises we couldn't keep.

One minute we're kissing on the veranda and the next stumbling through the front door. I lose contact with her while we're moving, so I pick her up and press her against the entrance wall to re-establish our connection. I swallow her inhale, pulling her legs up until I feel them tighten around me. Only then do I carry her to the bedroom, wondering where the line sits today. I lay her on my bed, tasting her neck and collarbone and rubbing my face against her skin until I'm marked with her scent.

Tugging up her T-shirt, I whisper against her stomach, 'Tell me when to stop.'

She takes hold of my head and pulls me up until I'm eye level with her. 'No more lines,' she whispers. 'No more rules or sneaking around.' Her eyes well up. 'No more guilt.'

I search her face for any hints of hesitation but find none. 'You're sure?'

She nods.

I kiss her, and I mean really kiss her. I kiss her until we're both barely breathing. I sit her up and lift her T-shirt over her head. She's wearing a green cotton bra, and she's perfection in it. I spend a full minute drinking in the sight of her, brushing my fingers over her skin. There's no rush. I want to appreciate every second.

'I lied to you,' she says.

I lift her onto my lap and reach back to undo her bra. 'What about?' I'm confident I'll forgive her for anything at this point.

'There wasn't another time.' She swallows. 'There wasn't anyone else.'

It takes me a moment to get what she's saying. I drop my head to her shoulder. 'Shit.'

She lifts my head. 'Don't say that.'

'You don't want your first time to be in this depressing house, inside this bland room.'

She looks around as though noticing where we are for the first time. 'Don't tell me what I want. I don't need a fancy setting. I just need it to be with you.'

And I need her to feel safe, desired, and thoroughly pleasured. So I make it my personal mission to ensure she gets all those things from me. In some ways it feels like my first time too. First time transfixed. First time *making love*.

It's two hours of exploration, learning, and restraint. When it's time to put on protection, Annie watches like an eager student, asking questions that most women her age know the answer to. I take it so slow, even when she demands more of me. I watch her face carefully the whole time, stopping at any hint of discomfort. But each time she brings me back.

'I want this,' she assures me. 'I want you.'

So I take what I don't deserve.

Afterwards, I lie on my back staring up at the fan. Annie's curled against me, her head resting on my shoulder and eyes closed. I'm afraid to move because it's been a long time since I've felt this good. I turn my head, lips brushing her hair. 'No regrets?'

'No regrets,' she murmurs.

I draw her closer even though she can't get any closer. 'I'm glad you came.'

She blinks up at me. 'To Chirnside? Or in your bed?'

'Both.'

A smile spreads across her face. 'Me too.'

'Do you want a shower while I attempt to cook for you?'

She nods. 'Okay.'

But then neither of us moves.

'Dad'll be going to prison,' I tell her. 'He's going to plead guilty, and they'll sentence him. I'm going to stay in Chirnside and run the farm while he's gone. I phoned Pete today to let him know.'

She doesn't reply.

'You have to go back after the funeral.'

She props herself up on one elbow. 'Let me at least stay until your dad's sentenced. Then we'll go from there.'

'What about work? And Bridget?'

'My sister's not going anywhere.'

The fact that she only answers the second question has me sitting up also. 'And what about work?'

'I'm going to look for another job when I get back.' She doesn't meet my eyes when she says this.

'Why? What happened?'

She drops her head to my shoulder, kissing it. 'Let's just say that you were right, and I learned a valuable lesson.'

Fucking James. 'Do I need to fly to Brisbane and break his face?'

I'm rewarded with the smallest of smiles from her. 'While I appreciate the offer, I've already handled it. I phoned him from the airport to tell him I won't be coming back.' She reaches up to touch my lips. 'I love you.'

The words make me feel hot and shaky. A response swirls inside me, words I haven't said in years. The last words Mum heard me say. Instead, I say, 'I'm sorry.'

Annie nods. 'It's okay. They're just words.'

I press my forehead to hers and close my eyes. 'We might be waiting months for the hearing.'

She strokes the back of my hair. 'Then I guess you're stuck with me for a while.'

37

ANNIE

It takes me three days to work up the courage to go see my mum. Three days of wondering what to say, of preparing myself for a reaction I can't predict. Tears? Door slammed in my face? Pleading me to return to Jehovah and beg for his forgiveness? I can't stay across the creek from her, potentially for weeks on end, and not tell her. So the day after Maggie's funeral, I go to the house.

'You sure you don't want me to come with you?' Hunter asks when he pulls the ute over at the top of the driveway.

He'd never admit it, but I think he's afraid I won't come back. And I don't blame him. Two months ago, I got baptised. Two months ago, I was all-in with the organisation—except I wasn't. That's what he needs to understand. The temptation to return will always be there, but my desire to live life on my own terms wins every time.

'I'll be fine,' I tell him. 'I'll meet you at the hospital.'

His dad has been transferred back to Chirnside,

making visitation easier. On Thursday he'll be released, remanded, plead guilty, and a court date will be set. And then we don't know.

We look at each other for a long moment, acknowledging the sinking ship we find ourselves on. At least we have each other—for now.

I watch Hunter in the side-view mirror as he pulls away, then head for the house.

Banjo jumps off his bed the second he sees me. He doesn't recognise me, so he trots around in circles barking at me. But then I whistle. I whistle *his* whistle, and straight away his ears go back and his entire rear end starts to wag. He runs over, and I crouch down, attempting to cuddle him while he cries and headbutts me repeatedly in the face.

'I've missed you too.'

I look around and see Mum's car isn't here. She's likely still at work. I feel like an intruder, but that doesn't stop me from heading out back to see Charlie. His rug hangs over the fence, and he's standing in the shade. Even though I'm sure Mum has complained every day about having to care for him, she's doing a great job.

Half an hour later, Mum pulls into the driveway. I'm seated on Banjo's bed, the dog on top of me. She watches me through the window for a moment, unsmiling, before climbing out of the car.

'I'd heard rumours you were in town,' she says, walking over.

Banjo runs to greet her, so I take the opportunity to stand up. 'I wanted to go to Maggie's funeral.'

She sighs. 'So very sad. I prayed for her when I heard.' There's a pause. 'Where are you staying?'

'With Hunter.'

Her nostrils flare slightly, and she slowly shakes her head. 'His father is the reason Maggie's dead, you know.'

'And Kevin's living the consequences. Hunter's here trying to clean up the mess he's left and keep a hold of the farm.'

She regards me a moment. 'I really hope that boy's not the reason you threw away your chance at everlasting life.'

I'm tired of this conversation already and it's only just begun. 'I wanted to say hello and see how you're doing. I hope that's okay.'

She looks me over again. 'You're tanned.'

'Yeah.'

'Did you find her?'

Not Bridget, 'her'. The fact that she still can't say her name aloud speaks volumes. I nod, unsure if she wants details. By the look on her face, I think it might be too painful for her.

'She's well' is all I say. It's up to her now if she wants any more information than that.

She glances over her shoulder. 'Sister Jane's popping over shortly. Dropping off that bundt tin she borrowed back in June.'

It seems I'm not receiving an invitation inside today. 'Great. You can make your famous upside-down pineapple cake.'

She nods. 'I suppose I can freeze it in portions.'

That hits me in the heart. Cake for one. I know she'd

give anything to feed her daughters cake again. Anything except her beliefs. 'Well, I'll let you go get changed.'

I'm waiting for her to insist I come in, ask questions and hear all my news. Instead, I'm met with silence.

'I'll be across the creek if you need to get in touch,' I say. 'I have a mobile phone now if you'd like the number? In case of an emergency.' *Or a change of heart.*

She's hating this moment as much as I am. I can see the pain in her eyes pushing outwards. 'I suppose it would be good to pass on to your father. He keeps calling me.'

That's sensible—and hurtful.

She pulls a pad and pen out of her handbag and closes the distance between us, looking away as she hands it to me. I scrawl my number on it and hand it back to her.

'I'll keep praying for you,' she says to the ground between us.

Am I supposed to thank her or tell her to stop? This grief is so senseless.

'Okay.' My eyes go to Banjo. 'See you, boy.'

His whining follows me up the driveway.

———

I walk to the hospital, grateful for the chance to clear my head and calm myself. At least it's out of the way and I don't have to worry about an awkward first encounter in public.

When I arrive at the hospital, thirsty and slightly

sunburned, I grab a drink from the water fountain and head to reception to find out which room Kevin's in.

'All the way to the end of the corridor, left, then second door on the right,' the woman tells me.

I'm not really sure how I feel about seeing him. Am I angry? Empathetic? I don't think it matters. Kevin's self-loathing will be darker than any shade others will throw his way.

As I'm walking down the corridor, my gaze drifts to the open doors. Faces flash in and out of view. And as I pass room 36B, I glimpse a familiar face that makes me stop.

It's Sister Maria.

As I'm debating whether to acknowledge the fact that we just made eye contact through the open door, I hear, 'Sister Annie?'

My pulse quickens as I peer around the edge of the door, waiting to see what she'll do next.

A smile spreads across her face. 'I thought it was you.'

I step into the room but stay close to the door. 'Hi.'

'You're back.'

Oh no. She thinks I'm *back* back. 'Not permanently. I just came down for Maggie's funeral.'

Her smile fades. 'Such a tragedy. I was so sad to hear that you've become inactive.'

I shake my head. 'Not inactive, disassociated. I left.'

Her face falls. 'Oh. I've missed a lot of meetings of late.'

This is incredibly awkward now, because she's just realised that she's supposed to be shunning me.

'Well,' she says, 'just remember that Jehovah loves all his children.'

I wet my lips. 'I'm sorry to see you in here. I hope it's nothing too serious.'

She touches the back of her head. 'I had a bad episode and ended up needing stitches.'

'Must have been quite a knock.'

Her hand falls to her lap. 'It's a good thing. They did a scan, just to be safe, and they found a low-grade glioma.'

My lungs squeeze. 'You mean like a brain tumour?'

'A slow-growing tumour, so that's positive.'

I think back to how many seizures this woman has had that were labelled as demonic attacks, cared for by people with no medical knowledge whatsoever. 'I'm very sorry to hear that.'

She gives me a weak smile. 'Nothing some prayer and radiation won't fix.'

I'm relieved she included radiation in that sentence. 'Lucky they did the scan.'

She nods enthusiastically. 'Jehovah always takes care of his flock.'

The doctors get no mention.

She settles back on her pillow. 'You know, it's no coincidence us running into each other. Something tells me we'll be seeing you back in the Kingdom Hall very soon.'

I don't have the heart to contradict her, so I tell her to take care, then flee the room.

As I round the door, I collide with someone. 'Sorry,' I say, looking up. I freeze when my eyes meet Brother Oliver's.

'Annie,' he says, just as taken aback as I am. 'What are you doing here?'

Flustered, I look behind me. 'I was passing by and happened to see Sister Maria...' Or is it just Maria now? My departure means she's no longer my sister.

I'm so hot suddenly.

'I wasn't aware that you'd returned.'

I shake my head. 'I haven't, really. I came down for a funeral.' And I'm sexually active and living in sin. 'I'll let you go in.'

When I go to step around him, his hand lands on my arm.

'It might be a good idea for us to sit down and have a proper talk while you're down. We didn't get the opportunity before you left. Is that something you would be willing to do?'

Is it? I'm shaking my head, but I'm having some difficulty telling him no. 'I'm sure Mum can answer all your questions.'

His hand falls away, likely burned by the devil within me. 'Such a shame. It's always sad when someone in the congregation steps out from Jehovah's protection.'

'Annie.'

I jump at my name from Hunter's lips. He's standing a few metres away, glaring at the man in front of me. Brother Oliver looks in his direction also.

'Everything all right?' Hunter asks.

I give him a reassuring smile. 'Yeah. I was just saying goodbye.' I start backing away. 'I really hope Sister Maria's treatment goes well.'

He searches my eyes. 'Can I leave you with one thought?'

I'm dreading it already, and the fact that Hunter's listening makes me dread it all the more.

'Flee from fornication,' Brother Oliver says. 'The Bible puts it as simply as that. For no fornicator has any inheritance in the kingdom of Christ and of God.'

Hunter closes the distance between us and pulls me behind him. 'Does the Bible say anything about being a judgemental prick?'

I press my eyes shut, because I absolutely don't want to see the expression on Brother Oliver's face right now. 'Let's go,' I say.

Hunter ushers me to safety. When we round the corner, he stops and faces me. 'Don't let him get in your head. No more guilt, remember?'

I look up at him. 'I remember.'

He pulls me to his chest in what's officially our first display of public affection. Not the most romantic setting, or circumstances, but a milestone nonetheless.

'It's only fornication if it's with someone other than me,' he says, lightening the mood.

I smile. 'Is that right?'

'Absolutely.' He releases me. 'You should've called. I would've picked you up.'

'I needed the walk.'

His eyes move between mine. 'No good with your mum?'

I shake my head.

'Let's get out of here,' he says, looking both ways down the corridor.

'But I haven't seen your dad.'

He looks back at me. 'Not even the doctors want to see him.'

I get it. Maggie's funeral was yesterday, and many of them attended.

'You forget that I was raised on a diet of forgiveness.'

'Within a religion that shuns people who make mistakes?'

'Exactly.'

He drapes an arm around my shoulders as we head off down the corridor. 'Stay close, and watch out for J-dubs armed with garlic.'

38

HUNTER

Dad's taken from the hospital to the courthouse, where he pleads guilty to culpable driving causing death. He's remanded into custody, and a court date is set for February.

It's crazy that one of the darkest times in my life is coinciding with one of the happiest. Dad's locked in a prison while I'm playing house with the best thing that's ever happened to me.

Annie helps me with farm work since the farmhand quit the day after the accident. The money I save keeps us fed and goes towards Dad's legal fees. I doubt there's a person in the district who would put their hand up for the job now anyway. Lucky for me, Annie's the best farm-hand I could ask for.

On Christmas Day, we skip all the festive crap that I don't like and she doesn't understand and head to the waterfalls outside Turram. We swim in the waterhole, and Annie squeals every time something brushes her leg. Turns out she doesn't like eels, and to her, everything she can't see below the surface is 100 percent an eel.

After a swim, we lie on the mossy rocks next to the running water and let the sound drown out the noise in our heads. We eat sandwiches and plums we picked from a tree on the side of the road on the way here, washing it down with Four X beer to remind ourselves that we're Queenslanders.

It doesn't really matter that neither of us likes it.

Over the New Year period, I also teach her how to surf, ride a motorbike solo, tie a farmer's loop knot, use a nail gun, and drench a sheep. She helps me with the accounting stuff and comes with me to the bank. She teaches me how to cook scrambled eggs that don't taste like rubber and ways to make the food money stretch further than it should.

We keep grocery shopping to once a week because people in Chirnside have a habit of treating us like lepers. The J-dubs cross to snub Annie, and the rest cross to avoid me. It doesn't bother me like it does her. She tries to let go of my hand when she sees someone from her old congregation coming, and I hold on a little tighter. I've waited too long for the privilege, and I'm not letting go before I have to.

I hate that she cares. I hate how quiet she is when we get home, how much power these people still have over her. All I can do is love her enough for all of them—and without conditions. That's the point, even if we fail at it sometimes. During the day, I love her in quiet ways. Then at night, under a blanket of darkness, I worship her like she's a fucking God, until she can barely remember her name, let alone the fact that some arsehole crossed the street when they saw her coming.

The day before her birthday, I drive to Turram to buy her a present, even though she insists she doesn't want to celebrate. I can't get my head around the fact that she's never had someone say 'happy birthday' on the day or make her a cake or let her choose what's for dinner that night.

'Doesn't it annoy you that you've missed out?' I ask her.

'It's like asking someone who's never eaten chocolate how they feel about missing out on it. How would they know if they've never eaten it?'

In the morning, I bring her scrambled eggs and real coffee in bed and say 'happy birthday' even though she can't look at me when I say it. Then I give her the gift.

'It's not a birthday present, it's a thank-you gift,' I tell her. 'For all your help.'

She gives me a doubtful look but accepts it. She's so careful unwrapping it that I can't help but laugh.

'What?' she asks, face turning red.

'Just rip it.'

She pokes me. 'I have unwrapped presents before. I was trying to save the paper because it's pretty.'

I raise my hands. 'Fine. It's your day. If you wanna spend a large portion of it removing gift wrapping, go for it.'

She suppresses a smile as the last piece of sticky tape comes away. She sets it aside and studies the box. Her face softens. Removing the cardboard sleeve, she places the wooden box on the table and lifts the glass lid, staring down at the silver clasps, earring hooks, and other bits I don't recognise.

The smile comes, slowly. 'This is so thoughtful. It's almost as if you've been paying attention.'

'Now you can add clasps and make earrings.'

She picks up one of the earring hooks and studies it. 'You know, I think this might be the best birthday present I've ever gotten.'

I put the box aside and tackle her back onto the bed. She starts squirming and laughing so hard that her eyes are closed. She sounds happy.

'There's two more things we need to tick off,' I tell her.

She opens her eyes and looks at me. 'Which two things are they?'

'First, I'm going to make you a birthday cake with candles.'

'To be clear, I have blown out candles before, just not birthday ones. And won't it be easier just to buy a cake from the bakery?'

I brush hair back from her face and kiss her. 'Easier, sure. But every kid needs to experience a homemade lolly birthday cake.'

Her eyebrows come together. 'Why a lolly cake?'

'Because every child has one at some point in their life. I'll make the cake, and you'll put the lollies on, picking out all the ones you don't like.'

She watches me a moment. 'What's the second thing?'

I slide a hand under her pyjama top. 'Birthday sex.'

The corners of her mouth lift. 'Is it better than normal sex?'

'Yes.'

'How so?'

'Because it's your birthday. It's not something I can explain. I have to show you.'

She catches my hand through her top. 'I assume that comes after cake.'

I drop my head and drag her top up with my teeth. 'No, Wilson. It most definitely comes before.'

Her hands go into my hair, and her eyes sink shut.

39

ANNIE

We eat cake for lunch, butter cake with messy frosting that has crumbs through it. The lollies cover the imperfections. It's moist and possibly undercooked but utterly delicious.

'What do you want to do now?' Hunter asks.

I think for a moment. 'I'd love to see Banjo and go for a ride, but I don't see that happening any time soon.'

He looks at the clock. 'What time does your mum get home from work?'

'I don't know. Four. Five.'

'So you're saying nobody will be home for at *least* another three hours.'

I drum my fingers on the table, wondering if I'm brave enough to take the gelding from his paddock without asking. 'I mean, I'd be doing her a favour. Charlie hasn't been ridden for months.' Excitement flutters in my chest. 'I could have him back in his paddock in under an hour.'

'Better get your boots on.'

And so my next birthday activity is decided.

I venture across the creek, and Hunter stays back to get a few jobs done around the farm. I watch the house from the safety of the trees and only step out once I've established that Mum's not home. When I whistle, Banjo comes at a run, and we go to saddle Charlie, who's actually more excited than the dog.

We head up into the bush, staying away from the roads, cars, and people. It takes Charlie half the ride to settle, but then it's just the sound of hooves padding the dirt and a panting dog in tow. I can't help but think about how great it would be to combine the best parts of these lives instead of having to choose between them. I'm all too aware that this moment is stolen. It doesn't belong to me.

'You need to stay here and keep being the best boy 'round these parts,' I tell Banjo after our ride. '*Stay*.'

He must understand, because for once he doesn't follow me.

When I arrive back at the farmhouse, I see Mum's car parked in front of the shed. I stop, blink. And then I hear her. My eyes go to the veranda. She's standing at the bottom of the steps shouting up at Hunter. It's clear she hasn't come to wish me a happy birthday.

'Mum,' I call.

She whips her head in my direction, eyes ablaze. Then she marches towards me. 'You came onto *my* property while I wasn't home and removed *my* animals without permission.'

I almost laugh because it sounds so ridiculous. I grew up on *that* property with *those* animals. 'Yes, I took

Charlie for a quick ride. And Banjo followed like he always does.'

'Without. Permission.'

Hunter remains on the veranda, listening.

I swallow. 'I thought you'd prefer not to see me.'

'So you trespassed and stole from me?'

'Easy,' Hunter says.

She whips her head around. 'Stay out of this. It's a family matter and nothing to do with you.'

Nervous laughter falls out of me. 'Mum, Charlie's back in his paddock, and Banjo's waiting at your front door.' But I know this isn't really about me taking the horse for a ride. 'I'm sorry. I won't do it again.' I want this conversation to be over, for the hate to leave her eyes.

The sound of a car approaching has us all looking in the direction of the drive. A police car appears. I glance at Hunter, who's equally as confused.

A realisation sinks in as I look back at Mum. 'Did you... call the cops?'

She sets her mouth. 'Since God's laws mean nothing to you now, I'm forced to rely on worldly law enforcement.'

'Mum,' I breathe. 'What have you done?'

'Look where you've ended up.' She points to the police car. 'This is where turning away from Jehovah has gotten you.' She walks over to the two policemen now climbing out of the car.

Hunter's down the steps and coming towards me. 'Tell me your mum didn't call the fucking cops.'

I nod, lost for words.

Hunter links his hands atop his head. 'Shit.'

Mum climbs into her car and drives away without so much as a glance in my direction, and the two policemen head for me. When Hunter takes a step towards them, I catch his hand.

'Don't. Let me handle this.'

He searches my eyes, head shaking, then returns to the veranda.

I recognise one of the men as Sergeant Harry. He's been a police officer in Chirnside for as long as I can remember. I've sold shoes to him and knocked on his door to share the promise of a paradise earth. Other than that, there's been no need to interact. Jehovah's Witnesses don't really have run-ins with the law. I've never even had a speeding ticket.

The other man I don't recognise, but judging by his age, I'd guess he's fresh out of the academy.

Harry looks almost apologetic as they come to a stop in front of me. Past them, I can see Hunter pacing the veranda like a Rottweiler. As though sensing the threat behind them, the men look over their shoulders.

'Annie,' Harry says, facing me once more. 'This is Constable Jarrod.'

I can only nod.

With a heavy sigh, Harry says, 'Your mum's filled us in on a few things.'

'I just went for a ride,' I say, struggling to keep my voice even. 'I didn't go in the house at all.' I can barely believe I'm having this conversation.

Sergeant Harry repositions himself, blocking my view of Hunter. 'Your mum has a number of concerns, the trespassing being one of them.'

Now I'm lost. 'What concerns?'

'In regards to your current living arrangement,' Constable Jarrod says.

I stare at him.

Sergeant Harry rubs the back of his neck. 'It's our job to make sure that not only are you doing the right thing but that you're safe. I think it's best we have this conversation down at the station.'

Blood pounds in my ears. 'I don't understand.'

'We need you to accompany us to the police station,' Jarrod says.

I take a large step back from them, and Hunter stills when he sees it. I have to be careful not to alarm him or this could end badly for both of us.

'Am I under arrest?' I whisper.

Sergeant Harry gives me a reassuring smile. 'It's just a chat. Your mum's a bit worried and stressed. She'll likely drop the charges once she knows you're safe and has a chance to calm down.'

I go from hot to cold in under a second. 'She's pressing charges?'

Hunter's patience has run out, and now he's striding towards us. I know the only way through this is with a level head.

'I'll come with you. It's fine. Just let me talk to him.'

Jarrod turns to Hunter, but Harry gestures for him to start walking.

'We'll wait by the car,' he says.

Hunter glares at the men as they pass one another.

'I need to go to the police station. It's not a big deal.' I place a calming hand on his chest. 'They just want to have a chat.'

Hunter's visibly agitated. 'Not a big deal? What the fuck was your mum thinking? I'll drive you.'

'They want me to go in the car with them.'

'What? Why?'

I swallow. 'I need you to call my dad. Tell him exactly what happened. Can you please do that for me?'

He shakes his head, jaw working. 'If those arseholes so much as make you cry, I'm burning that station to the ground with them in it.'

I press my eyes shut when he turns away and heads for the house.

Hunter looks in the direction of the car. 'It's her birthday. You better make her a proper coffee with that fancy machine of yours.'

I walk over to where Harry's holding the back door open for me and climb inside.

Breathe.

40

ANNIE

Four thousand questions and three cups of coffee later, Sergeant Harry leaves me alone in the small interview room at the police station with nothing to stare at but the walls. Downing the final dregs of caffeine from my cup, I drop it into the bin beside the table and wait.

Trying to convince strangers that a former Jehovah's Witness is safe in the arms of the town's delinquent was no easy feat. Mum tried to convince them that I'm being manipulated. Leaving the religion is one thing. Choosing to remain outside is unfathomable in her mind and therefore must be Hunter's fault. The fact that I'm sitting here at the police station demonstrates the extent of her grief.

The door opens, and Dad steps inside. Aside from a few extra grey hairs and a slight shift in his hairline, he looks the same as the last time I saw him and appears as awkward as I feel. I don't think either of us imagined our reunion taking place here.

'You okay?' he asks, eyes moving over me.

It's funny how triggering that question can be from someone you've missed. Tears that weren't there a few seconds ago now threaten to spill over. I blink them back. 'Great.'

Great is probably a bit much.

He exhales slowly and peers through the open blinds to the policemen at the desk. 'I spoke to your mum. She's agreed to drop the charges.'

I laugh, relieving some of the tension. 'I don't even know how to respond to that.'

He nods like he understands.

'You got here fast,' I say.

'I promised myself when I moved out that I wouldn't miss any of your big life events. First arrest seemed worthy of a mad dash across the state.'

I can't help but smile. He reminds me so much of Bridget when he says things like that. 'Father of the year.'

Harry returns to the room. 'You're good to go.'

Dad thanks him. I'm not sure what for. The coffee? Or not cuffing me, perhaps.

'Ready to get out of here?' Dad asks.

'Yeah, I'm ready.'

We exit the police station and stand awkwardly in the middle of the street, looking everywhere but at each other. It's nearing five in the afternoon.

'You didn't tell me you'd left the organisation,' he says.

I'm not entirely sure why. Maybe I was afraid he would insist I come stay with him. Or maybe I was afraid he wouldn't. 'I left a few months back.'

'Months?' He drops his gaze. 'Does that mean I should wish you a happy birthday now?'

'Only if you want to make things more awkward.'

He snorts.

He was never a bad dad. He was just so mentally far away—then physically. I know it stemmed from how deeply unhappy he was in that life and marriage. And he wasn't allowed to leave either, so all his energy went into surviving, which meant he had nothing left for us girls. 'How about a birthday beer instead?'

He lifts his gaze. 'At the pub?'

I look past him to the pub on the corner. 'Or we could get takeaways and drink them in the park like rebellious teenagers. But I don't really feel like getting in trouble with the police today. Again.'

His mouth tugs up. 'I can't believe you're twenty.'

He says it with such affection that I'm momentarily lost for words.

'Come on.' He gestures for me to start walking. 'My shout.'

We walk side by side, with at least three feet between us. There are a few curious looks in our direction when we step inside, so we head to the booth at the far end. Dad goes to the bar and returns with two pots. We stare at our beers while we figure out what to say.

'Tell me when you first started having doubts,' Dad says, looking up from his drink. 'Then keep going from there.'

I nod. 'Okay.' And I do.

I tell him about everything that happened in the

house after he left, about Bridget, school, and the tense conversations I had with Mum. I tell him about Tamsin.

Then I tell him about Maggie.

'Sorry to hear that. She was a nice person,' he says, taking a moment. 'Now I want to hear about this thing with Hunter.'

So I tell him about that too—sparing him some of the details.

'Your mother thinks he's Satan himself.'

I'm not at all surprised to hear that. 'Hunter's not a bad person. He's just learning to be a better human, like the rest of us.'

Dad nods. 'Tough thing to lose your mum at that age. And his dad probably wasn't much help.'

He asks more questions, and I continue to answer them. It feels good watching him soak up my responses, enjoying the small details of my life. I'm not sure why I share them so readily. Perhaps I'm scared of ending up like Bridget, with walls so high no one can penetrate them. Or maybe I just missed him more than I'm prepared to admit.

'What now?' Dad asks me. 'You can't stay in Chirnside.'

'I know.' I twist the bracelets on my arm.

He reaches across the table and inspects them. 'Can't believe you're still making these. You've gotten better, though.'

I look down at them. 'I actually sold some when I worked at Maggie's. She had a display on the counter.'

Dad's brow creases. 'Have you tried selling them up north?'

I shake my head. 'I've been too busy pouring beers.'

'And now you're not too busy.' He takes a sip of his drink. 'You know how to make them. Now you just need to learn how to *sell* them. You could do a business course.'

I pick up my beer. 'I need an income. You know Bridget. She won't let me bludge off her for too long.'

'You'd qualify for youth allowance, and you could still work part-time.' He pauses. 'It's great the two of you are living together.'

I note the sad edge to his tone. 'She's really made a life for herself up there.'

He smiles. 'I'm happy to hear that.'

I wipe at the condensation on my glass. 'I don't understand why the two of you aren't in contact. You both left the organisation, and now you have nothing in your way except lost time.'

'It's a little more complicated than that.'

'Complicated how?'

He drags his gaze up to mine. 'This beer with you is the highlight of my year so far.' He pauses. 'If it's all right with you, I'd like to keep that conversation for another time and enjoy this moment a little longer.'

I nod. 'Okay.'

We watch each other across the table.

'I'm seeing someone,' he says, sounding nervous.

I'm not at all surprised by this announcement. 'Does she make you happy?'

He pushes his empty glass away. 'She does.'

I can't remember ever seeing him happy with Mum. 'What's her name?'

'Carol.'

'Does Carol have children?'

'Two. Thirteen and fifteen.'

I sit with that information for a moment. 'So she's younger than you?'

'Only by three years.' He smiles. 'Don't worry. This isn't some midlife crisis.'

The corners of my mouth lift. 'That's reassuring.'

He's quiet a moment. 'She's great company, and we have an enormous amount of trust and respect for each other.'

I turn my glass in my hand. 'What about love?'

'Love looks a little different when you get to my age.' He studies me a moment. 'Do you love Hunter?'

'You must remember what it's like at our age. You love first, then figure out the rest later.'

He smiles down at the table. 'Or you don't.'

I laugh quietly. 'Or you don't.'

'I remember him as a hot-headed kid. Hope he's grown out of that.'

I crinkle my nose. 'I'd describe him more as *growing* out of that.'

'Ah. A work in progress. So long as he keeps his temper in check around you, then I'll stay out of your business.'

It's the perfect fatherly response.

I finish my beer and set the empty glass down on the table. 'Don't suppose you can give me a lift?'

He nods and slips from the booth. 'Of course.'

We walk to his car in silence, and when I climb in, it smells different to what I remember. It smells like another family.

I look out the window.

'I'm going to tell you something,' he says to me. 'But what I'm about to tell you must stay between us. I need your word on that.'

I'm immediately nervous. 'Okay.'

'Bridget was adamant that she didn't want you to know.'

My heart beats a little harder in my chest. 'Didn't want me to know what?'

He takes his time, carefully selecting his words. 'Do you remember Derek Harding?'

My mind reaches for details. 'As in Brother Derek?'

'Yeah. You would've been eleven or so when he was disfellowshipped.'

I struggle to remember the people who didn't come back. Kids tend to remember the ones who do. The people at the back of the Kingdom Hall we're told not to talk to. I still remember the shame-filled faces of those shunned.

Derek never returned. By memory, there was an announcement one evening before the song, and then I never saw him again. My adolescent brain would've assumed he'd gone off into the world to live an empty, miserable life, a life without purpose and protection— because that's what we were told.

'Why was he disfellowshipped?' I ask. The elders don't announce the reason. You have to rely on congregation gossip for that, and I was too young to be privy to it.

'Because—' Dad chokes up, and now I'm terrified of his answer. 'It was discovered that he molested one of the younger sisters in the congregation.'

I blink, fingertips digging into my legs. 'Tell me it wasn't Bridget.'

I'm met with silence.

I feel hot and cold all at once. 'How did... When?'

His hands knead the steering wheel. 'He was living at home at the time. I'm sure you remember his sister, Karli. She was Bridget's best friend. They slept over at each other's houses all the time. And why not? The family were trusted brothers and sisters, after all.'

I remember Karli well. She used to come over a lot, until her family moved. Now I know why.

'It was a Saturday night,' Dad says. 'Karli's family would bring Bridget to the meeting on Sunday, like they normally would.' He scratches his nose. 'Karli woke up during the night, heard something. She probably didn't really understand what she was seeing, but at sixteen, she definitely knew her brother wasn't supposed to be there in that room. There was a lot of confusion initially.'

'Karli was sixteen?' She was a year above Bridget at school. 'That means Bridget would've only been fifteen.'

'And Derek was twenty-two.'

I close my eyes for a moment. 'Did Bridget... did she want him there?'

Dad chews his lower lip. 'We wondered the same thing. Young sisters get crushes on brothers all the time.' He pauses. 'But Bridget had no interest in Derek. She woke up, and he was there... She told us she froze.'

I can't move, can't breathe.

'Karli woke before he...' The pause is necessary. 'But the damage was already done.'

My sister's wary face comes to mind. 'So he was disfellowshipped. Then what? No one blamed her, did they?' It wouldn't surprise me if they had. Maybe her knees showed at a meeting.

Dad shakes his head. 'No. No one blamed her.'

There's more. I can feel it, so I wait for him to continue.

'I wanted to go to the police,' he says quietly. 'The elders wanted to deal with it internally.'

There's the missing piece. 'What did Mum want?'

'She wanted it to never have happened in the first place. She wanted it over, forgotten about.' He draws a shaky breath. 'She felt the swift action of the elders and the support they gave us was adequate.'

I rest my head back. 'Was that the thing that finally ended your marriage, do you think?'

'Our relationship had run its course long before then, but yes. I suppose it did.'

I roll my head to look at him. 'What did Bridget want?'

It takes him a moment to reply. 'At first, she wanted to bury it. The less fuss the better. Then she could move on and forget all about it.' He pauses. 'But trauma doesn't work that way. When she realised the memories couldn't be buried, she got angry.' The faintest smile comes and goes on his face. 'Then she wanted blood.' He indicates and pulls into the farm. 'She *wanted* Derek strung up from the nearest tree. What she *needed* was her parents to act in her best interests.'

I understand then. 'She never expected Mum to go against the organisation,' I say, 'but she expected you to.'

'I was one foot out anyway at that point.' He sniffs. 'But I chose not to upset the apple cart.'

I probably should feel angry at him, but I don't. We're trained to trust in Jehovah, in the elders. And in their minds, they had done everything they could—except they hadn't.

'If you had your time over, would you go to the police?' That's what matters at this point.

He stops the car in front of the house. 'That decision was a constant thorn in my side. A few months after I moved out, I phoned Bridget and said I'd pick her up and take her to the police station that afternoon. I told her it wasn't too late, that we could still press charges.'

'And?'

'And she told me, in no uncertain terms, that my chance to play the protective father had passed. That if she wanted to go, she would go alone.' He swallows. 'She stopped taking my calls after that.'

A drop of rain lands on the windshield. The sky is a turbulent grey.

'So that's the story,' Dad says after a minute of silence. 'I keep hoping that one day she'll forgive me for not stepping up the way I should've. Then I'll work on forgiving myself.'

My heart is heavy with those words. 'Maybe you should work on forgiving yourself anyway.'

He doesn't reply.

Hunter comes out of the house and leans against the veranda post.

'I still can't believe you have a boyfriend,' he says.

'Must have been a fairly impressive play to win you over at that time in your life.'

'It was impressive.' My eyes are locked on Hunter's. 'He built me a swing.'

Dad frowns. 'Kid's making me look bad.'

I smile. 'Thanks for the beer.'

He nods. 'Anytime.'

I climb out, watch him drive away, then wander over to Hunter.

'Do I have to burn the police station down?' he asks as I approach.

I shake my head. 'Not today.'

He searches my eyes. 'What happened?'

'Well, I had a birthday beer with my dad at the pub. Fairly sure the beer was VB.'

He winces. 'Jesus, Annie. For a moment there I thought you were telling me a happy story.'

'And I liked it.'

He throws his hands up. 'This day just keeps getting worse.'

I smile and look up at the sky when a drop of rain hits my face.

'It's about to bucket down,' Hunter said. 'Come inside.'

My feet don't move. 'Fancy a walk?'

His eyebrows lift slightly, and then he looks up at the thunderous clouds swirling above us. 'Sure.' He steps off the veranda and takes my hand just as the heavens open up. 'Let's go.'

41

HUNTER

I leave the lamp on in my room because I need to see Annie's face when she climaxes beneath me. She's so responsive that it's testing my restraint. It started out as a distraction from tomorrow's court hearing, but it's turned into something else. She's giving herself to me in a way that's both utterly gratifying and completely terrifying.

'More,' she breathes into my mouth.

But I'm already giving her everything. She has my mind, heart, body. It's clear she wants my soul too.

I can tell when she's close by the way her fingers dig into my neck and her back lifts off the bed. When her eyes sink shut, I say, 'Look at me.'

She opens her eyes and falls over the edge, and I'm right there with her. I don't kiss her during this part—I watch. And she watches me right back. Afterwards, I stay inside her until she stops trembling, then settle her on top of me so her head is resting on my heart.

The silence that follows is necessary. We're piecing our minds back together while allowing our bodies to recover.

When we can, Annie's the first to speak.

'They say baptism is a bit like being reborn. You're fully submerged, cleansed of all your sins.'

I'm drawing circles on her back with my finger. 'Should I be worried that you're thinking about washing away your sins right now?'

She looks up at me. 'That felt like a baptism of sorts.'

A lazy smile appears on my face. 'I may have been fully submerged, but I'm fairly sure I gained a few sins just then.'

She studies my face. 'Do you ever think about after? When this all ends?'

I think about her leaving and returning to Brisbane, but I never think about it ending. Is it even possible to sever a connection like this? 'You're baptised now, Wilson. There is no end.'

'I'm serious.'

'So am I.'

She exhales and falls silent for a while. 'I could stay.'

'You're not staying. You're going back to Brisbane where you belong.'

'And where do you belong?'

'In hell, probably.'

She blinks up at me. 'Your dad's being sentenced tomorrow.'

'I know.'

'And we don't have a plan.'

Whatever she needs from me right now, I'm not sure I can give it. 'We do have a plan. You're going to Brisbane, and I'm staying here to run the farm until Dad's released.'

She hesitates. 'The lawyer said it can be up to twenty years.'

'I know what the lawyer said, Annie. I was the one who told you, remember? And he also said a sentence that length was unlikely because he had no prior convictions.'

My tone has her withdrawing, but I hold her in place. I'm not angry at her. I'm angry at the inevitable separation. I fucking love this girl.

'I'm sorry,' I whisper. 'This farm's been in our family for five generations. Mum would be so heartbroken if we lost it this way.'

She relaxes against me. 'How can a person feel so happy and so sad at the same time?'

'Years of practise.' I drop my forehead to hers. 'You're so much better than this place.' I don't want her to go, but I also can't hide her away on this farm forever. She deserves to live in a place where people smile in her direction, where they stop her in the middle of the street to ask how she is.

I kiss her. I kiss her because it's the only form of comfort I can offer right now. My words are useless.

'More,' she says, dragging my hand beneath the sheet.

I know this girl owns me body and soul now, because despite having given her everything I could just minutes ago, I meet her demands.

On the morning of Dad's court hearing, I leave Annie asleep in bed and walk the long drive with Tess at my heel to collect yesterday's mail. The local paper is wet from the rain, so I remove the partially dry classifieds from the middle and flick through them on the walk back.

I freeze when I see the following ad:

For sale: 15.3h, 8yo, bay thoroughbred gelding. Charlie is a former racehorse currently being used for pleasure riding. He would be best suited to a competent rider. He has established paces, enjoys jumping, and would be perfect for eventing with some additional education. Charlie is well mannered, good to shoe, clip, and float. For more information, contact Dawn Wilson on 53822904.

I lower the paper and resume walking. But instead of returning to the house, I head for the creek and go pay Dawn a visit.

She sees me through the glass, and I see her hesitate before making her way to the door.

'What are you doing here?' she asks, opening it wide enough for her head only.

The corners of my mouth turn up. 'That's not a very Christian greeting now, is it?'

'Do I need to call the police again?'

I release a breath and hold up the classifieds ad. 'I'm here about the horse.'

She narrows her eyes at the page. 'You're joking.'

'Nope. How much?'

She opens the door the rest of the way and crosses her arms. 'Did Annie send you?'

'Annie has no idea I'm here. How much for the horse, please?'

She scowls at me. 'That girl can't be bought with gifts and grand gestures, no matter how gallant.'

I don't take the bait. 'I would like to buy the horse. If you tell me the price, I'll go to the bank when it opens and return with cash.'

She tilts her head at me. 'You don't have the money to spend on horses.'

'Let me worry about that.'

She shakes her head. '$4000. Do you have $4000?'

'There's no way you paid $4000 for that horse.'

'No, we didn't,' she admits, 'Charlie's a failed race-horse my daughter rescued from a kill pen for $80.' She pauses and looks me straight in the eye. 'But the price is $4000.'

I chew my lip as I attempt to keep my cool. 'Is that the price for everyone or just me?'

She doesn't reply.

Banjo appears from inside and runs out to greet me. When he jumps up for a pat, Dawn calls him back inside.

'I'll be honest,' she says. 'Even if you had $4000, I wouldn't sell him to you.'

I nod slowly. 'I see.'

Her eyes are full of contempt. 'I would've gotten her back if it wasn't for you.'

My brow creases. 'Gotten her back from where? She never left you. She left the religion. You can have her back any time you please. She'd run here right now if you asked her to.' I step back from the door. 'You're pointing the finger in the wrong direction.'

'I suggest you get off my property before I call the police.'

'Okay.' I nod slowly and turn to leave. 'Good luck with the sale.'

42

HUNTER

Five years.

Those were the words from the judge's mouth. Culpable driving causing death, something, something, then five years.

Five years.

I'll be twenty-five years old when he gets out.

None of us are surprised, yet all of us are in shock. My eyes meet Dad's before he's taken away. He's aged about ten years in the two months he's been locked up. I can see the toll of detoxing, regret, and self-loathing. But I also see genuine remorse, not only for taking Maggie's life but for taking mine too.

He glances once at Annie, like he's acknowledging this is a sentence for her also. Then he's gone, out the side door and hustled into a car to be driven back to the prison, leaving his lawyer to put away his notes and return to his comfortable life. I want to be angry at the man, lay blame at his feet, but I know five years is at the lower end of what Dad could have gotten. His clean record prior to the accident was his saving grace. He never drank and drove on my watch.

We file out of the courthouse, and Annie doesn't bother asking me if I'm okay. Neither of us are okay. Tom's coming to collect her tomorrow to drive her to the airport. In the end, I was forced to make plans directly with her dad because Annie was stalling.

'She needs to go back to Brisbane' was the first thing he said to me when I phoned him that evening.

If he was expecting an argument, he didn't get one. 'I know.'

'Not because of you or your dad,' he went on. 'Despite what you think, Dawn's suffering as much as Annie. Her daughter's within arm's reach but living a life she can't accept. Plus you've got an entire congregation circling like righteous wolves. Don't underestimate the power of the pack.'

'Can you help me get her back to Brisbane?' I asked him quietly.

'Of course.'

Tom booked her a one-way flight from Melbourne to Brisbane the moment he hung up. When I told Annie of the plan we had made, without her consent, she didn't speak to me for two days. Two days of not speaking, not touching. Two days of torture.

Annie slips her hand into mine as we head for the ute. My fingers instinctively close around hers. Letting go requires conscious effort now.

'How will you manage everything at the farm by yourself?' she asks for the four hundredth time.

I open the passenger door and gesture for her to get

in. 'The same way I've managed for the past nine years.' I close the door and head around to the driver side.

The second I climb in, she starts up again. 'Farmers don't get days off. *You* told me that. If I leave, I'll never see you. That will be it, right?'

I doubt it'll ever be it for me, but I don't say that aloud. As tempting as it is to tell her to come visit, I know every trip will leave another scar on her. 'Five years is a good outcome.'

She looks out the front window as I put the ute in reverse. 'Dad wants me to do this diploma business to learn how to sell my jewellery.'

Through the tightness in my throat, I reply, 'I think it's a great plan. Go to Brisbane. Go study, learn, create stuff, be with your sister. Go have the life you've waited twenty years to live.'

Her eyes well up. 'I'll be two states and five years away from you.'

The burn at the back of my nose is uncomfortable, but I don't dare sniff. If she glimpses any thread of hesitation on my part, she'll grab hold of it with both hands.

That night we eat the quietest dinner we've ever had in the house, and then Annie goes for a two-hour walk without me.

'Charlie's not in his paddock,' she tells me when she returns.

I haven't had the heart to tell her Dawn was selling him. 'I probably should've mentioned this earlier, but I saw an ad for him in the classifieds.'

'Oh.' She presses her lips together. 'I suppose it had to happen eventually.'

'I would've bought him if I could.' I don't tell her I tried.

She tilts her head. 'And done what with him?'

'Probably put him in a paddock and hope he learned how to be a sheep.'

Annie stares at me a moment, then closes the distance between us. The second she enters my personal space, I know this isn't going to be a sweet moment between us. She pushes up onto her toes to kiss me, and heat explodes like pain through me. I back her up all the way to the bedroom while she tugs at my clothes. I try to slow things down, because it's our last night together, but she ignores my cues. The whole thing is frantic and rushed. Annie's too rough and demanding, and my body can't quite read hers, so it's awkward too. She comes without telling me she's close, without telling me to come with her, without uttering a sound. Her silence feels like punishment. And the second I finish, she untangles herself from me and turns to face the wall.

What the hell just happened?

I hear her crying next to me, and I press my palms to my eyes. I have no idea how to comfort her, so I don't.

Neither of us sleeps. We lie facing away from each other, and I hate every second of it. Then finally, when she's ready, she rolls over, her fingers brushing my back. I meet her in the middle of the bed watching her in the dark.

'I love you,' she whispers.

I'm silent—and an arsehole. I just can't say those words ahead of a goodbye. I do kiss her tears away, though. I kiss her whole face, her neck, breasts. She's relaxed this time and content to let me lead. She's also tender and vocal, breath hitching and fingers pressing.

'I'll miss you,' she tells me later when we're watching the clock.

I drag her closer to me. 'Will it be better or worse if I call you?'

She thinks about that for a moment. 'Worse, I think. But if we're not in contact, then it's really over.'

'We'll text,' I say. 'Infrequently. At random times. No expectations, but no end either.'

'Like friends?'

I don't answer her. Trying to reduce this relationship to friendship is senseless.

'Am I waiting for you?' she asks when I don't respond. 'Is that the plan?'

I roll my head in her direction, my lips finding her hair. 'You're not waiting for anybody, Wilson. You've waited long enough to start living. Please don't waste another five years.'

She's crying again. 'I wanted a life with you.'

'I'll be right here on the sidelines, cheering you on.' I kiss the top of her head. 'You're going to have a full, amazing life up there.'

She rubs her cheek on my chest. 'And what will you have?'

I think about that for a moment. 'I'll have this place ready to hand back to Dad when he's out.'

She blinks, eyes heavy with fatigue. 'It's really only four years and ten months because he's served two months already.'

I stroke her hair. 'Four years and ten months will fly by.'

Sleep takes her before she can reply.

43

ANNIE

'You're doing the right thing,' Dad tells me in the car on the way to the airport.

My eyes keep going to the side-view mirror, because that was the last visual I had of Hunter. He's more than a hundred kilometres behind me now, but I continue to look.

Dad reaches down next to my feet, picks up a stack of papers, and hands them to me.

'What's this?' I ask, running my eyes over the first page.

'Enrolment details. You start next week.'

I look at him. 'You already enrolled me?'

'Consider it a well-meaning push.'

I could pretend to be annoyed that he didn't ask me first, but this is the most fatherly thing he's done in years. 'How much was the fee?'

He shakes his head. 'Doesn't matter. Let me do this small thing for you.'

My eyes return to the mirror. 'You said that about the flight to Brisbane.'

'Then let me do these two small things for you.'

My mouth twitches.

'There is one thing you can do for me in return.'

I look back at him and wait.

'I'd love you to meet Carol.' He keeps his eyes on the road ahead. 'Maybe we'll come to Brisbane for a holiday, meet up for dinner.' He sneaks a glance at me. 'And you know you're welcome to visit us here in Melbourne anytime, right?

It's clear he doesn't want me to disappear again. 'I'd love to meet her.'

The muscles in his shoulders relax upon hearing that. 'Okay. Great. We'll figure something out.'

It's starting to feel comfortable with him again. We almost resemble something normal, something *healthy*.

'Make sure Bridget knows she's welcome too,' he says.

I nod, feeling sad for him. 'I'll tell her.'

Our goodbye at the airport is rushed, but it's fine. We've already said everything we need to in the car on the way there.

'I'll see you soon,' I tell him when we hug goodbye. It's the first time we've touched since the day he moved out. We both hold on a fraction longer than the people around us. Then he's climbing back into the car and driving away.

As I head into the terminal, I text Bridget to let her know I'm at the airport. I phoned her the day Dad booked my flight, asking if she still has a bed for me there or should I go back to the hostel.

She texted back, *Who's this?*

So I wrote back, *The pretty sister. I'm bringing the latest issue of the Watchtower with me. There's a great article in it titled "Being Funny—Why God Skipped You".*

And she wrote back, *I've changed the locks.*

When I exit the plane in Brisbane, I look around for the baggage sign and freeze when I see my sister standing amid a group of chauffeurs holding signs with names printed on them.

'Mark Webber - Emporium Hotel'

'Lisa Thatcher - Hilton International'

My gaze goes to the sign Bridget's holding. It reads 'Annie Wilson - Metro North Incontinence Clinic'.

I press my lips together to stop from smiling. She's even printed a logo on it to make it look official. The smart thing to do would be to walk by and pretend I've no idea who she is. But that's not what I do. Instead, I walk straight up to her and do something I should have done months ago, the day I found her drawing in a park—I wrap my arms around her and hold on. Hers remain stiff at her sides. She's thoroughly uncomfortable. Undeterred, I squeeze her tighter. I squeeze until the muscles in her arms finally relax, until the wall she built for protection begins to crack beneath the weight of my affection.

'I missed you,' I tell her.

Finally, she bends one arm and places it lightly on my back. 'Careful,' she says. 'If you squeeze too hard, you might pee yourself.'

I release her and snatch the sign from her hand, folding it in half. 'I need coffee.'

She gestures in the direction of the baggage claim. 'Then let's get you caffeinated.'

44

HUNTER

I'm not prepared for the train wreck of emotions that hits when Annie returns to Brisbane. I feel her absence all the time, but especially at night. I miss the feel of her curled against me, her scent, and the way she always starts a fresh conversation just as I'm falling asleep.

Annie's gone.

Dad's gone.

The loneliness never leaves.

Running the farm is a lot of work for one person, but it's a great way to pass time. Rise early, work hard all day, sleep. No time for self-pity.

On the weekends, I visit Dad, and it's surreal, and hard, and sad. I know he's responsible for Maggie's death, but it still feels like he shouldn't be in there. This man raised me solo through my teen years. He taught me how to drive. Now he's locked up for culpable driving causing death.

I guess if I just keep showing up every morning for

work and showing up at the prison on weekends that this will eventually feel like my life instead of someone else's.

A month into this new existence, Sammy shows up at my door carrying a duffel bag similar to the one I left home with. I can tell by his face that all is not well.

'What's going on?' I ask, gesturing to the spare seat on the veranda. Tess is off the chain and jumping all over him.

'I dropped out of uni.'

I wasn't expecting that. 'Why?'

'Turns out it's not for me.'

I frown. 'The degree or uni?'

He leans back, continuing to rub Tess's head. 'Both.'

Sammy got his first preference at the best university in Melbourne. His parents were so proud, and he was happy. That's life for you.

'I need a place to stay away from the disappointed stares of my parents. Need some time to regroup.'

'Then I guess you came to the right place.'

He looks down. 'My Centrelink payments have stopped, so I have no money coming in right now.'

I laugh through my nose. 'I don't need your money. I need your labour.'

He angles his head at me. 'My dad's a dentist. You know I know nothing about farming.'

'Well, hunger's a great motivator.'

So he moves in, and it all feels a little easier with him there. Not just the work but the meals and idle moments. Amazing how having someone else in the room while you stare silently at the television in the evenings equates to company. I'm not one to verbally express my appreciation, so I show him by stocking up on his favourite foods and beer when I head into town instead.

'One day at a time' is our motto right now.

I give Annie some time to settle back into Brisbane life before texting her to check in. The last thing I want is to disrupt her while she's finding her feet.

Me: Learned anything useful yet?
Annie: Yes. There's a second-hand bookshop in the city where you can buy textbooks at half the price.
Me: Did you find that out before or after buying your textbooks?
Annie: After.
Me: Ouch.

That's enough. It's enough for her and enough for me. If we can keep it light, then that'll surely reduce our suffering.

A few weeks pass before she texts me.

Annie: Tamsin told me Sammy's living with you. How do the sheep feel about it?
Me: Weirdly, they seem to like him.
Annie: Well, there's no accounting for taste ;)

In March she texts again.

Annie: I got a part-time job at a kids' shoe shop.
Me: Congrats. Hope your new boss isn't a sleazy fuck like the last one.
Annie: So far she's been well-behaved.

Me: :)

In April I text her.

*Me: Did you know your mum sold the house? She
bought that little cottage behind the mechanics.*
Annie: Oh. She take Banjo with her?
*Me: Yeah. Saw him in the yard when I passed
yesterday.*
Annie: He hates fences :(

It's well into May when I hear from her again.

*Annie: Any idea where Charlie ended up? Bridget's
been asking about him.*
Me: Did you tell her he won't fit on the terrace?
Annie: *eye roll*
Me: He was sold to the Wilkons.

I actually showed up at their house when I found out,
offering to buy the horse they had just purchased for
their daughter. Needless to say, the door was politely
closed in my face.

Annie: The Wilkons are a nice family. Thanks x

I stare at that *x* on my phone for an embarrassing
amount of time. It's the most intimate thing to have taken
place between us in months. I go to text her back, then
delete everything I've written and put the phone down.
Four years and six months.

45

ANNIE

'I don't understand what the rules are between the two of you,' Bridget says over her wine glass.

After biting her tongue for months, she's finally asking me outright about where Hunter and I stand. 'There are no rules.'

She appears confused. 'Because you broke up?'

'We didn't say those words. We just kind of agreed to be... separate.'

Her eyebrows come together. 'Like a long-distance relationship?'

I draw a breath. 'He doesn't want me to wait for him.'

'Oh. So it's an open relationship, then.'

I give her a tired look. 'We never had a conversation about starting the relationship, so I guess there was never a need to have one around ending it.'

Bridget crinkles her nose. 'So it was a casual country fling, and now you're friends?'

There's nothing casual about us. It was intensely serious from the second I stepped up onto that veranda.

'We're just living the lives we need to right now, and then we'll...' *Look at me pretending I have answers to these questions.* 'See what happens in the future.'

She leans against the countertop, watching me. 'So Hunter would be fine if you went out tonight and met some guy, because you're living the life you need to right now?'

Hunter wouldn't be fine with that. *I* wouldn't be fine with that. 'It's not something I'd mention in a casual text.'

'But you *could* technically do it.'

I'm chopping potatoes for dinner, and this conversation is making me clumsy with the knife. 'I suppose I could.'

'You *suppose*? I can't believe you didn't clarify all this stuff before you left.'

'He didn't want to talk about it.' Or face it. Knowing the status of our relationship and saying it aloud are two very different things.

She takes a drink. 'Are you expecting *him* to be celibate for the next four and a bit years?'

The blade of the knife slips, narrowly missing my finger. 'Of course not.'

She sets her wine glass down, takes the knife from me, and starts chopping. 'But you're hoping he will,' she says without looking at me.

Hoping. Praying. Sacrificing small animals in fire rituals. 'I'm a little more realistic than that.'

She tosses the potatoes into the pot. 'When did you last text him?'

'June.' I manage to keep my voice casual despite feeling choked.

'As in two months ago?'

I nod.

'And what did you say?'

'I said... "How are the sheep?"'

She bites down on her top lip to stop from smiling. 'And did he reply to this profound message?'

I pick up the pot and carry it to the sink. 'I got one word back.'

'Which was?'

I swallow. 'Woolly.'

She shakes her head. 'Why can't you just ask him how he is?'

We've never asked each other that. It might be the one rule we have. Asking how the other is could lead to someone admitting that they're not good, lonely, broken. That they're missing the other person. And that would be like pulling that loose thread on a garment that makes the whole seam come undone.

Bridget picks up my phone. 'This is silly. I'm going to text him for you.'

'No.' I snatch my phone from her hands.

'Why not?'

So many reasons, but I go with 'Because I sent the last text.'

'So?'

'So it's his turn.'

Bridget picks up her glass again and takes a large sip. 'You know what I think?'

'I'm sure you'll tell me.'

'I think his intentions are noble but ultimately damaging. Because he didn't have the heart to end things properly, you're left living half a life instead of the full one he wanted for you.' With that said, she leaves the kitchen.

I look down at my phone where my last text message to Hunter sits open. Leaning against the sink, I start typing.

Annie: I love you. I miss you. And even though you don't want to hear this, I'm waiting for you.

I read it three, four, five times. Then, deleting the message, I place the phone back on the bench.

46

HUNTER

On my birthday, I get a present in the mail from Annie. The card has a prawn with a face on the front. It reads 'Hope your day is shrimply the best.' Inside she's written, 'Don't forget the lolly cake.'

She's managed to make it personal and keep it casual at the same time. It's friendly, funny—except for the *x* following her name at the bottom.

I open the box, and inside is an Akubra. My eyes are drawn to the band as I pick it up to look at it. The corners of my mouth lift. The band's made from Annie's signature braided leather and held together with a silver clasp engraved with my initials. I put the hat on and tug my phone from my pocket.

Me: You trying to make all the other farmers around here jealous?
Annie: Can't have you blending in.
Me: It's perfect. Thanks.
Annie: Happy birthday x

There's that *x* again.

A few months go by. A few months of silence. I wonder if I should send Annie something for Christmas, then decide against it. She doesn't even celebrate it, and I don't want to set any patterns that tie her to me. It's been nearly a year since I've seen her, or even heard her voice, and all I can think is that Dad has four more to serve.

Sammy's offered to take care of things here so I can escape for a few days. He thinks I should go to Brisbane, visit Pete and the family, see Annie. It's tempting. *So* tempting to show up and disrupt the life she's spent the last year building, only to disappear once more. Then what? Does it become an annual thing? I go up every Christmas, we fall hard all over again, then spend the rest of the year counting down the days until the next one?

That's not the life I want for her.

Christmas comes and goes in mutual silence.

New Year's Eve rolls around. The century is coming to a close, and no one knows if all the technology we've spent the previous one hundred years inventing will still work tomorrow.

Sammy convinces me to go to some eighties night at a pub in Turram. He's been giving me shit about only leaving the farm for supplies or to visit Dad. I agree to go because that's what people my age do. It's normal, and maybe I need a bit of normal. So I put on the shirt and mullet wig Sammy hands me that evening and drive us to the pub.

Thankfully, everyone has gotten into the spirit of the theme, so we're not left looking like idiots. Sammy orders me a pot of light at the bar, and we spend the next few hours running into people we know from high school. Funny how everyone acts like we were best mates back then, even though I fought with most of them at some point during those years.

Tamsin shows up with one of her city friends and spots me by the bar. She walks over with her arms outstretched.

'Hey, you,' she says.

I hug her. 'It's been a while.' I can tell they had a few prior to coming.

'Have you spoken to Annie recently?'

Just her name said aloud changes the direction my blood is pumping in. 'Not since my birthday.' And I'm trying very hard to be okay with that.

Tamsin's friend returns from the bar and hands her a drink.

She nods. 'Thank you. Have you met Hunter?'

The girl extends a hand to me. 'Charlotte.'

When I take hold of her hand, she maintains eye contact.

'I was in Brisbane a few weeks back, and we had breakfast,' Tamsin says, drawing my full attention back to her.

'How'd she seem?'

'Really good. She's made some great friends through TAFE. They all hike and do this fitness boot camp thing together twice a week. She looks fantastic.'

I'm soaking in every word, every image.

'She's considering dyeing her hair,' Tamsin says, sipping at her wine, then making a face.

I'm trying to imagine another hair colour wrapped around my fingers. 'And what did you say?'

'I told her that girls would kill for her hair, and going darker won't work with her complexion.'

I'm weirdly relieved. 'Fair enough.'

She takes another sip of her drink, then says to Charlotte, 'Should've gone with a premix.'

Charlotte nods in agreement, then pushes her dark hair over her shoulder. 'I think the bottle's been open a while.'

'Not a lot of wine drinkers here,' I say.

She meets my gaze, a faint smile on her lips. 'Beer country, huh?'

I might be in the middle of a very long dry spell right now, but I recognise flirting when I see it.

'She asked about you,' Tamsin says. 'I told her I hadn't seen you in months.'

I nod. 'Busy time on the farm.'

'Next time I see her, I can tell her you're venturing out. And have a mullet.'

I exhale through my nose. 'She'll love that.'

'Break-ups are tough,' Tamsin says with a sigh. 'I don't think she's over it.'

I fucking hate that phrase. Annie and I never broke up. We just... broke.

'Why'd you split?' Charlotte asks.

I barely even talk to Sammy about it, so I'm hardly going to confide in this stranger.

Tamsin answers for me. 'Hunter's stuck here in Chirnside, and this is one place Annie can't be. It's such a sad outcome, but you never know what the future holds.' She squeezes my arm, a gesture of comfort, then looks over at the band when a U2 song starts. 'Oooh, we should dance.'

'I'll pass,' I tell her.

Tamsin drags Charlotte onto the dance floor, calling over her shoulder, 'Have a good night.'

I raise my nearly empty glass.

We end up staying well past my preferred finish time. Sammy's flirting up a storm with Tamsin on the dance floor, and I don't have the heart to ruin his night. He's worked as hard as I have this past year and has earned a night of fun.

People have reached the point of drunk where they form one large messy group and are singing along to all the songs while spilling their drinks everywhere. And I'm stuck at the bar with Charlotte.

'You know, I happen to look great in flannel,' she tells me.

She's like a bolder version of Tamsin. 'That right?'

'I'd be adorable on a farm.'

I watch her flirt, wondering if I could break the drought with this girl before me. A year is a *long* time.

'Maybe you should invite me back to yours, and I can try on your clothes,' she says, sipping seductively from a short black straw.

I'm fairly sure she'd be great company in bed. I'm single. She's single. We're worlds apart in real life but have been brought together for this one night. It doesn't get much simpler than that.

Then I wonder what Annie would say if she were here witnessing this. I imagine her wounded expression as she says to me, 'It's okay. We're not together. You can be with whoever you want.'

And just like that, I can't fuck this girl. 'Not tonight, sorry.'

Charlotte sighs. 'I know you don't have a girlfriend, so naturally I'm going to assume the issue is me.'

I might not have a girlfriend, but I do have a soulmate. Not something I'd ever say aloud—especially in the middle of a busy pub. 'It's not you—'

'I swear to God, if you finish that sentence with "it's me".'

'Okay, then, it's you.'

Her eyebrows rise.

'Your obvious bad looks and awkward personality.'

She relaxes. 'Oh. You're one of those hilarious farmer types.'

We're silent a moment.

'She messed you up good, huh?' she says, expression turning serious.

I turn the leather band on my arm. 'I think we did a pretty good job on each other.'

She nods. 'Well, if you change your mind, I'll be with the rest of the drunk folk on the dance floor.'

'Better-quality guys out there anyway.'

'Your modesty just adds to the appeal, so you're better off saying nothing.' She flashes me a smile. 'I'll leave you to lick your wounds.'

I watch her walk away. Actually, I watch her arse. I'm not perfect.

The moment she's swallowed up by the unruly crowd, I take out my phone and type a text message to Annie.

Me: I'm at a pub in Turram wearing a mullet wig.
Annie: I have the visual, and I'm not disappointed. I think I'm the only person in Brisbane in bed right now.

I glance at my watch. It's 11:56 p.m.

Me: Did I wake you?
Annie: I have a stall at the local market tomorrow. I'm still fiddling with jewellery. This is how jewellers 'ring in' the New Year.
Me: I see what you did there. Your jokes are getting worse. Tamsin's here btw.
Annie: Now I'm jealous.
Annie: Everything okay?
Me: Did you dye your hair?
Annie: Not yet. Why? Are you pro or against?
Me: It's none of my business what you do with your hair... but 100% against.
Annie: :)
Annie: Are you okay?
Me: You already asked me that.
Annie: And you didn't answer.

The music stops, and the drunken crowd starts counting down from ten. At midnight, my phone beeps in my hand.

Annie: Our phones still work!
Me: Going home to check the fridge ;) I hope tomorrow's a raging success.
Annie: Thank you. Happy New Year x

I stare at the *x* on the screen. Minutes go by.

Me: Wish you were here.

I delete the message.

Me: I fucking miss you.

I delete that also.

Me: Happy New Year, Wilson.

47

ANNIE

The graduation ceremony feels like a lot of unnecessary fuss, but the moment Dad phones to tell me they're flying up for it, my feelings change. His pride is contagious. I mention to Bridget that he and Carol will be there, and she assures me it's fine and makes no difference to her plans. But I see her grow more nervous as the day approaches, despite how hard she works to conceal it. This will be the first time she's seen Dad since he moved out of our family home and her first meeting with Carol. It's a lot.

'Tonight's not about me or Dad or Carol,' she tells me on the day. 'It's about celebrating your accomplishment.'

'It's just a TAFE course.'

'Don't do that. Don't diminish it. You could've gotten into uni if you were encouraged and supported.'

'You got in without those things.'

She reaches for my arm, looking me straight in the eye. 'Don't you dare compare yourself to me. You were the last daughter standing. The pressure on you was twice what I had. Still, you trusted yourself, your mind, and you got out.' She lets go of me and straightens. 'This might seem like a small deal to outsiders, but you and I both know it's not. Dad knows it too. That's why he's flying across the country. To watch you take a step in a direction of your choosing.'

I scrunch up my nose when I feel my eyes begin to burn.

'Your eyes are leaking,' Bridget says.

I press my lips together to stop from smiling. 'Your fault.'

She gestures to the door. 'Let's go before you mess up the floors.'

The ceremony's held in one of the amphitheatres on-site. We're called up one at a time to collect our diplomas to the applause of family. Afterwards, they serve refreshments in the next room, enabling students to say goodbye to teachers and peers.

The best part of the night is looking across the room and seeing Dad, Carol, and Bridget having what appears to be a normal conversation. No one would suspect any tension between them. It makes me optimistic that their relationship can be mended. We could start behaving like a family.

'It's going to be weird not seeing you every day,' Chris says as he keeps me company at the food table.

He's been a solid friend over the past two years, even if the lines have blurred at times. We went on a few dates earlier this year. He wore me down. One of those dates even ended with a kiss, which another friend later told me is called a pity-pash.

I've never been able to give things a proper go, though Bridget assures me this will change when the right guy comes along. But I take relationship advice from my sister with a grain of salt, because she's been thoroughly single since leaving home.

Chris is a nice guy—and he's not secretly married, which is another plus. He's also not Hunter. It's nearing two years apart, and still he keeps a firm hold on my heart. I've received a total of four text messages from him this year. I don't want to be dramatic and say he's moved on, but the separation is easier for him now. At what point will it become easier for me?

'Well, this just got awkward,' Chris says, raking a hand through his sandy hair.

I laugh. 'Sorry. That silence was a bit brutal. Yes, it'll be weird for me too. But we'll see each other at boot camp.'

'And New Year's. Party at my place, remember?'

Difficult to forget when he reminds me of it every day. 'And New Year's.'

Dad wanders over, Carol in tow. 'Want to go get some real food?'

I look over at my sister. 'What about Bridget?'

Carol gives me a warm smile. 'We invited her too, of course.'

'She said she'd go along with whatever you wanted,' Dad says.

And so we go out for dinner as one big awkward family. Aside from Bridget insisting on paying for her own meal when the bill comes, and me scrambling to fill in all the uncomfortable silences, it borders on enjoyable.

At the end of the evening, I hug Dad and Carol goodbye and thank them for flying up. Bridget stands back, watching the road. Some walls remain firmly in place.

When we arrive home, there's a bouquet of pink lilies sitting on the doormat.

'Chris going with the less-subtle gestures now?' Bridget asks.

I pick them up, knowing full well that if Chris was going to give me flowers, he'd do so in person.

'Here,' Bridget says, plucking the card from the foliage. She opens it and reads the message. 'Happy graduation.' Then she lowers her brows as she flips it over. 'No name.'

I take it from her and check it for myself. Two words with no name. And now my heart's thrumming away like that means something.

'Tamsin?' Bridget asks, shoving the door open.

Tamsin, of course. Who else would buy me flowers? She's the only person who wasn't there who I told about it. 'I'll call her later to thank her.'

Bridget puts the flowers in a Mason jar because we don't own a vase. 'Where do you want them?'

'Bedroom.' I take them from her and carry them into my room, placing them on the desk that I sit at when I'm making jewellery. I sink down onto the bed and stare at them for the longest time. I flinch when my phone rings in my pocket. It's Tamsin.

'Hey, you,' she says when I answer.

'Hey.'

'Sorry it's been a while. Tell me all your news.'

After chatting for a few minutes, it becomes clear that she's forgotten about my graduation. I have to ask her to be sure. 'This might be an odd question, but did you by any chance send me flowers today?'

The silence on the end of the line answers me. 'Oh God, what have I missed?'

'Nothing. Never mind.'

There's an intake of breath. 'Your graduation.' She groans. 'Sorry. How was it?'

I can't look away from the flowers. 'It was great, actually.'

We chat for a while longer, and when I hang up, I lie down on the bed.

Two years of missing him. Two *long* years.

'Nightcap?' Bridget calls from the kitchen.

I close my eyes for a moment, then, with enormous effort, push myself up.

'Make it a large one.'

It's a celebration, after all.

48

ANNIE

The lilies dominate my desk, my room, and my mind for ten intense days. When they start to wilt, I remove them from the jar, tie the stems together, and hang them upside down to dry. It takes them three days to die. I leave them hanging there until Christmas, until all the life and colour are gone. Once I've cleaned and dried the jar, I return the flowers to it. According to the internet, dried flowers can last up to one year. Hopefully by then I'll be ready to bin them.

On Christmas morning, Bridget and I eat cereal for breakfast while the rest of the city open presents and telephone loved ones. We sit on the terrace listening to the city until it's too hot to remain outside, then retreat indoors for a movie marathon. We still have an enormous backlist of films we're working through, filled with swearing, sex, and graphic violence.

'I love Christmases with you,' I tell Bridget late that night under the fog of gin. We're seated in the middle of the sofa instead of at either end.

'I love Christmases with you too,' she says without looking at me.

'Even when the sex scenes come on and we both have to pretend we're not embarrassed?'

Now she looks at me, eyes creasing at the corners. 'Especially then.'

Five days later, Bridget has agreed to be my plus-one at Chris's New Year's party. She gravitates towards intelligent conversation and always has something remarkable to contribute. She's surprisingly social in these situations, maybe because she gets to be whoever she wants with strangers. It's the people who know her that she struggles with.

A little before midnight, I gather with my TAFE friends, and we count down from twenty. We shout the numbers in unison, plastic flutes in hand. Then everyone yells, 'Happy New Year!'

Fireworks sound in the distance, far from our limited view. People turn to those around them, clinking cups and hugging. Chris turns to me, and we're both smiling. I think he's going to hug me, but he kisses me on the mouth. And just like that, my mood deflates. I knew it was coming, though. He's spent most of the night at my side, refilling my cup and trying to anticipate my hunger. And if I'm honest, it felt nice for a while.

Having someone tell you that you look beautiful is nice.

Having someone bring you nibbles on a plate is nice.

Feeling wanted, *desired* is nice.

I've enjoyed these things a little too much tonight. I've

led him on. That's why he kissed me on the mouth and no one else.

Chris drapes an arm over my shoulders, and it feels a lot like a claim I haven't agreed to. My eyes meet Bridget's across the room, and I feel exposed and ugly. The pity in her eyes has me slipping out from under his arm and seeking out a hiding place.

'Where are you going?' Chris calls to my back.

I look over my shoulder. 'Bathroom.' It's the only place he won't follow me.

Only when I lock the door and the noise dulls do I realise I'm drunk. One glance at the mirror confirms it. My make-up's a little smudged, and my eyes are wobbly. At least I can draw breath in here. The weight of Chris's arm was too much, and now I'm trying not to cry.

I stare at myself in the mirror, missing someone who isn't Chris.

There are moments when I'm fine and moments when I'm paralysed by feelings I can't for the life of me move past. How is it that I'm still in this place *two years* on?

Pulling out my phone, I open a text message to Hunter. I'm drunk, so it's fine. I excuse the bad behaviour before it's even occurred.

Annie: I'm so exhausted.
Hunter: Big night?
Annie: Sure, but that's not why I'm exhausted. When will it get easier?

A few minutes go by before I get a reply.

Hunter: I'll let you know when I get there.

I cover my mouth to stop the sob rising up my throat. It's the closest we've come to saying 'I miss you' since I left. It's dangerous territory. If I'm not careful, one of us will end up calling, and there will be no turning back once I hear his voice.

Hunter: Whatever happened tonight, it's okay.

He knows. Of course he knows. He knows like I knew last New Year's Eve. It doesn't even matter if we act on our temptations or not. It's having them in the first place that feels like betrayal.

Hunter: You at a party?
Me: Yeah. You wearing a mullet?
Hunter: Nah. That's so 1999. Where are you?
Me: Locked in the bathroom. I should go back out there.
Hunter: Back to him?

I stare wide-eyed at that last question. He broke so many of our unspoken rules with that one.

Hunter: Should've sat on that a bit longer before hitting Send.

He's jealous. He's jealous, and I couldn't be happier about it. That's how little I've moved on. So I throw all caution to the wind and make a proper mess of things.

Me: Tell me not to go back to him and I won't. Tell me to go straight home instead. Tell me you'll call me in the morning.

I'm gripping the phone with both hands as I wait for his response. A knock sounds on the door, but I don't move or respond. Seconds slip by. Maybe even minutes.

'Annie?' comes Bridget's voice through the door. 'Open up.'

I'm holding my breath, willing my phone to beep. But it doesn't.

Hunter doesn't text back.

He doesn't text me back before leaving the bathroom or even that night.

He doesn't text me the next day, or the day after that, or any time in the months that follow.

49

HUNTER

The same bitter wind has been blowing up from the south all week, making winter feel eternal. I've just put Tess back on the chain when I hear Sammy's car pull up out front. He climbs out and shrugs his coat on before heading in my direction. He came to me looking like a city boy, but he's every bit the farmer now.

It was supposed to be temporary, until he found his feet. No one expected him to fall in love with this life. Now he's moved in permanently and earns a full-time wage as a farmhand. It's taken his parents some time to adjust to the fact that he's chosen a much simpler life than the one they had planned for him.

'Did you hear the Wilkons are selling the milk bar?' Sammy says when he reaches me.

I throw some kibble into the rusted food bowl. 'No. You know why?'

'Marg at the supermarket told me they're heading to the peninsula.'

I lean against the shed wall, nodding. 'So they're selling the house too?'

'Why? You interested?

I shake my head.

Sammy studies me a moment. 'Wait. You asking about the house or their horse?'

I start walking towards the house. 'Why would I care about their horse?'

He follows. 'Because if my memory serves me, they bought that horse off Dawn Wilson a few years back—after you tried to buy it.'

'That was a long time ago.' When we reach the bottom step of the veranda, I turn to him. 'Don't you have work to finish?'

He crosses his arms, seeing through my deflection. 'You spoken to her since New Year's?'

'Nope.'

'Then maybe you should give her a call, use the horse as a conversation starter.'

The last thing I'm going to do is disrupt her life right now. I ran into Tamsin last month, who informed me that she's kicking arse up there at the moment. Annie's officially launched her jewellery business, Entwined. Not only does she sell at markets but also to local boutique stores in her area.

'The best thing I can do for Annie is continue to stay out of her life,' I tell Sammy.

He rubs his forehead. 'So I guess you can throw away that arm band you still wear.'

I give him a tired look. 'I said I didn't want to mess up her life, not erase all memories of her.'

He stuffs the keys into his pocket. '*Years* have passed, and still I can't say her name without you looking like a kicked puppy. Your feelings haven't changed one bit. Why do you assume hers have?'

'I don't assume anything, but I *know* nothing good'll come of me reaching out to her. Nothing has changed. I'm still stuck here, and she's all the way up there. And for now it has to be that way.'

'What about when your dad's out? It doesn't have to be that way then. I'll stay on here, and you can go wherever you like.'

'That's two and a half years away. It's the time we've both served all over again.' I rest my hands on my hips. 'I want the next few years to be easier for her.'

Sammy doesn't speak for a long moment. 'Okay. If that's how these things work, then I guess the next few years will be easier for you too.'

I climb the steps and go inside, slamming the screen door so hard that one of the hinges pops off, leaving it hanging at an awkward angle.

'Things feeling easier yet?' he calls through the broken door.

I snatch up my keys and kick it open with my foot on my way out, jogging down the steps and past a smirking Sammy.

'Where are you going?' he asks. 'To see a man about a horse?'

I unlock the ute and slide into the driver seat. 'Door needs fixing while I'm gone.'

50

ANNIE

I dial Tamsin's number as I lock the car and head for the apartment. The humidity has me sweating before I've even reached the building. As I'm preparing to leave a voicemail, she answers.

'Well?' she asks, anticipating the reason for the call. 'Did you do it?'

I smile into the phone as I put in the door code. 'I did. I finish next week.'

Tamsin squeals into my ear. 'Look at you go.'

Today I gave notice at the shoe shop. After reducing my hours midyear, Entwined has now officially replaced my, albeit modest, income. I can now focus on growing the business, which includes outsourcing some of the production to save my hands from certain death.

'I know I said this was going to be your year, but I think next year's going to be even better.'

I'm smiling like a madwoman. 'I don't know about that. It would take a lot to top this one.'

'You're still missing a few key ingredients.'

I roll my eyes. 'As I've said before, I'm perfectly happy being single.'

'Have you said that before?'

'Many times.'

Tamsin sighs dramatically. 'I think a childish part of me hoped that Kevin's early release would breathe new life into old love. But alas, my star-crossed lovers appear to have moved on.'

I'm almost to the stairs when I register what she just said and grip the handrail for balance.

'You know, when I saw Sammy on the weekend...'

She continues to speak, and I catch none of it.

'You still there?' Tamsin asks after a long silence at my end.

I swallow. 'Did you say, "Kevin's early release"?'

A few beats of silence follow. 'Didn't Hunter tell you? Kevin had his parole hearing last week and might be out before Christmas.'

Parole hearing? 'I haven't heard anything about a parole hearing.' And I can't quite believe I'm hearing about it from Tamsin instead of Hunter.

'Assuming Kevin doesn't start a drug smuggling ring in the coming weeks or make one of those tiny knives from a toothbrush and go on a killing spree in the meantime.'

I resume my climb.

'I get the impression Kevin kept the whole thing a bit hush-hush to avoid getting anyone's hopes up—including his own. But he's served 60 percent of his sentence, which means he was eligible to apply.' She pauses. 'Hunter really didn't send you a text?'

'No. No, he didn't.' I reach our apartment and unlock the door. 'We haven't spoken since New Year's.'

'Really?' Tamsin exhales. 'I mean, I knew communication was sporadic between the two of you, but you failed to mention that it's been non-existent of late.'

I walk into my bedroom, eyes going to the dried flowers in the jar. They are so far past their expiry date it's not funny. I keep waiting for Bridget to bin them while I'm out. Way back in February, she asked me if they might be from Mum. I told her I didn't know, which is the truth. But she would have signed the card. Jehovah would have seen her send them, so she may as well sign her name.

Hunter sent the flowers. That's why they're still sitting in the jar.

'Maybe he didn't want to get your hopes up,' Tamsin says. 'You know what he's like.'

I close my eyes. 'Yeah. I know what he's like.' But that doesn't stop me from feeling cheated. This is big news. This changes everything, and... and he chose not to tell me.

Me.

Me, who was with him through the entire mess. Me, who has wanted this for as long as he has.

'From what Sammy told me, it was a long shot given his already short sentence length and the serious nature of the crime.' She exhales into the phone. 'I'm so sorry. I've ruined today for you, and that's the last thing I meant to do.'

I force a smile so she hears it in my voice. 'It's not ruined. I was just a bit surprised is all. It's great news, obviously. Kevin getting out early is more cause for celebration.' I barely know what I'm saying.

'I wish I was there to drink champagne with you. Make sure Bridget steps up in my place, okay?'

'I doubt she'll drink that much,' I tease.

'Ouch.' There's a pause. 'You're really okay?'

I nod even though she can't see me. 'Of course.'

'Well, congrats again, my clever, creative little bunny. I'm wearing your earrings, by the way.'

The smile remains on my face. 'I couldn't ask for better advertising than that. Speak soon.'

My smile fades the second I end the call. I stare at the flowers. These were the last thing he gave me, all that's left of us. The jewellery accessories I got for my birthday all those years ago are now long gone, which makes the flowers the only remaining proof I have that he once cared.

Shooting up off the bed, I swipe the jar off the desk and watch it shatter on the tiles between the rug and the wall. I remain there in that spot until I'm certain I'm not going to cry, then head to the laundry for the dustpan and vacuum. When the mess is cleaned up, I go to the kitchen and grab a bottle of sparkling wine from the fridge, then fetch two glasses from the cupboard. I pop the cork as my sister enters the apartment.

'Looks like I'm home just in time,' she says, dropping her handbag on the floor. 'I gather you've officially retired from the shoe biz to concentrate on your role as founder, owner, and CEO of Entwined?'

I hand her one of the glasses. 'Don't forget CFO, head of sales, marketing director, and production manager.'

She clinks her glass to mine. 'To all the things.'

I drink. 'To all the things.' Then I drink some more.

51

HUNTER

I t's one of those car trips where you pull up at your destination and realise you don't remember anything about the drive. Did I stop at all the stop signs? Give way when I was supposed to? The fact that Dad is already waiting outside for me is a strong indicator of the speed I was travelling. Well under the limit, it seems.

The sight of him in regular clothes is enough to make me choke up. There's no guard with him. He's free to walk to the car and drive away with me. And when we get home, he won't go straight to the fridge for a beer. He won't pass out before dinner. He'll be sober, and I'm going to make sure he stays that way.

He spots me and heads for the car. I'm not sure whether I'm supposed to get out, maybe hug him. But the closer he gets, the more I realise that I'm not emotionally stable enough for that. So I sit in the car and wait for him to climb in.

'Sorry I'm late,' I say when he closes the door.

'All good.' He brushes a finger down his nose. 'I haven't been waiting long.'

I look over at him. 'I guess you don't have any stuff that needs to go in the back?'

He shakes his head. 'Need to get used to having things in my pockets again. And wearing jeans.'

I start the ute and pull away from the entrance, relieved that I won't be back here again—hopefully.

On the drive home, we talk about the farm, like we always do, but then he asks, 'So Sammy's happy to stay on?'

I nod. 'He can do it all now. I've basically retired.'

Dad chuckles. 'I'll have to build my strength up again so I can be of some use around the place.'

'That'll make for a refreshing change.' The words fall out of me before I can catch them. 'That was a bit harsh, sorry.'

He looks around. 'Harsh but fair. I haven't been much use to anyone for a while. It'll be different now.'

I really want to believe that. 'When's your parole officer coming by?'

'I need to report to the community corrections centre within the next two days.'

We pull out onto the main road. 'And you understand all the conditions? You've got them written down or something?'

He looks at me properly for the first time. 'I know you've had to shoulder a lot of this stuff over the years, but it's not on you anymore. I'll manage everything myself from this point on. You can put that stuff out of your head and focus on what's next for you.'

My hands work the steering wheel. 'Someone needs to make sure you stay sober. That can't fall to Sammy.'

'It falls to me.'

I blink. 'Given your track record—'

'Pull the ute over.'

I glance at him, confused. 'What?'

'I said pull over.'

I indicate and stop the car on a gravelly stretch of grass.

'Get out,' he says, opening the door and climbing out.

At first I don't move, but his pissed-off stance has me reaching for the handle a moment later.

'What's wrong?' I ask as I approach.

He turns to face me, jaw set. 'I should've thanked you. Before all this, I should've thanked you for everything you did. And I probably should've apologised a lot more than I did.'

I cross my arms. 'I didn't need your gratitude or meaningless apologies.'

He nods. 'But I should've done it anyway.' He steps up and pulls me into a hug, the first since Mum's funeral when I was twelve years old. 'Thank you for stepping up when I failed,' he says. 'And I'm sorry for all of it.'

I'm not prepared for this, so I'm frozen in place with no words.

He claps me on the back before letting go. 'But like I said earlier, I'll manage everything myself now.'

I swallow and nod. 'Okay.'

'You called Annie yet? Made plans to go see her?'

This part of the speech I was most definitely not prepared for. 'No.'

'Why not?'

I throw my hands up. 'Because I didn't know how all this would turn out.'

'Well, it's turned out pretty good, don't you think? Might be time to give her a call.'

My mouth is open, but the words are sticking. 'I haven't spoken to her in months. Haven't *heard* from her in months. I have no idea if she even *wants* to hear from me.'

'Only one way to find out.'

I chew my lip. 'You get why I'm hesitant to leave, right? If you start drinking again—'

Dad takes a firm hold of my shoulders. 'I'm gonna stop you right there. That's between me and my parole officer. I don't need a babysitter. I have people for support and meetings I can go to. I'm good.' He releases his hold on me. 'You've taken care of the farm, managed the debt. You've done everything you said you'd do while I was in there. Now I'm out, and that means we're *both* free.'

His words begin to penetrate.

It's been close to a year since our last text exchange. She's likely moved on from the drama of us, got herself some safe boyfriend who says 'I love you' after they finish their bland lovemaking. And I'm the guy who broke her heart and let some random girl blow me behind the gas bottles at the RSL two towns over in an attempt to move on.

'I'm going to get back in that car, and you're going to call her right now,' Dad says, sounding more like a father with each passing second.

'Because that's not awkward.'

He waves a hand. 'I won't look.'

I watch him walk away and climb into the ute. He makes a point of looking away.

I can't just call her. I need to think about what I'd say.

The horn sounds, and I jump a foot in the air. I glare in Dad's direction. He brings his hand to his ear in a phone gesture. Shaking my head, I turn my back to him and fetch out my phone.

———

Annie

My head is buzzing and heart thudding from adrenaline as I exit the building where the Mother Bling offices are located. The purchasing director has just confirmed that my jewellery will soon be available in every one of their stores in Australia.

I did it. I thought he was going to laugh me out of the building, but I'm leaving with a contract instead. All I need now is for my lawyers to look over it. And to hire some lawyers. And hope that the good people at Mother Bling don't discover that I'm a giant fraud figuring all this stuff out on the go.

Opening my bag, I retrieve my phone and text Bridget.

Me: Success! Mojitos for dinner?
Me: Mojitos are basically a meal, right?
Me: Fruit, greens, etc.

My phone rings, and I bring it to my ear without bothering to check the screen. It'll be Bridget saying she's going to be a few minutes late, which is code for half an hour late.

'I'm literally across the road from the pizza shop, so don't worry. Actual food is coming.'

I'm met with silence, which has me lowering the phone to check the screen. I almost drop it when I see Hunter's name glowing before me. Even then, my brain can't quite figure out why it's there. Did he accidentally call me? Did I accidentally dial his number when I was searching for my phone earlier?

Slowly, I bring the phone back to my ear and move to the side of the footpath. 'Hello?'

'You didn't check who it was before you answered, did you?'

It's the first time I've heard his voice in three years. It's like a jolt of electricity through my brain. It's deeper, older sounding, but it's still his voice. 'I thought it was Bridget calling.'

'Only me.'

Only him. Only Hunter Reed. Only the man who still manages to steal the breath from my lungs with a few simple words.

I gather myself as best I can. 'Hi.'

'Hi.'

I'm going to need more words. 'Is everything okay?'

He clears his throat. 'Dad got out early. On parole. Today, actually.'

I'm not sure if I'm supposed to know, but since I'm a

terrible liar, I go with an honest response. 'I actually heard he might be getting out.'

'Ah. Tamsin?'

'She assumed I knew, which obviously I didn't.'

He's silent a moment. 'I wasn't sure it would happen. Usually if it sounds too good to be true—'

'It probably is.'

'Yeah.'

I watch the busy street a moment. The fact that he phoned to tell me the news should make me feel better, but it doesn't. Too much time has passed, too much damage done to each other. 'I'm really happy for you both.'

'Thanks.'

I look up at the sky. 'I appreciate you letting me know, especially given how much easier a text would've been.' When he doesn't respond, I ask, 'What will you do to celebrate?'

'Well, the grass needs cutting on the spillway.'

My lips turn up. 'Don't go too crazy. You don't want to wake up in the morning with dam maintenance regrets.'

'True.'

I hear the smile in his voice when he says that.

'Listen,' he says, 'I was thinking I might fly up to Brisbane.' He pauses. 'I'd like to see you, but I don't want you to feel obligated or uncomfortable—'

'I want to see you.' It comes out before he's even finished speaking. And in case that's not embarrassing enough, I then start to cry. I try to do it silently, but years of pent-up emotions are trying to escape my body all at the same time.

'Annie.' He says my name so gently. He doesn't need to see me to know I'm crying.

I hold the phone away from me for a few seconds and take some calming breaths.

'You still there?' he asks.

I bring the phone back to my ear. 'Yeah.' I try to make my voice cheerful—and fail.

'Good tears or bad tears?'

I press my lips together as they continue to spill down my cheeks. 'Hard to tell with us. The two seem to blend.'

He doesn't speak for a full minute. 'I wasn't sure if I should call. Feels a lot like tearing scabs off wounds.'

'Scabs? Scabs cover superficial wounds. You and me, we're misaligned broken bones.'

There's another spell of silence. 'If you want me to stay away, I'll stay away. If it's too hard, too much, too late...'

It's all those things. 'Come anyway.'

'Okay.' I hear him swallow. 'I'll come.'

He doesn't hang up.

'Don't you have a celebration at the spillway?' I ask.

'Don't you have pizzas to order?'

I laugh once. 'Yeah, I do. I've got lots to tell you when I see you.'

'Good things?'

I close my eyes, savouring the sound of his voice. 'Yes.'

'Great. Well, I'll call you when I have dates figured out.'

I sniff. 'And I'll answer the phone in an appropriate manner.'

'Don't do that. The inappropriate way is much more entertaining.'

When he hangs up, I continue to hold the phone to my ear as I process the conversation. This impossible hope is soaring inside me. My heart is so full from one phone call, one I've waited three years to receive. So I remain there, feeling everything, until a stranger eventually stops and asks if I'm all right.

I assure them I'm fine, and they walk on.

Only when I feel tears running over my lips do I realise I'm crying again. I brush them away. Hunter's coming to Brisbane. His dad's free. *He's* free. I'm not really sure what that means yet, but I know I'm not going to waste any time being angry at him.

I take a moment to pull myself together, slipping my phone into my bag and wiping my face with both hands. I look across the street to the pizza shop, then, drawing a breath, step down off the kerb, pausing for the car approaching on my right.

I don't see the motorbike behind it.

52

HUNTER

One phone call, and I feel myself coming back to life. It's like my lungs are remembering how to breathe again. It's the Annie effect. I guess nothing's changed these past three years.

We've been home a few hours now, and the sun has sunk behind the pines on the hill. Dad and Sammy are seated on the veranda, cans of Coke in hand, discussing plans for the irrigation project. I'm half listening while changing the oil in the ute when my phone rings in my pocket. I wipe my hands and dig it out.

'Annie?' Sammy calls to me, smirking.

I ignore him as I check the screen. It's not Annie. It's Bridget. We've conveniently lost touch over the past three years. Annie's needed her sister all to herself, and I wanted that for her too. I wonder if this is going to be the phone call where she tells me that Annie's finally moved on with her life, that she's happy, and I need to stay the hell away. I wouldn't blame her.

'Bridget,' I say when I answer.

The second I hear her crying into the phone, my stomach twists. Bridget's not a crier, which means something's very wrong.

'What's going on?' I ask, wandering away from listening ears.

'There's been an accident.'

The pure misery in her voice makes every muscle in my body grow rigid. 'Who? Annie?'

'Yeah.'

I walk in tight circles. 'Tell me what happened.'

She lets out a shaky breath. 'I just got to the hospital. She... she was hit by a motorbike crossing the road.'

I still, ears roaring.

'She has a ruptured spleen. She's having surgery.'

I let that sink in a moment. 'Which hospital?'

'St Andrews.' She exhales hard into the phone. 'They told me she was conscious in the ambulance on the way here.' There's a pause. 'She was asking for you.'

I press my eyes shut. 'Shit. We spoke on the phone earlier. She was upset...'

'This isn't on you. That's not why I called.'

I'm walking towards the house now. 'Can you do me a favour and keep me updated? If my phone's off, it's because I'm in the air.'

'You're going to fly up?'

I step past Dad and Sammy, who exchange a look, and head straight to my room, where I start throwing clothes into a bag. 'Yeah. I'll be there as soon as I can.'

When I hang up, Dad's standing at my door with a worried expression.

'What's going on?' he asks.

I explain the situation while I finish packing, disappearing into the bathroom at one point to grab a few toiletries. Sammy's waiting at my door when I return.

'I'll drive you to the airport,' he says.

Dad runs a hand down his face. 'You'll keep us posted?'

'Yeah.' I zip the bag up and throw it over my shoulder. 'Let's go.'

On the drive to the airport, I call Tom to make sure he's been informed. Bridget has phoned him already. We agree to meet at Tullamarine Airport and fly up together.

'Call me when you know what's going on,' Sammy says, stopping in the drop-off lane.

'I will.' I climb out and turn to look at him. 'Thanks for the lift.'

'Go,' he says, waving me off.

Tom's waiting at the baggage check-in with my boarding pass.

'Any update?' I ask.

He shakes his head. 'We'll know more post-surgery. I phoned Dawn to let her know what's going on. Didn't think Bridget was up for that particular phone call.'

We join the line of passengers, emptying our pockets onto trays. 'And?'

He stares down at the watch he's removing. 'And... now she knows. She didn't say much. Shock, probably. I'll keep her posted.'

It's a hard situation for me to get my head around. I know she loves Annie, so why isn't she here at the airport right now?

We arrive at the gate just as boarding opens.

'Bridget mentioned that you and Annie spoke before the accident,' Tom says, eyes ahead. 'Didn't realise you two were still in touch.'

I glance at him. 'If you want to blame someone, you can blame me. It might be my fault.'

He eyes me as we creep forwards in the line. 'I've already spoken to the police. The bike was behind a car. She didn't see it in time. Her phone was in her bag.'

That does little to ease my conscience.

The next few hours pass in a blur of agitation and crying infants. When we land, we take a taxi straight to the hospital. The tired nurse at the front desk asks if we're family. Tom tells the woman he's Annie's father, then glances at me.

'And he's... with me.'

The nurse looks up Annie's information and informs us that she's in recovery, then directs us to the waiting room. I like the idea of Annie being in recovery. It gives the illusion that she's on the up.

It's close to midnight when we step into the dimly lit waiting room. We find Bridget curled up in a chair, half asleep, with an open bag of chips on her lap. She stands the moment she sees us.

'Hey,' she says.

Tom approaches his daughter slowly, like one does a nervous horse, and I head over to the vending machine, where I spend a few minutes browsing the items in order to give them some privacy. They fall silent when a doctor in scrubs enters.

I wander closer, bracing.

He tells us his name is Dr Singh. Then he talks about

the surgery, saying things like 'blood pressure', 'stopping the bleeding', and being 'stable'. My brain takes in only fragments, but judging by Tom's relieved expression, it's predominantly good news.

'Can I see her?' Bridget asks.

Dr Singh looks at her. 'She's still asleep, but I'm happy for one of you to visit with her for a few minutes.'

'You go,' Tom tells Bridget.

She follows the doctor, and we sit and wait. When she returns, she's a little red-eyed. I know too well how confronting it is seeing people you care about unresponsive, with tubes everywhere. I swallow down my questions, and Tom does the same.

At some point I fall asleep, and when I wake up, I see Annie's mum is here. She actually came. She and Tom are speaking on one side of the room while Bridget remains on the other. Rising, I walk over to check on her.

Dawn's face hardens when her eyes land on me. 'What's he doing here?'

I could ask the same question of her.

'He's here for Annie, like the rest of us,' Tom says quietly.

I focus on Bridget. 'You okay?'

She nods, barely.

The clock reads 2:55 a.m. 'I'm going to find us some coffee.'

'I'll have one too,' Tom says.

I look to Dawn, and she shakes her head. Time to leave them to their family reunion and go in search of coffee.

The hospital cafe is closed. One of the nurses points

me to a kitchen where there's a kettle and a big supply of instant. I have no idea how Tom takes his coffee, so I throw in some sugar and milk and carry all three cups back to the waiting room.

The tension hits me like a freight train when I step inside. I pause at the door and look around, trying to gauge what level of family drama I've walked in on. It takes me a moment to notice Dr Singh among them.

'What's going on?' I ask, continuing forwards and handing out the coffees. I know it's bad news when they immediately set their cups down on the coffee table beside the torn magazines.

'He's not family,' Dawn says. 'He shouldn't even be here.'

Tom brings a hand to his forehead. 'Not now, Dawn.'

Bridget's staring at the ground, Dawn hates me, and Tom looks stressed out of his mind.

I turn to the doctor for an explanation. 'Is Annie okay?'

He glances at Dawn before replying. 'Annie's blood pressure's very low. We need to get her haemoglobin levels up. She requires a blood transfusion.'

'Okay.' I'm confused by everyone's inability to look at me right now. 'So give her one.'

Dawn holds up a small folded white card with red-and-black print on it. 'He can't. This was in Annie's purse. She still carries it.'

My eyes narrow on the card. The words 'NO BLOOD' are written in red. Underneath is a picture of a blood bag. A red circle with a line through it is stamped over the top.

That's when I remember that Jehovah's Witnesses don't accept blood transfusions.

I put down my coffee and snatch the card from Dawn.

'Advance decision to refuse specified medical treatment,' I read aloud. Opening it up, I run my eyes over the text, all the way to Annie's signature at the bottom. 'This is no longer valid,' I say, handing it back to Dawn. 'Annie left the organisation years ago, as every person here can attest to.'

Dawn shakes her head. 'It doesn't work like that. Becoming inactive doesn't mean her beliefs or wishes have changed.'

'She's not inactive,' Bridget says quietly. 'She left.'

'Her wishes have changed,' I say. 'She no longer believes the bullshit she was force-fed through childhood. I can tell you with absolute confidence that she would want the transfusion.' I look to Tom to back me up. 'Right?'

He clears his throat. 'I haven't spoken to Annie about this particular issue.'

My eyes go to Bridget. 'You know her better than anyone here. You would've spoken about this stuff.'

She can barely meet my gaze. 'Not this.' On an exhale, she adds, 'I got rid of my card after I moved out. I don't know why she still carries it.'

I can't believe we're standing here debating this while Annie's a few rooms away needing blood. 'She probably just forgot she had it.'

Dawn's eyes flash at me. 'Or perhaps she still believes it's the right thing to do in this situation.'

Tom raises his hands, gesturing for calm. 'What are our options here?'

'If she needs blood, we give her the blood,' I say. 'We all want her to live.'

Silence.

Dr Singh rubs his forehead. 'The card's valid, and she was carrying it at the time of the accident.' His hand falls to his side. 'But if you tell me her wishes have changed, I'll act in the best interest of the patient.' He looks between us. 'Right now you're all telling me different things.'

Bridget looks up. 'I think she'd want the transfusion.'

Finally, someone speaking sense.

'I agree,' Tom says. 'If it's life or death, I think she would choose life.'

The doctor looks to Dawn, and I can tell by the way she sets her mouth that I'm not going to like her response.

'I was there when Annie signed that card.' She swallows. 'She was not a minor. She was an adult. It was her choice.' Releasing a shaky breath, she adds, 'There are lots of safe and effective alternatives, right, Dr Singh?'

Bridget steps away from the group, and Tom drops his chin to his chest.

'That card's over three years old,' I say. 'The emergency contact details list this lady right here, her mother. What it doesn't tell you is that the pair have barely spoken in that time.'

'I'm going to get Annie started on some tranexamic acid,' Dr Singh says. 'You can let me know your decision when I return.' With that, he exits.

Dawn levels me with a hard stare. 'Annie's wishes are here in writing.'

'That card's bullshit, and you know it,' I snap.

Tom casts a warning glance in my direction. 'Easy. We all want the same thing here.'

'No we don't. Dawn here wants to obey the scriptures, and the rest of us want Annie to fucking live.'

Tom shakes his head, like my language is the problem here.

'Mum,' Bridget says quietly. 'You heard what the doctor said. The blood transfusion is her best chance.'

Dawn starts walking towards the door. 'I need some air.'

Some air? Annie's in there fighting for her life, and she needs some *air*?

I follow her out into the corridor, ignoring Tom's protests behind me.

'My beliefs won't be swayed by your vulgar words,' Dawn says when I fall into step with her. 'So save your breath.'

'Then I'll try something else.'

'I'm walking away from you for a reason.'

I draw a breath for patience. 'Will you just hear me out?'

She continues walking without so much as a glance in my direction. I follow her all the way to the front entrance, and we step out into the balmy Brisbane weather. I'm sweating in seconds. When she doesn't stop walking, I step in front of her, giving her no choice.

'I know you blame me for her leaving. You wanted her to meet some nice, God-fearing J-dub and have a lovely, chaperoned courtship. You hate me. You're disappointed. I get it. But you need to put all that aside for a minute and think about what Annie wants for once.'

She appears unmoved by my little speech. 'Do you think it's easy for a mother to stand before a doctor and instruct him *not* to give life-saving treatment to their child?'

It's a rhetorical question, so I don't respond.

'It's my job as a mother to consider her well-being long-term,' she continues. '*You* want her to wake up in that hospital bed and go on to live another sixty, seventy years in this world. *I* want her to live forever in paradise.'

This is when I realise I'm never going to win this argument with logic, because she believes every word coming from her mouth. 'If Annie dies today, it will be because of you. And forever is a long time to carry the weight of her death—even while living in paradise.'

Before she can respond, the automatic doors open, and Bridget comes running towards us. Her expression confirms it's not good news.

'Her blood pressure dropped,' she pants. 'The doctor said there was a heart arrhythmia.' She takes a moment to compose herself. 'They had to shock her.'

The colour drains from Dawn's face. She looks ready to fall down. I place an arm around her and guide her towards the door. 'Let's go.'

Inside, Dr Singh and Tom are talking. Tom steps forwards when he sees us, helping Dawn into a nearby chair.

'Is Annie okay?' I ask the doctor.

'She needs blood—right now. It's likely we'll lose her without it.'

Bridget covers her face with her hands and starts to cry. Tom links his hands atop his head and turns in a tight circle.

My eyes go to Dawn. 'Please,' I say, voice breaking.

She looks to her crying daughter, then drops her gaze. 'Give her the blood.'

53

ANNIE

There's a part of us, no matter our age, the condition of the relationship, or the damage done to it, that always wants Mum in a crisis. Waking up in hospital after being hit by a motorbike is one of those moments. Do I wish that wasn't the case? Absolutely. But I wanted her at my graduation, wanted her there the day I had my first stall at a market, and wanted to phone her when it was a success. I also wanted her when I got bronchopneumonia last year, and at the dinner I had for my twenty-first birthday, even though she never acknowledged the twenty birthdays before that one. And now as I look around the foreign room filled with beeping machines, barely able to move, I want her again.

This time I even admit it aloud.

'Mum,' I say to the middle-aged woman in scrubs who's scribbling on a chart.

She looks up from her notes and smiles at me. 'Awake

at last. Your mum's in the waiting room with the rest of the fam, love.'

'She is?' I blink and feel tears run down into my hair.

Mum's here.

With the rest of the family.

It must be more serious than I realise.

'Let me just check a few things here, and then we'll sit you up a bit. You gave everyone a bit of a scare.'

'I did?'

'Dr Singh will come speak with you shortly.' She's flitting around the room, pressing buttons and checking readings.

I move my arms and legs to make sure they're still attached. My body is numb and heavy. 'Did a motorbike hit me?'

She glances in my direction. 'Yes, sweetheart. Going at around fifty kilometres per hour. Dr Singh will talk to you about your injuries. He did a wonderful job stitching your spleen back together.'

I swallow. My mouth is so dry. 'It ruptured?'

'You're very fortunate that's all that ruptured.' She looks to the door as a man walks in. 'Here he is.'

'Ah, she wakes,' the doctor says, giving me a smile. He takes the chart from the nurse and comes to stand beside the bed while he looks it over. 'My name's Dr Singh. If you're feeling up to it, let's have a little chat about the past twenty-four hours.'

'Okay.'

He gives me all the details he knows about the accident, then goes through my injuries one at a time. The ruptured spleen, a fractured rib, and a number of superficial wounds. He talks about the surgery, the blood loss, and the decision made by my family to give me the transfusion.

I'm silent a moment. I don't know why I still carry the card, but I know it has little to do with not wanting a transfusion. 'Mum... agreed?'

'You can probably thank your boyfriend for that,' Dr Singh says with a tight smile. 'He was quite insistent.'

'My boyfriend?' *How hard did I hit my head?*

'Hayden is it? No, Hunter.'

Hunter's here.

Of course he is.

'She asked for Mum when she woke,' the nurse tells him, 'so we'll send her in first.'

There's some guilt on my part, because Mum gave up the right to be first in the room. But I don't object. I watch the door, waiting for her to appear.

She looks like any other anxious mother as she steps into the room. There's comfort in that. Despite everything that's transpired over the past few years, every belief she holds so dearly, she can't shake her instincts. I'm triumphant in that moment—and deeply sad.

The nurse drags a chair over to the bed, then leaves us. I'm relieved, because I don't want anyone else to witness our discomfort.

'How are you feeling?' Mum asks, finally meeting my eyes.

I start to reach for the cup of water next to my bed. 'Like I've been hit by a motorbike.'

She leaps up to get the water for me, waits for me to

drink, then sets the cup back down before sitting once more. It's such a motherly act.

'I'm surprised you came,' I say after an awkward silence.

She shifts in her chair. 'Did I make the right choice with the transfusion? Is that what you wanted?'

'Yes. I wanted to live.' I swallow. 'That's the reason I left—to *live*.'

She draws a shaky breath. 'In this temporary world?'

She's relentless. And I don't expect anything less from her. 'We both have to live in this world.'

'For now.' She looks around the room. 'And this good news of the kingdom will be preached in all the inhabited earth for a witness to all the nations, and then the end will come.'

'Matthew 24:14.'

Her eyes meet mine once more. 'Surprised you still remember.'

'Hard to forget. Hard to let go. I suppose that's why I still have a blood card in my purse.'

We watch each other for a moment.

'I should go,' Mum says with a sniff. 'Bridget's keen to see you. I hardly recognised her at first. She's a proper woman now.'

'An amazing woman.'

She purses her lips. 'Is there anything you need before I go? Something to read, perhaps?' Before I can answer, she picks up her handbag and pulls out a copy of the latest *Watchtower* and *Awake*, placing them beside the water jug.

'Oh.' She can't help herself. 'Thanks.'

'There's an interesting article in the *Awake* about food.' Then, seeing my face, she adds, 'I could grab you something from the newsagent if you'd prefer.'

The corners of my mouth lift. 'It's fine. Thank you.'

Her face contorts, and she inhales sharply. 'Sorry.' She attempts to compose herself.

I know how hard this is for her, how torn she is between being a good disciple and being my mother. I *know* she loves me. I reach a hand out to her, but she doesn't take it.

'Mum,' I say quietly. 'I know you have to go. I know nothing has changed. Hold my hand before you leave.'

She brushes a tear away with one impatient swipe, then takes hold of my hand.

'It's all right,' I tell her. 'I understand. It's okay. You can go.'

Her eyes are brimming with tears now. 'I'll tell Bridget to make you some broth. I've seen the meals coming out. They won't help you heal.'

I nod. 'Sure. Okay. Thank you.'

She releases my hand and takes hold of the strap of her handbag. She's struggling to leave.

'You said yes to the blood,' I tell her. 'It's more than enough.'

She nods, sniffs. 'I'll keep praying that you find your way back to Jehovah. "Return to me, and I will return to you."'

'Malachi 3:6.'

She looks around as if she might have forgotten something, because that's easier than looking at me. 'You have my number if you need anything. Medical information, that sort of thing.'

I need my mum. 'I do.'

She starts backing out of the room. 'I'll send your sister in.' Then she's gone from sight, and I have no idea when I'll see her again.

I love you.

I forgive you.

———

Hunter

Dawn says an awkward goodbye to Tom and Bridget, then turns to me, nodding once in place of words. She might hate my guts and not want me anywhere near her daughter, but acknowledging my existence feels a lot like progress. I can see she's either been crying or is trying not to.

Bridget goes to see Annie. Then Tom goes to see her. I'm pacing the room when he returns.

'She fell asleep while I was in there,' he says, giving me a sympathetic look. 'The nurse will let you know when she's awake.'

Bridget stifles a yawn. 'Why don't you both come back to the apartment for a shower and something proper to eat? She's not going anywhere.'

I can't leave until I see her. 'You two go. I'm happy to wait.'

After they leave, I head to the now-open cafe and grab

a bacon and egg sandwich with the largest coffee they have.

Two hours pass before a nurse comes to find me. I'm out of my chair, heading down the corridor before she's finished speaking.

Annie's sitting up when I enter, propped up by pillows and blending with the linen framing her. Her face and arms are bruised, and there are grazes everywhere. My throat closes involuntarily at the sight. I fucking hate this. It's a painful reminder of how close I came to losing her.

'Hey.' Her voice barely carries the short distance. She searches my face. 'That bad, huh?'

I force my feet forwards and sit in the chair beside her bed. 'Is this my fault?'

'No.'

'You were crying on the phone.'

She shakes her head. 'Honestly, this was just a ploy to get you here sooner.'

It's far too soon for jokes. 'Well, it worked.'

Her eyes move over my face. 'You've changed. You're more stubbly.'

I rub my jaw. 'It has been nearly three years.'

'It has.'

When she opens her hand to me, I take it, relieved to find it warm. I've waited so long to touch her.

She lifts my hand, pressing it to her cheek. Her eyes close. 'I've missed you.'

The burn in my throat is instant.

'I can say stuff like that and simply blame the morphine,' she says.

I glance in the direction of the IV pole. 'Can we turn that shit up?'

She laughs, then winces.

Seeing her in physical pain is a special form of torture. 'Might be too soon for belly laughs.'

She nods. 'I think you might be right.'

I wrap my other hand around hers. There are things I want to say, but I'm not good at this kind of thing.

Annie watches me with a drugged-up smile. 'What's going on in that head of yours?'

I really need to get this out. 'I've missed you too. Every day. And there were some bloody long days.'

'So long,' she agrees.

'I wish I'd told you that before today.'

She's silent now, watching and listening.

'I wish I'd told you a lot of things.' I draw a breath before continuing. 'Like how I loved you all the way back in high school, when you were going door to door carrying your Bible and wearing those ugly blouses.'

Annie's smile grows, but she doesn't say anything.

'And how I still loved you after I left and when I was waiting for *you* to leave. I loved you when we were together in Chirnside and for the three years we were apart.' I pause. 'I still love you. Never stopped. I mean, I *really* fucking love you.' I wait for the tightening in my throat to ease before continuing. 'And I know if you went away for another three years, nothing would change.' I search her tear-filled eyes. 'I need some time to get things in order, and then I'm coming for you, Wilson.'

Light fills her eyes, bringing some life back to them. 'I have some things to get in order too... like my spleen.'

I rise, pressing my forehead lightly to hers. She smells like medicine and hospital grade bleach.

'I would've waited the five years,' she whispers. 'The full sentence.'

She's killing me.

'I'm tired,' she says, blinking.

'You need to rest.' When I straighten, I realise she's holding on to my T-shirt.

'Don't leave yet. Can you lie down with me?'

I couldn't walk away now even if I wanted to. 'I'll be right here in the chair. I don't want to hurt you.'

'You being all the way over there hurts me.'

I'm defenceless against this girl, so I carefully climb onto the bed, making sure I'm not lying on any tubes. She can't really move much, but she turns her head into my shoulder, closes her eyes, and falls asleep.

54

ANNIE

After thirteen days in hospital, I'm finally deemed well enough to go home. Bridget picks me up and even takes a few days off work until she's sure I can manage on my own.

'I'm more than fine,' I assure her on day three. 'Go.'

I spend the rest of the week doing small amounts of work and taking plenty of short walks, slowly regaining some strength while giving my rib a chance to heal. In the evenings, I cook dinner so Bridget doesn't have to. We eat on the terrace, sipping frosty beer from tacky stubby holders.

Hunter calls me every single day to check on my progress and update me on what's happening at the farm. Then he calls me with the best news of all.

'Pete phoned. Their farmhand's moving back to Toowoomba. He's offered me my old job back.'

I'm so ridiculously happy for him. I know how much he loved that job and that family—and they loved him right back. There's no one more deserving of this second chance.

It all feels too easy. I keep waiting for something to go wrong, for Kevin to start drinking, or Sammy to walk out, or Hunter to realise he doesn't love me after all.

'You sure your dad's okay with you leaving?' I ask.

'Don't,' Hunter says. 'We're done with guilt, remember?'

I smile into the phone. 'Then I guess I'll see you in a few weeks.'

'Love you.'

My heart can barely hold this amount of joy. 'Love you too.'

Two weeks later, I get the phone call I've been anxiously awaiting ever since Hunter confirmed the date. He calls me early morning to tell me he's at the Leroys' farm and could Bridget please drive me over there.

She agrees because she doesn't want me driving.

Forty minutes later, we pull off the main road onto a dirt one. Cattle are gathered beneath tall gums in the paddocks on either side. At the end of the long drive, we spot a large brick home. Hunter's ute is parked in front of the bungalow located a hundred metres from the house. He wanders out when he hears us pull up, and I can't stop the smile that takes over my face. I'm out of the car and running towards him before Bridget's even turned the engine off. He's grinning now. He's happy, and I'm the reason.

'Slow down,' he says right before I fling myself at him.

He catches me with an 'Oof', then laughs. 'You trying to refracture your rib?' His arms tighten around me. 'Hi.'

I bury my face in his neck, his scent, his familiarity. This moment has been a long time coming.

A car door closes behind me, and a moment later Bridget calls, 'Right. Well, I think I'll head off, then.'

Hunter lowers me to the ground and takes hold of my hand. 'I wouldn't go just yet.'

'If you're wanting a long cuddle from me, you might be disappointed,' she replies, leaning against the car.

A high-pitched whinny rings out around us. The sound has Bridget straightening and looking around and the hairs on my arms standing on end. It's impossibly familiar.

Hunter gestures to a paddock beyond the trees. 'Like I said, I wouldn't go just yet.'

I'm not sure if Bridget hears him, because she's already walking off in the direction he pointed.

'What's going on?' I say, looking up at him.

He tugs me along with him. 'You're going to want to see this.'

We trail Bridget through the trees to the fence on the other side. She stops suddenly, both hands going over her mouth. I follow her line of sight to where a tall thoroughbred stands, head hanging over the fence and ears pricked in our direction.

It's Charlie. One piece of my sister's heart, her horse soul mate. He still knows her. He recognised her voice the second she spoke. And as if to prove my point, he whinnies again upon seeing her.

I watch as Bridget rushes towards her 'heart horse', ducking beneath the fence post and taking hold of the gelding's face. He smells her while she stands there crying. Of course, I start crying too, because there's no one more deserving of a horse's loyalty and love.

I press a kiss to Hunter's shoulder. 'Thank you.'

He lets go of my hand and drapes an arm around me. 'Sorry it didn't come with a kelpie.'

'I think my mum needs Banjo more than I do right now. That dog is all she has left of her family.' I continue watching my sister. 'I have enough.'

Hunter turns to me, cradling my face with both hands and looking in my eyes. 'This has been the hardest, longest wait of my life, but so bloody worth it.'

I wipe my face. 'You're going to have a lot of trouble getting rid of me now.'

'Good.'

He kisses me slowly, and there's no need to hide anymore, no one here to tell us it's wrong.

'Gross,' Bridget says.

Except my sister.

Hunter kisses me again before facing Bridget. 'This paddock's his. You can come here as often as you like, so long as you bring Annie with you every time.'

Bridget frowns in his direction. 'I suppose that's one way to keep your girlfriend close.' She pauses. 'Thank you, by the way. This is... I'll pay you back.'

Hunter shakes his head. 'You already have. Three years watching over her when I couldn't.'

Bridget swallows, then looks back at Charlie.

The sound of a door opening and closing makes us look in the direction of the house. An older man steps outside, presumably the infamous Pete Leroy. He peers in our direction, looking from the two of us to Bridget.

'Sue's got more chops in the slow cooker than she knows what to do with,' he says. 'Come and get something to eat.'

Hunter nods and looks over at Bridget. She's standing with her face buried in Charlie's mane.

'Leave her,' I say, tugging him in the direction of the house.

He threads his fingers through mine as we walk. 'Sue's probably going to fuss and ask you a lot of questions.'

I smile at the ground. 'That's okay.'

'Not too much too soon?'

I lean into him. 'A welcomed change. Normally it's not enough and too late with us.'

'That's because we're... was it misaligned broken bones?'

I laugh once and push up onto my toes to kiss his stubbly cheek. 'Yes. Misaligned broken bones.'

EPILOGUE

'You can't live here. It looks like it'll collapse at any moment.'

That's what I said to Hunter when I saw the house he bought on four hectares in Ripley, a run-down three-bedroom timber Queenslander precariously balanced on stilts.

'What are you talking about?' he said, hugging me from behind. 'The structure's the only thing it's got going for it. It just needs some love.'

Admittedly, it had a lot of charm with its pitched ceilings and oak hardwood floors.

'I'm gonna build a deck the whole way round,' he said. 'Treetop views from any part of the house.'

I stared at that house for a long time, envisioning it sanded back and painted white with windows ajar, praying for a breeze. 'Then I'll help you.'

I'll never forget the exact shade of his eyes when they landed on me a moment later, pure adoration radiating from them.

We spent every weekend for the next six months at that house. Repairing, sanding, and painting. We did everything within our capabilities before outsourcing the bigger jobs. Then Pete helped build the new deck, and Sue helped me restore the yellow 1960s GE stove that I insisted he keep.

By the time the house was ready to be lived in, I was totally in love with it.

'When are you going to move in?' I asked him the day it was completed. We were lying on our backs on the deck, watching the cockatoos shred the gums above us.

He turned his head to look at me. 'The same day you do.'

We had talked about the future many times. It's just that we were so comfortable in the present that we hadn't taken any real steps towards it. 'You want me to move in with you?'

'Are you really asking me that?'

The following week, Bridget helped me pack up my things.

'You really don't mind?' I asked her.

'Of course not. I've been waiting *years* to get my studio back.' She winked at me before resuming packing.

Still, I couldn't shake this guilty feeling, like I was doing something wrong. And I couldn't pinpoint it either.

'For nineteen years you were taught that it's a sin to live with a man out of wedlock,' Bridget pointed out. 'Some lessons are so deeply ingrained we can't unlearn them.'

She was right, of course. I wasn't free of the religion simply because I left it.

When I brought the subject up with Hunter, he stared at me for the longest time.

'Why are you looking at me like that?' I asked.

He leaned forwards, resting his elbows on his knees. 'I think we should get married. Problem solved.'

I smiled down at my lap. 'Just like that, huh?'

'Just like that. We both know this is forever. If you'll feel more comfortable with a certificate hanging on our wall to prove it, I'm in.'

I laughed at that. 'I don't think people hang them on their walls.'

'We would.'

'We would?'

'Sure.'

My adoration for him grew a little more that day. 'Let's finish moving in before we go planning a wedding.'

A week later, we moved into our first home together. Aside from personal belongings, a few furniture items donated by friends, and a washing machine Dad bought us as a housewarming gift, the place was relatively empty in those initial months. And it didn't matter at all.

Hunter continued to work at the Leroys' farm Monday to Friday, and I ran my business mostly from home. The weekends were ours. Breakfast with friends, horse riding, early morning hikes, and lazy afternoons dozing on the deck. We embraced this simple existence, the mundane, because we'd never had it before. The simple act of grocery shopping together was a reminder of how far we'd come and how hard we'd fought to love each other out in the open.

'When are you going to marry me, Wilson?' Hunter

asked me one night out on the deck. We were seated in the chairs I'd rescued from a nature strip earlier that week.

I took a sip of my beer, eyes meeting his. 'She wouldn't come, you know. I'd invite her, and she wouldn't come.'

He didn't ask me who I was talking about—he didn't need to. 'Who says we need to invite other people?'

The following week, Hunter drove us to the Brisbane registry, and with Bridget as our witness, we got married.

'Come back to mine,' she said afterwards. 'I'll barbeque.'

What she failed to mention was she'd invited some additional guests. Sammy and Tamsin had flown up for what Bridget described as a super-casual hang with no presents, cake, dancing, or empty chairs to stare at.

She lied about the dancing, though.

That night remains one of my happiest memories to date, and I'll be forever grateful to my sister for bringing the two people who loved us through our broken years together to celebrate the best decision I ever made.

Dad and Kevin phoned in their congratulations. They knew of our plans and were both genuinely happy for us. They even collaborated in buying us a clothes dryer to get us through the wet summers. We would do a family celebration when Kevin had more freedom.

It took me a week to work up the courage to phone Mum and tell her the news. I was happy, and I didn't want that feeling to end. But I knew hearing about it from someone else would sting. So I told her, giving her a chance to express her grief and disappointment.

I would only give her that chance once.

She didn't cry. Nor did she express her disappointment—though I'm certain she felt it.

'What's your address?' she asked me after a long, uncomfortable silence. 'I'd like to send you something.'

It took me a moment to respond. 'You don't have to send us anything. I just wanted you to know.'

'I want to.'

So I gave her my address.

I'd be lying if I said I didn't check the mailbox every day for the next week. I did it when Hunter wasn't around so he wouldn't witness my disappointment every time it was empty.

Two weeks later, a man showed up at our door with a large crate. It wasn't until I heard the whining coming from it that I realised what it was. I dropped to my knees and peered inside, then promptly burst into tears at the sight of a greying kelpie.

My wedding present was Banjo.

The visibly uncomfortable man handed me an envelope before leaving. It was a wedding card with 'Mr & Mrs' printed on the front. Inside, Mum wrote out scriptures containing marriage advice. Then at the bottom, it said:

I'm pleased to hear you have plenty of land at your new marital home. Banjo will love having space again. Perhaps I'll come visit him one day.

I read this card often. Every time I miss her. It's been

two years since she sent it, and I'm still waiting for that visit.

Lots has happened in those two years. Banjo sleeps far more than he runs nowadays, and my jewellery business has expanded to New Zealand. That growth has enabled me to outsource all production, freeing up my time for designing, sourcing quality materials, and mindless cockatoo watching.

Hunter still works at the farm. Pete wants him to manage it when he retires. They're very much family now, and Sue takes her role as substitute mother very seriously. We always have more casserole in our fridge than we can possibly eat.

Kevin's still sober. He hasn't had a drink since the accident. Hunter likes to fly down and spend a few weeks with him over Christmas. Both times they've completed a farm project of some kind because neither of them can sit still for long.

I like to spend Christmas with my sister, *not* celebrating Christmas. We do get merry though—except for Christmas 2006.

This Christmas, Bridget hands me a glass of champagne as I enter her apartment, then directs me to the lounge room where we'll spend the entire day watching movies and snacking.

'Horror, graphic violence, or sex scenes?' she asks, picking up the TV remote.

We do have *some* Christmas traditions.

'All the above.'

We spend a few moments selecting a movie, then settle in to watch.

A few minutes in, Bridget narrows her eyes. 'Why aren't you drinking?'

I can tell by her expression that she already knows the answer. 'Because I'm pregnant.'

She sits up slowly and sets her glass on the coffee table. 'How pregnant?'

'Eight weeks.'

She slides closer to me on the sofa and proceeds to hug me for longer than one second. It reeks of sisterly affection. Then, retreating to her side of the sofa, she says, 'We're not watching a violent horror movie. It's PG films with happy endings from now on.' She looks at the food on the coffee table. 'I bought so much Camembert.'

I laugh. 'Well, now you don't have to share.'

Her eyes meet mine. 'You're going to have to cut down on caffeine.'

'How very dare you.'

Her eyes crease at the corners. 'I'm happy for you. That's one lucky baby.'

We fall silent and watch *Black Beauty*.

Hunter tells his dad the news in person during his annual trip, and Kevin tells him that he wants to be called Pa. When Hunter returns to Brisbane, we tell my parents together over the phone. Dad cries happy tears, which then makes me cry. Mum cries too, but for very different reasons. She's grieving the grandchild she would have helped raise. Her choice to disassociate from me means settling for yearly school photos in the mail and an occasional phone call.

Tamsin's absolutely thrilled for us, and Sammy's already claiming the role of uncle. Everyone who matters is happy about it. Happiness *is* the "correct" reaction to the news. And even though I know this, I'm still bracing for disgrace, because deep, deep down, I'm still that Jehovah's Witness girl who was led astray. I fell out of the truth, as they say. I'm a sinner. I'm a lost sheep. I'm worldly. I'm a bad influence. In the eyes of the congregation that raised me, I'm a failure.

I'm *weak*.

Only those with the courage to walk away will ever understand the strength required to do so.

Whenever Hunter catches me in one of these moods, these guilty moments, he'll call me out on it.

'What's going on in that head of yours, Wilson?'

I'm a month from my due date, and he's just found me standing in front of the open fridge, staring into it. I turn, unsure how long he's been watching me—or how long I've been standing there, for that matter.

'I was just thinking that I'm too tired to cook.' Deflection is always my go-to.

He eyes me carefully, then decides to let the lie go. 'It's a good thing Sue brought over another casserole, then. You go rest. I can heat a bit of dinner.'

The closer I get to my due date, the more insistent he's getting with rest. I can't wipe a bench without him taking over. But I need to be busy. Much better to be moving than still with my thoughts.

The following day, I'm seated on the front deck, sketching earrings, when he appears before me all hot and sweaty. 'I want to show you something.'

I look up at him. 'Okay.'

He pulls me to my feet with an exaggerated groan. I

playfully flick his arm, then follow him downstairs and through the back door. Straight away, I notice a swing hanging from one of the trees, and a smile lights me up from the inside.

'You built us a swing,' I say.

'I did.'

Walking over to it, I run my fingers along the polished timber seat, then climb on.

'Like it?' he asks.

I nod. 'It looks far safer than the last one you built me.'

He laughs, then catches the swing. Bending, he slides a hand over my belly and brings his mouth to my ear. 'I don't want you feeling guilty anymore. Not about this.'

I close my eyes and place a hand over his. 'I'm sorry.'

'And we're not apologising for it either. The correct response is "I love you".'

I open my eyes and feel the beginnings of a smile. 'I love you.'

'Better.' He straightens and gives me a small push. 'We never did hang that certificate.'

I laugh. 'That's Bridget's fault for giving us too much beautiful art. Higher, please.'

He pushes me again.

'Higher!'

He shakes his head. 'That's as high as you're going.'

I lean all the way back, watching him as I swing.

'It'll all work out,' he says. 'Just have a little faith.' He winks when he says that last part.

'Oh. I see what you did there.' I continue watching him upside down.

Banjo wanders over, clearly feeling left out, and Hunter guides him away from the swing.

'It's called malalignment, by the way,' he says. 'That's the medical term.'

It takes me a moment to realise what he's referring to. Misaligned broken bones.

'And it's easily treated by rebreaking the bones and realigning them so they heal correctly,' he adds.

'That easy, huh?'

His blue eyes shine down on me. 'I suggest we just go forwards one bone at a time.'

I sit up. 'What was once a dark and poetic analogy is now sounding oddly sexual.'

He laughs, and the sound fills me.

Banjo takes my sitting up as an invitation. A few moments of chaos follow as Hunter tries to stop the swing and save the dog from being crashed into while ensuring I don't fall off.

It's the laughter that ensues that's meaningful. These moments are nothing and everything.

These moments add up to a life of our choosing.

ACKNOWLEDGMENTS

I would like to express my gratitude to the many people who contributed to this book. My biggest thanks goes to my readers. Without you guys, I wouldn't get to do what I love. Next, a huge thank you to my rock star husband who supports and encourages me even though my writing takes time away from him. I love you to bits. A big thank you to Kristin and the team at Hot Tree Editing for polishing the manuscript into something beautiful. A shout out to my proofreader, Rebecca Fletcher, for catching everything I missed. A huge round of applause for my cover designer, Stuart Bache (Books Covered), for this *gorgeous* cover. And finally, a huge thank you to my ARC readers for your encouragement, honest reviews, and being the final set of eyes on my work. You guys are amazing.

ALSO BY TANYA BIRD

You can find a complete list of published works at

tanyabird.com/books